To my beloved daughters, Olivia and Isobel, the
brightest stars in my firmament.

THE BRIGHTON GUEST HOUSE GIRLS

Lesley Eames

FT
Pbk

First published in the United Kingdom in 2019 by Aria, an imprint of Head of Zeus Ltd

Copyright © Lesley Eames, 2019

The moral right of Lesley Eames to be identified as the author of this work has been asserted in accordance with the Copyright, Designs and Patents Act of 1988.

A CIP catalogue record for this book is available from the British Library.

ISBN 9781788545723

Aria
c/o Head of Zeus
First Floor East
5–8 Hardwick Street
London EC1R 4RG

www.ariafiction.com

One

Dear Miss Fairfax,

We were most grateful to receive settlement of our account for services rendered in regard to the funeral of the late Mr Herbert Ambrose. Your esteemed custom at this sad time was—

Huh. Thea tossed the undertaker's letter back onto the kitchen table. Sad time indeed. She felt no grief at all for the dissipated scoundrel she'd had the misfortune to call her stepfather. But that part of her life was over now. It was the future that was important.

Thea had no idea what that future might hold but one thing was surely certain. It wouldn't be the sort of future her parents had expected for Miss Theodora Fairfax of Clarendon Place, Brighton.

Although not precisely rich, Robert Fairfax had enjoyed very comfortable circumstances. Had he been able to see his daughter sitting here in the basement kitchen reviewing her stricken finances, he'd have felt shock and distress. Thea's mother would have shared that distress though instead of feeling shock she'd have been tormented with guilt because it was her marriage to Herbert Ambrose that had brought the stricken finances about.

Thea was reading papers by the light of a single candle to save on electricity and although there was a fire in the grate it was meagre to save on coal. To stop herself from shivering she was wearing an old greatcoat of her father's and, having washed her hair, she'd spread it around her shoulders to enjoy the illusion of warmth created by the candlelight raising shimmers of gold from its coppery depths.

The rest of the house – all four storeys of it – was dark and cold above her. It was emptier than it had once been too. Most of the heavy furniture remained but many smaller items – graceful side tables, paintings, silver and china – had gone, sold by Herbert to fund his drinking and gambling.

Despite that, Thea couldn't feel harshly towards her mother. Cecily Fairfax had been kind and loving but also the sort of woman who felt all at sea without a man to guide and support her. And even if Thea had never warmed to Herbert's oily charm, she'd understood how her more delicate mother had been flattered by the attention of flowers, chocolates and compliments after two years of loneliness following the death of Thea's father.

Of course, the courtship hadn't lasted past the wedding day five years ago. Disillusion had set in rapidly along with ever-reducing circumstances. One by one the servants had been given notice because there wasn't the money to pay them – first the cook, then the maid and finally even the woman who came in to help with the rougher work.

There hadn't been money for Thea's school fees either. Sixteen at the time of the marriage, she'd left her education behind to run the household and look after her delicate mother. Never strong, Cecily had grown steadily weaker with a heart complaint and five months ago she'd died. Repellent Herbert had sickened soon after and Thea had nursed him too. Not out of affection, but because his only son lived abroad and there was no one else to do it.

Still, at least the house was hers now though she hadn't the income to cover the running costs going forward. Thea had no income at all at present and needed urgently to find some sort of job. She might have been brought up genteelly by parents who'd expected her to marry comfortably rather than work but needs must and—

A bang from the door knocker cut off her thoughts. Thea frowned. She wasn't expecting anyone and it was late for someone to be calling. She shrugged out of the greatcoat and pinned her hair into a loose bun.

Hastening upstairs, she was tempted to glide into the drawing-room to identify the visitor via a glance through the side of the projecting bay window but the knocker sounded again. Switching the hall light on, Thea paused at the door – a dark, heavy door without windows, of the sort that was common to the tall, white-painted terraces in Brighton's more pleasant streets – then opened it just enough to see outside.

Familiarity stirred then sharpened into recognition. 'Mr Ambrose!'

It was a formal way to address a stepbrother but Stanley lived in America and Thea had only met him briefly before. That had been two years ago when he'd called in three or four times while in England on a visit. She opened the door wider, shivering in the chill wind that raced along Clarendon Place after sweeping over the English Channel and across Marine Parade. 'Come in.'

A big man in his forties, he stepped into the hall. Thea closed the door then led the way into the drawing room, switching the light on and pulling the curtains across the window. She gestured to the empty hearth and smiled apologetically. 'I'm afraid you've caught me unprepared. If you wrote to me, the letter went astray.'

'I didn't write.'

'I didn't receive a telegram either. Not since the one that instructed me to proceed with the funeral.'

'I didn't send a telegram.'

'I see.' Thea hadn't warmed to her stepbrother the first time she'd met him and she couldn't warm to him now.

That first time he'd treated Thea and her mother as irrelevancies in his world, sparing them barely a nod when he'd come to the house. Ever gracious, Cecily had invited him to stay but he'd declined with a grunted 'No', without even adding thanks.

Instead he'd slept elsewhere but holed up with his father in the old book room to drink whisky during the evenings. The room had stunk of it in the morning. It had stunk of Herbert and Stanley too, a combination of hair oil, breath mints and alcohol oozing through their pores. Thea had found it deeply unpleasant.

She hoped Stanley wasn't expecting to stay now. He'd brought no luggage but he could have left it at the station while he saw how the land lay. She hoped he wasn't expecting a meal either. Thea had only half a loaf, a little cheese and four eggs in the house. She should offer him tea, though.

'Would you like a warming cup of—'

'No.'

Goodness, he was difficult. 'I'm sure you want to hear about the funeral, however.'

It hadn't been well attended. Herbert had lived his life separately from Thea and her mother, treating their house as little more than a source of funds and a place to lay his head when he returned from who knew where, crashing about drunkenly in the small hours. Not knowing his cronies, Thea had spent money she could ill-afford on an obituary in the newspaper but only five people had come to the funeral: three old sots with blood-shot eyes, and two bold, blowsy women. None of Cicely's old friends had come because shame over her second husband had kept Cicely isolated for years.

On a brighter note, surely Stanley would offer to reimburse Thea the funeral costs now. 'Several of your father's friends attended and—'

'I'm here about his Will.' Stanley's eyes were hard and unemotional. They were hooded eyes set in a fleshy face above a beefy neck.

Thea acknowledged the change of subject with a nod. 'I was intending to write to you about your father's things. I didn't know which of them you wanted to keep so I've left his room untouched.' If Stanley had travelled from America hoping for a substantial inheritance, he was going to be disappointed. His father had left very little behind. Not even photographs of Stanley's late mother.

'I'm here about your mother's Will too.'

Thea was surprised then a little concerned. If Stanley thought he was a beneficiary of her mother's Will, he was set for more disappointment. Cecily had left all her estate to Thea. What remained of it that was.

But perhaps he merely wished to be sure that everything had been done properly so he could return to his own life without giving her further thought. 'I haven't seen a solicitor about my mother's Will yet, but I intend to do so soon,' Thea told him.

Herbert had fallen ill soon after her mother's death and Thea had mostly been tied to the house. Then one day Herbert had grabbed her wrist and pulled her closer. Fighting her revulsion, Thea had allowed him to gasp in her ear, 'Your mother's Will. Don't. Do. Anything.'

Assuming he feared she'd put him out on the streets, Thea had agreed to wait.

'I have your mother's Will,' Stanley said now.

Thea realised he must be referring to her mother's old Will, made after the death of Thea's father and in anticipation of her marriage to Herbert. Oh dear. This could be awkward. Dismayed at the way Herbert was running through her money, Thea's mother had made a new Will in secret that left the house in Clarendon Place entirely to her daughter.

'Even if there's no money left, you'll have a roof over your head,' she'd said and, comforted by the thought of it, she'd mentioned it often. 'At least you'll have a place to live... At least you won't be without a home...'

Thea braced herself for anger on Stanley's part. 'My mother made a new Will three years ago.'

'The Will I have was made two years ago.'

Thea blinked. 'That isn't possible.' Her mother would have told her about a third Will.

'I assure you it *is* possible. It's lodged with my solicitors.' Stanley took his wallet out, extracted a business card and slapped it onto the mantelpiece. 'Sneath & Landis of North Street. I suggest you call on them soon.'

There had to be a mistake. Surely there was some sort of mistake? A feeling of dread crept over Thea. 'What are the terms of this Will?'

'Your mother left her jewellery to you.'

Only a few pieces remained. Herbert had taken most of them.

'She left the rest of her estate to my father and he left everything to me.'

'Including this house?'

'Certainly including this house.'

Thea's hand grasped the back of a chair. She felt suddenly unsteady but was determined not to show it.

'I'm prepared to be generous,' Stanley continued. 'I'm in England for only a short time on this occasion but I'm arranging to return permanently. My business affairs in America will occupy me for the next few months but then I'll be back. It's almost the middle of February now. Provided you've vacated the house by the end of May and left the contents intact, I'm prepared to give you a gift of one hundred pounds. My solicitor will see to it.' He nodded towards the business card. 'The end of May, Miss Fairfax. Not a day longer.'

With that he headed for the hall and would have barged past Thea if she hadn't darted out of his way. He didn't wait for her to open the door but pulled it open himself and walked out into the night without a backward glance.

Thea closed the door after him then slumped against it. One hundred pounds wouldn't last long at all. And once it had gone she'd be destitute.

Two

Bermondsey, London

Anna knew from the malicious triumph on her father's face that her days in this house were numbered. Her mother knew it too judging from the way her anxious fingers pleated and re-pleated the worn tea cloth. So did the children.

Mary, four years younger than Anna at sixteen, was taking short, sharp breaths as though summoning the courage to leap to her darling sister's defence. Anna shook her head to warn her against trying because it would do no good for Anna and might bring their father's wrath down on Mary too.

Lizzie, the youngest at just five, had tears pooling in her eyes. She didn't understand what was happening but she did know her beloved Anna was in trouble. Anna sent Lizzie a bracing smile then repeated the smile for the boys – Joe at fourteen as keen to spring to Anna's defence as Mary, and Tom at ten confused but concerned.

Jed Watson sucked on his Woodbine then blew smoke out slowly, savouring his moment. 'Some daughter you've turned out to be. Where are all your fine ways now, eh? So much for thinking you're better than us working folk.'

'I've never considered myself to be better than anyone,' Anna pointed out quietly.

'So much for all them books and outings to look at pictures too. Ideas above your station, that's what you've always had.'

'I've tried to make the children see the value of an education, that's all. To give them choices about their futures.'

'Futures like yours, you mean? With a bastard baby on the way by some fancy man who's left you high and dry?'

'Piers hasn't left me. He's travelling.'

'So you say. And you're dumb enough to believe it despite all your book-learning.'

'Piers is a gentleman.'

'Gentlemen don't lie with girls before they marry 'em.'

'We're engaged.'

'Then where's the ring?'

There hadn't been time for a ring. Not a proper ring. Piers had wrapped a buttercup around her finger instead. 'A token of my love and commitment,' he'd said with a smile. 'To keep us going while I'm away. I'll buy the biggest diamond I can afford when I return.'

'I don't need a big diamond,' Anna had told him. 'All I want is you.'

But she wished she had a proper ring now.

'You've let that man make a whore of you,' her father said. 'And I won't have a whore in my house.'

'Jed, please,' her mother begged. 'Don't say things like that. Not about your own daughter.'

'She's no daughter of mine.'

'She's –'

'Shut up, woman. Or I'll shut you up, and you know what that means.'

Janet Watson did know, and so did Anna.

'It's all right, Ma.' Anna smiled reassurance at the faded, harassed woman who'd given birth to her, but felt the heavy weight of dread. Where on earth could she go?

'Away with you,' her father said. 'Get out of my sight.'

Anna hesitated for just a moment then ran upstairs to the room she shared with her brothers and sisters where she leaned her palms on top of the small chest of drawers and let her head drop forward, breathing deeply to try to quell the mounting panic. But it was only a matter of time before her mother and the children came up, and Anna didn't want them to find her looking scared. Pushing herself upright, she studied her reflection in the small mirror that hung on the wall.

Her face was even paler than usual while her dark eyes were large with fear. Swallowing, Anna smoothed her hands over the heavy brown hair that she kept drawn into a bun on the nape of her neck like a Victorian governess, then attempted a smile. She didn't linger to see if she'd succeeded but turned away from the mirror to pack her things.

The tiny house – surely long overdue for demolition – had only two rooms upstairs, a crude curtain separating the bed in which Anna slept with her sisters from the bed in which her brothers slept. Having brought home cardboard boxes so they could keep their possessions in an orderly fashion under the beds, Anna kept the room spotlessly clean and tidy.

Those possessions were admittedly few. There were the books, writing tablets and pencils that Anna had bought, the doll that had been passed down between them and scraps of fabric that Anna had used to teach the girls sewing. There were also wooden carvings made by the man at number twenty-six who'd been blinded by gas in the war, catapults, a ball and things scavenged from the banks of the Thames when the tide was out – small bottles, pipes, a model boat with the rigging missing, and bits of glass worn smooth after years in the river.

Anna took a bag from her box, opened a drawer and began to pack her modest collection of clothes, aware that her fingers were shaking badly. Her mother and the children crowded into the room after her. They were white-faced and saucer-eyed, and little Mary was crying openly now.

Anna took a deep breath and renewed her attempt at a smile. 'It's going to be fine.'

'But where will you go? How will you manage?' her mother asked.

'I have friends, Ma. I'll cope.'

'Your pa says you mustn't even write to us.'

'I'll write care of Mrs Fawley next door but don't fret if you don't hear from me for a while as I get myself established.' Anna turned to Mary. 'You'll keep up the lessons?'

Mary worked in a bakery but the other children were still in school and Anna had always given them extra lessons. ''Course I will,' Mary promised.

'What's happened to me changes nothing,' Anna insisted. 'The better you're educated, the more choices you'll have about how you earn a living.' Earning a good living was the way out of slum housing and poverty. The way to dignity and satisfaction too.

'Listen to what Mary tells you,' Anna bade the others.

'We will,' Lizzie promised, then she held out her shiny sixpence. 'I want you to have it.'

Anna's throat tightened.

'I've got tuppence you can have,' Joe said.

'And I've got ninepence,' Mary said.

'Here, love.' Anna's mother held out five or six coppers. 'It's all I've got till your pa gets paid.'

Anna swallowed. 'You're all wonderfully generous but I can't take your money.'

She took her mother into her arms instead and kissed her, then did the same to each of the children. 'I love you all dearly,' she told them.

Afraid she might cry or let her fear show if she lingered, Anna picked her bag up and hastened downstairs. She said not a word to her father and he said nothing to her.

The door opened straight onto the pavement. Anna stepped outside and shivered in the chill then walked away as though she had a clear destination in mind. She hadn't, but she guessed her mother and the children were watching from the bedroom window and didn't want to upset them even more by looking lost and helpless.

It started to rain as she rounded the corner. Anna quickened her pace and reached a row of shops. They were closed but the doors were set back from the pavement and offered at least a little protection from the rain. Stepping into the shelter of the cobbler's shop, Anna tried to formulate a plan of action.

She had indeed made friends at work in the women's wear section of Selfridges department store but none of them knew about the baby. She'd kept her pregnancy secret so she wouldn't lose her job and also so no one would condemn Piers as a bounder for getting her into trouble.

But Piers didn't know about the baby either because Anna had wanted to save him from the distress of imagining what she was going through while he was thousands of miles away. He'd have been mortified with guilt and might even have left the expedition on which they were pinning their hopes for the future.

It was just a pity the expedition had overrun. Or so Anna assumed, not having heard from him for several weeks and preferring to believe in a delay than in the alternative possibility – that something bad had happened to Piers. An illness, an accident, an attack by a poisonous spider, snake or other deadly creature... Piers might love adventure but he loved life more and wouldn't take foolish risks. No, he'd warned her from the beginning that communication over a distance of thousands of miles was likely to be difficult.

Hanging on for Piers's return, Anna hadn't even told her family about her pregnancy until today. Luckily, she hadn't felt sick and her body hadn't expanded as much as many women's did in the early months. She was taking after her mother in experiencing a general thickening around her middle rather than 'carrying it all in front,' as she'd heard some women call it. So far she'd been able to hide the changes under the dresses she'd made for herself – two black drop-waisted dresses worn with loose jackets or cardigans to disguise her shape still further. But now she was into her sixth month she'd known that the days of hiding her condition were numbered.

She'd also feared that Selfridges might refuse her a reference or write about her in disapproving terms if they learned of her pregnancy. To be sure of receiving a glowing reference that would help her to get work in the future Anna had felt she had no choice but to resign her job and throw herself on her father's mercy. Now she had no roof over her head, no job and little prospect of getting one in her current condition. She didn't have much money either. Anna had always been careful with money but most of her wages had gone to her mother.

None of her old colleagues were in a position to help even if she explained her circumstances. Agnes lived with strict parents who'd be appalled at the idea of accommodating a fallen woman. Emily lived with her widowed mother in rooms scarcely big enough for the two of them while Hilda's family was reeling after losing their youngest child to tuberculosis.

There was only one set of people to whom Anna could go. She hadn't wanted to meet them like this but, again, she hadn't a choice.

Sighing, Anna stepped out of the doorway into the rain.

Three

Daisy gave the horse's muzzle a reassuring stroke. 'It's over, darling. Didn't I tell you there was nothing to worry about?'

Claude hated having his hooves shod even though Daisy's dad was a calm and efficient farrier. Daisy didn't mind holding the horse's head and whispering sweet nothings into his ears to calm him, though. She much preferred the forge to the kitchen.

She led Claude to the paddock behind the forge, not letting the fact that she was barely five feet tall undermine her confidence in handling a large horse like him. There wasn't a horse alive that frightened Daisy.

The farmer would send someone to collect Claude shortly. In the meantime, he could recover from his ordeal in peace. Releasing him, Daisy patted his neck and watched him start to crop the grass. It was chilly, wintry grass but still welcome.

Daisy wasn't needed for the next horse. Mr Oaks, who'd taken over Downs Edge, the smallholding along the lane, was bringing his children's pony and would look after it himself.

Reluctant to return to the cottage despite the cold, Daisy climbed the fence and sat on the top, looking out across the Downs. She could see horses in the distance, dusky in the shadows of trees. They put her in mind of her cousin and the horses he looked after. There was nothing Daisy wanted more than to work with Max but he'd told her he couldn't afford to employ her yet.

'You won't always be poor,' she'd reasoned, because no one had more energy and drive than Maxwell Moore.

'To be sure I won't. If I can help it. But until then…'

Daisy supposed she'd just have to be patient though patience wasn't her strong point.

Meanwhile it was pleasant to daydream of the day she'd join him at Clareswood, helping to look after his employers' horses and also his own mare and the foals she brought into the world. Max wanted to train horses too, ideally for racing, but that was unlikely to happen for some time.

Eventually, the need to prepare supper worked its way through the reverie. Daisy's cooking wasn't up to much but her father had to eat and so did she.

Jumping down from the fence, she realised she must have been daydreaming for quite a while because tall Mr Oaks was already leading the newly-shod pony home. Daisy's conscience stirred and she moved into the forge at speed.

'I'm going to start on supper now,' she assured her dad.

'I'll brace myself, shall I?'

Scowling at the teasing, Daisy turned to leave.

'Wait on,' her father said then.

Daisy turned back again.

'Daniel Oaks was here.'

'I saw him.'

'He mentioned you.'

'I didn't think you needed me to look after the pony. She's a placid little thing.'

'You weren't needed for the pony. But Daniel asked if I'd object if he paid some attention to you.'

'Paid some…?' Daisy was puzzled, but then she realised what her father was suggesting. 'Pay attention to *me*?' It was the stupidest suggestion she'd ever heard. 'I hope you told him no.'

'I told him I'd talk to you and that's what I'm doing.'

'You should have told him no straight away, Dad.'

'He's a fine-looking man. Good with animals too. I'd have thought that would be a point in his favour.'

'He's ancient!'

Frank Flowers laughed. 'The man's not yet thirty, girl.'

'And I'm not yet twenty. Not yet nineteen even. He's a widower. He's got children.'

'I don't see how that disqualifies him.'

'He's just looking for someone to keep house and look after his family.'

'With all due respect, girl, I don't think you'd be top of any man's list if he were looking for a housekeeper.'

'He doesn't know I'm hopelessly undomesticated. He doesn't know me at all.'

'Neither do you know him. Daniel hasn't been here a year yet but he's already well regarded in the village and he's making a real success of Downs Edge. Even your cousin gets tonics and potions for his horses from him. Mebbe spending time with Daniel is a chance for you both to get to know each other and see if you'd suit.'

'I don't want to get to know him.' A sudden thought struck her with horror. 'You're not going to make me see him, are you?'

Frank laughed again. 'I might just as well try to catch hold of a rainbow.'

'So you'll tell him no?'

'I think you should tell him no.'

'Me?'

'It's you he wants to court.'

'Yes, but –' Daisy broke off and chewed her lip.

'You're not afraid of facing him?'

'No! It's just… embarrassing.'

'Much of life is embarrassing. It doesn't hurt to practice dealing with it.'

Daisy rolled her eyes and stomped out of the forge. The cottage was just a few yards away. Walking into the kitchen, she threw herself into a chair.

What was she supposed to say to Daniel Oaks? She could hardly tell him that the thought of being courted by him appalled her. It would sound less insulting if she told him she wasn't ready to be courted by anyone yet. On the other hand it might make him think she'd come round to the idea.

Perhaps she should tell him she'd decided never to marry anyone because she was devoting herself to looking after her father. Would she have to add that she was honoured by his interest and other guff like that? Daisy didn't know, but she was sure she was going to make a hash of it. Even the thought of having to face the man made her stomach tighten.

Daisy looked across at the photograph of her mother that stood on the dresser. Alice Flowers would have known exactly what to say. Daisy shared Alice's daintiness, fair hair and blue eyes but sadly she'd inherited none of her finer qualities. Aside from her lapse in judgement in saddling her daughter with the awful name of Daisy Flowers, Alice had been gentle and tactful with a cosy appreciation for hearth and home. She'd relished domesticity, in fact, but Daisy loathed it.

Glancing around the kitchen, she felt a stab of guilt for failing to keep it up to the standards of her mother and Mrs Beddows, the neighbour who'd helped in the first years after Alice's death. The room was neither dirty nor particularly untidy but nothing sparkled with freshness or gleamed with care. Daisy did the bare minimum.

Would things have been different if Alice had lived long enough to guide her daughter through the turbulent years of change from girl to woman? Daisy had only been eleven when her mother died. But no. Daisy was cut from a different cloth and always had been.

Max's mother had been sister to Daisy's mother but he wasn't made in the family tradition either. Even so he might be able to give her some advice about the best way to let Mr Oaks down.

Getting up, Daisy fetched notepaper from the dresser and began to write.

Dear Maxie,
Something awkward has happened. Could you come over to see me?
Love, Daisy x

She paused then added:

PS No one is ill or anything like that.

She paused again then added:

PPS Hope you are well.

She should probably have put that at the beginning but she wasn't going to waste time and paper writing the letter again. Max preferred straight talking to sugar-coated nonsense anyway.

She addressed the envelope:

Mr M Moore,
Stable Cottage,
Clareswood,
Near Pulborough,
Sussex

Then she added a stamp.

It was getting late but she might still catch the last post. Daisy shrugged into her coat and wrapped a scarf around her neck but hesitated when she reached the lane. If she walked straight into the village, she'd pass the entrance to Daniel Oaks's smallholding. She cringed at the thought of meeting him before she'd got her answer clear in her head.

She pushed her way through a hedgerow instead, working her way towards the centre of the village through a field and hoping no one would see her because she must look furtive and odd. She emerged next to old Dolly Cartwright's cottage and hid in its shadow until she was sure the coast was clear. Darting across the road, she dropped the letter into the red pillar box and returned home the same way she'd come.

She found her father in the kitchen. He'd cut two thick slices of ham and was frying them along with some eggs. 'I didn't see any signs of supper cooking and I didn't fancy starving,' he said.

'I popped out for some air.'

'I don't know about popping. You look like you've been dragged through a hedge backwards.' He picked a dry brown leaf from her hair.

She didn't explain that she'd pushed her way through a hedge frontwards but laid the table for supper, hoping Max would come to her rescue soon.

Four

Thea decided there was something reptilian about Mr Sneath of Sneath & Landis. His handshake was cold and lifeless, his eyes hard and unblinking in a pale, narrow face from which thin dark hair was held back by grease. He was devoid of colour too, his jacket black, and his shirt white. Even his lips appeared to be bloodless.

He'd said nothing as Thea was being shown into his office. Now he gestured her to the chair in front of his desk and sat in his own seat behind it, linking his long, white fingers together and watching her, still without saying a word. Had she been a butterfly caught in a jar, Thea felt he could have watched her death throes with utter indifference.

Thea didn't consider herself to be a hate-filled person but she disliked Mr Sneath intensely. Perhaps it stood to reason that repellent people like the Ambroses would choose another repellent person to serve their interests.

So be it. Thea would have to serve her own interests. 'Stanley Ambrose is your client, I believe.'

'That is correct.'

'He tells me you have a Will made by my mother. Cecily Ambrose. Formerly Cecily Fairfax.'

'That is also correct.'

'I'd like to see it, please.'

'It provides for you to inherit your mother's jewellery.' His voice was flat. Lacking expression.

'So I understand. But I'd like to see the Will for myself.'

'It's a legal document written in legal language.'

'Legal language is still the English language, is it not?'

He stared at her for a long moment then reached under a pile of papers on his desk to withdraw a long document that had been sewn along the side with black ribbon. He passed it to her.

The paper was thick and creamy, the handwriting black and decorative but still legible.

Thea read:

This is the last Will and Testament of Cecily Anne Ambrose.

The rest of the Will was written in old-fashioned language but the meaning was clear: Thea was to inherit what remained of her mother's jewellery and Herbert was to inherit everything else.

'May I see Mr Herbert Ambrose's Will too?' Thea asked.

'That Will doesn't mention you.'

'Perhaps not. But is there any reason why I can't see it? Wills are documents of public record, are they not?'

'Once probate has been granted.'

'Which means I'll get to see it eventually anyway.'

The white fingers brought out another document that had been sewn with black ribbon. Thea read it swiftly, unsurprised to find that all of Herbert's estate had indeed been left to Stanley. Putting it down, she took a notepad and pencil from her bag.

'I assume I can make a note of the details?' she asked. 'I can use the outer office if I'm inconveniencing you in here.'

'Here will do very well,' he told her.

Both Wills had been made on the same date two years previously. If memory served Thea correctly, the date coincided with Stanley's visit.

'You're not aware of a later Will?' Mr Sneath asked.

'Only an earlier one.'

His mouth moved. It wasn't a smile but a smug grimace. 'Old Wills become invalid once a new Will is made.'

So Thea understood.

She wrote the date of the Wills into her notebook then turned to the most puzzling thing: her mother's signature. She stared at it for a long time before looking up and meeting Mr Sneath's cold gaze. 'Did my mother come here to sign this Will?'

'She signed it at home, I believe. There's no legal requirement for a lawyer to be present when a Will is signed.'

'Did you even meet my mother?'

'I did not. Again, there's—'

'No legal requirement,' Thea guessed. 'Your instructions came from Stanley Ambrose, I suppose.'

'From his father too. There was nothing extraordinary about a married man putting his affairs in order and assisting his wife to do the same, particularly as I understood your mother to be a lady of delicate sensibilities.'

'My mother never mentioned this Will to me.'

'Perhaps she considered it inappropriate to discuss such matters with a young lady.'

Thea was twenty-one now and she'd been nineteen when the Will was made. Hardly a child. Besides, she'd grown up fast after her father's death. It had been Thea who'd provided emotional and practical support to her mother rather than the other way round. 'My mother was open with me about her financial affairs.'

He gave the smallest of shrugs. 'It must be disappointing to learn that she wasn't as open as you'd thought.'

What an unpleasant man he was. 'According to these Wills, my mother made Herbert the principal beneficiary of her Will yet she didn't benefit from his Will at all.'

'Had Herbert Ambrose been the first to die your mother would still have had the house in Clarendon Place,' Mr Sneath pointed out.

'Neither Will made provision for me.'

'Doubtless your mother assumed her husband would have allowed you to continue living in the house. Or perhaps she imagined you'd soon have a husband of your own to provide for you.'

That made no sense at all. Cecily had been desperately worried for her daughter's future and many a time she'd mentioned how she feared Thea might never find a suitable husband now they no longer had genteel connections.

'She also left you her jewellery,' Mr Sneath reminded her.

'A modest collection, much depleted during her marriage.'

'It was not my business to enquire into its value.'

He couldn't have cared less about it. Thea moved on. 'The people who witnessed the Will. Did you meet them?' she asked.

'I did not.'

'Do you even know who they were?'

'I know no more than you're reading there.'

The two witnesses had signed their names under Cecily's signature and added their addresses. Thea wrote them down.

Jeremiah Jarrold, 16 Ships Passage, Brighton and Albert Strupp, Apartment C, 11 Ballard Street, Brighton.

'I trust you're not suggesting there was some sort of irregularity to your mother's Will?' Mr Sneath asked, the snake eyes reminding her that there was such a thing as slander.

'I'm not suggesting anything.' Nothing she was ready to share with Mr Sneath anyway.

'Stanley Ambrose is sensible of the fact that you may find yourself in some financial difficulty and has authorised me to pay you one hundred pounds when you vacate the property. This is an ex gratia payment. That is to say it's a voluntary payment given free of any obligation on his part and conditional upon you vacating Clarendon Place by the end of May. Being voluntary, the offer can be withdrawn should Mr Ambrose encounter resistance or other impediment.'

In other words Thea had to shut up if Stanley was to pay up.

Mr Sneath rose to his feet, a gaunt figure but a threatening one too. 'It will be appreciated if you apprise me of the likely date of your removal once you've made your arrangements. A telephone call to my clerk will be sufficient. I can then release the funds. Good day to you.'

Thea stood too. 'Good day to you, Mr Sneath,' she said, her tone just as glacial as his.

Outside she walked towards Clarendon Place, avoiding passers-by through instinct rather than conscious thought as she struggled to make sense of what she'd learned. Shock had kept her awake last night but she considered each possibility with as clear a head as she could manage:

1. Her mother had signed the Will and made no mention of it for the reasons Mr Sneath had suggested. Thea rejected the possibility instantly. She hadn't imagined that she'd been the strong one in her relationship with her mother. Cecily hadn't trusted Herbert at all and worry about Thea's future had been the major concern of Cecily's last years. Right until the end, Cecily had taken comfort in her belief that Thea would have the house. No, Cecily hadn't knowingly signed a Will that placed her daughter in such a difficult position.

2. Might she have been tricked into signing it? Thea pictured the scene. 'Just sign here,' Herbert might have said. 'It's only a subscription to a magazine. Quickly, Cecily. I need to go out...' But Cecily hadn't been stupid, and there was no way she'd have signed a document in front of two witnesses who were strangers to her without ascertaining what, exactly, she was signing. In fact the very presence of witnesses would have alarmed her. Herbert might have tricked Cecily into signing

and arranged for the witnesses to sign later but Thea considered the third possibility to be more likely.

3. Cecily's signature had been forged.

Sneath & Landis weren't the only solicitors in Brighton. Thea's parents had used Mr Lawley of Lawley & Pearce. He was a nice old gentleman who'd given Thea mint imperials when he'd drawn up the Will that ensured she inherited the house. It was to old Mr Lawley that she'd go for advice.

Five

Anna woke wincing at the stiffness in her neck. Sitting up, she rubbed her aching muscles then opened her eyes, a moment's confusion being followed swiftly by the memory of the circumstances that had led to her spending the night dozing uncomfortably in a station waiting room.

It had been late by the time she'd reached the station. It would have been later still by the time she reached Worthing and she had no idea how far Ashfyld House was from the centre of town. Nor did she know how she might get there. All things considered, it had felt wiser to delay her journey until morning when she could arrive at a more civilised hour.

Unsure of her welcome at Ashfyld House, Anna had decided to spend not a penny more than was essential so she'd headed for the waiting room instead of a guest house. People had come and gone but eventually she'd found herself alone. When a station attendant had entered, keys in hand, he'd looked surprised to see her. 'Missed your train, Miss?'

Anna had sent him a non-committal smile.

'If you're looking for somewhere to stay, there's—'

'Actually, I thought I'd wait here and catch the early train.'

For a moment she'd thought he might tell her that waiting all night wasn't allowed but he'd studied her for a moment then nodded kindly. 'As you will, Miss.'

Anna hadn't liked being pitied. She'd always worked hard and been determined to make her way in the world. But sympathy had been helpful just then.

To occupy the long wait until morning and take her mind off the future, Anna had sought solace in remembering the past. The happy past, starting with the time she'd met Piers.

She'd gone to the Natural History building of the British Museum one evening to hear a talk on a recent African expedition and had just taken a seat when Piers walked in. It would have been difficult not to notice Piers because he was taller than most men and had a head of bright fair hair that gleamed beneath the lights. He was smartly dressed too, his pale jacket showing that he was broad in the shoulders but otherwise trim, and there was a rare energy in the way he walked that suggested he believed that life was a gift to be grabbed with both hands.

He took a seat on the opposite side of the room and, as the lecture started, Anna turned her attention to the speaker. His stories of the animals and people he'd encountered in Africa were captivating and she applauded enthusiastically at the end. Getting to her feet, she moved towards the door, wondering how long it would take to save enough money to take the children to London Zoo. The zoo wasn't Africa, but they'd still be able to see some wonderful animals.

'Did you enjoy the talk?' someone asked her.

Looking up, she saw Piers though she didn't know his name then. What blue eyes he had. Anna found herself blushing. 'I thought it was wonderful,' she told him. 'Did you enjoy it?'

'I always enjoy hearing about people's travels. Travel is a passion of mine.'

'You've been overseas?' Anna was intrigued.

'Many times. My next trip is to Brazil.'

'How wonderful!'

They continued talking as they walked through the building and finally reached the street.

'If you're not in a hurry to get home, I could tell you more about my trip over a drink,' he said.

Anna felt a rush of pleasure followed by the dampening weight of disappointment. She'd promised to go home and tell the children all about the talk and it wasn't in her nature to let them down.

'Tomorrow?' Piers asked. 'I could take you to supper.'

'I'd like that.' She'd like it a lot.

They arranged to meet after Anna had finished her shift at Selfridges. 'I'm Piers Rutherford, by the way,' he said then. 'Sorry. I should have introduced myself earlier.'

'Anna Watson.' She'd never felt self-conscious shaking someone's hand before but the light in Piers's eyes brought a glow to her cheeks.

He walked her to her bus stop and saw her safely aboard her bus. Anna waved as it pulled away from the kerb then sat back feeling oddly but pleasantly flustered, another new sensation.

She spent the next day fearing he might decide not to meet her after all. It was one thing to spend a few minutes in conversation with someone and quite another to spend a couple of hours with them. He might worry they'd have little to say to each other, especially as his clothes and his voice had suggested someone several notches above her on the social scale.

Anna told herself that it wouldn't matter if he showed up or not as he was practically a stranger. But she knew deep down that it would matter because she'd been very taken with what she'd seen of him. That smile in particular.

He was exactly where she'd asked him to be. Not outside the store but further along Oxford Street at Bond Street underground station because Anna hadn't wanted her colleagues to tease her about meeting a man, especially as she wasn't sure if they were meeting only as people who shared an interest or because… well, because there was a spark that might lead to them walking out together. Anna had never walked out with any man before and didn't know how to read the signs about what a man had in mind.

Even when she spotted that golden head she wondered whether he regretted his impulsive invitation and was meeting her only because he felt good manners required it. How awkward that would be! But his warm smile reassured her that he'd had no such regrets.

'I hope you're hungry,' he said. 'There's a restaurant on Brook Street I thought we might try.'

A restaurant? Anna had never been to a restaurant in her life. A Lyons Tea Room was the height of luxury to her and to everyone she knew. And Brook Street was in Mayfair, a very expensive part of London. 'I'll be happy with a simple café,' she told him, adding, 'I'm still dressed for work.'

'You're my guest and I think you look very well indeed,' he assured her, the softness of his voice leaving her in no doubt of his sincerity.

A thrill of pleasure squeezed Anna's stomach and to Brook Street they went. The restaurant Piers had chosen was small with subdued lighting so she didn't feel self-conscious as she took off her coat to reveal a black dress that reached to mid-calf and was relieved from severity by velvet trimming around the neckline and cuffs.

On Piers's recommendation they feasted on Dover sole, lamb cutlets and toffee pudding. 'Delicious,' Anna declared, without exaggeration.

They also drank ruby-coloured wine which made her head swim a little. She drank rarely because she hadn't the money to spare for it and didn't want to behave like her father who became even nastier after evenings at the Anchor. But this wine was very nice indeed.

Urged by Anna, Piers talked of his love of travel as they ate. He'd seen historic frescoes in Italy and fairy-tale chateaux in France. He'd tasted oranges freshly plucked from trees in Spain and olives he'd gathered in Greece. But what really fired his passion was travel to remoter parts of the world.

'I went to Greenland then onto Nova Scotia in Canada last year,' he told her. 'At times it was so cold that we couldn't touch the rails of the ship in case our skin stuck to them, and we had ice crystals in our hair. But it was a magical experience. We saw the Aurora Borealis several times. Great plumes of pink and green dancing across the sky. We saw seals, whales and polar bears too.'

He'd also trekked through the Egyptian desert, visiting the pyramids of Giza before moving into Turkey. 'We rode on camels,' he said. 'Wonderful creatures if you overlook their habit of spitting.'

In Africa he'd seen lions, tigers, elephants and giraffes. 'Some people go to hunt them. I went to admire them. And to write about them, of course.'

'To write?'

'It's how I earn my living. I write about travelling for the *National Daily Herald*. George Acaster – he's the owner as well as the editor – helps to fund expeditions on condition that I can be a part of them.'

'It sounds as though you have the best job in the world.' Anna smiled.

'It's certainly one of the best,' Piers agreed.

'Is Mr Acaster helping to fund your expedition to Brazil?'

'He is. We'll be travelling down the Amazon, hoping to avoid being eaten by alligators.'

'How long will you be away?'

'Five months. Possibly six.'

'Goodness.'

Anna hadn't been thinking about the future as they talked – not consciously anyway – but now she was aware of a pang of regret as she realised this dinner was just a brief interlude between expeditions. Ah, well. 'When do you leave?'

'In six weeks' time.'

'You must be excited.'

'Of course. But...' He hesitated and Anna waited, curious but not wanting to prompt him for fear of treading on sensitive ground.

Piers smiled lopsidedly. 'I hadn't anticipated meeting you, Anna. The expedition has begun to feel terribly ill-timed.'

Warmth rushed across Anna's cheeks as his meaning sank in.

'At least we have six weeks to get to know each other before I leave,' he said. 'Assuming you'd like that?'

'I… I'm not sure,' Anna admitted.

'Is that because you think there isn't much point in getting to know me when I'm going away?'

That was certainly one of her concerns.

'I'm not going away forever,' Piers pointed out.

But he'd be taking in wondrous sights that might make him forget all about her while she'd be left behind nursing what she suspected might be a bruised heart.

Anna wasn't a frivolous person by nature. She'd never been attracted to any man before but being here with Piers was exhilarating. Wonderful. If she allowed him to touch her feelings, those feelings would run deep.

Piers appeared to understand her concerns without Anna needing to explain them. 'Neither of us knows what the future holds,' he said. 'We've spent… What? Two hours in each other's company? They've been the happiest two hours of my life and, unless I'm much mistaken, they've been happy hours for you too. It might be the sort of happiness that fades as quickly as a rainbow but it might be the pot of gold at a rainbow's end. I'd rather find out what it is than spend the future wondering if we've let something precious slip away.'

There was another possibility. Happiness might fade for only one of them and that way heartbreak lay. But it felt cowardly to run away from even a chance of happiness and Anna loathed the thought of being a coward. 'I'd like to find out too,' she agreed, while vowing to place a cautious guard on her heart.

They didn't see each other every day while Piers remained in England. Anna had to work and help at home. Piers had to prepare for the expedition. But they met as often as they could for supper, the theatre, a film or just a walk through a leafy London park. The rainbow shone brightly for Anna and for Piers too, it seemed.

On their last day together Piers borrowed a car and drove her to the South Downs for a picnic. Sussex was Piers's county. He'd been brought up there and his parents still lived in the same house just outside Worthing.

Anna hadn't met his parents and he hadn't met hers though she'd been honest about her modest background. Anna might have a thirst for education and choice in life, but she had no wish to pretend to be someone she wasn't, and the shame she felt for her father arose from his character rather than his financial circumstances.

She told her mother and Mary about Piers but urged them to say nothing to the other children. 'They'd feel terrible if they let something slip,' Anna explained, shuddering as she pictured her father jeering.

Then she implored her mother and sister not to get their hopes up about Piers. 'He'll be away for months and absence doesn't always make the heart grow fonder.'

'We won't,' they chorused, but Anna suspected they'd got their hopes up already.

She tried her best to enjoy that last day but by then there was no doubt in her mind that, despite her caution, she'd fallen in love with Piers. His departure was going to hit her hard.

'I know it's a lot to ask you to wait for me,' he said, as they walked through a small wood before heading home. 'But believe me when I say I love you, Anna.'

'You love me?' Anna came to a halt, needing to see the truth of it in Piers's eyes.

'I love you to the end of the world and back again. I wasn't going to tell you before I left because I didn't want you to feel obliged to wait for me, but I can't keep it back any more. In fact, I wish I'd gone further and –' He broke off, looked around then walked to a nearby tree.

Returning with a buttercup he got down on one knee and offered it up to her. 'I wish I'd bought a ring,' he said. 'I'll buy a ring as soon as I return but in the meantime I'll make do with this flower. Will you marry me, Anna?'

Anna was shocked. And thrilled. 'Yes, I'll marry you, Piers.'

He leapt up and wound the buttercup stalk around her finger, leaving the flower on top in place of a diamond. 'No ring could be more beautiful,' she said, then laughed and reached her arms around his neck to kiss him.

Piers kissed her back, gently at first but then with more passion and urgency than he'd shown before as though he had to drink his fill of her to last him through all the months of his absence. They sank onto a log without breaking the kiss then they were moving to the soft ground beneath the trees…

Afterwards, Piers lay back and drew her head onto his chest. But eventually he propped himself onto an elbow so he could look down on her. He stroked her cheek with his thumb. 'Should I apologise?' he asked. 'It feels wrong to apologise for loving you but I should have waited before –'

Anna touched a fingertip to his mouth. They'd taken things too far but she was as much to blame as Piers. 'We love each other,' she told him.

He kissed her again but gently this time. Then he helped her to her feet. Anna slid her arm through his as they returned to the car, hoping to reassure him that he'd done her no wrong because she could see that guilt weighed heavily on him.

He helped her into the car then walked around to the driver's door and got in beside her.

'You'll let me know if you need me?' he said, and she guessed he was thinking of a pregnancy. 'Just send word and I'll return straight away.'

'What about the expedition?'

'You're more important.'

His warm smile left her in no doubt that he meant it. Anna smiled back though she was thoughtful as they drove towards London. Who'd have thought that disciplined Anna Watson would be carried away in a man's arms like that? But Piers wasn't any man. He was the man she loved.

The waiting room door opened. Cold and aching, Anna got to her feet, her hand travelling instinctively to the still-small curve of her belly to reassure herself that all was well with the child. The baby stirred comfortingly.

A woman had entered and now another woman left. Clearly, the day had come to life while Anna was dozing. She headed for the ladies' cloakroom, feeling stale and creased. She would have liked to bathe or at least give herself a proper wash but all she could do here was splash her face with water and, while no one was around to think her strange, clean her teeth.

Pulling the pins from her hair, she brushed the heavy tresses then re-pinned them at the nape of her neck. The mirror told her she looked neat but she also looked wan. Anna wasn't surprised but she'd have preferred to present a more vibrant appearance at Ashfyld House and have all her wits about her too.

A cup of tea and a currant bun in the station café did little to help. The exhaustion didn't lift but there was nothing more Anna could do. She took the train to Worthing and arrived mid-morning.

'Chilford?' the station guard repeated when she asked for directions. 'It's two or three miles away, Miss.'

Anna set off walking and after half an hour reached a signpost that told her she still had two miles to go. Clearly, the guard's estimate had been wrong. After another half hour she was out in the country and saw a white house with what looked to be extensive gardens in the distance. If this was Ashfyld, it was even grander than expected. But perhaps it wasn't Ashfyld at all.

The white house was lost to her view as the road turned and became flanked by trees. In time she came to a high brick wall and then to a set of ornate iron gates. A sign on the nearest gatepost announced that this was indeed the entrance to Ashfyld House.

The gates were open so Anna walked through them onto a neat, curving driveway. Just one curve along, she saw the house again. Anna's fastidious heart approved the cleanliness of the white paint and the loveliness of the wide black door set under a pillared porch but the gulf between this place and the tiny terraced house that was her family home in Bermondsey felt huge. Anna might believe that it was the character of a person that mattered most but not everyone shared that opinion.

There were three tall windows on each side of the door and two rows of windows above them. Was anyone watching her approach? Wondering who she was and why she was here?

Squaring her shoulders, Anna walked up to the door, passing a car that was parked on the gravel sweep. Did it belong to the Rutherfords or to visitors? Hoping the Rutherfords were free to see her, Anna rang the bell. She blew out slowly, wishing she had an alternative to throwing herself on the Rutherfords' mercy, but this was what Piers would want and expect.

The door was opened by a maid in traditional black and white. 'Would it be convenient for me to see Mrs Rutherford?' Anna asked. 'Or Mr Rutherford, if he's home?'

'Are you expected, Miss?'

'No, but—'

'I'm sorry. Mr and Mrs Rutherford are busy.'

Anna realised the maid was agitated. Perhaps the visitors were causing a lot of work.

'If you'd like to leave a card?' the maid added.

'I don't have any calling cards but my name is Anna Watson. Would it be more convenient for me to return a little later?'

'I don't know, Miss. Perhaps you could telephone.'

'I don't have the number,' Anna began, but the harassed maid had already closed the door.

What now? Anna couldn't wait here on the doorstep. She retraced her steps to the road, tiredness dragging on her feet and shoulders. She'd been a fool not to buy food and something to drink while in Worthing but she couldn't face returning there only to have to walk back again later.

Perhaps she'd find a shop in the village. She headed towards it but Chilford proved to be little more than a hamlet. There was no shop but two farm labourers paused to stare at her and so did a woman who was washing her cottage windows. Doubting the Rutherfords would be pleased if she became an object of curiosity, Anna turned around and walked back, continuing past Ashfyld House to a copse she'd noticed further along the road. Anna scrambled into it and sat on a fallen log, glad to be able to put down her bag.

The copse reminded her of the wood in which Piers had proposed but barely had that thought registered than the rain started. It pattered on the canopy of leaves above her then slithered off the edges to fall on her in ice cold drops. Unstrapping her umbrella from her bag, she put it up and held it over her head, tucking her legs under it too. Walking had made her warm but the heat drained from her rapidly and soon she was shivering and wretched.

A sound reached her. An engine. Anna peered through the trees to see the car that had been parked on the Rutherfords' gravel move past in the direction of Worthing.

Hoping the Rutherfords might see her now, she scrambled back through the copse and returned to the house, aware that she must look even more bedraggled than before but drawing herself up with as much dignity as she could muster.

The same maid opened the door but showed no inclination to let Anna enter. 'Miss, this really isn't—'

'It's important.' Anna couldn't bear the thought of being put off again. Her attention was caught by movement further back in the hall. A slender woman dripping black lace had started up the staircase. 'Mrs Rutherford?' Anna called.

The woman stopped but didn't look round and spoke only to the maid. 'Who is it, Edna? I've told you we can't—'

'My name is Anna Watson,' Anna called. 'If I might just have a word, Mrs Rutherford, I can—'

'Impossible.' The older woman waved a dismissive hand and took another step up the staircase.

'It's about Piers.' Anna was growing desperate. 'He'd want you to talk to me. I know he would.'

Mrs Rutherford stopped again. For a moment she did nothing. Then she turned and looked at Anna though she still spoke only to the maid. 'The library, Edna.'

The maid opened the door wider and Anna stepped through into a spacious hall. 'This way, Miss.

Anna glanced at Mrs Rutherford who'd turned away again then followed Edna into a beautiful room that was lined with books.

The maid left, closing the double doors without inviting Anna to sit. A moment later Mrs Rutherford entered. She was a handsome woman, but Anna was dismayed to realise she'd been crying. A lace handkerchief hung from her bony fingers which plucked at it in distress.

Was there bad news of Piers? Anna clutched the back of a sofa.

'Well?' Mrs Rutherford demanded.

'I hope you haven't—'

'What do you want?'

Anna was going to have to blurt it out. 'Piers and I. This isn't the way we'd have chosen to…' She broke off, unable to bear not knowing what had happened to bring that glitter of tears to this proud, hostile woman. 'Please, Mrs Rutherford. Have you—'

A man entered. Doubtless Mr Rutherford. Anna could see Piers in both of his parents: their height, their fair colouring and their blue eyes, though Piers's eyes were summery instead of glacial like these. Mr Rutherford walked to his wife, touched her shoulder protectively then turned an accusing look on Anna. 'Yes?' he asked.

'Piers and I are engaged to be married,' Anna said.

The Rutherfords exchanged looks. 'Leave this to me,' Mr Rutherford told his wife.

He turned back to Anna. 'It didn't take long,' he sneered.

Anna shook her head. 'I don't understand.'

'I suppose you read it in the newspaper and decided this was a chance to make money.'

'I haven't read anything. If something has happened to Piers, please tell me. I love him.'

'You would say that, of course.'

'It's true! I love Piers and he loves me.'

'Perhaps you were a little acquainted with him. Perhaps not. But don't insult us by asking us to believe there was any love between you.'

'I'm having his child!'

His gaze lowered to her belly where her hand outlined the slight swell and his mouth twisted in disgust. 'You're having someone's child but it's nothing to do with Piers.'

Did he think her pregnancy didn't look far enough advanced to have started before Piers left England? 'I may not look very big but—'

Mr Rutherford's disgust only deepened. 'Piers wouldn't have involved himself with someone like... Well!' He sniffed in distaste.

'Someone like me?' Anna asked. 'You're wrong. We're engaged.'

'I see no ring.'

'Piers intends to buy one when he returns. But you're talking of him in the past tense. I beg you to tell me –'

'The *Adonia* has been lost.'

That was Piers's ship. 'Lost?'

'No survivors have been found.'

Anna felt sick. Dizzy. Her fingers tightened on the back of the sofa until her knuckles turned white.

'But you already knew that,' Mr Rutherford continued. 'You saw an opportunity to take advantage of our grief with this ridiculous story, but you'll foist neither yourself nor your bastard child onto us.'

'Is there no chance that Piers may have survived?' Anna asked.

'We've been warned against false hope. Not that it's any business of yours. I suggest you buy another evening paper and find a different grieving family to exploit for money because that's why you're here, isn't it? For money?'

Mr Rutherford walked to the library doors and thrust them open. 'Please leave. And don't come near us again.'

Anna stared at him, wild-eyed. Piers was dead. Her beautiful, loving Piers was dead.

She let go of the sofa and swayed.

'Enough of your play-acting. You should be ashamed.' With an impatient oath, Mr Rutherford strode towards her and grabbed her arm, bustling her through the hall and out onto the porch. He closed the door behind her with a resounding bang.

Moments later the door opened again and her bag was thrown out after her. The door banged shut again and this time it stayed shut.

Anna picked up her bag and staggered down the drive in the rain, her heart breaking into pieces with every step.

Six

Daisy's plan was simple. She'd stay close to the cottage and forge today, and that way she'd be in little danger of meeting Daniel Oaks. Yes, she had to talk to him eventually, but she'd prefer to wait until after she'd seen Max.

Doubtless Max would laugh at the thought of anyone trying to court his little cousin, but afterwards he might have something useful to suggest about what she could say to the man. Not that Max was courting anyone himself because he was too focused on his work. But Daisy had seen the way women looked at him, sometimes boldly, sometimes slyly, and she was sure he had experience of romance. He was clever too. Shrewd, even. And Daniel Oaks was his friend.

It was possible that Daisy's letter would arrive at Clareswood today but it was more likely that Max would receive it tomorrow. Clareswood was only seven or eight miles away so he might come straight over. On the other hand, he was always busy so might not get to her for several days. Unfortunately, the forge had no telephone so Max couldn't call to let her know when he'd be coming.

Daisy would just have to wait and avoid Daniel in the meantime.

'What's all this?' her father asked when he came across to the cottage for his midday meal.

A ladder stood propped against the wall, a pail beside it on the floor along with rags, old newspapers and a bottle of vinegar.

'I've been cleaning windows,' Daisy told him. 'The sun came out and I noticed they were dirty.'

'The sun came out, did it? I must have missed that.'

'It wasn't out for long.'

'Just long enough for you to see the dirt. Naturally, you couldn't rest until you'd cleaned it off.'

'If you need me to help in the forge, I could come back to the windows later.'

'You could take a walk up to Daniel's place and come back to the windows later,' Frank pointed out.

'I could,' Daisy admitted. 'But if I wait for a day or two he'll start to realise I'm not keen on his suggestion.'

'So you'll be letting him down gently?'

'Preparing him, yes.'

Frank looked her up and down as though the sight of her puzzled him.

'What are you doing?' Daisy asked.

'Just trying to make out if something's happened to your backbone.'

'Dad! I didn't ask Mr Oaks to take an interest in me so it's only fair that I have time to deal with it in my own way.'

'Just don't leave it too long. The poor man's waiting. And that ham's burning.'

Daisy turned to the stove and saw smoke rising from the frying pan. 'Oh, heck!' She snatched the pan away from the heat and threw the kitchen window open, flapping a tea towel to encourage the smoke to go outside.

'Sorry about that,' she said, then poked the ham with a fork. 'It isn't too badly burnt.'

Frank peered at it over her shoulder. 'It'll do. I'm used to burnt offerings.'

Daisy slapped his arm and he returned to the table.

'How many eggs?' she asked.

'Two. Preferably with the yolks unbroken.'

Daisy scowled then reached for the eggs. She fried three but despite her care one yolk broke. She kept that one for herself.

They ate at the table where Daisy had already put roughly-sliced bread and a dish of butter. Afterwards, Frank patted his stomach experimentally. 'Well, I think I'll survive.'

'Very funny.'

'Harry Riggs is bringing Rambler in this afternoon,' he told her then.

Rambler was a nervous horse who didn't ramble as much as stampede when he came near the forge. 'Call me when he arrives and I'll come and help,' Daisy said.

He nodded, drank a mug of tea then returned to work. Daisy put the bread and butter into the pantry and carried the dishes to the sink. She was washing them when the sun came out, showing up the smears she'd left on the window.

And what on earth was that? Daisy peered closer and saw that her father had drawn a face with a downturned mouth in the biggest smear. Doubtless it was supposed to be an entertaining dig at her poor housekeeping skills.

Daisy rolled her eyes then finished the dishes, inspecting each one carefully to avoid giving Frank any more excuses for exercising his awful sense of humour. She boiled some water, poured it into the pail and carried it outside so she could wash away the smear. She hauled the ladder back outside too along with the newspaper and vinegar bottle.

Climbing the ladder, she paused as she heard a voice out in the lane. Those gruff tones belonged to old Reuben Banks from Cutlers Farm but who was with him? Another man spoke. Daniel Oaks. Oh, heck. The voices were getting louder. Any moment now, the men would pass by the forge gate and be able to see her.

Daisy had to get out of sight. Flustered, she took a step down the ladder but her foot slipped and caught between two rungs. She tugged it out but twisted the ladder in the process. The ladder teetered for a moment, then it clattered to the ground and took Daisy with it.

It wasn't a big fall and Daisy wasn't hurt beyond a bruise or two, but she'd made a lot of noise. The voices in the lane had stopped.

Frantically, Daisy pushed the ladder aside, trying to be quiet but making it clang against the metal pail. 'Bugger,' she muttered, getting to her feet at last.

Bugger was Frank's favourite swear word. His only swear word, in fact.

'Bugger indeed.' Daniel Oaks had come across to help her. He stooped down and picked the ladder up. 'Are you all right?' he asked.

'I'm fine.' Daisy was vexed with herself for making such a hash of things, but realising she'd been surly, she added a begrudging, 'Thank you.'

'Comfrey is good for bruises,' he suggested.

How awkward this was.

'I stepped in because I heard you fall,' he said gently. 'I'm not here to press you for an answer.'

She glanced round, wondering if old Mr Banks was in earshot, but he was standing by the gate. A wave from Daisy to confirm that all was well sent him on his way again. 'If you need more time…' Daniel began.

'I don't.' How blunt that sounded! She tried to lift her gaze to his but got no higher than the top button of his shirt. 'It's very… nice of you to want to walk out with me but I don't feel… What I mean is…'

How could she explain that he was too old? That the thought of settling down on his smallholding and playing mother to his children horrified her? She couldn't. 'I don't think I'm the right person for you,' she said instead.

'Shouldn't I be the judge of what's right for me?'

Oh, heavens.

A moment passed. 'I understand,' he said then.

Really? Daisy risked a glance at him. He was a fine figure of a man in many ways. Handsome even, with twinkling green eyes, bronze-coloured hair and regular features. But he wasn't the man for her.

'You don't have feelings for me,' he said.

Was he annoyed? Resentful? He gave no sign of it. 'I don't have feelings for anyone,' Daisy pointed out, trying to soften the blow. 'I'm sorry.'

'None of us can choose where our feelings settle. I just hope I haven't embarrassed you.'

'Not at all,' Daisy lied.

'I wouldn't like to think I'd made you uncomfortable.'

'You haven't.' Another lie.

'If you're sure you're all right—'

'I am.'

'Then I'll bid you good day.'

She nodded, grabbed the pail and hastened inside. She leaned back against the door to give him time to get away but he must have lingered for a moment, because when she moved to the window she saw he hadn't gone far at all.

Her eye was caught by something on the window itself. Someone – it could only have been Daniel – had drawn another face in the smear but this one was smiling. Which meant what exactly? That he really didn't mind that she'd rejected him? Or that he realised he'd had a lucky escape because she couldn't even clean a window properly?

Daisy felt a moment's humiliation at the thought of the latter possibility but a worse feeling soon followed. Dread. In a village the size of Pixfield, there was no way she could avoid Daniel Oaks for long. Every time she saw him she was going to squirm.

Seven

Thea wasn't offered mint imperials by Mr Lawley. A wind of change had gusted through the offices of Lawley & Pearce, Solicitors, taking dust, untidiness and old Mr Lawley with it. They'd been replaced with gloss, efficiency and young Mr Lawley. He smiled just as much as his father, but Thea suspected it wasn't good humour that glinted in his eyes. It was the determination to acquire as many pounds, shillings and pence as possible.

'We do indeed have the Will that your mother made in 1920 but it won't be valid if she made a later Will,' he told her. 'Assuming there was no irregularity about the later Will, of course.'

'What counts as an irregularity?' Thea asked.

'If your mother was unduly influenced, misled or tricked into signing it.'

'So if she thought she was signing a different sort of document…'

'That would be an irregularity, though naturally you'd need evidence to support the allegation. There are technical irregularities too. Your mother should have signed the Will in the presence of two witnesses who were both present at the same time.'

'I have the names and addresses of two witnesses,' Thea said.

'Then they should be able to shed light on the circumstances in which the Will was made.'

'Unless they were involved in a conspiracy to swindle my mother's property,' Thea pointed out.

'Quite so,' Mr Lawley agreed. 'My firm can investigate the witnesses on your behalf, if that's what you'd like?'

It was indeed what she'd like.

'There'd be a fee, of course.' The pound signs blazed brightly.

'Might that fee be paid once the enquiries are completed? If I'm right, the house in Clarendon Place will be mine.'

'But if you're wrong, it'll pass to your stepbrother.' Clearly, Mr Lawley wasn't going to risk non-payment. 'If you wish to instruct my firm, we'll need a retainer against services of twenty-five pounds. Naturally, any unused part of the retainer will be repaid should the business be concluded quickly and inexpensively.'

On the other hand, more money might be demanded if the business took longer.

Thea didn't have a spare twenty-five pounds. Not at the moment. 'Thank you, Mr Lawley. I'll give it some thought.'

She got to her feet, shook his hand and left.

With no clear plan in mind, she walked down to Marine Parade, crossed to Aquarium Terrace, an island in the middle of the road on which the clock tower and aquarium stood, then crossed to the promenade above the stony beach. Beyond that the English Channel stretched to France.

It had been a chilly afternoon with rain threatening but not materialising. People had been out and about when Thea had walked here before her meeting. They'd kept warm with activity – exercising dogs, pushing perambulators, flying kites, or skimming stones across the water. Now dusk was falling, most of them had gone home.

Thea turned in the direction of the Palace Pier, hoping a walk would clear her head for decision-making. She was more convinced than ever that her mother hadn't knowingly signed a Will that left everything to Herbert and it felt monstrously unfair that Stanley should get away with whatever trickery or forgery he'd used. But how could she raise twenty-five pounds?

If Thea sold what remained of her mother's jewellery – even her wedding and engagement rings – along with everything else she possessed, she might just have enough but it felt like betraying her parents to part with the only items they'd been able to leave her. Besides, the investigation might prove fruitless in which case she'd have lost precious heirlooms for nothing.

Whatever happened to the house, Thea needed to earn an income. Might she find work that would allow her to save enough money to pay Mr Lawley's fee as well as maintain herself? Thea dismissed the idea as hopelessly unrealistic. She'd never save enough before Stanley's return, even if she could get a job.

She'd wanted to find work as soon as she'd realised that Herbert was intent on running through the Fairfax money but the thought of it had made her mother cling to her in dismay. 'Don't leave me here with that man, darling. Please don't leave me alone with him.'

After a lot of tears and trembling on Cecily's part, Thea had agreed to stay at home. From time to time she'd brought the subject of work up again but it was only when she realised she was dying that Cecily had begun to regret holding her daughter back, because by then their world had shrunk to just the two of them.

'And now you're going to be alone,' Cecily had lamented. 'I wish I'd been stronger. I wish I'd thought less of myself and more of you.'

'I'm strong enough for both of us and I'm going to be fine,' Thea had assured her.

Brave words that she remembered with a sigh.

Of course, there was an alternative to paying Mr Lawley to make enquiries. Thea could make them herself instead. Theoretically, simply visiting the witnesses in their homes might lead to the information she needed to confirm her suspicions. But instinct warned her that it was unlikely to be so easy. Even if the witnesses were easy to find – and there was no guarantee of that – she might have an uphill battle to persuade them to help her, especially if they'd been involved in the fraud. She might have to find some other way of proving the truth but how would that be possible if she were also holding down a job?

Evening was closing in rapidly now, draining colours and bringing shadows. Having reached the halfway point between the Palace Pier and the West Pier, Thea was turning for home when her gaze fell on the buildings on the other side of the road. They were tall, impressive buildings. The Palladium Theatre. The Grand Hotel. The Metropole Hotel…

A thought blossomed in Thea's head. She had her house for the next three months. Three and a half months to be exact. Might she let out some of the rooms to paying guests to provide an income? Doubtless there'd be work involved in getting the rooms ready, keeping them clean and preparing meals, but surely her time would be freer and more flexible running a guest house than working outside the home? It was certainly worth considering.

She retraced her steps and crossed back over to Aquarium Terrace. She was about to continue onto Marine Parade when she heard an anguished female voice shout, 'Stop! Please stop!'

Looking around, Thea saw a man running in her direction from further along the esplanade and another person – presumably the woman who'd cried out – on the ground behind him. He was carrying a bag and Thea guessed he'd just snatched it from the woman.

She raced back across the road to intercept him, her gaze scanning the street for someone she could call to help but there was no one around. The man was big. Not fit but doubtless still able to swat Thea aside with ease. 'Out 'o my way!' he yelled, as he neared her, and he put out a hand to show he'd push her away if necessary.

He grinned as she stepped aside but his triumph was premature. Thea grasped her umbrella with both hands and swung it at his shins. He bellowed in pain, dropped the bag and in trying to catch it lost his balance, falling to the ground like a collapsing hippopotamus.

Thea grabbed the bag and darted back, brandishing the umbrella as a weapon as she waited to see what he'd do.

Cursing, he sat up, recovered his cap from where it had fallen, and got to his feet. 'Bitch,' he sneered, and he spat at the ground in front of her feet. Fortunately, the fight had gone out of him. He backed away a few paces then turned and limped off.

It frustrated Thea to let him go free but she could still see no one else who might help. And checking on his victim was more important. Hastening towards her, Thea crouched down at her side.

She was young – twenty or thereabouts – and she reached out gratefully when she saw her bag. 'Thank you. It was good of you to help but I'll be fine now.'

'Forgive me for contradicting you, but you don't look fine to me,' Thea said. There was blood at the girl's temple and she was trembling too.

'I hit my head on the wall. It stunned me, but now I'm—'

'Still shaking. Here, let me help you.'

Thea put her arm around the young woman who got to her feet and leaned against the wall, saying, 'I just need a moment.'

She was shorter than Thea but still of average height. 'Take as a long as you need and then I'll help you home,' Thea said.

'There's really no need.'

'There's every need.'

The girl looked awkward. 'I don't actually live in Brighton.'

'But you're staying nearby? Or were you heading for the train station?'

'Yes,' she said. 'The train station.'

'Is anyone waiting for you at home?'

'Not exactly. But—'

'If no one's waiting, it makes sense to come to my house for a steadying cup of tea before you attempt the journey.'

'I can't impose on you.'

'I'm only offering the help I hope someone would offer me if I'd been attacked. You needn't stay long if you start to feel stronger.'

Thea linked her arm with the young woman's and led her the short distance to Clarendon Place. 'It's warmer in the kitchen,' Thea said, letting them in.

Down in the basement she added coal to the fire, took the girl's coat and steered her into one of the two armchairs.

'You're very kind,' the girl said. 'I'm sorry, but I don't know your name.'

'Theodora Fairfax, but I'm known as Thea.'

'I'm Anna Watson.'

'Well, Anna. Rest there while I heat some water.'

Thea set the kettle to boil. She also fetched gauze and cleaned the graze on Anna's head before passing over a cup of tea. 'Don't rush to drink it,' she urged, seeing the exhaustion in her new friend's face.

She wondered about the circumstances that had led to the exhaustion but decided against asking questions. What Anna needed just now was to rest.

Eight

Anna surfaced from sleep slowly as though it involved pushing her mind through a great heavy force that wanted to draw her back into oblivion. Anxiety gnawed on the edges of her consciousness. Something was wrong, but what was it?

Memory slammed into her brain and pierced her heart. Piers was gone. Her darling Piers was gone and Anna would never see him again. She'd cried an ocean of tears since hearing the news but more tears flooded her eyes now. Turning, she buried her face in the pillow and sobbed.

But in time awareness of her whereabouts caught up with her. Lying in bed was a luxury she couldn't afford because she was still in the house of that tall, slender and rather beautiful young woman who'd come to her rescue on the seafront. Theodora Fairfax.

With her upright bearing and silvery voice, Thea was as much a lady as any of the grand women Anna had served in Selfridges. Yet she'd also been kind, practical and brave.

Anna hadn't meant to fall asleep in the chair but she'd been utterly weary after spending one night in the waiting room at the station and another night huddled in an alley somewhere in Worthing, having been too distraught about Piers's death to do more than wander the town in a daze of grief.

She'd been mortified to be woken by a gentle shake of her shoulder. Fearful too in case her sleeping position had exposed the slight swell of her pregnancy but enormously relieved to see that her clothes had bunched up to disguise it.

Thea had changed into a long white nightgown and a brown dressing-gown that looked as if it had been made for a man. Released from their pins, Thea's fiery curls had tumbled over her shoulders like a coppery waterfall that gleamed in the light.

'What time is it?' Anna had asked.

'Eleven-thirty.'

Eleven-thirty! 'I'm so sorry. I didn't intend... I must leave.'

'It's far too late to go anywhere so I've made a bed up for you here,' Thea had told her. 'I've warmed some milk for you too as you haven't eaten.'

Thea had also given her a plate on which stood a little bread and cheese. Overwhelmed by such kindness, and ambushed by another flood of grief, Anna had been unable to utter more than a choked, 'Thank you.'

She hadn't been conscious of feeling hungry but the supper had been just what her empty stomach required. Leaving her to eat it, Thea had moved quietly about the kitchen, returning clean dishes to cupboards and filling two glasses with water. 'Ready?' she'd finally smiled.

Anna had nodded. 'This is extraordinarily kind.'

'You need a bed for the night. I have one to offer.' Thea had made it sound straightforward but in truth it was a huge leap of trust and generosity.

Anna had been led up to the ground floor and then up another flight of stairs to a large room overlooking the front of the house. 'It's rather chilly, I'm afraid, but I've put a hot water bottle between the sheets,' Thea had told her. 'I'm in the room next to this one so do knock if you need anything. There's a bathroom further along the landing.'

Placing a glass on Anna's bedside table, she'd moved to the door. 'Goodnight, Anna. Please don't rush to get up in the morning.'

Now Anna reached for her watch. It was ten o'clock. She'd never slept until ten o'clock in her entire life. She still felt exhausted but her mind was clearer. Perhaps now she could—

There was a tap on her door. Anna sat up and arranged the covers to hide her shape, not wanting to see Thea's expression turn to disgust at what she'd doubtless take to be Anna's loose morals. 'I'm awake,' she called.

Thea entered with a cup and saucer. 'Tea,' she announced. 'Shall I open the curtains?'

'Yes, please.'

Thea did so then returned to stand by Anna's bed. In daylight Anna could see that Thea's eyes were a vivid green. 'I'm making breakfast,' she said. 'Come down when you're ready but drink your tea first. Oh, and mind it doesn't cool. This house is cold.'

Alone again, Anna reached for the tea and realised Thea was right about it cooling quickly. Drinking it, she looked round the bedroom she'd been given. It was a high-ceilinged, elegant room with a large three-sided bay window, ornate cornices at the top of the walls and a beautiful wooden door. The furniture was old and substantial, the curtains heavy and the carpet ornate.

But everywhere there were signs that Thea had fallen on hard times: a worn patch on the carpet, lighter squares on the papered walls that suggested paintings had once hung there but had since been sold, and an absence of ornaments, clocks and other fripperies. Then there was the chill and the fact that there appeared to be no servants in the house.

Anna felt bad about eating food and drinking tea that Thea might not be able to afford. She'd leave straight after breakfast but where would she go?

Anna needed a plan. So far she'd simply reeled from the tragedy of Piers's loss but she had to move forward. The child she carried was all she had left of Piers and she had to do her best for him. Or for her.

Because she had to go somewhere, she'd walked all the way from Worthing to Brighton yesterday. But she couldn't begin another day of useless wandering. She had to find a place to stay and a way of supporting herself. Thanks to Thea, she still had the bag containing her money and clothes, but that money wouldn't last long at all.

Perhaps she'd been wrong to stay at Selfridges once she'd realised she was pregnant. If she'd got a job out of sight of the public, she might have proved her worth to an employer who'd have been sympathetic to her situation and let her keep working until she literally went into labour. But it was no use thinking about the past. She had to plan the future.

Perhaps she should see if Brighton had anything to offer in the way of work before she returned to London. There were hotels and boarding houses at the seaside. It was winter so visitors would be fewer but there might still be work for a willing chambermaid or cleaner.

She got up and went to the bathroom where she washed herself all over, glad to feel clean again. She was glad to be able to change her underclothing too, though as yet she had no way of washing what she'd worn. Clean and neat, she packed her bag then went downstairs to the basement kitchen.

'I'm boiling eggs,' Thea told her. 'They'll be ready in just a moment.'

'You must let me pay for them.'

'That would make me feel like a terrible hostess. If you want to repay my hospitality, you can give me your opinion on a little venture I have in mind.'

'Venture?'

'I'm thinking of turning this place into a guest house temporarily but I've no experience of such things.'

More proof that Thea had fallen on hard times.

'Do sit down,' Thea invited. 'You could slice some bread if you like to be busy.'

Anna sat and cut two perfect slices. At home in Bermondsey, with seven mouths to feed on small incomes, it was important to be careful and fair with food. Not that Bermondsey was home any more. Anna swallowed down the sudden panic that rose up inside her.

'There's more tea in the pot,' Thea told her, so Anna poured a cup for each of them.

Thea brought the eggs to the table. 'Of course, if I offer rooms, I'll have to prepare more substantial breakfasts than this.'

'Have you cooked for people before?'

'Not professionally. I've never had any sort of job but circumstances change.'

Thea had spoken without a trace of self-pity but underneath the courage Anna saw a young woman who was no stranger to suffering.

'It's lucky you have the house,' Anna said.

'Actually, I don't have it. Not yet.'

Thea told Anna the story of a greedy stepfather and a deeply unpleasant stepbrother who intended to take the house because of a Will her mother had supposedly made.

'Supposedly?' Anna questioned.

'I don't believe my mother made that Will knowingly. Either she was tricked into making it, or it's a forgery.'

'Goodness.'

'I need to prove it somehow.' Thea described her plan to question the witnesses. 'If I can find them. Whatever happens, I'll need money so I hope that letting rooms will provide me with income. But do say if you think my idea is foolish.'

'I think it's a good idea. If you got a job it would leave you little time for pursuing witnesses.'

'Precisely.'

Silence descended as they ate their eggs but it wasn't an entirely comfortable silence for Anna. Thea had confided her story. Was she expecting Anna to return the confidence?

Anna couldn't tell Thea about the baby but she could tell her about Piers. In fact, Anna wanted to talk about Piers. It would be a way of declaring to the world that Piers's life had mattered.

It was impossible to stop the tears from flowing as she spoke about him.

'He sounds a lovely man,' Thea said.

'The best.'

'As for your father…'

Anna had described her family situation too.

'He sounds the sort of man who feels threatened and insulted by anyone who wants to improve their lot in life.'

Thea had caught onto Jed Watson's personality instantly.

'Piers was lucky to have someone like you to love him,' Thea said then.

'I keep thinking of how he must have suffered.' Anna shuddered, imagining his terror as the storm raged and he realised the ship was floundering. 'He might have survived in the water for hours, getting weaker and weaker, and hoping for a rescue that never came.' The thought of his despair appalled her.

'He might equally have been knocked out by a blow to the head and had no time to suffer,' Thea pointed out. 'Besides, it isn't the manner of death that's important. It's the quality of the life that goes before it. Piers's death doesn't change what you shared together. Hold onto those memories and treasure them. Isn't that what Piers would want?'

It was. Anna wiped her eyes and pictured the way Piers used to smile at her, his blue eyes soft and loving.

'I imagine you're going to look for work now,' Thea said.

Anna nodded, though fear crept back at the thought of her pregnancy. Anna was hugely relieved that Thea hadn't noticed it, but another couple of weeks would make it impossible to miss.

An idea suddenly struck Anna's mind. 'I thought I might try Brighton for work,' she said. 'As you're looking for paying guests I wonder if I might stay here? Just for a night or two. I have the money to pay you.'

Thea didn't answer for a moment and Anna began to think she'd blundered in making a suggestion that was obviously unwelcome. Doubtless Thea had a higher class of guest in mind. 'I'm sorry. I didn't mean—'

'I have a better idea,' Thea announced. 'I need to get started on finding the witnesses but I also need to prepare the house for guests. Today is Friday. If you stay and help for a couple of days – until Monday, perhaps – we can consider that as payment. I won't take all of your time. Just some of it. How does that sound?'

'It sounds wonderful.'

'Then finish your tea and we'll get to work.'

Anna picked her teacup up and drank. It was a relief to know she had somewhere to sleep for the next three nights.

On the other hand, she hadn't told Thea the whole truth about her situation and that made Anna feel she'd won sympathy through deceit. It was shameful, but Anna was desperate. All she could do was to work hard for Thea and move on elsewhere before Thea realised how badly she'd been taken in.

Nine

Daisy knew it was unreasonable to expect Max to drop everything to see her in what was hardly a life or death situation. But he must have had her letter for two days now and her patience was wearing thin. She might have told Mr Oaks that she didn't want to walk out with him but she still felt horribly awkward about the situation.

'So you've spoken to him,' her father had said yesterday, emerging from the forge in his heavy leather apron after Daniel had walked away.

'I have.'

'How did he take it when you told him you weren't interested?'

'All right, I think.'

'The man's a gentleman. So it's back to normal for you, girl.'

'I suppose so,' Daisy had agreed, but even a day later she didn't actually feel back to normal.

She was throwing corn to the chickens to entice them into the coop for the night when her ears picked up a distant phut-phutting sound. Max's motorbike? 'Get in quickly or the big bad fox will get you,' she urged the chickens.

She shooed them all inside, fastened the coop and hastened round to the front of the cottage just as Max turned in from the lane. He pulled his goggles off, the strap ruffling his dark hair, then surveyed her with shrewd but amused grey eyes. 'What's up, little coz?' he asked.

'Come to the paddock.' They were less likely to be disturbed there. Linking her arm with his, she pulled him off the bike.

'Wait,' Max laughed. 'Whatever the crisis, I can't overlook the courtesies due to my welcoming committee.'

The committee comprised Shep, the family sheepdog, and Catherine, the family cat. Both had come out to greet him because all animals loved Max.

He stroked them and talked to them then grinned at Daisy. 'Come on, then. I can see you're twitching as though you've got ants in your pants.'

Daisy led him to the paddock where they sat on the fence, hunching their shoulders against the chill.

'Daniel Oaks asked if he could… pay his attentions to me.'

'Seriously?' Max burst out laughing which wasn't the response she wanted though perhaps it was the one she'd expected. 'The poor sod,' Max finished. 'If he married you, he'd starve to death on your cooking and his clothes would be in rags.'

True, but that wasn't the problem. 'I turned him down.'

'Did you now? And why would that be?'

'Why?' Daisy looked at Max as though he'd just dropped down from the moon. 'He's old, he's a widower, he's got children and he needs a housekeeping sort of wife. And, as you just pointed out, I'm not much of a housekeeper.'

'He's only a few years older than me,' Max said. 'But that isn't what matters. What matters is how you feel about him. You don't love him?'

'No!'

'You don't even like him?'

'I don't know him. And, before you ask, no, I don't want to get to know him.' Daisy gave a cringing sort of shudder. 'It's all so embarrassing!'

'Have you told him you're not interested?'

'Yesterday.'

'Was he offended?'

'I don't think so.'

'Then the embarrassment – if there is any – will pass soon enough.'

Not soon enough for Daisy's comfort.

'I'm going over to see him anyway as he's made up some tonics for the horses,' Max said. 'I'll report back in half an hour.'

He sprang down from the fence with his usual easy athleticism and strode purposefully towards the lane, leaving Daisy to follow as far as the cottage.

Her father stepped out of the forge a few minutes later. 'Was that Max's motorbike?'

'He'll be back soon.'

'Gone to Daniel's, has he?' Frank Flowers grinned then returned to the forge.

Daisy drifted into the cottage and wondered what she might prepare for supper now Max was here. All things domestic bored her but even so it stung to be treated as a joke by both Max and her father. She wished she'd thought of supper before because there wasn't much in the house.

She'd been too concerned with avoiding Daniel to go to the village shop.

Stew would take too long to cook so it would have to be ham and eggs. Again. But Daisy could fry potatoes to make the meal more substantial. She set to work, holding the eggs back until Max's return but going to the trouble of warming the plates.

He wasn't long. 'Well?' she asked, as he stepped into the kitchen and leaned his trim frame against the wall.

'He had my tonics ready,' Max reported.

'That isn't what I—'

He'd only been teasing her. Pushing away from the wall, he came to inspect her cooking. 'Daniel wishes you well. There are no hard feelings on his part.'

'Is that all?'

'What more do you want?'

What she really wanted was for Daniel's excruciating suggestion to be erased by the wave of a magic wand.

'If there's any awkwardness, it's all on your side, little coz,' Max said.

Hmm. Daisy picked up an egg and took a deep breath to ensure she'd be careful. She tapped it with a knife to drive a slit into the shell then separated the parts slowly. The egg slid into the pan and the yolk promptly broke.

Max shook his head despairingly, picked up another egg, tapped it against the rim of the pan to open the shell and slid the egg into the pan with the yolk intact. He did the same again and again until there were six eggs in the pan, all perfectly whole apart from the one Daisy had broken. Daisy took her frustration out on a frying potato, stabbing it with a fork.

'Do you want to know what I think?' Max asked, lounging against the wall again and folding his arms across his middle.

'About what?'

'About you. Your situation. I don't think it's just Daniel that's got you in a mood. It's everything. I think you need to spread your wings before you settle down with a husband.'

'How do I do that?'

'By leaving home for a while. By getting a job.'

'With you?' Daisy turned shining eyes on him. 'Max, that would be wonderful!'

'You know I can't afford more help just now. But you could look for a job in Worthing or Brighton. It would be a change for you. A new experience.'

'Who'd look after Dad?'

'Daisy, dearest. Don't take this the wrong way, but whether he gets Mrs Beddows or someone else to help, that person will do a better job than you.'

Daisy slapped his arm. But he was right. What Daisy needed was to get away for a while and, not having much money to her name, she needed a job in order to do it. What sort of job, though? Daisy had no idea but surely there was something suitable in the world beyond the little village of Pixfield?

Ten

'I think we've done enough for the moment,' Thea announced late on Saturday afternoon. 'I want to take these sheets to the laundry and start looking for my witnesses.'

She was also worried about overtaxing Anna. The poor girl worked hard and would have worked harder still but Thea could see that she was both exhausted and wracked by grief. She never complained but her face was white and Thea caught the occasional glitter of tears. It meant that progress was slower than Thea would have liked but at least it was moving forward.

They'd made an assessment of the drawing room and dining room, and decided how they might make them comfortable for paying guests, moving mirrors and pictures around to cover the bare patches on the walls though none were large enough to cover a patch over the drawing-room fireplace where a gilt-framed mirror had once hung. Thea decided to look out for an inexpensive mirror to cover that. They'd also assessed what remained of the china, cutlery and glasses and decided there were enough of them, even if they didn't all match.

Moving upstairs they'd inspected the bedrooms. The first floor had three bedrooms – Thea's own room, her late mother's room where Anna had slept, and another room that had been occupied by Herbert. There were three more bedrooms above them and three attic rooms at the top of the house. 'I thought I'd move up to the attic floor and offer the good bedrooms to guests,' Thea had explained, though the attics were full of clutter.

There were beds in all of the rooms, but an investigation of the linen cupboard established that most of the sheets needed washing after being stored for years. There weren't enough sheets or blankets to enable beds to be changed rapidly between guests but, not knowing if she'd have any guests at all yet, Thea had decided against buying more until she was sure they'd be needed

She parcelled up the sheets then gave Anna a key. 'I want you to feel you can come and go whenever it suits you.'

Anna looked surprised by so much trust. Tears welled up in her dark eyes again.

Not wanting to embarrass her, Thea picked up the parcel and left. She deposited the sheets at the laundry then headed for the address of the first witness, Albert Strupp.

Ballard Street was in north Brighton. It wasn't the best street but neither was it the worst.

Strupp's building had started out as a family home but been divided into flats at some point in time. Steps led down from the street to a basement door but that was Apartment A according to the sign painted on the wall beside it. More steps led up from the street to where the main door had once stood but the original had been replaced with two crudely-made narrow doors. Thea wanted Apartment C and there was a letter C on the right-hand door. Mounting the steps, Thea banged on the dingy brass doorknocker.

No one came to answer so she banged it again. Still no one came. Clearly, she'd have to come back another time.

Jeremiah Jarrold's address, Ships Passage, was in the Lanes, a warren of narrow streets that were filled with small shops, many of which sold antiques or items the sellers claimed to be antiques. A shop selling dusty books occupied the ground floor of number sixteen. Presumably Mr Jarrold lived in the rooms above it, accessing them via a door set into the wall beside the shop entrance. There was no door knocker or bell so Thea banged on the door with her hand. Once again nobody answered.

Frustrated for the time being, she called in at a second-hand shop nearby. It had stuck in her memory because she'd once walked past and seen her father's writing set for sale. Herbert Ambrose had taken it along with so many other things.

She negotiated a price on a mirror that was large enough to cover the patch above the fireplace. The frame was plain but at least it wasn't ugly. It was too heavy for Thea to carry home so she arranged for it to be delivered on Monday.

She also called in on several shops to ask if she might have any empty cardboard boxes she could use for packing away the things that had belonged to her mother and Herbert. There were a couple of tea chests in the attics but more boxes would be useful and Thea was pleased to go home with four of them.

They began the packing the following morning. It brought a lump to Thea's throat when she packed her mother's things but when they moved into Herbert's room she could only grimace at the smell. It permeated everything and Anna suggested it was better to open the window and feel cold than to feel disgusted. His clothes were greasy to the touch and when the boxes were packed Thea threw in mothballs because the awfulness of their odour was better than the awfulness of Herbert's.

She returned to Albert Strupp's address the following afternoon hoping that, being a Sunday, she'd find him at home. When two knocks went unanswered, she turned away only to turn back when she heard movement inside. Movement and cursing. Lots of cursing.

The door was finally opened by a short man of fifty or sixty with wispy hair, slouching shoulders and a heavy belly that gravity had dragged low. He hadn't dressed with visitors in mind as his shirt was collarless and soiled with the stains of several meals.

'Mr Strupp?' Thea asked brightly. 'Mr Albert Strupp?'

'No.'

'Is Mr Strupp at home?'

'How would I know?'

'He doesn't live here?'

'No.'

'Perhaps he's a neighbour? Do you know your neighbours?'

'No.'

'Or perhaps he lived here before you? Do you know who lived here before you?'

'No.'

Thea sighed. 'Could I trouble you for the address of your landlord? He might have a forwarding address for Mr Strupp.'

She'd spoken too late. The door had closed in her face and she could hear curses fading into the distance.

After a moment's hesitation, she knocked twice on the door for Apartment A but no one answered. She walked down the steps to the basement apartment and this time her knock had the door opening a crack and an eye appearing in the space.

'I'm sorry to disturb you but I'm looking for Mr Strupp,' Thea said. 'I understand he's moved on.'

The crack widened to show two eyes belonging to an old woman. 'Year or two back,' she confirmed.

'Do you have a forwarding address?'

'For 'im? Not likely.'

Clearly, Albert Strupp hadn't endeared himself to this old neighbour.

Thea asked for the landlord's address instead.

'I'll have to look it up.'

'I'll be happy to wait here,' Thea told her. 'Please don't feel uncomfortable about closing the door. I live alone too. We have to be careful, don't we?'

The woman nodded and duly closed the door. Five minutes passed and Thea was wondering if she'd been forgotten when the door opened again and a small sheet of paper was passed out. The writing was spidery but legible: *Mr Mortimer Clark, 42 St Agnes Road, Hove.*

'Telephone number?' Thea asked.

'I've never used a telephone in my life. Don't trust these new-fangled things people keep inventing.'

'Well, thank you for the address. It's appreciated.'

Thea returned to the street. Hove lay to the West and blended into Brighton but Thea decided to call on Jeremiah Jarrold, the second witness, next.

She knocked on his door three times but again no one answered. Turning away, she saw a girl – a young woman rather – watching her from further down the passage. Realising she'd been noticed, the girl's eyes widened and, spinning swiftly, she bolted.

'Excuse me!' Thea called, but the girl didn't stop.

Thea set off after her. The girl burst onto Queen Street and raced across the busy road. Thea made to follow but a bus came to a halt in front of her. By the time she'd run around it, the girl was nowhere to be seen.

Thea spent fifteen minutes searching for her but in vain. Was she Jarrold's daughter? Thea hadn't taken particular notice of what she'd been wearing but had an impression of an ill-fitting brown coat, a tired brown hat and a shabby brown bag.

Judging from the girl's appearance, the Jarrolds weren't prospering. That was hardly surprising if Jeremiah had been a drinking and gambling crony of Herbert's. And if the girl had assumed Thea was calling to collect money Jeremiah owed, it explained why she'd bolted.

Thea decided against retracing her steps to Ships Passage to await the girl's return. She might be gone for hours and make herself scarce all over again if she saw Thea waiting. It would be better to return another time and hope for a chance to explain that she wanted information, not money.

The walk home took Thea back to Queen Street. She was thinking about Anna and the grave misfortune that had cost her a much-loved sweetheart when a voice penetrated the reverie.

'Miss Fairfax?'

Thea looked up to see a young man in army uniform standing in front of her.

'It is Miss Fairfax, isn't it?' he asked.

'Yes.' Something about him stirred recognition in Thea too. Those deep brown eyes and hair, that neat moustache... 'Mr Kirby-Laws! Major Kirby-Laws, I should say.' She'd spotted the crown on his epaulette.

He held out a hand which she shook. 'It's been what? Seven or eight years since I last saw you?' he said.

'It must be.'

Their mothers had been friends but Herbert Ambrose's behaviour had put an end to that friendship along with all the others.

'Your mother is well, I hope?' he asked.

'I'm afraid she died last September.'

'I'm sorry.'

'I trust you have better news of your parents?'

'They're both well,' he reported, then gave a delighted smile. 'My mother will be glad indeed to hear that I've seen you. Are you still living in... Clarendon Place, isn't it?'

'It is. And yes, I'm still living there.' For the moment.

'I expect my mother will wish to write a letter of condolence.'

'That would be kind. You're home on leave, I assume.'

'Yes, but I'm leaving the army to take a position in my father's office.'

Mr Kirby-Laws Senior was something to do with finance. A stockbroker, Thea thought.

'I imagine that will please him greatly.'

Ralph was his parents' only child as she'd been her parents' only child.

'He's very pleased,' Ralph confirmed. 'As is my mother. I must let you go on your way, Miss Fairfax, but I hope I'll see you again.' His dark eyes shone with both admiration and sincerity.

For all that their mothers had been friends, Ralph and Thea had barely known each other as children. He was six or seven years older, often away at school and then he'd joined the army. But they were both adults now and Thea discovered that it was a very pleasant thing to be admired.

Not that she held out much hope of seeing him again. Once his mother enlightened him about the sorry tale of Herbert Ambrose… No, Thea wouldn't expect to hear from Ralph or his mother again.

She smiled a little sadly and walked away.

Eleven

Anna was feeling much better after four nights at Thea's house. Physically, that was. Emotionally, she was still fragile with grief and worn down with worry for the future. But she couldn't afford to wallow. She had to make plans for the baby's sake.

'I know I suggested staying until tomorrow,' Thea had said on Sunday night, 'but I'm happy for you to stay longer as there's still so much to be done.'

Busy washing the china, cutlery and glasses the guests would use, washing and ironing table cloths and napkins, airing blankets in the garden then mending some of the bindings that had come loose, they hadn't even started on the heavy cleaning or on clearing an attic room for Thea. But sooner or later Anna would need to be independent.

Having washed guest towels, squeezed them through the mangle and hung them in the garden to dry, Anna went out on Monday with four errands in mind. The first was to make enquiries about how much Thea could expect to charge for her rooms. Thea had proposed that task for herself but it had occurred to Anna that it might be hard for Thea to advertise her reduced circumstances to all and sundry. Thea was no snob but she might still feel that letting rooms wasn't what her parents would have liked.

The other tasks were to look for work, to send a postcard to her family to let them know she was safe and to find more information on what had happened to Piers. Knowing the details of the shipwreck wouldn't turn the clock back but Anna needed to understand what Piers had been through, as though by understanding she could somehow hold him closer.

His expedition had been sponsored by the *National Daily Herald*. Perhaps that paper would carry a report on the shipwreck.

Anna went to the tourist office for advice on guest house charges. She'd agreed with Thea that she wouldn't mention the plan to open a guest house in case it led to awkward conversations about rules and regulations. 'I'm normally a law-abiding person,' Thea had said. 'But just this once I'm desperate enough to turn a blind eye to officialdom.'

Instead, Anna made up a story about wanting prices in case her family came to stay. She was given a range of prices which depended on the location of the guest house, whether it was plain or elegant, and the time of year. Reflecting that Thea's house was certainly elegant, Anna wrote the prices into a notebook and also asked questions about meals

Afterwards she walked along Marine Parade. She'd been attacked just across the road from here, unaware of the man's approach until he'd run up, grabbed her bag and pushed her to the ground. The memory of it made her shudder but without that attack Anna might never have met Thea.

She reached the clock tower and aquarium where signs indicated that feeding of the creatures it housed would take place at twelve noon and three in the afternoon. How the children would love to see that!

Continuing further, she reached what Thea had told her was the Palace Pier. There was a theatre at the end, and apparently Charlie Chaplin had performed there before making films. Boat trips could be taken from the pier as well, passengers being offered a choice of local trips along the coat, crossings to the Isle of Wight and even trips to France. The children would love that too but the only treat Anna could manage just now was the postcard.

She found a shop which sold them and chose a photograph of the Pavilion, a building which looked as exotic as an Indian palace with its domes and clean white walls. She bought a stamp too then stood in a corner to write her message.

Just a quick note to let you know that I'm in Brighton. I'll write again when I'm more settled but please don't worry about me. Love to all, Anna x

She said nothing about Piers's death, knowing how much they'd worry if they knew the truth. It would be better to wait until she had a plan for the future before she shared her terrible news.

Fortunately, Anna had always been vague about Piers's return date. 'Brazil is thousands of miles away,' she'd said. 'And being on an expedition means Piers has to see everything that sounds interesting.'

She addressed the postcard to her mother care of their neighbour, Mrs Fawley, spotted a red pillar box and dropped it inside. Walking on, she entered another shop to buy a copy of the *Herald*.

Outside again, she looked quickly through the paper but saw nothing about Piers's shipwreck. She looked again, more carefully, but still found nothing. Remembering what the Rutherfords had told her, the first reports must have appeared several days ago.

Anna went back into the shop. 'Do you have any old copies of the *Herald* left? From the past few days?'

'Got rid of them all,' the assistant told her.

How frustrating! Was there another way of getting hold of back issues? 'Could you tell me if there's a library nearby?'

'Over by the Pavilion, Miss.'

She followed his directions and found the library in a beautiful old building which appeared to be part of the Pavilion estate. She found a sympathetic librarian too. 'I'm not sure we'll have kept last week's papers but I'll have a look for you,' he said, but he returned shaking his head. 'Sorry to disappoint you, Miss.'

'Thank you for looking.' Anna walked back outside feeling vexed with herself. Why hadn't she thought of finding a newspaper before?

Turning towards the town centre, she barely registered that she was walking past a shop selling fried fish until the smell penetrated her consciousness and gave her an idea. She went inside.

'Hake's good today,' the shop assistant told her.

'Do you wrap the food in newspaper?'

'Clean paper on the inside. Newspaper on the outside. All nice and proper.'

'I'm sure. Might you have old copies of the *Herald* amongst your newspapers?'

'We've got a lot of papers,' he said.

'I know it might feel like looking for a needle in a haystack, but would you mind looking for copies dated four or five days ago? It's important.'

He hesitated, then took pity on her. 'All right, I'll look. But the moment a paying customer comes in is the moment I stop looking. I've got a living to make.'

'Thank you.'

He ducked down below the counter and Anna heard him dragging a crate from under it. 'Let's see. No, no, no, no, no... Yes, here you are, Miss.'

He stood up triumphantly and offered her a newspaper.

Anna saw that the shipwreck had been reported on the front page and felt a wave of dizziness. She swallowed hard. 'Can I pay you for it?' she asked.

'It's only an old paper and I've plenty more of them. Take it with my blessing.'

'You're very kind.'

Hastening outside, Anna rounded a corner then leaned against the wall and began to read.

It is with great sadness that we report the loss of HMS *Adiona* off the coast of Brazil. The ship was caught in a storm in the Atlantic Ocean and wreckage found in the area suggests that it went down with no survivors. The *Herald* offers its sincere condolences to the families of those lost and will report further when more information becomes available.

Poor Piers. It was impossible to avoid thinking of the terror he must have felt.

Anna read the report again and lingered on a single word: *suggests*. Wreckage found *suggests* that the ship went down with no survivors. Did that mean it was uncertain? But Piers's parents had entertained no hope of his survival. They must have more information than was printed here, but what?

Agitated and fighting back tears, Anna walked up and down the seafront but time was marching on and she had to start looking for work. Thea had mentioned an employment agency she'd considered trying herself.

The door to Miss Kimble's Employment Agency was sandwiched between shops. Finding it open, Anna pushed through into a narrow hall with stairs leading upwards. There was another door at the top. She knocked on it and a woman's voice called, 'Come in.'

A thin woman with a pinched face got to her feet as Anna entered a small office. 'Miss Kimble?' Anna asked.

'Correct.'

Anna forced a smile. 'Good afternoon. I'm Anna Watson. I'm looking for work and wonder if you might know of any suitable positions?'

'Sit.' The thin woman gestured Anna to a chair in front of her small desk, waited for her to settle then sat back in her own chair. 'What experience have you?'

'I'm from London. I worked in Selfridges department store – women's dresses – and have an excellent reference although I'm open to suggestions for any sort of…'

Anna's voice trailed off in dismay as she realised Miss Kimble's witch-like eyes were staring at her middle. Miss

Kimble was no Thea Fairfax, a genteel young woman who knew little of pregnancy. Neither was she someone from Anna's past whom it was easy to fool with loose clothing because it never crossed their minds that sensible Anna Watson would get herself into trouble. Miss Kimble had a business to run and it would do that business no good at all to place girls of loose morals who'd soon have to leave.

Probably, she subjected every girl who crossed her threshold to the same scrutiny and Anna might have brazened it out had a guilty flush not warmed her cheeks. 'You'll find the workhouse on Elm Grove,' Miss Kimble sneered.

The workhouse? Anna got up, despising the woman's unkindness. The love Anna and Piers had shared hadn't felt crude or dirty. It had felt beautiful.

But the world didn't see it that way. Thea Fairfax wouldn't see it that way either and Anna would be hurt by her disgust far more than she was hurt by Miss Kimble's. Thea would think Anna had abused her hospitality. Come what may Anna would leave Thea's house tomorrow.

Thea was in the kitchen when Anna returned. They sat at the table to share the outcome of their enquiries over a cup of tea. Thea had had no luck in locating one witness but thought the other might still be living in Ships Passage. 'I'll make another attempt to speak to him tomorrow,' she said.

Feeling it was her turn to report, Anna passed the notebook to Thea and explained the notes she'd made at the tourist office. She paused then said, 'I didn't have any luck finding work but I did find out a little more about Piers's ship.'

She handed the newspaper over.

'I'm sorry,' Thea said, when she'd read the *Adiona* story.

The sound of a horse and cart pulling up outside had them both looking through the basement window. 'I bought a mirror,' Thea said. 'That'll be the delivery cart.'

Anna followed her upstairs in case her help was needed. They watched the delivery man take the mirror from the cart. 'Want this inside, Miss?'

The cart was blocking the way of a car whose driver didn't look pleased. 'Thank you, but we can take it,' Thea said.

Anna stepped forward and lifted the mirror from the cart but its heaviness surprised her. Fearing she might drop it, she arched backwards to take some of the weight on her body. 'Careful!' Thea cried, but the weight eased as someone else came to hold one side of the mirror.

'I'm stronger than I look,' the girl said, for she was a tiny thing with fluffy fair hair and a bright smile. 'You shouldn't be carrying heavy things in your condition.'

Oh no. Anna looked to Thea whose face registered puzzlement and then shock as the meaning of the girl's words sank in.

Twelve

Oh, heck. Daisy hadn't meant to cause trouble but only to save the pregnant girl from injury. After all, Mrs Donovan in the village had hurt her back lifting hay bales when expecting her first child and needed help for weeks afterwards, while the butcher's wife had miscarried after helping her husband to replace roof tiles.

But the moment that Daisy spoke, she realised she was exposing a secret. The pregnant girl's face drained white while the green eyes of the coppery-haired girl widened in shock.

A stunned sort of silence followed until the delivery man touched his cap and said, 'I'll be off, then.'

The green-eyed girl roused herself. 'Thank you for your help,' she told him, then moved towards Daisy. 'Thank you for your help too, but we're fine now.'

She took hold of Daisy's side of the mirror and Daisy stood aside to watch the two girls carry it into the house and close the door behind them.

She groaned at the thought of the conversation that must be going on inside. The argument, rather. The girls – young women really because they both looked a little older than Daisy – bore no family resemblance. Perhaps the dark-haired girl had found herself out on the streets as a result of her pregnancy and thrown herself on the mercy of a distant cousin or old friend without telling her the truth of her situation.

What if she found herself out on the streets again thanks to Daisy's big mouth? Daisy couldn't just walk away and abandon her. A glance at her watch showed she had almost an hour free before she needed to catch the train to Worthing where her father would meet her in the trap. Sighing, she walked up the steps to the house and sat on the top step to wait and see what happened next.

Her father had been surprisingly relaxed about Daisy leaving the village to work elsewhere. He and Max had gone out to the forge after their supper and Daisy guessed that Max had talked to her father on her behalf. 'So you want to spread your wings,' Frank had said, as they'd waved Max off on his motorbike.

'I think it would be good for me.'

'So do I.'

'You do?' Goodness. She'd expected to have to plead her case because Frank thought life in Pixfield was just fine and dandy.

'Not because of Daniel,' he'd explained. 'He's just brought things to a head. You need to go because you're restless and you'll stay restless until you work the kinks out of your system.'

Restless wasn't a bad word for describing how Daisy felt.

'Go and see what's out in the world, girl. And don't worry about me. I'll manage.'

So here she was in Brighton, away from home but not so far away as to make visiting Frank troublesome. She hadn't had a lot of luck finding work today, but she'd only tried the places she thought might be fun – the aquarium, the pier, the theatres and cinemas. There were plenty of other places to try the next time she came as Brighton had numerous shops, restaurants and cafes.

Daisy had noticed the mirror being delivered after she'd walked along the seafront then turned up a side street to explore some of the grander-looking roads. Max would say she should have paused to think before opening her mouth and doubtless her father would agree. But – Daisy's eye was caught by movement in the basement window to her side. Glancing down, she saw the green-eyed girl looking up at her. The steps were private property, of course. Daisy got up and moved to the pavement but the door opened behind her anyway and the coppery-haired girl looked out.

'May I help?' She was beautifully spoken. Rather grand, in fact.

'I'm worried about your… friend,' Daisy told her. 'She looked… She didn't look quite well.'

An exasperated sigh came Daisy's way. 'What you mean is that you're worried you blurted out something tactless and got Anna into trouble.'

'Yes,' Daisy admitted, glad to have things out in the open. 'Exactly that.'

'I'm not a heartless ogre, I'll have you know.'

'I never suggested you were.'

'But you're not ruling the possibility out?'

Daisy shuffled her feet.

'I suppose you'd better come and see Anna for yourself.'

Daisy was led down to a basement kitchen. 'Our visitor was worried about you,' the grand young woman told her friend and Daisy was surprised to see her pick up the kettle and fill it with water. Wasn't there a servant to do that?

Daisy turned to the pregnant girl who was sitting at the table. 'I'm sorry I blundered in like that. I hope I haven't caused any… problems?'

'Thea isn't throwing me out onto the street,' the girl admitted with a smile.

'Good.' Daisy committed their names to memory. Anna and Thea. She'd never met anyone called Thea before. Perhaps it was short for Theodora.

'She thought I was annoyed,' Thea said. 'To be honest, what I mostly feel is stupid. I should have realised.'

'No,' Anna protested. 'I deliberately hid my condition from you.'

'Our young visitor noticed it.'

'Only because I saw you from the side when you leaned back,' Daisy pointed out. 'Besides, I'm used to farm animals. Horses, especially. Not that I'm suggesting you're like a horse, Anna. Or a cow or a pig or—'

Thea burst out laughing. 'I should hope not. I still feel stupid but let's not argue about it.'

She brought the tea pot to the table together with a third cup which Daisy was astonished to realise was intended for her.

'I'm afraid I've no cake to offer,' Thea said. 'No scones or crumpets either.'

'I wasn't expecting anything,' Daisy told her. 'But thank you, Miss…?'

'Fairfax. Theodora Fairfax but call me Thea. This is Anna Watson and you are…?'

'Daisy Flowers.' Daisy grimaced. 'Dreadful name, I know.'

'I think it's a pretty name.' Thea smiled, and Anna nodded agreement.

Daisy drank her tea and looked from one young woman to the other, fascinated by both of them. Thea's face was alive with colour and expression. Anna's was as still as an exquisite alabaster statue until she looked up and showed dark eyes that were full of feeling. Daisy wanted to know more about the girls but suspected it would be rude to ask questions. In fact, it was probably rude of her to have imposed herself upon them in the first place.

'You must let me help you to put the mirror up,' she said, wanting to make up for it.

Thea looked inclined to decline the offer but a glance at Anna seemed to change her mind. 'I'd appreciate that, but let's finish our tea first.'

'It was kind of you to be concerned about me,' Anna told Daisy.

'Sometimes my mouth opens before my brain's had a chance to think about what I plan to say,' Daisy said ruefully.

She felt very young next to these girls. They were only two or three years older than her but both of them had the air of being quietly capable and clever.

'Do you live in Brighton?' Thea asked.

Daisy told her about living in Pixfield with her father. By then the tea had been drunk and she was eager not to outstay her welcome. She also had a train to catch. 'Shall we hang the mirror now?'

Thea fetched a box of tools and they filed back upstairs. The mirror had been left in the hall temporarily. Daisy and Thea carried it into a parlour that was large and stately if a little bare. A patch on the wall above the fireplace indicated where the mirror was destined to hang. Had the mirror that had hung there before been broken? Daisy didn't like to appear nosy by asking.

'Is it all right if I stand on a chair?' she asked instead, conscious of her limited height.

'Of course.'

There was no need for the toolbox. Hooks remained in the wall and, reaching out to test them, Daisy found them to be secure. The mirror already had wire attached so Daisy and Thea had simply to lift the wire over the hooks and adjust the mirror for straightness according to Anna's instructions.

'I think it'll pass muster with guests,' Thea said.

'You're expecting guests?' Daisy would never have taken up their time by drinking tea if she'd known guests were coming. 'I didn't realise. I'll get out of your way.'

'We're not expecting anyone today,' Thea assured her. 'But hopefully soon. I'm planning to open this house as a guest house.'

Daisy was surprised but realised she shouldn't have been. The signs of hard times were obvious: the lack of domestic help, the plainness of the mirror, the Spartan feel of the house and, now Daisy came to think about it, even the dress Thea was wearing. Daisy was no expert on fashion but even she could see that the dress looked old-fashioned somehow. Not that it looked bad on her. Thea was so tall and striking that she'd look elegant in anything.

'Anna will be staying to help me,' Thea said.

Anna's smile was a mixture of gratitude and guilt that suggested this was an arrangement that had only just been agreed to give her somewhere to live.

'I could help too,' Daisy said, suddenly excited by the idea. 'That's why I'm in Brighton today. I'm looking for work.'

The house was five storeys high and although Anna looked to be a hard-working sort of person it wouldn't be easy for her to trek up and down all the stairs in her condition. 'I could run up and down these stairs all day because I'm never tired,' Daisy continued. 'I could run errands too. And you wouldn't have to pay me much because what matters more than money is getting away from Pixfield for a while.'

'I can't afford to pay anything so I'm not taking on extra help at the moment,' Thea told her.

Daisy's imagination had taken flight but now it fell back to earth with a bump.

'I'm sorry,' Thea added.

But it was Daisy who was sorry. Her mouth had run away with her again. Doubtless she'd embarrassed Thea as well as insulted Anna by suggesting she couldn't cope. 'I shouldn't have asked,' Daisy admitted. 'Thanks for the tea but it's time I was leaving. I hope all goes well with the guest house. With the baby too.'

Eager to get away now, she was walking as she spoke. 'Bye!' she called, over her shoulder, as she left the house.

She ran down the steps and turned towards the station, vowing to learn some tact and adopt a more mature air next time she came to Brighton to look for work.

Thirteen

Thea stood in the hall, thinking rapidly. Then she opened the door and called, 'Wait!'

Daisy couldn't have heard because she kept walking into the distance at a cracking pace. Thea set off after her. 'Daisy, wait!'

At last the younger girl glanced over her shoulder, saw Thea and came to a halt. Catching up with her, Thea saw she was frowning. 'The mirror hasn't fallen off, has it?' Daisy asked.

'Nothing like that. I've been thinking about your offer and the truth is that I would welcome some additional help.' Especially now she knew Anna was expecting a baby and couldn't – or shouldn't – do the heavier work. All three attic rooms would need to be cleared if Daisy joined them – goodness knew where the clutter could go – but an extra pair of hands had become a necessity.

Thea had expected enthusiasm but Daisy's fresh, pretty face remained sombre. 'Please don't worry about me,' she said. 'I'll find another job.'

Clearly she suspected the offer had been made out of pity.

'To be honest, I'm not worried about you,' Thea told her. 'You strike me as being the sort of resourceful girl who'll find work easily. But I'll be glad to have you join us, if that's what you'd like and provided we can agree terms.'

'I don't understand. You said—'

'I find myself in unexpected circumstances. I need to keep expense to a minimum but I also need to be realistic. Could you come back to the house so we can talk about it more comfortably?'

'I'd love to, but I have a train to catch.'

'Then I'll explain briefly now, if you're willing to listen?'

Daisy didn't move so Thea gave her a brief account of her mother's Will, watching as Daisy's eyes grew bigger and bigger.

'What a slimy toad your stepbrother is,' Daisy concluded.

'Indeed. But I need to be able to prove it and I've begun to suspect I may have to spend a considerable amount of time searching for evidence. It may be hard for me to look after paying guests as well so your help could be invaluable. Besides, I'm concerned that Anna may try to do too much.'

Daisy nodded as though her impression of Anna was the same.

'Unfortunately, I'm not in a position to pay you a proper wage,' Thea said. 'I can only offer to share the money I make from paying guests. If I can find any guests.'

'You'll find them. Your house is lovely, and just a short walk from the beach.'

'I hope you're right. I should also point out that, as staff, we'll be sleeping in small attic rooms and even our food will have to be basic.'

'None of that matters,' Daisy assured her. 'I'd love to work for you.'

'As I can't pay you a wage you'd be working *with* me rather than *for* me,' Thea pointed out.

'Even better.'

'It might not be for long either. If I can't prove that I'm right about the Will, we'll all be out on the streets in three months' time.'

'A lot can happen in three months.'

'Yes, it can. Do you need your father's permission to work with us? Forgive me, but I assume you're not of age?'

'I'm eighteen but my father won't object.'

'Excellent. When might you join us?'

'Saturday? I think I should spend a little time with my father first.'

'Perfect.'

Grinning, Daisy ran off to catch her train.

Had Thea done the right thing in taking Daisy on as well as Anna? She hadn't had a choice with Anna because where else could the poor girl have gone? To the workhouse? Thea could never have allowed that to happen when she had a home to offer, even if it was only a temporary home.

Anna had looked distraught but dignified when they'd gone inside after Daisy had dropped her clanger. 'I'm sorry,' Anna had said. 'It was dishonest of me to conceal my situation.'

'You were desperate.'

'That doesn't excuse deception. I'll fetch my things and leave.' Anna had moved back to the door.

'Stay,' Thea had urged. 'I don't blame you for not telling me about the baby. I might have kept quiet about it myself in your position.'

'I wouldn't like you to think that I'm... I mean, I've never...'

'You loved Piers and he loved you.'

Anna had swallowed down emotion. 'There's never been anyone else.'

'If Piers hadn't needed to go on his expedition, you'd have been safely married by now. You can't bring Piers back but you can do your best for his child and for yourself as well. That means staying here. For a while anyway. When is the baby due?'

'The middle of May.'

'That means you should be back on your feet before Stanley returns. Don't think of yourself as a charity case. You can still help me with the guests.'

'Oh, I can! I'm not unwell. You've only seen me at my lowest but I'm a hard worker.'

'I don't doubt it. I'll feel more secure having a friend in the house with me, and a guest house might be considered more respectable if it's run by two people rather than one young woman alone.'

'Respectable? With me in my condition?'

'You're a widow to all intents and purposes so why not pass yourself off as one? No one will question your respectability then.'

'I could call myself Mrs Watson.'

'Or Mrs Rutherford, if that's what Piers would want.'

Tears had glistened in Anna's eyes. 'It is,' she'd agreed.

'I can lend you a ring to make it look official. I managed to save three wedding rings from Herbert. My mother's and both of my grandmothers'. One of them should fit you.'

'I'll take good care of it,' Anna had promised.

Now Thea turned for home and re-joined Anna in the kitchen. 'I asked Daisy to help after all.'

'Not because you think I won't cope?' Anna was worried.

'An extra pair of hands will leave me freer to pursue the witnesses,' Thea pointed out.

She didn't mention that she hoped Daisy would help to keep an eye on Anna too. Thea knew nothing about babies. She could remember her mother's friends cooing over infants once they'd been born, but pregnancy and childbirth had been shrouded in mystery. Certainly they hadn't been considered suitable subjects for discussion in front of the young girl Thea had been back then. Daisy had struck Thea as being much more unlikely to panic when Anna went into labour.

Thea had warmed to Daisy. She'd liked the younger girl's merry smile and pretty dimples. Even her tactlessness had been endearing because she'd been so openly honest about it.

Why was she so keen to get a job in Brighton, though? Daisy had spoken of her father with obvious affection. Thea decided she wouldn't pry but wait for Daisy to decide if she wanted to confide in her.

It was going to be strange having another two people in the house. As the only child of parents who were themselves only children, Thea had never shared her home with young people before. It might be difficult to adjust to the loss of privacy. On the other hand, it might be fun.

With Daisy coming to help to prepare the house and Anna still busy with washing, ironing, mending and devising inexpensive but appealing menus for the guests, Thea decided to focus on finding the witnesses over the next few days. The Jarrolds' door remained closed but she had more luck in finding Strupp's landlord at home.

'One day Strupp was there owing me a month's rent. The next day he was gone, still owing me a month's rent,' he said.

'You don't have a forwarding address for him?'

The landlord pulled a face that suggested she was hopelessly naïve if she expected a man who owed money to leave behind a means of tracing him.

'He might not have left the address with *you* but he could have given it to a friend or neighbour,' Thea pointed out.

The landlord's expression conceded that perhaps her enquiry hadn't been entirely dim-witted. 'My other tenants told my rent collector that they barely knew Strupp. I didn't have the neighbours questioned because paying my man to make enquiries would likely have been throwing good money after bad.'

'Do you have a previous address for Mr Strupp?'

'I might have. Owes you money too, does he?'

'I just want to talk to him about a document he witnessed.'

The landlord invited her into the house while he looked through his papers. '26 Tea Street,' he finally said. 'That's in London though I can't be sure Strupp actually lived there.'

'Do you have an address for the landlord of that property?'

Mr Clark looked back at his papers. 'Archibald Ward, 32 Caton Avenue, Highgate. If he actually exists.' The landlord wrote both addresses on a sheet of notepaper and handed it over.

'I don't suppose you'll find any trace of Strupp but just in case you happen to be lucky, I'd appreciate you letting me know,' he said.

'Of course. And perhaps you'd be good enough to let me know if you happen to hear anything of him.' She left the landlord with one of her mother's old visiting cards on which she'd written her own name neatly.

She wrote to Strupp's Highgate landlord that evening. Not because she expected a letter to bear fruit but because it would be foolish not to find out.

The next day she returned to Ships Passage and ducked into a recessed shop entrance after knocking on Jarrold's door in case he or his daughter looked down at her from a window. It still did no good.

Neither did it help when she waited further up the passage in hopes of one of the Jarrolds appearing. She was too conspicuous in such a small space.

By the time Friday afternoon came Thea had decided not to knock on the Jarrolds' door for a few days. If they were avoiding her on purpose her absence might persuade them that she'd given up and make them less vigilant about avoiding her. And with Daisy coming the following day it was time to switch her attention back to opening the guest house as soon as possible, especially considering she'd have three mouths to feed in future.

She went home with more cardboard boxes for packing up things in the attics. Inspecting the rooms earlier that morning, she'd felt a rush of emotion as she identified her father's old school trunk, the bag containing his cricket things, and another bag containing his golf clubs. She'd found her mother's painting easel and box of watercolour paints in another attic, together with some of her pictures, inexpert but precious to Thea though heaven knew where she'd put them if she lost the house. Behind them she'd spotted the cradle, rocking horse and dolls' house from her own childhood. They were precious too but luckily, she'd also seen several items she was happy to throw away – a chair with the seat worn through, a chipped glass lampshade and a scuffed suitcase to name a few.

'A letter came for you,' Anna told her on her return.

The envelope she passed over was of excellent quality, the handwriting ornate and feminine. Thea opened it, and read the letter it contained.

Dear Thea,

I hope you won't consider it impertinent of me to address you by your Christian name but you were Thea to me as a child in those happy days when you visited frequently with your mother. I was very sorry to hear of her passing. I wonder if you might join Ralph and me for tea at the Grand so we can talk of those happy days and renew our acquaintance? Would the afternoon of 16th March be convenient? I'd suggest an earlier date but I'll be away visiting friends.

Kindest regards,
Maria Kirby-Laws.

Thea felt a sudden tug of longing for those happier times. Yes, she would take tea with Mrs Kirby-Laws. In fact, she was looking forward to it.

Fourteen

'That'll be Daisy,' Anna said, when the doorknocker banged.

Eager to be of use while she still could, she hastened towards the basement stairs to answer the door before Thea had a chance to move. Halfway up the stairs the baby kicked and Anna smoothed her hand over her gently-curving middle. She'd been in Thea's house for little more than a week but already the baby seemed to have grown. What would have happened if she hadn't met Thea? Even the thought of it made Anna shudder.

She opened the door and Daisy stepped inside to dump her bags in the hall and beam broadly. 'What do you want me to do first?'

'Come down for a cup of tea and Thea will tell you what needs to be done.'

'We need to prepare space in the attic rooms for us to sleep in them,' Thea said, as they sat around the kitchen table. 'They're full of clutter, I'm afraid – old things belonging to my family and odd bits of furniture too. We can get rid of some of them but whatever remains will just have to be stacked neatly. I've been collecting boxes for packing things up.'

Clearing the attics took the rest of the day but eventually each contained a bed, a wardrobe or chest of drawers and a fair share of the clutter. 'You take this room, Anna,' Thea said of the largest attic.

Anna was shocked. 'I couldn't. This room should be yours.'

'You'll need space when the baby comes,' Thea reasoned, gesturing Daisy to help her move the cradle into the room.

'I'm happy with the smallest room,' Daisy declared.

Thea decided they'd done enough for one day. 'Time for supper, I think.'

'I'm not the best cook but I'll be happy to run to the shops if we need to buy anything,' Daisy offered.

'I hope you're not the worst cook?' Thea asked.

She was teasing but Daisy looked guilty as though she believed she really might be the worst. 'Um…'

'I can cook,' Anna said. 'Coming from a family of seven I'm used to cooking on a budget too.'

Feeling she wasn't pulling her weight with the heavier work, it made her feel better to be able to contribute her cooking skills. She made a stew for supper and the next morning offered to scramble eggs for breakfast.

'I adore scrambled eggs,' Daisy said, only to glance at Thea as though concerned she might have spoken out of turn seeing as Thea was paying for their food.

'Eggs will be lovely,' Thea confirmed.

'Delicious,' Daisy declared, after they'd eaten. 'The eggs I scramble end up speckled with burnt bits.'

'Try to cook them more slowly,' Anna advised.

'I do try, but the slower I cook them the more likely I am to be distracted by something else. A fight between the chickens, the cat wanting to be stroked, the dog barking at someone passing in the lane… The next thing I know, the eggs are burning.'

Daisy suddenly looked horrified and Anna guessed she'd remembered she was here as domestic help. 'I hope I haven't given the impression that I can't cook at all,' she said. 'I can. Sort of.'

Anna saw Thea was hiding a smile. 'Perhaps I could show you how I cook seeing as I'm more experienced,' Anna offered.

'I'd like that,' Daisy said.

They set to work cleaning the attic rooms, making up the beds and moving their things up there too. Afterwards, Thea insisted they do no more as it was a Sunday. They took a bracing stroll along the seafront then returned to Clarendon Place for a quiet evening at home.

Anna wrote a longer letter to her family.

> *The house where I'm staying is a lovely place just two minutes' walk from the sea. I'm staying here because the owner is going to open it to paying guests and I'm going to help her.*

Anna's conscience stirred as she wrote that. She still felt guilty over the way she'd virtually forced herself on Thea.

> *The owner is a Miss Fairfax. She's a rather grand young woman but friendly. She insists on being called*

Thea which is short for Theodora. She's tall and elegant with striking good looks and beautiful manners. I'm very happy living with her.

I'm working with another girl called Daisy. She's two years younger than me and looks like a tiny fairy with untidy fair hair but she has more energy than anyone I've ever known and she's very friendly too.

Do write back and let me know all your news,

Your loving daughter and sister,

Anna x

There were two pieces of information Anna had decided not to share. She'd didn't mention that the guest house was only a temporary venture because it would worry them, and she still didn't explain that Piers was gone because it would worry them even more. Besides, putting his loss down in writing would feel too final. Too terrible. No, that desperate news would have to wait for another day when Anna was feeling stronger.

Grief was still sweeping over her at night and ambushing her at moments during the day. Feeling another wave building, Anna blinked it away, addressed her envelope and fixed a stamp to it, ready for posting in the morning.

She was up and out of the house early. She posted the letter then bought a newspaper and took it to the seafront, holding the pages down against the chilly breeze. She'd been buying a paper every day but there was still no more news about the shipwreck.

Perhaps the *Herald*'s editor, George Acaster, had told Piers's family about details that weren't being made public.

Might he share them with Anna too? It was certainly worth thinking about what she might write to persuade him to share his information.

Sighing, she folded the newspaper and put it in her basket then walked down the steps to the fish market being held on the stony beach, bargaining for a small quantity of mackerel for their supper.

Thea and Anna were in the kitchen when she returned to Clarendon Place. 'Any news?' Thea asked, seeing the newspaper.

'Not yet.'

'I'm sorry.'

Thea patted Anna's arm and Daisy sent her a smile. How kind they were.

They set to work cleaning the rest of the house. The rooms were neither dirty nor even untidy but Thea had a proper spring clean in mind. They rolled up rugs, carried them outside and beat the dust from them then dusted and swept the rooms. 'Would you start cleaning windows, Daisy?' Thea asked.

'Um, yes. If that's what you'd like.'

Anna supposed that Daisy's window-cleaning skills ranked alongside her cooking skills.

'On second thoughts, I'll clean the windows if you keep me supplied with hot water,' Thea said tactfully.

Anna washed skirting boards and doors.

After three days the house was gleaming and each guest room was looking as attractive as they could make it, the furniture polished and bearing such homely touches as they'd been able to manage, from books to one or two of the cheaper ornaments Herbert hadn't pilfered. Thea had been to the stationery shop and bought stout sheets of card. Now she fetched pen and ink from a drawer. 'We need to make a *Vacancies* sign to put in the window,' she explained.

She outlined the letters then used a small paintbrush to fill them with ink so they stood out clearly. 'We should put small cards up in shop windows and places of interest too,' Thea said.

She cut a sheet of card into smaller cards, wrote on one of them then said, 'What do you think of this?

> *Guest House in Clarendon Place*
> *(two minutes from sea).*
> *Reasonable rates for bed and breakfast.*
> *Evening meal optional.*
> *Enquiries to Miss Fairfax,*
> *18 Clarendon Place, Brighton'.*

'I think it'll do the job very well,' Anna said, and Daisy nodded.

'I'll write several cards and perhaps you could go around town arranging for them to be put up tomorrow, Daisy?'

The younger girl nodded enthusiastically and Anna imagined she'd race around town like a whirlwind. It would be the first day of March. 'A good day to open with the worst of the winter behind us and spring in the air,' Anna suggested.

'Let's hope so,' Thea said. 'Anna, would you mind staying at home tomorrow just in case anyone sees the sign in the window and enquires about rooms?'

'Of course.' It was a welcome opportunity as Anna was keen to write to the *Herald*'s editor about Piers. 'You'll be back out hunting for your witnesses, I assume?'

'I will. Hopefully they'll think I've given up and be more likely to open the door.'

Anna wrote to Mr Acaster when she was alone in the house the following morning. Describing herself as a close friend of Piers, she begged for information about the shipwreck.

Feeling restless afterwards, she got up and walked around the kitchen, torn between dread that she'd learn that Piers's last moments had been terrible and hope that she might learn that his passing had been quick.

She was nursing another hope too. She knew it was ridiculous after what she'd read in the paper and heard from the Rutherfords but she couldn't help hoping that there'd been some mistake and Piers wasn't dead at all.

The sooner she knew exactly what had happened, the better because the hope was torturing her. But George Acaster might not bother to write back. If that proved to be the case, might there be another way of uncovering information?

Thea had mentioned that Major Kirby-Law and his parents lived near Worthing and they sounded as well-to-do as Piers's family. If the families moved in the same circles then the Kirby-Laws might know more about the shipwreck than had appeared in the *Herald*. Could Anna ask Thea to find out what they knew? Or would that be imposing on Thea's good nature too far?

Anna heard the front door open and close on the floor above her. Rapid footsteps sounded on the basement stairs then Thea came in, her breathing as fiery as her hair and her green eyes sparkling with frustration.

'They've gone,' she said. 'Jarrold and his daughter have done what the neighbour called a moonlight flit. No forwarding address, of course. That means I've lost both witnesses.'

'I'm sorry,' Anna said, but it felt a wholly inadequate response to Thea's distress and to the hollow feeling that was opening up inside Anna herself.

With the disappearance of the witnesses it was more likely than ever that Thea, Anna and the baby would be out on the streets when Stanley returned.

Fifteen

Daisy sipped her tea thoughtfully, wondering whether to say what was on her mind. The guest house had been open for a week now and a strained quietness had set in as each new day had brought no guests at all.

They'd kept the house spotless, taken turns to wander the Brighton streets and seafront, read books, written letters and made encouraging comments about how business should pick up now March was advancing and the trees were in bud. Thea had pursued her witnesses too, making enquiries of their neighbours and local shopkeepers but her efforts had led nowhere. There'd been no reply to her letter to Strupp's London landlord and neither had there been a reply to Anna's letter to Piers's editor. Life in Clarendon Place felt suspended in time as they waited for guests and information, but time was in fact marching on relentlessly.

'I know we can't afford to waste money but I'm going to buy some flowers to put in the window,' Anna said now. 'It might be worth a few pennies to make the house look cheerful.'

Perhaps she was right. Flowers might appeal to guests as well as help Anna to feel useful. Daisy had no ideas for helping with the lack of guests or the fact that there was still no more news of Piers but she did have an opinion on why Thea had got nowhere with questioning the Jarrolds' neighbours about where they might have gone.

'What is it?' Thea asked.

Daisy realised her thoughts must have shown on her face. 'I hope you won't take this the wrong way, but I don't think any of the neighbours will talk to you unless they want to get the witnesses into trouble. You're too grand, you see? You're obviously not a friend so people will guess there's been some sort of bother. By the sound of it, no one cares about Strupp and they might not care about Jarrold either, but they might care about the girl you thought could be Jarrold's daughter.'

'I'm practically a pauper but I take your point,' Thea said.

'Would you like me to see what I can find out?' Daisy offered.

'That would be wonderful, Daisy. Thank you.'

Daisy would be glad to repay Thea's kindness any way she could. 'Let me think of a plan.'

Just then feet passed by on the pavement beyond the window. The postman's feet. Daisy ran up to collect the post he pushed through the letterbox. There was only one envelope. Picking it off the doormat, Daisy had mixed feelings when she saw it was addressed to her in her father's handwriting. It was lovely to hear from him but it meant another day with no replies for Thea and Anna.

'Just a letter for me,' she said, returning to the kitchen.

She opened it and rolled her eyes at her father's mockery.

Well, girl, you've still not come home so I suppose you haven't poisoned the good people in Brighton with your cooking. Or have you been arrested and no one's told me?

'News from home?' Thea asked.

'From my father. Teasing me again.'

'He sounds like a nice man,' Thea said.

'He is.' Daisy supposed Thea and Anna must be wondering why she'd been so keen to get away from such a nice man. They'd been open about their situations. It was only fair that she should return the confidence.

'I didn't want to leave home because of my father,' Daisy told them. 'We have a neighbour and he… well, he's interested in me. Which is ridiculous, of course.'

'I don't see why,' Thea said.

'Neither do I,' said Anna.

'He's old and he's been married before,' Daisy explained. 'He's even got children. He wants a wife who'll keep house for him but I'm completely the wrong person for that sort of thing.'

'You don't want to get married?' Thea asked.

'I'd rather work with horses,' Daisy said.

'Don't you already work with horses at the forge?'

'I want to work with my cousin, Max. He's going to breed racehorses one day. Train them too. But he can't afford to employ me yet. If I stay here for a while, the neighbour will find someone else and I'll stop feeling awkward.'

By Sunday evening Daisy had thought of a plan to help Thea. 'Do you have a necklace I could borrow?' she asked.

'A necklace?' Thea looked puzzled.

'Just a cheap one. It isn't for me to wear but I've got an idea of how it might be useful.'

The next day Daisy left the house and headed for Ships Passage where the Jarrolds had lived. She banged on the door then opened the letterbox and shouted through the slot. 'It's Daisy. I've got your necklace.'

No one answered but Daisy hadn't expected that anyone would. She stepped back and looked up at the windows then shouted through the letterbox again.

'They've gone,' someone said.

Daisy's antics had attracted the attention of the woman from the sweet shop next door.

'Gone?' Daisy questioned.

'Sneaked out in the night a week or two ago. Couldn't pay the rent, I suppose.'

'But I borrowed a necklace.' Daisy held up the string of blue beads by way of evidence. 'I need to give it back.'

The shopkeeper was sympathetic. 'Jessie can't afford to lose a necklace or anything else the way that father of hers keeps her short of money.'

Jessie. A name. 'Do you know where she's gone?'

'I don't, love. And I don't know if she's still got her job but you could try her there.'

'Thank you, I will.' Daisy smiled gratefully then made a show of being struck by a sudden thought. 'Could you remind me where she works? I've only just moved here so I haven't actually known Jessie for long. I was hoping I'd made a friend but if she's gone…' Daisy pulled a sad face.

'Wainwrights on Keppel Street. She'll finish at six if she's still there.'

Daisy summoned another smile and walked away. She hadn't found the Jarrolds yet but she'd made a good start and was eager to report back to Thea.

She'd turned into Clarendon Place when she saw a middle-aged couple staring up at the house. Daisy slowed her pace and waited to see what they'd do. They exchanged a few words then walked up the steps and knocked on the door.

Moments later Daisy heard the door open. There was a murmur of voices then the couple stepped inside. Daisy waited a few moments longer, noticing the bowl of bright yellow daffodils Anna had placed in the drawing-room window, then used the key Thea had given her to let herself in and tiptoe down to the empty kitchen.

Two minutes later a smiling Anna joined her. 'We've got a Mr and Mrs Mitchell staying for three nights while they visit a great aunt who lives in a rest home. Thea's showing them to their room.'

'Wonderful! Those flowers of yours really did the trick. Should we make the Mitchells some tea?'

'They're going straight out but they'd like dinner tonight. I'll go to the shops later once I've decided what to cook.'

Thea looked as pleased as Anna when she came down, and her smile broadened when she heard what Daisy had learned about Jessie Jarrold. 'Daisy, you're a marvel.'

The praise felt premature to Daisy. 'Jessie might have left Wainwrights,' she pointed out. 'But if that's the case there might still be someone there who knows where she's gone. I'll go along later and see if she comes out. I need to know what she looks like, though.'

Thea's smooth forehead furrowed as she tried to remember. 'Neither particularly short nor particularly tall.

Slender. Light brown hair. Pale skin. Her coat was brown and loose. A hand-me-down from someone with a fuller figure perhaps. Her hat was brown too and so was her bag.'

'I won't confront her if I see her,' Daisy said. 'I'll follow her home instead so I can find out where she's staying.'

The idea of it gave Daisy a thrill of excitement. 'What sort of business is Wainwrights?' she asked, but Thea didn't know.

By the afternoon the guest house had another booking. Mr Jeffries, a commercial traveller wanted to stay for four nights and also wanted evening meals. Deciding that onion soup, lamb cutlets and a suet pudding would make for a satisfying dinner without breaking the bank, Anna went shopping then settled in the kitchen with Thea to prepare the meal. They were planning to serve the guests then eat their own dinner later once Daisy had returned from her mission to find Jessie.

Daisy arrived at Keppel Street early and soon found Wainwrights, a business that made mackintoshes. There was only one entrance as far as she could see. Large double gates set into the wall presumably allowed vehicles to come and go while a small single gate looked designed for people to use.

Crossing the road, she lingered outside shops as though browsing the windows, deciding that being small and ordinary had its advantages. Thea's striking good looks would have attracted attention. So would Anna's air of dignity. No one took any notice of Daisy.

Just after six the small gate opened on a swell of chattering voices but oh, heavens!

There was a whole crowd of women and many of them were wearing brown coats. Calling out, 'Goodnight', and,

'See you tomorrow', they rushed off so quickly that it was hard to see ages and hair colours under their hats.

Taken by surprise, Daisy dithered for a moment then set off after a group of three women purely because the middle one was slender and her brown coat looked loose.

'It wasn't Ivy's fault,' one of the girl's companions was saying as Daisy drew near.

'Mrs Beckett always picks on her,' the other agreed.

'That's because Ivy is pretty and Mr Beckett has an eye for her.'

The girls lowered their voices and Daisy guessed they were whispering bad things about their Mr Beckett. They reached the end of the road. ''Night, then,' the middle girl said.

''Night, Sally.'

Not Jessie, after all. Daisy ran back to Wainwrights but the other women had scattered out of sight. Blast. She'd have to come back another day but, if the Jarrolds hadn't left Brighton already, they could be making plans to leave any moment now. Daisy returned to Clarendon Place feeling frustrated.

Sixteen

Thea opened her wardrobe and sighed. She'd had pretty clothes as a child but by the time she'd outgrown the last of them her mother had married Herbert and money had become tight. These days Thea's clothes were both inexpensive and old. Without a doubt she'd be the least well-dressed woman taking tea at the Grand Hotel on Friday.

Anna spoke from the open doorway. 'Would you like me to help you choose something?'

'By all means,' Thea told her, 'though there's little to choose from.'

Anna walked into the room and looked in the wardrobe. 'The Kirby-Laws won't expect you to wear mourning clothes?'

'Because of my mother?' Thea shook her head. 'My mother loathed seeing people dressed in funeral black because they reminded her of crows. She made me promise not to wear mourning on her death and six months have passed since then anyway. I can't imagine anyone expects me to wear mourning for Herbert.'

'No,' Anna agreed.

'This is my best dress.' Thea took a green dress out of the wardrobe. 'I mostly make do with skirts and blouses.'

'The colour is perfect for you,' Anna approved. 'But the style… it's just a little severe and the waist is unfashionably high. Do you have any braid or other trimmings?'

'Nothing suitable.'

'Not even on other clothes? Your mother's things, perhaps? I noticed some lovely fabrics and trimmings when we packed them away.'

Thea felt a pang of dismay at the thought of cutting up her mother's clothes but knew Cecily would gladly sacrifice them if they helped her daughter to rebuild her friendship with the Kirby-Laws.

'Let's see.' Thea pulled a box from a corner of her room, and invited Anna to explore the contents.

Anna rummaged for a moment then pulled out an old evening coat. 'This braid will do nicely.' It was the colour of old gold and embroidered in red and blue. 'It's fraying in places but there should be enough to trim the dress. If you'd like me to try?'

'Please do. Use anything in there. Not just to alter my dress but to make things for the baby too.'

Anna was visibly touched. 'Are you sure? I've been worrying about preparing for the baby but I'd hate to take advantage, particularly if these clothes have sentimental value.'

'Take them with my blessing,' Thea said, knowing Cecily would like to help Anna too. 'And do tell me if I can help. I don't have any special talent when it comes to sewing but I can sew a straight seam and embroider a little.'

'Thank you.'

Thea paused then said, 'I don't mean to interfere, but have you seen a doctor about the baby?' Anna was noticeably bigger now and only two months away from her expected confinement.

She blushed. 'Not yet. I didn't dare visit a doctor when I was living at home in case someone saw me.'

Thea supposed she was worried about the doctor's fee too. But Anna's health and the health of her child were more important than money. 'I'll happily give you the name of my family doctor and help with the fee,' Thea offered.

'I'd appreciate the recommendation, though I think I've enough money put by to pay the fee.'

Thea wrote down the name and address of Doctor Maddox. 'He's a kind man.'

'I'll still tell him I'm a widow,' Anna said.

'Perhaps that would be wise.'

Thea patted Anna's arm and went to see Daisy who was planning on returning to Wainwrights for a third time in another attempt to find Jessie Jarrold.

'The women all come rushing out together,' Daisy explained again. 'I've no chance to eavesdrop on conversations before they scatter and I can only follow one person or a small group of people at a time.'

'You're doing your best and I'm grateful,' Thea told her, but she was growing ever more anxious.

Daisy had no luck that day either, or the following day. 'But I'm not giving up,' she said.

Thea forced a smile then thrust anxiety aside, determined to enjoy her tea with the Kirby-Laws that afternoon. She was delighted when she saw the dress Anna had altered. Anna had lowered the waist by inserting a panel of green velvet. She'd also stitched braid onto each side of the V-shaped neckline and around the panel's upper and lower edges.

'It's simple but I hope it's attractive,' she said.

'How clever you are!' Thea declared. 'I won't feel half as dowdy now.'

She walked the short distance to the hotel, wondering why Mrs Kirby-Laws had chosen to meet her there. Because she had other business in Brighton? Because it was convenient for Thea? Or because she wanted to see what sort of person Thea had grown into before inviting her into her home?

As far as Thea was concerned, Mrs Kirby-Laws had no need to fear Herbert's influence. Thea was her parents' daughter and determined to do them proud.

She held her head high as she was shown into the lounge and was pleased to see that her arrival brought a look of pleasure and approval to her hostess's face. Relief too, most probably.

Ralph got to his feet to greet her. He was in civilian clothes, his collar crisp and his tie straight. He was a fine-looking man and open in his admiration of Thea. After all the troubles of recent years she felt again how very pleasant it was to be smiled upon so warmly.

'My dear girl!' Mrs Kirby-Laws presented a cheek for Thea to kiss. 'It's such a delight to see you again. I always thought you'd grow into a beauty and I was right. Do sit down.'

The waiter moved to pull a chair out for Thea but Ralph got there before him. 'Thank you,' Thea said, then turned to his mother. 'It's very kind of you to invite me.'

Mrs Kirby-Laws waved a hand to suggest that it was nothing, the lace at her cuff dancing as she moved. 'I was so sorry to hear about your poor mother,' she said. 'You must miss her.'

'I do,' Thea admitted. 'But she wouldn't want me to grieve more than I can help.'

'She'd want you to be happy, of course. It was such a pity we fell out of the way of seeing each other.'

Thea's feelings were mixed when she heard that comment. It was true that her mother had withdrawn from social engagements due to embarrassment and shame. It had been hard to bear her friends' disgusted looks when they encountered Herbert, particularly if he was drunk and boorish.

It had been equally hard to bear their pity and perplexity over why a fastidious woman like Cecily had married such an uncouth brute. But her friends could still have taken a more compassionate view instead of letting her cower from disgrace inside the walls of her home.

'Let's be blunt,' they could have said. 'You've married a man we can't receive in our homes and have no wish to see anywhere else, but you're our friend and that mustn't change.'

None of them had said anything like that as far as Thea was aware, but the past was the past and nothing would have thrilled her mother more than to see Thea renewing old friendships. 'Circumstances changed,' she said and Mrs Kirby-Laws patted her hand as though approving of the way Thea had steered them past any awkwardness.

No condolences were offered regarding Herbert's death. Mrs Kirby-Laws didn't mention him at all. He was a part of history she preferred to ignore. Thea would have consigned him to history herself were it not for the awful mess he'd left behind.

There was something troubling her hostess, however. 'I hope you're not all alone in Clarendon Place, Thea?'

'No, no. I have company,' Thea assured her. 'Anna and Daisy.'

'Thank goodness.'

Realising Mrs Kirby-Laws took them to be servants, Thea was wondering whether to correct her when their tea arrived. It looked scrumptious with tiny sandwiches, scones, cakes, and dishes of preserves served with gleaming china and silverware. Thea hadn't experienced such luxury in years and only wished she could take some food home in a napkin for Anna and Daisy.

By the time they'd begun to eat Thea had decided against explaining why Anna and Daisy were in her house. Admitting that she'd had to let their servants go would be admitting she was poor and she didn't want the Kirby-Laws to feel embarrassed or obliged to help in some way. For the same reason – and also because she didn't want them thinking badly of her mother – she decided to say nothing about her mother's so-called Will.

Thea asked about the Kirby-Laws instead. 'We've extended the rose garden,' Mrs Kirby-Laws told her. 'Your mother would have loved it. She was so fond of a rose garden.'

'The house has been redecorated too,' Ralph said.

'Yes, we have new paper on the walls. That's why I couldn't suggest an earlier date for this tea. We stayed at my cousin's house in London while the paper was being put up. Ralph was away with his regiment, of course.'

Thea smiled at him. 'But now you're home again.'

'We're delighted,' Mrs Kirby-Laws said. 'Ralph always intended to go into business with his father eventually, and it will be wonderful to have him living at home.'

She paused then added, 'You must come and see the house, my dear. We're having a dinner party on the thirty-first of the month. Do say you'll join us. Ralph can collect you and take you home again.'

Thea guessed she'd passed whatever test had been set to ensure she hadn't been contaminated by Herbert's vulgarity. 'I'll be happy to join you,' she said, not missing the flare of pleasure in Ralph's brown eyes.

The conversation moved on to Mrs Kirby-Laws's shopping earlier that afternoon. 'I went to Needham's for handkerchiefs but the selection was very dull today. How are you finding Needham's, Thea?'

'I can't say I've shopped there recently.' She hadn't had the money for it. 'But I always find shopping to be a game of chance. Sometimes we can't see anything we like. On other days we're spoilt for choice.'

'And then we can't make our minds up.' Mrs Kirby-Laws laughed.

The hour passed pleasantly. They talked about Ralph's army years, the new gardens and boating lake that were planned for Brighton, and a reception the Kirby-Laws had attended in Brighton Pavilion.

'It was perfectly proper to use it as a hospital during the war years but all the fencing they put up around it was so drab. It's lovely to have the place open again,' Mrs Kirby-Laws said.

Anna hadn't asked Thea to try to find out information about Piers but, assuming she'd been held back by the fear of making her uncomfortable, Thea decided to mention him anyway. 'I read in the newspaper about a young man from Worthing who lost his life overseas recently. Perhaps you knew him?'

'I suppose you mean Piers Rutherford. We move in similar circles to his family though I wouldn't claim we're on intimate terms,' Mrs Kirby-Laws told her. 'I hear his family are devastated.'

'A shipwreck, wasn't it?'

'In a storm, I believe.'

'A storm?'

'We don't have details. Such a tragedy. We're so relieved to have Ralph home safely after his adventures in the army.'

'I'm delighted to be home,' Ralph said.

Eventually Thea judged it time to leave. 'It's been lovely, seeing you again.'

'I'm pleased it won't be long before we see you again,' Mrs Kirby-Laws said.

'I have the car here,' Ralph told Thea. 'It'll be no trouble to drop you in Clarendon Place.'

'Thank you, but a walk will do me good.'

He stood politely as she got to her feet, waited as she kissed his mother's cheek again, then said, 'I hope you'll allow me the pleasure of accompanying you on your walk?' He turned to his mother. 'Unless you wish to leave now, Mama?'

Mrs Kirby-Laws waved a complacent hand. 'I'll happily sit here for a while.'

Ralph took Thea's arm as they walked along Kings Road and across Kings Junction to Marine Parade. 'Mother's party isn't for another two weeks,' he said. 'Would you give me the pleasure of your company before then? For dinner, perhaps?'

They agreed on the Saturday of the following week. Turning into Clarendon Place, Thea came to a halt outside her house. She intended to shake Ralph's hand but he leaned towards her and kissed her cheek, his moustache a light tickle on her skin. 'We're old friends,' he said to justify the familiarity, though they'd barely exchanged more than a few words in the past.

Not that Thea minded. 'Goodbye, Ralph.'

She ran up the steps to the door, opened it then paused to smile back at Ralph and receive a glowing smile in return. She'd gone inside and reached the top of the basement steps when a thought struck her. Walking back to the drawing-room, she saw that the *Vacancies* sign was still in the window but perhaps Ralph hadn't noticed it.

Thea had no intention of lying about her situation. If her friendship with the Kirby-Laws flourished, she'd have to be open about it. But until then she felt the same reluctance to explain her circumstances as had come over her when she'd mentioned Anna and Daisy. It wasn't because she was ashamed or embarrassed – she rather enjoyed talking to the paying guests – but because she wanted to meet the Kirby-Laws as their equal instead of someone who needed help.

Thea was looking forward to seeing Ralph again but in the meantime there was work to be done. The *Vacancies* sign might still be in the window but three of the rooms had been taken by a Mr and Mrs Hackett, their son and their daughter. They were Americans who were visiting England from their home in Boston. They'd come to Brighton for three days of their visit as this was where Mr Hackett's family had lived in the past.

Thea went downstairs to help Anna to prepare the dinner. Chopping carrots, she wondered if Daisy would have any luck identifying Jessie Jarrold today.

Seventeen

Anna could understand why Thea liked Doctor Maddox. His manner was indeed kind though he was clearly curious about how she fitted into Thea's life.

'You're residing with Miss Fairfax?' he asked.

'For the moment.'

'Your husband is looking for a property of his own, perhaps?'

'My husband is...' Anna swallowed, overwhelmed by an avalanche of grief. Piers would have hated to see her like this – vulnerable and afraid that Doctor Maddox might somehow divine her unmarried status and judge her unworthy of his care.

'I'm a widow,' Anna finished.

'I'm sorry. I didn't mean to distress you.' He gave her a comforting pat on her hand then examined her thoroughly and kindly. 'All appears to be well,' he confirmed, and Anna felt a rush of relief. 'Have you decided where you'll give birth?'

'Not yet.'

'I recommend a nursing home. You'll receive the best medical attention during and after the birth.'

But nursing homes cost money. Lots of money.

'I'll give it some thought,' Anna assured him, but even with a little money coming in from paying guests Anna was concerned that a nursing home might be beyond her.

'It would be prudent to decide in advance on the sort of confinement you'd prefer,' he advised, giving her a note of the nursing home's name and address. 'You may have another two months before you expect to be confined but babies have a habit of arriving to suit their convenience rather than ours so I suggest you make arrangements sooner rather than later.'

'Of course. Thank you.'

Anna sighed as she left the consulting rooms. Childbirth wasn't as mysterious to her as it must be to a gently brought-up young lady like Thea. In the crowded terraces of Bermondsey, privacy was impossible, and childbirth couldn't be hidden. Anna had even helped her mother to give birth to little Lizzie and once helped a neighbour too. She was aware of the triumph and joy of delivery but also of the devastation that followed when childbirth went wrong.

Anna wasn't afraid of the pain but she was afraid that she might not be able to provide the medical attention that would give her child the best chance of a healthy start in life. All she could do was to work and save as much as she could.

She still hadn't heard from the editor of the *Herald* in reply to her letter. Not knowing what had happened to Piers was torturing her dreams so that she often woke with a scream forming in her throat. The tiny flicker of hope that there'd been some sort of mistake tormented her too. What if Piers were lying ill or injured somewhere and she'd made no effort to help him? It was unlikely, Anna knew, but even so…

If only the editor would write back.

She reached Clarendon Place, hoping to finish hemming a cot sheet before making dinner for the guests. Thea had been extraordinarily generous in giving Anna old clothes, sheets and blankets that still had enough good material in them for baby linen. Thea was helping with the sewing too.

'Just say if you want me to help,' Daisy had offered, but her grimace had suggested her sewing skills ranked at the same level as her cooking and window cleaning.

She was worth her weight in gold when it came to fetching and carrying, though. Her energy was as boundless as she'd promised and she'd thrown herself into tracing Jessie Jarrold too. Frustrated when Wainwrights closed on Saturday and Sunday, she'd begun questioning more neighbours of the other witness, Albert Strupp, but so far none of them had even admitted to knowing his name.

Anna had seen Thea's anxiety about the missing witnesses growing by the day and wondered where Major Kirby-Laws fitted into her thoughts. There'd been a trace of self-consciousness in the way Thea had reported on their tea then added that she'd be going to dinner with him. Anna guessed there was a romantic element to the major's invitation though perhaps it was too soon for that.

If a romance did develop, would the house be more or less important to Thea? The major was comfortably off as far as Anna knew and well able to maintain a wife. But perhaps the house was important for sentimental reasons or simply for Thea's pride. Whatever the future held for Thea, Anna couldn't depend on her for a place to live indefinitely.

'How did you get on?' Thea asked, when Anna returned.

'Doctor Maddox told me that all appears to be well.'

'Thank goodness.'

Anna didn't mention the nursing home, not wanting Thea to feel obliged to contribute to the cost. On the other hand Thea might welcome the reassurance that Anna didn't expect to give birth here. Anna decided to visit the nursing home soon so she could learn what sort of expense she was facing

Daisy came downstairs a few minutes later and it was obvious from her downturned mouth that once again she'd had no luck locating Jessie. 'I don't think she works at Wainwrights any more. I'm not giving up, though. I'm going to talk to one of the other girls and see what I can find out that way.'

Eighteen

There was a dark-haired girl at Wainwrights called Rose according to the names Daisy had heard being called out as the staff parted at the end of the working day. As Rose tended to walk away by herself, Daisy decided to approach her first so she wouldn't scare other girls off with her questions and make them close ranks against her.

She waited until Rose turned a corner then ran to catch her up. 'Excuse me!'

Daisy smiled in what she hoped was an affable manner. 'I'm trying to find a friend but I'm not sure she works at Wainwrights any more. I wonder if you might know where she's gone?'

'If she's your friend, wouldn't she have told you where she was going?'

Clearly, Rose was no fool.

'It was a new friendship. I've only just moved to Brighton,' Daisy said.

Rose didn't answer so Daisy pressed on. 'Her name's Jessie Jarrold.' At least Daisy assumed that was her surname.

Rose's eyes turned hostile. Obviously, she knew Jessie and felt protective about her.

'I'm not after Jessie for money or anything like that,' Daisy assured her quickly.

'Then why are you after her?'

'I want to talk to her about her father.'

Rose's lip curled at the mention of that man and Daisy realised she might be onto something if Rose saw Jeremiah as his daughter's enemy. 'Have you met Mr Jarrold?' Daisy asked.

'I have.'

'I don't blame you for not liking him. It must be hard for poor Jessie to be dragged down by him all the time. The drinking, the gambling, the hiding from debt collectors…'

It was guesswork on Daisy's part but it fitted with Thea's suspicions and seemed to be hitting home with Rose.

'Not to mention the way she's beaten black and blue by that oaf,' Rose said.

Goodness. 'Maybe there's a way to help Jessie,' Daisy suggested.

'How?'

Daisy didn't know. Not yet. To buy herself thinking time she said, 'We can't talk properly out in the street. Is there a tea shop nearby?'

'Not one that'll be open at this time. But there's a pub not far from here.'

Daisy had only been into one pub in all her life and that was the Wheatsheaf in Pixfield. She'd stepped in a handful of times to deliver messages from her father and she couldn't remember ever seeing a woman in there. The thought of going into a noisy Brighton pub was exciting as well as mildly alarming.

Rose led her to a pub called the Admiral's Fancy but steered Daisy away from the first door they reached. 'That's the public bar. We want the saloon.'

Daisy understood Rose's thinking as soon as they were inside. The public bar – visible across the counter – was occupied only by men while the saloon contained a mix of men and women. There was an empty table not far from the counter. Rose headed for it and sat down. Daisy sat too, wondering if she should go to the counter for drinks the way men were doing in the public bar. But a waiter approached.

'What's your fancy, ladies?'

'Port and lemon, please,' Rose told him.

Frank Flowers drank a pint of best, which was beer, but it didn't feel the right sort of drink for Daisy to order. 'I'll have a port and lemon too.' She didn't actually know what that was but she'd find out soon enough.

The drinks arrived and Daisy paid for them, adding a tip for the waiter. She hoped one drink would be enough to unleash Rose's cooperation otherwise it would be an expensive evening.

Daisy's head swam a little after the first sip of her port and lemon but it was a rather pleasant sensation and didn't stop her from thinking about the best way forward. 'Jessie's dad is making her life a misery,' Daisy began.

Rose nodded. 'It was only because Jessie paid the rent that they managed to stay in Ships Passage for so long but he found where she hid her money and the arrears built up. Before Ships Passage, they lived here, there and everywhere so I suppose that's how it's going to be again.'

'Jessie needs to get away but he doesn't want her to go,' Daisy continued.

'He's a nasty piece of work, especially after he's been drinking. Which is every night. Jessie's tried to get away but he always comes after her and drags her back.'

'He couldn't drag her anywhere if he were in prison. Jessie would have the chance to get far away where he'd never find her.'

'Jessie's much too scared of him to report him for beating her.'

'Maybe we can have him locked up for something else. For fraud.'

'Fraud?'

Daisy told Rose about Jarrold witnessing the Will.

'So your friend thinks he was paid to add his name to the Will and never even met her mother? It sounds exactly the sort of thing that oaf would do if there was money in it,' Rose conceded. 'Though I don't see how you can prove it.'

'We're taking one step at a time,' Daisy told her.

Rose drank some port, her expression thoughtful. 'I don't actually know where Jessie is at the moment,' she finally admitted.

'You don't?' Daisy was dismayed.

'She said she'd write when she was settled.'

'Will you let me know when you do hear from her?'

'I'm not promising, but give me your address.'

Daisy had already written it down in readiness. 'Thanks,' she said, handing it over.

'You've nothing to thank me for. I've done nothing except drink at your expense.'

'Perhaps you haven't done anything yet, but I hope you *will* help us.'

'Don't hold your breath waiting,' Rose said, and with that she left the pub.

Daisy's glass was still half full. She sipped it slowly, self-conscious at being alone in a pub but fascinated by her surroundings. There was a group of six women who looked as if they'd just finished work and were enjoying their release from drudgery. There was another group of two men and two women who were flirting outrageously. A young couple appeared to be out together for the first time because they were painfully shy with each other. An older couple stared into space.

The public bar was noisier, mostly with young men's voices. They were teasing a friend who must only just have got engaged.

'Tied you to her apron strings for life, she has,' one said.

'There's no escaping now,' agreed another.

'You'll be nagged to death,' said a third.

Didn't it occur to them that the man's fiancée might be the one who was feeling trapped?

The noise level dropped suddenly and Daisy guessed the young men had left. Perhaps they were drinking their way around Brighton.

It meant she could hear the voices of the two middle-aged men on the table next to hers.

'The knacker's coming tomorrow,' one said.

The knacker? Daisy felt a pang of sadness for whatever poor old creature had outlived its usefulness and was being sent off to be made into food for other animals.

'It means I've lost money on the bugger but what can I do? I reckon McGinty fed the bugger brandy or summat to quieten 'im down when I bought 'im. Years of hard graft in 'im, I were told. Years of biting and kicking, more likely. But McGinty won't take the bugger back. Buyer beware, 'e says.'

'You've tried to sell the 'orse on?'

''Course I 'ave. But would you buy an 'orse that's a savage? 'Course you wouldn't. 'E may be a young bugger but it's the knackers for 'im.'

Young? Daisy felt a stab of horror. She got to her feet. 'Excuse me, but I couldn't help overhearing. Did you say you were going to send a young horse to the knacker's yard?'

'What business is it of yours, if you don't mind me asking, Miss?' The man who owned the horse was defensive.

'The horse may be difficult now, but if he's given a chance he might—'

''E's had more chances than I've 'ad 'ot dinners. 'E's too wild and savage for a working 'orse and that's that.'

'He just needs the right training.'

The men exchanged the sort of glances that dismissed Daisy as one of those sentimental females with no sense of a world in which men had livings to earn.

'Beggin' your pardon if I'm being rude, Miss,' the owner said, 'but you've never even seen the 'orse.'

'I work with horses. At least my father does. So does my cousin.'

'If they want to come and buy the bugger, they're welcome. But they'll 'ave to come quick.'

Could Daisy get Max to come? Perhaps. Max couldn't afford to keep a horse out of charity, but he was a wonder with difficult horses. If he could work out the kinks in this horse, he might be able to sell it on. Daisy should see it first, though.

'Show me,' she said. 'Show me the horse.'

The owner sighed as though he found her tiresome but downed his beer and said. 'All right. Seeing as I'm 'eading 'ome anyhow.'

He led her through the night time darkness to an alley that ran between the back yards of small terraced houses. There were lights on in some of the houses but the only light that reached the alley came from the moon. Peering down it, Daisy saw that it was lined with brick walls behind which rose a hotchpotch of tumbledown outbuildings.

The owner set off along the cobbles and Daisy followed, unable to see where she was putting her feet and hoping she wasn't treading in anything horrid. He reached the middle of the alley, opened a gate and stepped into a yard. Instantly, there came the sound of kicking and angry neighing. Daisy hastened in after him. He walked up to the back of his house, went inside for the moment and lit the gas jets in what Daisy saw was a kitchen. The light didn't reach to the bottom half of the yard but when he emerged he was carrying a lantern. 'Keep back,' he warned.

He stepped further down the yard and Daisy saw that the outbuilding was a crude stable. The top half of the stable door was open and for a moment it looked like an empty black square but with more furious neighing the horse launched himself forward, thrusting his head over the door with his teeth bared ready to be sunk into human flesh.

Finding none, he kicked the door and thrust himself against the bottom half of it again and again, so hard that Daisy feared the wood might splinter or the bolt might not hold.

'You see?' the owner said.

'No horse behaves like this unless they've been cruelly treated,' Daisy argued.

'Now you look 'ere. I've never—'

'Not by you. By his previous owner.'

'Humph. Well, I can't say as I'd call McGinty a gentle man but mebbe this 'orse just 'as the devil in 'im.'

He was a big horse, black all over as far as Daisy could see. And a mess. He hadn't been groomed in an age so his forelock and mane were tangled while his coat was filthy. Daisy couldn't blame the current owner for not wanting to risk life and limb by grooming him.

The horse's bedding was out of sight behind the stable door but the smell of urine was sharp. Probably, the owner simply threw hay into the stable and didn't dare to remove the soiled stuff.

Yet the horse tugged on Daisy's emotions. It wasn't his fault if he'd been cruelly treated, and being cooped up here in this mean little stable without light or freshness couldn't be helping.

'Seen enough?' the owner asked.

'I want him to have another chance but you need to give me time to make some arrangements,' Daisy told him.

''Aven't got time. The knacker's due first thing tomorrow.'

'I'll come back as soon as I can.'

Daisy rushed to find a telephone kiosk but the girl at the Exchange told her no one was answering the telephone in Max's cottage. He could be nearby with the horses or he could be out on a visit. Daisy paced the streets of Brighton for half an hour then tried again. Still no answer. Grgh!

She ran to Clarendon Place instead and rushed down the stairs to the kitchen where Thea and Anna were clearing up after the guests' dinner. 'Thea, you've got to come,' Daisy begged.

'Come where?'

'There's a horse that's going to be sent to the knacker's yard if we don't save him.'

'A horse?'

'A young horse. Too young to die.'

Thea looked confused. 'Why would anyone kill a horse when it's young? Horses are valuable.'

'He's... he's got some problems.'

'I'm not a vet, Daisy. I don't know the first thing about horses.'

'I don't mean he's ill, though I suspect he's half-starved. Mostly he's upset. A bit...' How could she explain what she meant without frightening Thea away?

'A bit wild?' Thea guessed.

'He'll die if we don't help him.'

'That's terribly sad but what could I possibly do with a horse, wild or tame? I've nowhere to keep one and I can't possibly afford to pay for someone to look after one.'

'My cousin could take him. Max is wonderful with horses. But I can't reach him on the telephone and this is an emergency.'

'You're telling me that if I buy this horse your cousin will repay me and take him off my hands?'

'Yes. Maybe.'

Thea sighed.

'At the very least he'll know what to do with him,' Daisy said. 'Please, Thea. If you saw the poor creature, you'd—'

'How much would I have to pay for this horse?'

'I don't know. A few pounds.'

'Daisy, a few pounds is a fortune to me at the moment.'

'I know. It's just –' Daisy broke off abruptly. She was frustrated and disappointed, but it wasn't fair to put Thea under pressure to spend money. 'Sorry. I got carried away.'

Thea sighed again. 'I'll look at the horse but I'm not making any promises.'

'Thank you! Thank you!'

Daisy waited impatiently as Thea fetched her coat and hat then led her back to the horse, aware that the streets were becoming shabbier the further they went. Thea was frowning when they reached the alley. 'This doesn't look an appropriate place to keep an animal.'

'It isn't,' Daisy told her, thinking of the paddocks of Pixfield and Clareswood.

'Perhaps we should go round to the front of the house and knock on the door instead of just barging through the gate.'

Daisy supposed that would be polite. The house was the eighth house in the terrace. Walking around, she banged on a shabby door. The horse's owner opened it in shirtsleeves. He was eating a pie. 'Well, well,' he said, seeing Daisy but then he looked at tall, elegant Thea and his eyes widened.

'I'm Miss Fairfax,' she told him. 'You're…?'

'Brown, Miss. Caleb Brown.'

'We'd like to see the horse, please, Mr Brown.'

'Right.' He looked undecided over whether to invite them to come through the house or send them back to the alley.

Daisy had no doubt that she'd have been sent to the alley but Thea was considered worthy of better manners. 'You'd better come through,' he said.

He stepped back to let them into the house and appeared suddenly to remember he was holding a pie. He put it on a table and wiped his hand down his trousers. 'The 'ouse isn't… I wasn't expecting company.'

'I'm sorry we're imposing,' Thea said, pretending not even to notice the dirty plates, overflowing ashtrays, empty beer bottles and cast-aside newspapers.

They walked through a small parlour and kitchen, paused for Mr Brown to light a lantern, then continued into the yard. The horse must have heard them coming because he gave another irate neigh and threw himself against the stable door.

'Goodness,' Thea said, then something about the horse caught her attention.

'May I?' She took Mr Brown's lantern, and stepped forward. 'What's that on his chest?'

'Looks like blood,' Daisy said.

'Is it blood?' Thea asked.

'The bugger thrust 'isself into a pitchfork I were 'olding to keep 'im off.'

'You haven't had a vet here to see him?'

'Vets cost money and I've already lost money on the bugger. Begging' your pardon for the bad language, Miss.'

'How much do you want for him?'

Mr Brown looked thunderstruck by Thea's interest. 'You thinkin' of buying 'im?'

'Perhaps. If the price is right.'

His expression turned crafty. 'Ten pounds.'

Daisy snorted. 'You won't get that from the knacker.' At least she didn't think so.

'You'll take five pounds and be glad for it,' Thea told him brusquely. 'You'll keep him overnight for us too. We'll make plans for his removal in the morning.'

With that they left. 'I don't know why on earth I let you talk me into buying a horse,' Thea said. 'Please talk to your cousin as soon as possible or the horse may have to go to the knacker after all.'

'I'll call him straight away,' Daisy promised. Then she grinned. 'That man Brown was no match for you, Thea.'

She went off to telephone Max. She'd told him about Thea and Anna in a letter but wondered what he'd make of them when he met them in person.

Nineteen

Thea had imagined Maxwell Moore to be a male version of Daisy: short and slight with blue eyes and fair hair. She couldn't have been more wrong.

He was taller than Thea by at least an inch or two, and his build was both wiry and strong. He was dark-haired too while his eyes were a cool, penetrating grey, surveying her with respect but expecting equal respect in return.

'Miss Fairfax.' He shook her hand with easy confidence.

'Thank you for coming, Mr Moore.'

'Call him Maxie,' Daisy said.

Thea thought Maxie was far too frivolous a name for this self-possessed and clearly intelligent man. He thought so too, judging from the pained look he sent his cousin. 'Just Max,' he corrected.

'I'm Thea. May we offer you some refreshment?'

'Thank you but Daisy is bouncing up and down in eagerness to rescue this horse,' he said, and Thea picked up a faint trace of Irish in his voice.

'Before we go any further, let me make it plain that I'm going to look at this horse but I'm not promising to take him,' he added. 'The horse may be beyond my help and, much as I'd like every horse to have a comfortable home, I've neither the space nor the funds to support horses that can't earn their keep.'

'I understand,' Thea told him, but a knot of anxiety tightened in her stomach. What would she do if he didn't take the horse?

Just then Anna returned from the shops. Max greeted her with the same easy confidence with which he'd greeted Thea. If he judged her for being an unmarried mother, he certainly didn't show it, and when a cabbage rolled out of Anna's basket he simply picked it off the floor and restored it to her without fuss.

Leaving Anna to look after any guest enquiries, they left the house and climbed into the horsebox Max had borrowed from his employers. They all had to sit in a row in the front and Thea was glad when Daisy sat in the middle. She'd have felt self-conscious squeezed up against this cool-eyed stranger.

He dropped Thea at the front of Caleb Brown's house and asked Daisy to direct him to the alley. Thea knocked on the door and the owner answered holding a thick slice of bread. A half-hearted attempt had been made to tidy up inside but Thea simply glided through so he wouldn't feel embarrassed. Opening the gate to the alley, she found Max and Daisy waiting outside.

There was no need for Max to ask the whereabouts of the horse because he was kicking the stable door again, his black head lunging over the top with teeth bared.

'Don't blame me if 'e's wilder than you were expecting,' Caleb told Max. 'I'd 'ave thought young women would have gone soft on puppies or kittens instead of a savage brute like 'im, but I 'id nothing from 'em.'

'What's his name?' Max asked calmly.

'I call 'im Evil Bugger but you can call 'im what you like.'

'What age is he? Two?'

'So I were told.'

'And what's his history?'

'I got 'im from McGinty over in Seaford. McGinty got 'im from a farmer who weren't right in the 'ed after 'is wife passed on. Or so I were told.'

'Step back, please.' Max's voice required instant obedience. 'All of you. Please step back and stay back.'

Thea, Daisy and Caleb retreated up the yard to stand by the house. They watched as Max stepped closer to the horse but remained out of biting distance.

'So what's been going on with you?' he asked, his tone conversational. 'You've had some troubles, to be sure. A bad master is my guess. Maybe more than one bad master. Some of them are bastards, aren't they? Bullying and beating breaks some spirits but not yours. What those masters don't understand is that they'd get far more out of their animals if they treated them kindly.'

Thea realised the horse had quietened a little under the influence of Max's mesmeric tones. He was still tossing his head and his hooves still gave the occasional skitter but he wasn't trying to bite any more. Even so, her heart jumped when Max took another step forward.

'I treat all of the animals in my care with respect,' he said, his voice steady and calm. 'The way I see it, man and beast are partners. Each needs the other in order to thrive. You'd like it where I live. There are fields instead of this mean little yard. Fields that look out on more fields and the rolling hills of the Downs. You can see the sky and watch the clouds pass overhead from one horizon to the other. The grass is deep green and lush enough to shine, and the air smells and tastes like air should. Fresh sometimes. Earthy at other times, especially after rain.'

Still talking, Max moved closer, small step by small step until he could lean his arms on top of the stable door. The horse backed away and Thea could see him in the shadows, trembling and snorting. If he sprang forward suddenly… Thea swallowed.

'I look after eight horses and ponies with the help of a local lad,' Max continued. 'Freddie and Ferdy are Mrs Leigh's carriage ponies. She drives them in competitions. Proud little ponies they are because they've won dozens of rosettes and Mrs Leigh adores them. Clara is Mrs Leigh's riding horse but mostly she's a pensioner. Eats her fill and takes life easy. Then there's Constable and Turner, Mr Leigh's riding horses. Magnificent in their day but becoming old gentlemen now. Constable is at stud and he's produced some fine progeny. Mr and Mrs Leigh also have two mares, Matilda and Madge, who've produced some nice foals too. Then there's my horse.'

Thea stifled a gasp as Max opened the door, paused for a moment then stepped unhurriedly into the stable, bolting the door behind him. He leaned back against it, folding his arms across his chest.

'I've got Aurora, a mare who's given me two foals so far with another on the way,' he said. 'It's hard to say how they'll turn out but the idea is that they'll race if they're good enough. Between you and me, what I want is to breed fast horses but when a man has no money behind him he has to start small and work his way up. That's why I'm looking after the Leighs' horses as well as my own. You'd like the Leighs because they love their animals just as I do. So what do you think about joining Aurora and the others? I can't promise it'll work out well, but to my way of thinking it's better to try it than head straight for the knacker's yard.'

He unfolded his arms and held a hand out. The horse skittered again then sniffed at the fingers before butting them aside.

'Right then, I'll be back in a moment,' Max told the horse.

He let himself out of the stable and loped up to where Thea stood with Daisy and Caleb. 'I'll take him,' he told her, 'but we need to agree terms.'

Oh, dear. Terms that involved Thea paying for the horse's keep would be beyond her means.

'Two options,' he said. 'The first option is for me to buy the horse from you at whatever price you paid.'

Thank goodness.

'The second option is for us to hold equal shares in him. You've provided the purchase price. I'll provide the stabling, feeding and training. Until we see what I can make of him, that is.'

Thea much preferred Option One. But it occurred to her that buying the horse from her might leave him short of funds.

'It all turns on whether you're curious and have a sense of adventure,' he said, a challenge in those cool eyes which rather knocked the wind from her sails. 'A decent horse could broaden your horizons.'

'Is this a decent horse?' Thea asked.

'It's too early to say, but don't you want to find out?'

Thea felt unusually flustered. She forced herself to think clearly. A good horse might earn her some money. A lesser horse might cost her every penny she'd spent. Max was willing to take on all the risk but wasn't it fairer to share it? Besides, part-owning a horse might be fun and there'd been precious little fun in her life in recent years. 'Can I change my mind afterwards if we start as joint owners?' she asked.

'Any time you like.'

It sounded reassuring in theory though Thea knew that in practice she wouldn't be able to demand the purchase price from Max if the horse proved to be of little financial value. It wouldn't be right.

But what the heck. 'All right,' Thea said. 'We'll share the horse for the moment and see what you can make of him.'

'He needs a name,' Daisy said. 'I don't think Evil Bugger will find favour with Mr and Mrs Leigh.'

'To be sure it won't,' Max agreed. He looked at Thea. 'How about Fairfax's Fancy?'

'Or Moore's Magnificence,' she countered.

Max laughed. 'We can leave my vanity out of it.'

'Mine too,' Thea told him. It would be especially awkward to have a horse named after her if she had to give him up.

'We can think about a name later,' Max said. 'The most pressing thing is to get him away from here.'

He propped the gate open and lowered the ramp on the horsebox, returning with a halter and blanket. 'To go over the horse's head,' he explained. 'So he can only see what's directly ahead of him. He's less likely to be spooked if he isn't distracted and overwhelmed.'

Max let himself back into the stable and spoke to the horse for another few minutes before introducing him to the halter and blanket then slowly fixing them into place. 'Stand clear,' he ordered, leading the horse out.

Despite Max's soothing, the horse reacted with alarm, his hooves scrambling on the flagged yard and his head pulling this way and that as he snorted in dismay. Max steadied him and talked to him, his mouth close enough to breathe warm air across the horse's muzzle. Gradually, the horse settled again.

Thea was tense as Max led him out into the alley. If he pulled away and bolted into the streets of Brighton, he might cause a terrible accident. But, crooning softly, Max got the horse up the ramp and into the box. He tied the halter to a hook then climbed out to raise the ramp and bolt it into position.

'The horse is black all over,' Daisy said. 'Could he be called Blackie?'

'That's a name for a pet dog who sits at your feet, not for a warrior who'll take a chunk out of your arm at the first opportunity,' Max told her.

Thea was thinking about names too. Blackness… Darkness… Night time… 'Night Warrior?' she suggested.

'That's a grand name,' Max approved, though he grimaced when Daisy said. 'We can call him Warry for short.'

Night Warrior kicked the horsebox wall. 'I don't like to abandon you ladies, but would you mind making your own way home?' Max said then. 'I need to get this horse back to Clareswood before he kicks the horsebox to pieces.'

'We can walk,' Thea assured him.

She and Daisy waved Max off then turned to Caleb who was staring after the horsebox as if he thought Max was a cross between a mystic and a lunatic. 'I'll wish you good luck with the bugger,' he told Thea. 'I reckon as you'll need it.'

Twenty

Anna had wasted her money buying a newspaper. Again. Either no more information about the shipwreck had come to light or the details were being kept from the public out of sensitivity for the families of those who'd perished.

Perhaps that second possibility explained why the *Herald*'s editor hadn't replied to her letter. He might have tossed it away, thinking that a genuine friend would have contacted Piers's family and only someone who was seeking to profit from his death would approach the newspaper.

The post had at least brought Anna another letter from her mother and the children. The first letter had been written by Mary as their mother wasn't good at reading or writing.

Dear Anna,

We all miss you badly but are happy you have found somewhere to stay. Write to us again to let us know how you are getting on and what Brighton is like. We are all well but missing you.

They'd signed the letter individually:

Love from Ma x Mary x Joe x Tom x and Lizzie x

Anna had written a longer letter in reply, describing Thea and Brighton, and including the sort of challenge she'd long set them to help their education: *Think of ten words for the colour blue.*

Opening their second letter – also written by Mary – Anna smiled when she saw they'd replied to the challenge with:

Turquoise, sky, navy, indigo, ink, sapphire, forget-me-nots, eyes, sea and – becoming desperate – Lizzie's doll's dress.

But their next words pierced her with the sharpness of glass:

Is Piers back yet?

For a moment Anna couldn't read on but then she forced herself to continue.

We would like to come and visit you one day. We could look at the sea and the beach.

Anna sensed wistfulness behind that hope. There wasn't money for visiting Brighton or anywhere else now Anna had stopped paying for treats. She felt guilty about it but maybe one day she'd be in a position to help out again.

Small bits of news followed. Mary had let down the hem of an old dress and it hardly showed thanks to Anna's careful lessons in sewing. Joe had got all his sums right in a school test. Tom had started reading *Just So Stories* and little Lizzie was practising writing her name every day. They all sent their love and wanted Anna to write back soon. Tears welled up in Anna's eyes as she saw that, once again, each of them had signed their name and added kisses.

Hearing voices out in the street, she glanced up through the kitchen window to see Thea and Daisy passing by. Moments later they came in through the front door and bustled downstairs to join her.

'We saved him!' Daisy crowed. 'Warry, I mean.'

'Warry?'

Daisy told Anna all about Night Warrior.

'So you own a half-share in a horse,' Anna concluded, looking at Thea and hoping she hadn't felt pressured into taking on another burden out of charity.

'Perhaps Max will make something of the horse so we can sell him on,' Thea smiled, but Anna wondered if she might be feeling exasperated by the fact that her efforts to save money were being thwarted.

The thought made Anna feel all the guiltier later. Daisy had gone to the laundry when Thea turned to Anna and said, 'You didn't tell me if you made any plans for the birth when you saw Doctor Maddox. I hope you don't feel I'm prying but—'

'I'm living in your house. You've every right to know,' Anna assured her, but then she hesitated. She really didn't want Thea to think she was asking for help. 'I have the option of giving birth in a nursing home.'

'Is that what you want?' Thea asked.

'I'm considering it.'

'You mustn't worry about the cost. We'll manage somehow.'

'No, *I'll* manage. I'm not expecting you to pay a penny.'

'Wouldn't you pay a penny if I were the one needing help?' Thea asked.

Anna was momentarily silenced.

'Of course you would,' Thea concluded. 'And of course I'll help *you*. I don't know the first thing about childbirth but if you'd prefer a home birth then I'll help with that too as best I can.'

How generous Thea was. 'Thank you,' Anna said. Then she paused, feeling awkward again. 'I hope you won't think I'm squandering money foolishly but I want to go to London one day soon.'

'To see your family?'

'Yes, but also to go the offices of the *Herald* to see if I can find out what happened to Piers. I know it won't bring him back, but I still need to know. And I need to stop...' Anna broke off, reluctant to put her lingering uncertainty into words though Thea guessed her meaning immediately.

'Oh, Anna, are you hoping Piers is still alive?'

'I can't seem to help it.'

'Of course you must go to London. Even if you hear that Piers was lost beyond all doubt, it'll help you to grieve for him properly. I might come with you as I've had no reply from Strupp's London landlord. I might learn more if I see him face to face.'

Anna was pleased. It would be reassuring to have company on the journey.

'Monday will be a good day to go as we've no one booked in after the Robertsons leave,' Thea said.

'Go where?' Daisy asked, returning from the laundry.

Thea explained their plans. 'You won't mind looking after things here, I hope?'

''Course not.'

'We'll be back in time to prepare the dinner in case we have any new arrivals,' Anna promised.

It felt good to be doing something positive instead of just waiting for news. The *Herald*'s Mr Acaster might refuse to talk to her, of course, but Anna wasn't going to think of that.

Twenty-One

Daisy knew Anna and Thea had only been trying to stop her from worrying when they'd promised to return from London in time to cook. Even so, the fact that they felt obliged to return confirmed Daisy's suspicion that she wasn't pulling her weight in the guest house venture. Anna was wonderful with cooking, washing, sewing and all things domestic while Thea was a superb hostess for the guests. Daisy fetched and carried but she was keen to do more, especially now she'd foisted Warry onto Thea.

She couldn't be sorry that the horse had been saved but it was a pity his life had come at a cost to Thea's purse. 'Owning a horse might be exciting,' Thea had said, but it was Thea's way to be brave and perhaps she'd been worried that Max simply couldn't afford to buy the horse from her.

It had been Tuesday when she'd spoken to Jessie's friend, Rose, in the pub. On Friday Daisy decided to pay her another visit.

Seeing Daisy waiting for her outside Wainwrights, Rose sighed resentfully and walked over. 'You again.'

'Have you heard from Jessie?'

'I told you I'd get in touch if I had anything to share.'

Rose moved away but having nothing to share wasn't necessarily the same thing as not having heard from Jessie. Chasing after her, Daisy overtook Rose then turned to give herself a clear view of Rose's face. 'Has Jessie written to you?' she asked.

'Like I said,' Rose began, but there was defiance in her eyes that made Daisy suspicious.

'You *have* heard from her! Where is she?'

'I've nothing to say to you.'

'Jessie asked you to keep her address a secret?'

Rose shrugged.

'That was only to keep debt collectors away,' Daisy said.

'How would you know? Are you a mind reader?' Rose was sarcastic.

'I don't need to be a mind reader to guess why people flee their homes in the middle of the night. You might think you're being a good friend by keeping Jessie's whereabouts secret but you're not.'

'Aren't you the fount of all wisdom?' Rose looked down her nose as though Daisy was an upstart child who knew nothing of the world.

'If you don't give me Jessie's address, she'll miss out on the chance to get her horrible father out of her life.'

'Not much of a chance as far as I can see.'

'At least you'll have tried to help her.'

'So you say,' Rose sneered, but then she sighed. 'All right. I can't think of a better way of helping Jessie.'

She dug in her bag for an envelope and drew a letter from inside it. '20 Roper Street, Stepney, London,' she said.

'Thank you!' Daisy turned away.

'Wait,' Rose called.

Daisy turned back again.

'Tell your friend to explain to Jessie that I'm only trying to help her. And don't dare set debt collectors on her.'

'No debt collectors,' Daisy promised, then rushed back to Clarendon Place.

'I've got it!' she cried, bursting into the kitchen. 'Jessie Jarrold's address.'

'Really?' To Daisy's satisfaction, Thea looked deeply impressed. Anna too.

'She's in London. A place called Stepney,' Daisy reported.

'That's just across the Thames from where my family lives,' Anna said.

'I'll call on her on Monday,' Thea smiled. 'Thank you, Daisy. You're a marvel.'

'I only hope Jessie tells you what you need to hear.'

Saturday brought a letter from Max but it was for Thea, not Daisy.

'Max, the horse and the horsebox all survived the journey home,' Thea reported. 'The horse has been turned out, apparently.'

'That means he's in a paddock,' Daisy explained.

'So I gather. He's got his own field at the moment as he can't be trusted with other horses yet. He's eating well. He also has a good action which I assume means he moves nicely.'

Daisy nodded. 'It does. I'd love to see how he's settling in.'

'Your cousin suggests we all visit,' Thea told her.

'I have to make London my first priority,' Anna said.

'As do I,' Thea agreed. 'But we might spare you for a day, Daisy.'

The thought of visiting Clareswood was exciting and Daisy was crossing her fingers that Warry would turn out to be the horse Max needed to change his fortunes – a racehorse, a stallion for breeding or preferably both.

Her fortune too, because Max might be able to offer her a job at last. Not that she was desperate for that job just at the moment. Daisy had come to Brighton to escape from Daniel Oaks but she was enjoying being with her new friends and felt far less guilty about her domestic hopelessness now she was helping Thea.

Twenty-Two

Thea studied herself in the mirror, amazed at what Anna had achieved with an old dress that had suffered a rip in the skirt.

'All I had to do was darn the tear and cover it with a sash,' Anna said.

The ancient dress in midnight blue crepe had the high waist of several years ago but Anna had positioned the sash so that the top of it covered the waist while the bottom of it sat lower on Thea's hips, tying at the side to give the dress a modern look. Being made of satin, the sash added a touch of glamour too.

Thea kissed Anna's cheek. 'Thank you so much.'

'He's here,' Daisy called from the drawing-room window where she'd taken up position as a look-out. 'At least I think it's him.'

Thea put her coat on, picked up her bag and went downstairs. Daisy had moved into the hall. 'Heavens,' she said, seeing Thea. 'You look like royalty.'

'I don't know about that, but Anna's worked a miracle with this sash.'

Daisy turned to open the door just as Ralph came up the steps. How handsome he looked in his suit and tie. 'Daisy, this is Ralph Kirby-Laws,' Thea said. 'Ralph, this is Daisy Flowers.'

He murmured a greeting but his attention was all for Thea. Luckily, Daisy appeared to be amused. Eyes twinkling merrily, she retreated to the kitchen.

Ralph put an umbrella up because a chilly rain was falling, then offered Thea his arm. 'Shall we?'

They walked down to the kerb where he'd parked a car which gleamed with pristine newness. It was a Morris Oxford which looked solid and dependable, rather like Ralph himself. He opened the passenger door for Thea and saw her into the seat then lowered the umbrella and walked around the car to get in the driver's side.

'Are we going far?' Thea asked.

'I've booked a table at Fitzpatrick's.'

Fitzpatrick's had opened near the Pavilion three or four years ago and Thea had always thought it looked delightful. It had a glass-roofed veranda across the front, supported by decorative black ironwork from which hanging baskets of flowers or greenery were suspended, depending on the time of year. The door and window frames were also painted black and the name Fitzpatrick's appeared in artistically flowing gold letters across the windows.

'You're familiar with Fitzpatrick's?' Ralph asked.

'From the outside. I'm delighted to be going through the door at last.'

They could have walked to the restaurant but Ralph appeared determined to cocoon her in courtesy. He parked across the road from it then hastened round to hold the umbrella ready as he helped her out. Once inside, their coats were taken and they were shown to a table. 'This is a lovely place, Ralph,' Thea told him.

'It's Mother's favourite. The food is wonderful.'

It was. Thea chose soup, Dover sole, beef wellington, a refreshing sorbet and apple pie, eaten with wine chosen by Ralph that made her head feel pleasantly muzzy. Thea's father had enjoyed wine and had left a modest collection behind including six bottles of champagne he'd told her he was saving for a special occasion.

'What occasion?' Thea had asked once.

'Your engagement.'

Being only fourteen at the time and having no thought of marriage, Thea had laughed.

'You'll be glad when the time comes,' her father had told her with a smile, but Herbert had taken the champagne as he'd taken so much else.

Thea had got up one morning to find that he'd carried it up to the drawing-room where he'd partied with his cronies, leaving the room littered with empty bottles, glasses and cigarette stubs. Some of the wine had spilled over a sofa and onto the carpet. Two crystal glasses had lain shattered in the hearth, and a cigarette had burned the arm of a chair. Gradually, he'd worked his way through the wine too.

Still, that was history and Thea was determined that painful memories shouldn't sour this wonderful evening.

Being with Ralph was like being wrapped in velvet. Everything was ease and luxury, and she was touched by the delicacy he showed in avoiding the subject of Herbert. Instead they talked about Ralph's years in the army and his decision to move into civilian life.

'I met some wonderful chaps over the years, from my training at Sandhurst onwards,' he told her. 'Of course, some of the chaps perished in the war but others were lucky like me. I miss the camaraderie of evenings in the officers' mess but I'll keep in touch with some of the chaps and there'll be reunion dinners, of course. I miss the daily discipline of the army too but civilian life also requires discipline if a chap is to make his mark. And civilian life offers other advantages, of course.'

His warm smile left her in no doubt that he counted Thea as one of them.

'I'm enjoying catching up with old friends and making new ones too,' Ralph continued. 'There's a lively set of people here. I hope to have the chance to introduce you to some of them, starting with my parents' dinner party.'

'I'd like that.'

In turn, Thea told Ralph about rescuing Night Warrior.

'How kind of you,' he approved. 'But I hope your kindness wasn't imposed on?'

'It wasn't. I'm just glad to think that the horse is having a second chance, even if he doesn't amount to much.'

At the end of the evening he drove her back to Clarendon Place. 'Thank you, I've had a lovely time,' Thea told him.

'Might I take you out again?' he asked. 'Before the dinner party, I mean. We could go to the cinema or theatre. Being in the army meant I rarely went to either and I'm keen to make up for that now.'

Thea hadn't been to the cinema or theatre in years either because she hadn't been able to afford it. 'May I telephone to let you know?'

'Of course.' Ralph helped her from the car then walked her up the steps to the house. 'I'll look forward to your call,' he said.

He looked into her eyes for a moment then leaned forward to kiss her cheek.

Smiling, Thea went inside.

Daisy and Anna were waiting in the kitchen. 'Well?' Daisy prompted.

'We went to Fitzpatrick's and it was wonderful.'

'Was the major wonderful?' Daisy asked.

'You can't ask that!' Anna protested, but Thea only laughed.

'He was good company, Daisy, but don't let your imagination run away with you. I've only just met the man to all intents and purposes.'

It had been nice to step out of her predicament for a few hours but as Thea got ready for bed her thoughts returned to the serious business of Monday's visit to London. It could help her and Anna too, but it could also cause them frustration and distress. Only time would tell.

Daisy waved them off on Monday morning with an encouraging, 'Good luck!' but Thea's smile was stiff and she suspected Anna's required effort too. There was so much at stake.

Thea had suggested taking the tram to the station out of concern for Anna, but Anna preferred to walk and save the fares. 'It isn't a long walk.'

But it was mostly uphill and Thea spent most of the walk worrying that Anna would find it too much. 'It's sweet of you to be concerned but I'm fine,' Anna insisted.

Hoping they wouldn't be wasting hard-earned money, Thea bought tickets out of the guest house profits and they settled on the train, neither of them talking much because they both had a lot on their minds. But they separated with a hug when they reached London Bridge station.

Anna went to visit her family in nearby Bermondsey while Thea took the underground railway to Highgate where Albert Strupp's former landlord lived – or so Strupp had told his Brighton landlord. Strupp hadn't lied, however. Thea found Mr Ward at home but there her luck ended.

'I haven't seen hide nor hair of Strupp since he left and I don't expect to,' he told her. 'And before you ask, I don't know anything about him except that he left owing me money.'

He gave her directions to the rooms Strupp had rented in Tea Street, not far from Old Street station. Thea managed to question three of his former neighbours who still lived in the same building. One had only recently moved in and had never met Strupp. Another vaguely remembered a bad-mannered man who'd never replied to 'Good mornings' or 'Good afternoons.' The third had decided to keep a distance after seeing Strupp stagger home drunk.

She could have knocked on the doors of nearby houses but from what she'd learned here and in Brighton, Strupp was a man who kept to his own cronies if he had any. Besides, it was time to see Jessie Jarrold.

Anxiety clawed at her insides as she travelled on to Stepney. If Jessie proved to be another dead end, Thea didn't know what more she could do to prove the Will wasn't genuine.

Stepney was a down-at-heel part of London though that was no surprise. By dint of asking for directions, Thea located

Roper Street where Jessie was apparently living. It was a street of tiny terraced houses with soot-blackened walls and doors that were mostly a depressing shade of brown. Curtains were a luxury here. Some windows had old sheets or sacks tacked inside them instead. A few had broken panes with yellowing newspaper crushed into the holes to keep out draughts.

Thea could imagine some of Brighton's ladies turning their noses up at streets like this. But Anna had described living in a similar street so Thea knew that warm, generous hearts lived here along with enquiring minds, courage and the dignity of honest work.

Number twenty was one of the better properties, having curtains in the windows and even an aspidistra plant in a brass pot. Fearful that identifying herself as Miss Fairfax might alarm Jessie's father should he be at home, Thea had decided to call herself Miss Lawson and try to entice Jessie outside. She raised her hand to knock but hesitated when she heard an angry voice inside.

'I won't 'ave it, Jess.' The voice was female. Not young. 'Your pa coming 'ome drunk like that… I won't 'ave it.'

Another voice answered but too softly for Thea to make out the words.

Then the first voice spoke again. 'Jess, I pity you. Truly I do. But I want 'im gone.'

Thea stepped back as the door suddenly opened and Jessie burst out, almost colliding with her. 'Sorry,' Jessie muttered, but then recognition dawned.

Jessie's eyes widened then darted to each side as though she were trying to decide which way to run.

'I'm not here to collect a debt,' Thea assured her. 'I just want to talk.'

'I've nothing to say.'

'Please,' Thea said. 'Spare me five minutes of your time.'

'I can't.' Jessie hastened up the road.

'I got your address from Rose,' Thea called.

Jessie's shoulders stiffened but only momentarily before she continued on her way.

'Rose wants to help,' Thea said, following, but Jessie shook her head to suggest no one could help.

Desperation made Thea take a firmer line. She didn't want to make threats but she couldn't keep returning to London in the hope of persuading Jessie to talk. It had to be today. 'I could tell your landlord in Brighton where to find you,' Thea threatened. 'That'll mean debt collectors pursuing you.'

Jessie stopped then, shaking her head in despair.

'I really don't want to get you into trouble,' Thea said. 'But I do need to talk to you. Is there anywhere we might get a cup of tea?'

Jessie led her to a cheap café that catered for working people with little money to spend. 'Would you like anything to eat?' Thea asked.

Jessie shook her head but Thea bought her a currant bun anyway because she was white-faced and thin with strain.

They sat at a table and Thea introduced herself. Jessie heard her out in puzzlement as though trying to work out what Thea could want with her if it didn't involve debt.

'My mother died recently,' Thea said, and caught a flash of sympathy in Jessie's expression.

'You've lost your mother too?' Thea asked.

'When I was twelve. She was a lady. Not a fine lady like you but a cut above most people. Her dad was a clerk in a shipping company.'

Jessie spoke with pride, clearly wanting Thea to understand that there was more to Jessie Jarrold than this mean, penny-pinching life.

'I was fortunate in both of my parents,' Thea said. 'But after my father died my mother married for a second time and the gentleman – I use the term loosely – proved to be unworthy of her.'

Just as Jeremiah Jarrold had proved to be unworthy of his wife. Jessie looked surprised to discover she shared at least a little common ground with Thea. She picked up her bun and began to eat.

Thea pressed on. 'My mother died last year and my stepfather died more recently. His son – my stepbrother, I suppose you'd call him – produced a Will allegedly signed by my mother. It left everything to my stepfather. In turn—'

'He left everything to your stepbrother,' Jessie guessed.

'Including my parents' house.'

Jessie grimaced and sipped her tea. 'You don't believe your mother really made that Will?'

'She was concerned about me. She wanted to protect me. Would your mother have disinherited you?'

'No.'

Thea explained her theory of trickery or forgery. 'The thing is, your father signed the Will as a witness.'

Jessie's eyes widened in horror as she worked out what Thea was asking of her. 'You want me to have my father put in prison for fraud?'

'I want you to tell the truth.'

'I don't know the truth. I never knew your mother.'

'You did know my stepfather. Herbert Ambrose.' It was a guess but Thea could see that the name meant something to Jessie. 'My stepbrother is Stanley Ambrose.'

Jessie jumped to her feet. 'I have to go.'

'Will you at least think about—'

'No! You don't know what you're asking. If my father…' Jessie shuddered. 'Please leave me alone.'

She headed for the door and Thea raced after her. 'I know your father is a bully but this is your chance to get away from him. If you can't find the courage to seize it, you'll spend your whole life in fear of him. Never having enough money. Never managing to settle. Never keeping friends like Rose because you're always running from debt.'

Jessie kept moving, through the door and onto the pavement outside.

'What would your mother want you to do?' Thea called. 'Would she be proud of you for protecting your father or would she feel ashamed?'

Jessie paused to glare at Thea. 'I'm not protecting my father. I'm protecting myself and *that's* what my mother would want me to do.'

With that Jessie hastened away, leaving Thea watching after her. Had Thea gone too far and alienated Jessie? Or had she planted a seed in Jessie's mind that might gradually take root and grow? There was no way of knowing.

Thea had meant to give Jessie her address but there'd been no chance for that. Stepping back inside the café, Thea sat down to write a short note on some paper she'd brought. She wrote Jessie's name on the envelope and carried it to Roper Street. It felt likely that Jessie wouldn't return for a while but Thea didn't want to drop the note through the letterbox in case Jeremiah found it.

She knocked on the door instead, hoping the landlady would answer. She did, though Thea heard a male voice shouting from within. 'Where's my tea? I asked for tea!'

Jeremiah, Thea supposed.

She spoke quickly, keeping her voice low so there was no danger of him overhearing. 'If he asks, tell him I'm Betty from around the corner who's called to let you know that her mother is unwell.'

As if on cue, the voice called, 'Don't gossip at the door, woman.'

'It's Betty from around the corner,' the landlady called back. 'Her ma's sick.'

'What's that got to do with you? I'm waiting for my tea, you idle…' The words got lost in muttered curses.

'This is for Jessie,' Thea whispered. 'She'll know who it's from.'

The landlady nodded and tucked the envelope into her apron. 'I'll see she gets it.'

'Thank you.' Thea gave the landlady a smile, then set off to meet Anna and her family.

The journey took her back over the Thames on the East side of London where ships unloaded goods from all over the world into warehouses that hunkered at the water's edge. Sugar, tea, exotic fruits, spices, frozen meat… Anna's father was a stevedore at Butler's Wharf. Was he amongst the men she could see at work? Some stood on board the ships hooking boxes, barrels and sacks onto cranes that swung from deck to wharf side. Others stood ready to unhook them and wheel them into warehouses on barrows. It looked like back-breaking work to Thea.

Anna had asked Thea to join her and her family in the churchyard of St Mary Magdalen's church where they were unlikely to be seen by anyone who might report the reunion to Jed Watson. Thea paused when she saw them and smiled at the picture they presented.

The day was grey and chilly but Thea doubted any of them were bothered by the cold. Anna was sitting on a bench and the smallest girl – Lizzie, no doubt – was sitting on her lap. Beside Anna was a faded woman who had to be her mother and a girl who had to be Mary. The two boys, Joe and Tom, stood just behind, each with a hand on Anna's shoulders as though they didn't want to let her go.

It was heartening to see Anna in the midst of so much love but Thea's smile faded as she realised they all looked too happy to have heard about Piers's death. It was understandable that Anna didn't want to worry them, but they had to know about it eventually and surely it was better for them to hear it from Anna's own lips rather than in a letter? They'd want to comfort her and hold her close, and that wouldn't be possible if they heard the news when Anna was back in Brighton.

Anna had admitted to nursing a tiny flame of hope that Piers had somehow survived but now Thea began to suspect that the hope was in fact burning strongly. Which meant that the worst of Anna's grief was yet to come. Oh, heavens.

Twenty-Three

Anna had mixed feelings when Thea arrived in the churchyard. On the one hand Anna was pleased that her family would see that she was living with a truly wonderful person and Thea's charm did indeed work like magic on breaking through her family's awe.

Thea won Anna's mother over by telling her that Anna was a daughter of whom any woman would be proud. She had something to say to each of the children too, complimenting Mary on her letter writing, talking of trains to Joe and of animals to Tom, and telling little Lizzie that she was growing into a fine girl.

On the other hand Anna was anxious in case Thea mentioned Piers or the fact that the guest house was only a temporary venture. But she was underestimating Thea's tact because she said nothing about either subject. Instead she produced sweets for all the children, sticks of pink rock which had the words, '*A present from Brighton*' running through the middle.

'Perhaps you'll be able to see Brighton for yourselves one day,' she said.

'It was kind of you to give the children sweets,' Anna told her, after they'd parted with hugs and kisses on all sides.

'You have a lovely family.'

'I have,' Anna agreed. 'Thank you for keeping quiet about Piers. I know you think I'm foolish to put off telling them. I *will* tell them when the time is right.'

'When will that be, Anna?'

'After I've seen Mr Acaster.'

Thea didn't ask what she'd do if Mr Acaster wouldn't see her and for that Anna was thankful.

The *London Daily Herald* was on bustling Fleet Street. They walked through tall doors and approached a girl who sat at a reception desk. 'I wonder if I might have a few minutes of Mr Acaster's time?' Anna asked.

'Do you have an appointment?' The girl knew she hadn't.

'No, but I only need—'

'Mr Acaster sees no one without an appointment. And he doesn't allow appointments to be made without knowing what they're about. Perhaps you could write in?'

'What if he doesn't reply?'

The girl smirked. 'If he doesn't reply it's because he isn't interested. This is a national newspaper. Every day dozens of people want to see Mr Acaster. He sees only a few of them.'

The important ones.

'Anna!' Thea grabbed Anna's arm and steered her around.

A man was entering through the doors. He was big and bluff, striding rapidly as an underling fawned over him. 'Is that –?' Anna began.

'I think it might be.' Thea moved towards him. 'Mr Acaster!'

He stopped to look at her but Thea nudged Anna forward instead.

'Might I have five minutes of your time, Mr Acaster?' Anna asked.

'Not now. I'm busy.' His accent was northern. 'You'll need to make an appointment.'

He nodded towards the reception desk and Anna saw the girl smirk again because she knew she'd be making no appointment.

'Good day,' he said, and continued towards a wide staircase.

Anna hastened after him.

'An appointment,' he called.

Anna was overtaken by Thea who moved past him then turned to block his way.

'This is not the way to win my co-operation,' he complained, sourly.

'I simply want information about Piers Rutherford,' Anna explained, catching her up.

'What's your interest?' Mr Acaster asked.

Anna looked at him steadily, a hand outlining her swollen middle.

'Miss Watson isn't seeking money from Mr Rutherford's family, your newspaper or anyone else,' Thea said.

'I just want to know what happened to him,' Anna confirmed.

'Why don't you ask his family?'

'The Rutherfords won't speak to me.'

'Then I don't think I should—'

'Did Piers never mention that he was engaged to be married?'

'Mr Rutherford and I had a business arrangement,' Mr Acaster told her. 'My newspaper paid for his services in writing about his travels. That was all.'

He stared at Anna as though expecting her to shrink away but then he sighed and said, 'I did get to know him a little. I liked the lad. And he did mention having a special girl to come home to.'

Tears filled Anna's eyes and Mr Acaster patted her arm.

'Come up, lass. Your friend too. I can give you five minutes.'

He led the way into an outer office where two secretaries jumped to attention. 'Good afternoon, Mr Acaster,' they chorused respectfully, and Anna saw them sliding her curious looks.

'Tea for three, please. Quick as you can,' he said, moving into an inner office.

It was richly carpeted and had walls that were lined with books and photographs. A huge mahogany desk stood in front of an equally huge window. Two Chesterfield sofas stood either side of a fireplace in which a fire burned brightly.

'Sit yourselves down, lasses,' he invited, gesturing to a sofa.

He warmed his hands at the fire then sat on the other sofa. 'Now then. You wrote to me, didn't you?'

'Yes.'

'When a disaster occurs – an accident, an earthquake or, in this case a shipwreck – all sorts of folk sniff around hoping for money or some other advantage. Frauds and chancers, mostly. I'll admit I thought you were one of them.'

'I'm not,' Anna said.

'I can see that. It's a pity young Piers didn't put things into proper order before he went off.'

'I don't blame him for that,' Anna protested, assuming he was talking about marriage and life insurance that would have provided for her and her child. 'We fell in love quickly and we never dreamt that… I don't blame Piers for anything,' she said.

'Can you tell us what happened to Piers?' Thea asked.

'I can tell you what I know. There was a storm in the Atlantic, two days after the ship had set sail. The ship made a mayday call saying it was in danger of floundering. A lifeboat was launched only to be swamped with everyone in it going into the water. The next call said the ship was breaking up. Nothing more was heard but wreckage was found and in due course… I don't want to distress you, lass, but there were bodies.'

Anna's stomach squeezed painfully. 'Piers?'

'No, but his coat was found, caught on some wreckage. His wallet was fastened into an inner pocket so there was no doubt about whose coat it was.'

'But Piers himself…' Anna couldn't go on.

'Most bodies will never be found. I'm sorry, lass, but you did say you wanted to know.'

He pulled a handkerchief from his pocket, passed it to her then got up and went to the door. 'Where's that tea?' he barked.

Anna felt Thea's arm move around her shoulders to pull her close so she could sob her heart out. The thought of what Piers must have gone through was unbearable.

The tea arrived within moments, carried in on a large silver tray by one of the secretaries. 'Mr Bates and Mr Simons are here to see you, Sir,' she reported.

'They'll have to wait.'

He busied himself pouring tea into cups. 'Help yourselves to milk and sugar.'

Thea moved her arm from around Anna's shoulder and prepared cups for both of them. 'It'll do you good,' she said, when Anna waved her cup away, not trusting herself to hold it steady.

Anna took a deep breath and eventually accepted the cup. It shook in its saucer but she managed not to spill the tea.

'You'll let Miss Watson know if any more information comes to light?' Thea asked, and Anna was glad to let her take over.

It had been foolish to entertain hope but… Oh! The pain of losing that hope was lacerating.

'I will,' Mr Acaster told Thea. But you'll need to give me an address. I didn't keep the letter.'

'I'll give you a card. It shows my mother's name but the address is correct.'

Thea passed the card over and Mr Acaster passed one of his to Anna. 'Just in case you need to get in touch again.'

'Thank you,' Anna said. 'And thank you for seeing us.'

'I'm sorry the circumstances are so tragic, lass.'

Anna nodded and moved, exhausted, to the door.

'Piers will live on through your baby,' Thea reminded her, as they made their way downstairs.

Anna felt the baby kick. Thea was right. Anna would be the best mother possible and ensure their child knew all about his or her wonderful father.

Twenty-Four

Daisy was desperate to see how Warry was getting on but she was worried about leaving Anna. The news about Piers had hit her hard and though she was insisting on working as much as ever, Daisy was scared that it might become too much.

Three days had passed since the London visit but Jessie hadn't been in touch with Thea. 'I'm going to see Rose again and find out if *she's* heard from her,' Daisy announced.

She waited outside Wainwrights again and, seeing her, Rose rolled her eyes. 'There's no getting rid of you, is there?'

Daisy told her that Thea had met with Jessie but heard nothing since.

'Jessie hasn't written to me either,' Rose said.

Daisy gave her a searching look but decided Rose was telling the truth. 'Will you write to her and urge her to help?'

'I've already betrayed her confidence by telling you where she is.'

'If you've upset her, shouldn't you put things right while you still have a chance? My friend heard Jessie's landlady threatening to throw Jeremiah out and that means Jessie will have to leave too.'

'So I lose touch with *my* friend because I've tried to help *yours*?'

'The landlady made the threats before my friend even knocked on the door,' Daisy pointed out. 'But if Jessie is annoyed with you, why don't you write and explain that you're trying to help?'

'I've had enough of this. Stop following me and leave me alone.' Rose walked off at speed.

Daisy had seen enough of Rose to know she was as prickly as a thorn but perhaps she'd cool down and see the sense of Daisy's suggestion eventually. How long would it take, though? The days were whizzing past.

Thea was going to the cinema with Ralph that evening. 'This will be my second night off,' she pointed out, when Daisy returned to Clarendon Place. 'You really should have a day off tomorrow, Daisy.'

'You should,' Anna insisted. 'You're supposed to be seeing the horse.'

Daisy didn't point out that it was consideration for Anna that had made her delay the visit. 'It wasn't convenient for me to go before,' she said, hoping Anna would think it was Max's convenience she'd been awaiting.

The following morning Daisy took the train to Worthing where Max met her on the motorbike. Daisy never minded riding on the back of it, not being ladylike.

Clareswood was a large rambling house with numerous gables. Driving around it, Max came to a halt in the stable yard and took Daisy straight to the small paddock into which Warry had been turned out.

'He looks well, doesn't he?' There was satisfaction in Max's voice.

'He looks wonderful.'

Warry was clean, for one thing. 'He lets you groom him?' Daisy asked.

'It's taken a while to get him to trust me but I've been working up to it slowly and managed the first decent groom yesterday.'

The horse's coat was shiny now, though Daisy guessed that was from the fresh air and better food as much as the grooming. The dried blood had been cleaned away and the scabs were healing. Warry looked up when Daisy approached the fence but didn't come over. He walked to his water trough instead and Daisy saw how fluidly he moved.

'I'm beginning to get excited about this horse,' Max said. 'It's early days, of course. He hasn't even had a saddle on his back and Lord knows if I'll be able to train him to sustain a gallop and behave himself in a race, but even so…'

Warry was a handsome devil who'd surely sire fine-looking foals whether he could race or not. But his value as a stud horse would rise dramatically if he did well in racing and besides, training a racer was part of Max's dream.

Daisy turned at the sound of a vehicle being driven into the yard. It was a dashing red sports car. She glanced at Max to see if he was expecting a visitor.

He wasn't, but he did recognise the driver. 'Rory Connor,' Max said, setting off towards him.

Goodness. Rory Connor was a rising star in horse racing. Max and Rory had spent their early years in the same part of Ireland but Daisy understood that Rory was some sort of landed gentry so was surprised when he greeted Max with a handshake followed by the sort of shoulder slap that a man might give to a brother.

Daisy had hung back but Max beckoned her over. 'My little cousin, Daisy,' he told Rory.

Little? It wasn't the way Daisy would have wished him to describe her. Trying to recover some dignity, she held out her hand. 'I'm pleased to meet you.'

'And I'm delighted to meet you, Daisy.' He took her hand but instead of shaking it he raised it to his mouth for a kiss.

Daisy blushed. How attractive he was. He wasn't as tall as Max and he was whipcord thin but his blue eyes danced with laughter and his smile was... Well, it was warm and teasing.

He held Daisy's gaze for what felt like a long time then turned back to Max. 'I was in the area and thought I'd look in on an old friend.'

'You've timed it well as there's a new horse to see,' Max told him.

He led the way back to Warry's paddock and Rory glanced around to check that Daisy was following. His smile made more colour rise to her cheeks.

Both men leaned their forearms on the paddock fence. Rory made a clicking sound to call the horse over but Warry gave him a contemptuous look and set off in the opposite direction. 'Moves well, so he does,' Rory said. 'Is he the Leighs' horse?'

'He's half mine. A friend of Daisy's owns the other half.'

'Thea rescued Warry,' Daisy explained.

'What a charitable lady she must be.'

'She is.'

'Good afternoon!'

They all turned to see Mr and Mrs Leigh approaching. 'I hope we're not interrupting?' Mr Leigh said.

'Not at all,' Max assured them.

The Leighs smiled at Daisy, recognising her from previous visits. They were nice people, wealthy but also friendly and comfortable. Mr Leigh's trousers and jacket were soft with wear. Mrs Leigh's faded dress drooped.

Max introduced them to Rory. 'We've read about you in the newspapers, of course,' Mr Leigh said. 'Are you hoping to be Champion Jockey soon?'

'I'd like to knock Steve Donoghue off his perch for sure.' Rory laughed. 'Nine times, he's been Champion Jockey. I'd like to stop him from making it ten times.'

'Perhaps we'll have a flutter on you next time you race,' Mrs Leigh said with a smile. 'We don't bet as a rule, but it's different when one knows the jockey.'

They chatted for a few minutes longer then Mr Leigh said, 'Well, we won't keep you. We only came out so Bernard here could stretch his legs.'

Bernard was the Leigh's Chow Chow, a big lion of a dog.

'I could show you what I meant about Ferdy's fetlock,' Max offered.

'You have guests.'

'It'll only take a moment.' Max raised an eyebrow at Rory to check he wouldn't mind.

'Daisy can keep me entertained,' Rory told him, and he gave Daisy a wink that made her blush deepen.

Max walked away with the Leighs. 'So, Daisy,' Rory said. 'You're just visiting too, are you?'

'I wish I could work here with Max but that isn't possible at the moment. I've come up from Brighton for the day.'

'Brighton's a grand place, so it is. I've often ridden at Brighton races. Have you been to Brighton races?'

'Not yet.'

'It's a treat in store for you. Maybe you could come and see me race there.'

'I'd like that,' Daisy said shyly.

'I'm feeling an urge to see Brighton today. I could take you home in the Aston Martin.'

How exciting it would be to ride in such a glamorous vehicle. In such charming company too. But it wasn't to be. 'That would have been lovely but Max is taking me to see my father later.'

''Tis a pity, so it is, but perhaps I'll look you up in Brighton another day.'

'I'm in Clarendon Place. Number eighteen,' Daisy told him.

Rory tapped his head to show he was committing the address to memory.

'You've known Max for a long time, I believe,' Daisy said.

'We ran around Kerry as boys. Wild, we were.' He grinned. 'I was the bane of my tutor's life. Always sneaking out of windows and disappearing for hours before coming back wet or filthy or both. Not even being sent away to school tamed me. I still ran wild in the holidays and twice I ran away from school. Eventually, the school decided it would be a finer institution without my disruptive influence so I went back to having tutors. Not that they did me any good, poor souls. I wasn't a man for book-learning. I preferred horses.'

'You've made a successful career out of riding,' Daisy pointed out.

'So I have. And if I'm lucky I'll earn enough to restore Castle Kerwig, the family home. Not that it's actually a castle. Some distant ancestor must have had delusions of grandeur when he named it. But it's a beautiful house, so it is. Long and low and white. Sadly, it's falling to pieces.'

'Does your family still live there?'

'My father passed away five years ago, God rest his soul. But my mother's still there, wrapped in furs and huddled in front of fires against the cold and the damp. The roof's rotten, you see.'

'Hopefully, you'll be able to replace it soon.'

'That's the dream.'

Daisy realised Max was walking back towards them. 'Cup of tea?' he offered.

'I'll be for pressing on,' Rory told him. 'Only called in to say top of the morning to you.'

They walked him back to the gleaming car. 'I'll call in again soon and see how that black beauty of yours is getting on,' Rory told Max.

He turned to Daisy, winked and drove off in a cloud of dust.

'Rory sounds more Irish than you do,' Daisy said.

'I've been in England longer,' Max reasoned, then he paused before adding, 'And he's full of blarney.'

Was that a warning that she shouldn't take Rory Connor seriously? Rory probably made himself agreeable to every girl he met. Doubtless out of sight would be out of mind and Daisy would never see him again. The thought disappointed her. Just remembering those dancing eyes and smile made her heart beat faster. It was a new but exciting feeling.

She became aware that Max was walking away and hastened after him. But Rory Connor kept coming into her thoughts all through the day. It was surprising – strange even – to discover she was susceptible to manly charms after all, but it brought home to her how right she'd been to flee from Daniel Oaks.

She was relieved to arrive at the forge having seen no sign of Daniel. Frank must have heard the motorbike approaching because he came out to greet them.

'Well, girl, I see you've brought no luggage so I take it you haven't been sacked from your job. Yet.'

Daisy gave his arm a playful punch then reached up on tiptoes to kiss his weathered cheek. 'How are you, Dad?'

'I'm doing fine. So are you by the look of you. Come inside. I've got the kettle on.'

The kitchen looked just as it always did: homely and shabby but no worse than when Daisy had last been here. 'How's the new horse my girl foisted onto you?' Frank asked Max.

Daisy had mentioned Warry in a letter.

'I'm pleased with him,' Max answered. 'The tonic Daniel mixed has worked wonders. I'm going to walk up there and get some more before I leave.'

Daisy stayed at home while Max was out. 'Are there any chores that need doing?' she asked.

'No, girl. Everything's fine.'

Daisy sat and drank more tea instead, stroking Catherine, the cat, and petting Shep, the dog. Her thoughts strayed back to Rory. She didn't expect him to remember her – that would be foolish – but wouldn't it be wonderful if by some miracle he did?

Twenty-Five

Thea sat at the kitchen table and counted money into piles: one for Anna, one for Daisy and one for herself. They hadn't yet had a night when all the guest bedrooms were occupied, but they usually had at least a couple of guests which meant a little money was coming in. Split three ways it didn't amount to much but Thea was glad she'd taken Daisy in to help as she and Anna couldn't have coped without her. Not with the guest house and not with finding Jessie Jarrold.

Thea's gaze moved to the letters that lay on the table. The top one was the note that had finally come from Jessie that morning:

Dear Miss Fairfax,
*   Please don't visit me again unless I invite you. I need time to think.*
*   Sincerely,*
*   Jessie Jarrold.*

Did she really want time to think or was she buying herself time in which to move on, leaving no trail for Thea to follow? Thea was reluctant to let Jessie slip through her fingers for a second time. On the other hand, putting Jessie under pressure might only harden her heart against helping.

Meanwhile time was passing rapidly and March was coming to an end. It was pleasant to have longer daylight hours, less bite in the weather and the beginnings of spring greenery. But in two months' time Thea, Anna and her baby would be out on the streets while Daisy would be forced to return to Pixfield.

Anna was being extraordinarily brave and dignified. 'Piers was full of life,' she'd explained. 'He positively sizzled with it and the last thing he'd want is for me to mope. If he could talk to me now he'd urge me to seize life as he did, as though every second is precious. That's how I'm going to bring up his child.'

'You'll be a wonderful mother,' Thea had assured her, wishing she could also assure Anna that she and her child had a home here for as long as they needed it.

Unfortunately, the future was as uncertain as ever.

Thea gave Anna her share of the money then went to give Daisy her share. Daisy was standing by the kitchen window, staring into the darkness outside though there was nothing to see. 'Dreaming of horses?' Thea asked, and, turning, Daisy flushed.

'Sorry, I was miles away.'

She'd been miles away ever since her return from Max's. 'You wouldn't recognise Warry,' she'd reported. 'He's filling out and looking beautiful. Max has been letting him rest and get used to living in decent conditions but he's going to start training him now.'

'Training him how?' Anna had asked.

'Teaching him to gallop for one thing.'

'Can't all horses gallop?'

'Racehorses have to be trained to settle into races, to keep going over a distance and to run upsides of other horses too. Max won't rush Warry, though. He'll let him take his time.'

Was it the thought that Max might soon be able to offer her a job that had brought about this uncharacteristic change in Daisy? It wasn't Thea's way to pry though she was delighted to hear of Night Warrior's progress.

'Max says you're welcome to go and see how Warry is settling in. Anna too,' Daisy had said.

Max had since written to confirm the invitation. His letter sat on the table alongside Jessie's note.

Dear Thea,

I hope Daisy reported favourably on the progress of Night Warrior. I've been making some telephone calls and the story Brown told us seems to be true. McGinty did indeed buy Night Warrior from a farmer who had some sort of breakdown. Apparently, Night Warrior's dam was pretty useful in a hunt and his sire had shown promise in a couple of races before an accident left him lame. The farmer had high hopes for Night Warrior but then his wife died and his life fell apart. The horses were kept in shocking conditions for months. McGinty bought all three of them for a song and sold them on. Cruel man, I suspect, but Night Warrior is doing well now.

If you'd like to see how the beast has transformed into a beauty, I'll be happy to collect you from Worthing

station though you'll have to ride on the back of a
motorbike and perhaps you're too grand for that?
    Yours,
    Maxwell Moore

His final sentence had sounded more of a challenge than
a question though maybe Thea was reading more into it
than was actually there.

'I should get ready,' she said now, because Ralph was
collecting her soon to take her to his parents' dinner
party.

She went upstairs to bathe, having already washed her
hair. Anna had performed another miracle with the dress
Thea was to wear. 'You can't wear that again,' she'd said,
when she'd realised Thea was intending to wear the green
dress she'd worn for the afternoon tea.

She'd already worn it for a second time when Ralph had
taken her to the cinema. Since then she'd been out to a late
supper with him and worn a blouse and skirt but the dinner
party was too formal an occasion for daywear.

'Then I'll have to wear the blue dress I wore to Frederick's.
If the Kirby-Laws think less of me because I wear the same
dress twice, I'll think less of them,' Thea had said, though
it bothered her that they might blame her mother for her
straitened circumstances.

Unfortunately, Thea had no more dresses for Anna to
adapt. 'Let me see what I can find amongst your mother's
things,' Anna had suggested.

'I'm considerably taller than she was,' Thea had pointed
out. 'She was a pretty, delicate creature.'

'There's nothing to lose by looking.'

To Thea's delight Anna had made a new dress by cutting up two of Cecily's dresses. She'd used an amber bodice as a starting point, inserting green panels down the front and back to accommodate Thea's broader shoulders. A matching sideways-running panel had lengthened the bodice, then Anna had made a skirt out of alternating squares of amber and green chiffon hung diagonally in fashionable handkerchief style. She'd also created a headband of amber and green chiffon to sit low on Thea's forehead.

'I'd never in a million years have been able to create this delicious confection,' Thea admitted.

'You haven't worked in women's wear in Selfridges,' Anna answered.

'You're immensely talented, Anna.'

'I suppose it helps that I've never had much money. It's amazing how inventive you become when your purse is empty.'

Ralph admired Thea's appearance openly when he arrived to collect her. 'You look beautiful.'

'And you look very smart.'

Ralph was wearing a dark evening suit, crisp white shirt, bow tie and white silk scarf. Smart indeed. He settled her in the car, tucking a rug over her lap.

'Tell me who I'll be meeting tonight,' Thea invited, as they set off for Worthing.

'The Carlyles are coming. Elizabeth and Charlie. Mother thinks you may have met Elizabeth before.'

Thea's memory supplied a picture of a humourless woman though perhaps she was confusing Elizabeth with someone else.

'Then there'll be Bill and Flora Trent. They're old friends of my parents but there'll be younger people too. Bunny and

Charlotte Catchpole are old friends of mine – Bunny and I were at school together – while Bertie and Anne Briars are new to the area. We should be a lively crowd.' Ralph looked eager to please her and Thea responded with a smile.

She felt a pull of nostalgia when the car turned into his parents' drive. Beeches Lodge was far from being a mansion but it was substantial in size and surrounded by lawns and shrubberies. She'd spent many happy hours as a child exploring this garden before joining her mother and Mrs Kirby-Laws for luncheon or tea.

A maid opened the door but Mr Kirby-Laws stepped out of the drawing room to greet them in the hall. Thea hadn't seen Ralph's father in years but he welcomed her with warmth and a kiss on her cheek. 'You'll forgive familiarity from an old man, won't you, my dear? Come and meet everyone.'

He guided Thea into the room as though she were a much-loved prodigal daughter. Mrs Kirby-Laws came to give her another kiss then Thea was introduced to the other guests.

Elizabeth Carlyle was indeed the po-faced woman of Thea's memory but the others were pleasant enough even if Charlotte giggled all the time and Lavinia wouldn't open her mouth without looking at her husband first.

Judging from the sympathy that was shown to her Thea guessed that the Kirby-Laws had warned their guests that she'd been bereaved not so long ago. Doubtless it had been done out of consideration for her feelings though a sickly mother also explained Thea's absence from Brighton society in recent years. There appeared to be a conspiracy in place to spare her from distress so the questions that were asked of her were about where she lived in Brighton and what she thought of the town, the shops, and the entertainment it offered.

'Not that you'll have had a chance to enjoy the entertainment in recent years with your mother being so unwell,' Flora Trent commented, patting Thea's hand.

No one acknowledged that Herbert had even existed.

Over dinner the conversation turned to Ralph and his recent change of occupation. 'Civilian life is going to suit me perfectly,' he said, and his smile came to rest on Thea with unconcealed warmth.

It was one thing to give her admiring looks in private. It was quite another to advertise his admiration in public. Thea glanced towards his parents, wondering if they might think he should be far more circumspect about his interest in a young woman he was only just beginning to know in any meaningful way. But they were exchanging indulgent looks as though it wouldn't trouble them at all if Ralph's interest grew serious.

It was much too soon to know how things would turn out, but after so many years of isolation it was lovely to feel that her company was appreciated. Everything about the evening was enjoyable – the guests, the food, the crisp white cloths and crystal glasses…

Of course, it didn't mean she was becoming too grand to ride on the back of a motorcycle.

Twenty-Six

Anna tied string around her parcel to secure the brown paper wrapping then wrote her mother's name and their neighbour's address on the outside. It had been good of Thea to allow Anna to send the scraps of fabric that remained from her dressmaking to Mary and Lizzie so they could practise their sewing and make a doll's dress or two.

'Heavens, they're no use for anything else,' Thea had said, then with typical generosity, she'd gone looking for other things Anna might include with the parcel, finally producing *Blackie's Children's Annuals* from 1910 and 1911, some sheets of drawing paper and a packet of old crayons. 'There's plenty of life left in them if you think the children might want them,' she'd said.

'They'll love them,' Anna had assured her, thinking that the gifts would be all the more precious coming from Thea. The children had told Anna that Thea was their idea of a princess.

The sound of letters being pushed through the letterbox upstairs reached Anna through the door which she'd left open specifically so she could listen out for the post. There were two letters today. One was addressed to Daisy in what Anna had come to recognise as Mr Flowers's rather laboured handwriting. The second was addressed to Miss A. Watson in spiky handwriting that looked as if it had been written by a man with no time to spare for niceties. Mr Acaster?

Tearing the envelope open, Anna pulled out a letter and unfolded it. As she did so, papers which had been tucked inside it fell to the table but Anna ignored them for the moment to focus on the letter itself. It had been written on the embossed notepaper of the *London Daily Herald*.

Dear Miss Watson,

I was sorry to have had only bad news to deliver when you called at my office. No further information has come to my attention and I think you must be braced for the possibility – the probability rather – that it never will.

Mr Rutherford's life was insured by the Herald *but as I imagine you either know or expect, the beneficiaries of the insurance policy are his parents and I am powerless to change that. However, I hope the enclosed will be of assistance at this difficult time. Please don't think of it as charity but as a small gesture of appreciation for my having had the privilege of knowing Mr Rutherford.*

Sincerely,
George Acaster

She picked up the papers that had fallen onto the table and saw that they were five pound notes. Four of them, making twenty pounds in total. Twenty pounds! Anna hadn't expected him to send her money, but how kind he was to help her.

She'd put off visiting the nursing home until she had a little more money put by because it had occurred to her that she might be expected to make a booking there and then, and she wasn't sure she could pay the fees. But surely she could afford them now.

Anna still had no idea what she'd do once the baby was born. Thea was no closer to saving the house and, even if she did save it, she might soon want to sell it – or move the major into it.

'That major looks smitten,' Daisy had reported, after he'd collected Thea to take her to Frederick's.

Since then Anna had observed it for herself. Last night she'd opened the door to him when he came to collect Thea and take her to the cinema then on for supper. She'd introduced herself as Anna and when his eyes had widened at the sight of her now unmissable pregnancy she'd guessed Thea hadn't mentioned it. He'd looked faintly alarmed and Anna was sure he'd have questioned Thea about the presence of a pregnant young woman in her household.

Tactful as always, Thea had said nothing about it to Anna. Probably Thea had used her customary charm to reassure him that all was well. There was no doubt that he was susceptible to that charm. When Thea had appeared the major's eyes had glowed with admiration and he'd presented her with flowers as though offering homage to a goddess.

Anna supposed it would be a rare person who wasn't susceptible to Thea's charm. 'I feel I'm in the company of a real lady,' one of the paying guests had told Anna.

Clement Camshaw was a sweet little man with a ring of white hair like a monk's. He'd come to Brighton for a short holiday after retiring from his watchmaking business.

'You're such a comfort too, my dear,' he'd added, patting Anna's hand like an affectionate uncle.

Anna took pleasure in thinking that her quiet efficiency was adding to the comfort of all the guests. It had been no trouble to her to sort out elderly Miss Beresford's knitting nor to comply with Mr Hackett's preference for fish over meat. Anna had even enjoyed spending time with the Hackett's daughter who wasn't as sullen as she looked, once she learned that Anna had worked in Selfridges department store and was able to talk about fashions.

Anna would have been pleased to work in the guest house indefinitely but whether Thea lost the house to Stanley Ambrose or married the major, the days of paying guests were surely numbered.

'Do you think they'll get married?' Daisy had asked Anna.

'It's much too soon for them to be sure of their feelings,' Anna had answered, but was that true? Hadn't Anna and Piers fallen instantly into love?

Thea certainly looked happy to be spending time with Ralph and the last thing Anna wanted was to be in her way. That meant finding a route to independence as soon as possible. The thought of finding work that paid enough to cover rent on a place to live as well as the cost of someone to look after the baby was as daunting as ever. But once she'd adjusted to this terrible sense of grief… once the baby was born… once her back had stopped aching and she was restored to her energetic and resourceful self… surely then she'd feel more optimistic.

In the meantime, Mr Acaster's money was a real boon. 'I'm going to see about booking the nursing home now,' Anna told Thea.

'Only if that's what you really want.'

Anna called in at Doctor Maddox's to let him know what she'd decided. She didn't ask for a consultation but he wandered into his reception area and recognised her. 'I'm pleased to hear it,' he said, when he heard what she had planned. 'You'll be well looked-after there. Besides...'

He hesitated, then said, 'Step into my surgery for a moment.'

Puzzled, Anna followed him into his room where he gestured her to a chair in front of his desk. He sat down behind it and studied her. 'Bringing up a child in reduced circumstances can be difficult.'

As if she hadn't already realised that!

'Sometimes there's a better way.'

'Adoption?' Anna shook her head. She wouldn't give up Piers's baby.

'Adoption can be a terrible wrench,' Doctor Maddox admitted. 'You mustn't think I underestimate it. But adoption can give a child advantages its natural mother isn't in a position to offer. A good education, a decent home, stability, security, opportunity... and the love of a father as well as a mother. That's particularly important when the child is a boy in my experience.'

He let that sink in then continued. 'There are advantages to the natural mother too. Adoption frees her to work and build a new life. Often to marry without any... complications from the past.'

'I couldn't,' Anna said.

'It's your decision, of course. But it's a decision that merits careful thought and if a little reflection persuades you of the advantages to all concerned, the nursing home will be able to advise you on the steps to be taken.'

'Thank you,' Anna said, but she couldn't manage another word.

She got up and merely nodded to the receptionist as she rushed past, desperate to get outside so she could release the tears that were stabbing her eyes like needles.

She hadn't given adoption a moment's serious thought before but Doctor Maddox had made it sound as though keeping her child would be an act of selfishness. Was he right?

After all, the best Anna would be able to offer was a mean little home somewhere, long hours spent in the care of a stranger and a basic education only. In short an upbringing quite unlike the privileged childhood Piers had enjoyed. What would Piers want for his child? A mean life with Anna? Or a world of opportunity with adoptive parents?

A large building loomed up on Anna's left. She realised it was the workhouse and shuddered.

Twenty-Seven

Daisy was daydreaming her way along Marine Parade when she heard her name being called. She glanced around but saw no one trying to attract her attention. But then a gleaming red car glided to a halt beside her and Daisy's heart kicked in excitement. A grinning Rory Connor leaned towards her from the driver's seat. 'How is my little colleen today?'

'If you mean me, I'm fine,' Daisy said. 'Are you—'

But he was blocking the path of a coach whose driver tooted impatiently. With a resigned wave Rory drove on and Daisy felt crushed with disappointment. He didn't drive far, though. He pulled in to the kerb at a more convenient place and Daisy rushed to catch up with him.

By the time she reached him he was out of the car and leaning against the door, showing none of the self-consciousness that was bringing a flush of colour to Daisy's cheeks. 'The day started dull but it's brightening up, so it is,' he said.

The clouds remained resolutely grey but he wasn't referring to the weather. Daisy's flush deepened.

'Hop in and we'll go for a spin,' he invited.

Daisy wanted nothing more than to jump straight into the car but Anna was waiting for the basket of vegetables Daisy was carrying as they had new guests staying. Mr Duke had come to study the Pavilion, being interested in history. He was a nice man though he'd mortified Daisy by asking to see her mother when he'd come to enquire about a room and called her, 'My dear child'.

Mrs Ainsley and her cousin Mrs Antrobus had come to scatter the late Mr Ainsley's ashes into the sea because he'd longed to live on the coast when he retired but died before he had a chance.

'I need to take this basket home but I think I can get away after that,' Daisy explained.

'You won't keep a poor soul like me waiting for long?' he said.

'I'll be as quick as I can.'

She raced the short distance to Clarendon Place, let herself in and hastened down to Anna and Thea in the kitchen. 'Might I be spared for a couple of hours?' she asked, hiding her flush by unpacking the basket. 'I've just met a friend unexpectedly.'

'You want to spend time with her?' Thea guessed. 'Of course you can be spared.'

Daisy didn't point out that her friend was actually a *him*. She supposed she was too shy and embarrassed to admit it having so recently declared that she wasn't interested in romance. And she didn't know yet if Rory had romance in mind or simply a treat for the little cousin of a friend.

She ran back upstairs and came to a halt in the hall, struck by a sudden thought. Tiptoeing into the drawing-room, she stretched up to see her reflection in the mirror above the fireplace. Her fair hair was dishevelled as usual. Should she go upstairs and tidy it? Perhaps change her serviceable skirt, blouse and knitted cardigan for her Sunday best dress of dusky pink?

For a moment she was tempted. She even wondered what it would be like to powder her face and brighten her cheeks with… what was it called? Rouge. That was it. Not that she had any rouge. Daisy had never worn cosmetics in her life. Thea didn't wear cosmetics either but she always looked wonderful when she went out with the major.

The urge to appear pretty was strong but Daisy was afraid she'd look foolish if romance was the last thing on his mind. And she shouldn't keep him waiting. Contenting herself with smoothing some wisps of hair from her face, Daisy left the house and hastened back to Marine Parade.

Her steps slowed when she saw Rory was no longer alone. He was talking to a young woman but then he noticed Daisy and smiled. Leaning closer to the young woman for a moment, he said something Daisy couldn't hear and the young woman walked off.

'I didn't mean to interrupt,' Daisy said, joining him.

'Interrupt what? The colleen was only asking directions to the Pavilion, so she was.'

Daisy felt foolish because the twinkle in Rory's eyes told her he was aware that she'd felt jealous. She chewed on her lip and didn't know what to say because denying her jealousy might only confirm it.

'There's only one colleen I'm after spending time with today,' Rory assured her, and he opened the car door so Daisy could climb into the passenger seat.

'Where are we going?' Daisy asked.

'Wherever the road takes us. You've a taste for adventure, I hope?'

'An adventure sounds wonderful,' Daisy told him. As long as it didn't take too long. She couldn't leave all the work of Clarendon Place to Thea and Anna.

He manoeuvred the car through traffic until they were heading east. 'You don't mind if I drive fast?' he asked.

'I like going fast on Max's motorbike. On horses too, if I get the chance. Which isn't often, sadly. Being a jockey and getting to ride fast horses all the time must be wonderful.'

'If only they were always fast!' He laughed. 'I've ridden horses which are so slow I've felt like jumping off and carrying them to the finishing post.'

Daisy smiled. 'But you're doing well as a jockey?'

'To be sure, I'm not doing badly. If I don't become Champion Jockey, it shan't be for the want of trying.'

They passed Rottingdean, Saltdean and Peacehaven, the sea managing the occasional sparkle as the sun took tentative glimpses from behind the clouds. Newhaven came next and then Seaford where Daisy knew there was a racecourse. 'Have you raced there?' she asked.

'Many times.'

'I haven't time to go further than Eastbourne today,' Daisy told him.

'Then Eastbourne it shall be,' he said, and she was relieved when he didn't appear disappointed.

'I've never actually been there before,' Daisy admitted, feeling horribly unsophisticated.

'No?' He grinned across at her. 'Then we'll have a little tour of the place.'

Eastbourne proved to be a pleasant town with tree-lined roads and a seafront lined with bathing huts. There was a bandstand on the beach too, held up on tall stilts. 'It looks like a birdcage,' Daisy observed.

There was a pier too and Daisy wondered if he might want to walk along it. But instead he asked, 'Have you ever been inside a pub, Daisy Flowers?'

'I have,' she was glad to tell him, not wanting to appear completely naïve.

'There's a pub I sometimes visit. The Sombre Sailor. Not that it's sombre. In fact it's lively.'

'I like the sound of that,' Daisy said, eager to please him.

He drove to the eastern side of town and parked near the pub. The Sombre Sailor was lively indeed. The landlord was Irish and Daisy soon saw that he was a pal of Rory's. The two men slapped shoulders and Rory was hailed by several others who were sitting drinking.

'What'll you have?' Rory asked her.

The only drink that occurred to her was the one she'd had in the pub with Rose. 'Port and lemon, please.'

He ordered Daisy's drink and a whisky for himself.

'So, Rory boy, what's your tip for the three-thirty at York?' A middle-aged man with a paunch and rather grubby shirt had sidled up to him.

'My money is on Ebenezer's Dream, though Gordonstown Lad's showing some form.'

'Shame the same couldn't be said for your mount at Doncaster last week,' the landlord told Rory.

'The horse was a slug, so it was,' Rory admitted. 'I wouldn't have taken the ride if I hadn't been promised a present on top of a fee. When a man has a house going to ruin for want of the money to repair it, he can't turn up his nose at an earning opportunity. Talking of which, Padraic…' He handed the landlord a five pound note. 'Put ten shillings to win on Mary's Delight at Kempton and a pound each way on Summertime Surprise at Leicester.'

'Right you are, Rory boy.'

'Mary's Delight could earn me a fiver and Summertime Surprise a clear twenty pounds,' Rory explained to Daisy. 'That'll pay for a few tiles on the roof of Castle Kerwig.'

'What if they lose?'

'Life is full of risks, is it not?'

He drank his whisky quickly. 'Another?' he suggested.

Daisy had hardly touched her port so he ordered only another whisky for himself. But when he suggested a third drink, Daisy said, 'Actually, I'd prefer some fresh air.' The smoke in the bar was making her eyes smart.

'I know the best place for fresh air,' Rory said.

He took her arm and steered her towards the door though progress was slow due to the number of men who stopped Rory along the way to congratulate or commiserate with him on his recent rides, or to ask for betting tips.

'We should take a trip on a paddle steamer,' he said, when they finally got outside.

Daisy felt a pang of dismay. 'I'd love to, but I haven't time today.'

Would Rory think her a dull sort of girl?

'You know how to break a man's heart, Daisy Flowers,' he said, but he'd bent to fasten a shoelace so she couldn't see whether he was genuinely disappointed or merely teasing her.

'I really would like to go on a paddle steamer another day,' she told him, hoping she wasn't making him feel awkward because he had no intention of taking her out for a second time.

He didn't look awkward when he straightened again but neither did he mention trying the paddle steamer on a different day. 'Now where did we leave the car?' he asked.

'We came from that direction,' Daisy said, pointing.

'So we did.'

He drove back as quickly as he'd come. Now the sea was on their left and the sun was beaming brighter, making shimmers of silver on the water. 'Isn't that a sight to gladden the heart,' Rory said, and Daisy was relieved to know that his mood remained cheerful.

'Is Castle Kerwig by the sea?' she asked.

'It is. And it faces west so the sunsets are glorious.'

'Do you miss it when you're away?'

'To be sure. But a man has to earn a living. Or at least this man does. My grandparents were fine folk who never lifted a finger in the name of commerce. The house had seven indoor servants and another five working outside. Now there's just a housekeeper, a maid of all work and a single gardener. No groom because the stables are empty.'

'Where do you live when you're not in Ireland?' Daisy asked.

'I'm a roving sort of man. I was staying with friends last night. The Morrells in Plumpton. Their Friarsgate is another fine house though it doesn't hold a candle to Castle Kerwig. Sometimes I put up in hotels and inns. I've stayed at the Grand in Brighton but if Lady Fortune hasn't favoured me, I've gone to the Mermaid Inn instead. That's where I'm staying now.'

'Let's hope you get to be Champion Jockey so all the best owners pay you presents for riding their horses.'

'All I need is a sprinkling of luck from Lady Fortune.'

'You can drop me here,' Daisy said, as they reached Marine Parade.

He eased the car to the kerb. 'Don't bother getting out,' Daisy told him. 'I've had a lovely afternoon. Thank you.'

'I've had a fine afternoon too,' he said. He leaned over and kissed her cheek then winked after she'd got out of the car. 'I hope to see you again, Daisy Flowers. You'll find me at the Mermaid.'

With that Rory drove off and Daisy touched her cheek where he'd kissed her. Had he meant it when he said he hoped to see her again or was that the sort of thing young men said in order to be polite? Daisy could only wait to see what, if anything, happened next.

Walking around the corner into Clarendon Place, she thought back to Rory's smiles and shivered deliciously. But then she thought of Anna and how terrible it must have been for her to have found love only to have it snatched away from her so cruelly.

Changing her mind about going straight home, Daisy made for Needham's department store instead and bought a baby's matinee coat in soft white wool.

She presented the wrapped parcel to Anna as soon as she got home. 'What's this?' Anna asked.

'Open it and see,' Daisy advised.

Anna drew the matinee coat out and held it up.

'It's only a little gift,' Daisy said. 'You can change it if you don't like it.'

'It's… beautiful,' Anna said. She got to her feet. 'Thank you, Daisy.'

'I thought you'd need something warm for the baby to wear when you bring him or her back from the nursing home.'

'That's very thoughtful of you, Daisy,' Thea approved.

'It is.' Anna smiled, but tears shimmered in her eyes. 'If you'll excuse me…'

She headed for the door and – presumably – the privacy of her attic bedroom.

Daisy frowned. 'Did I do the wrong thing?' she asked Thea.

'I don't see how. It's just that kindness can be overwhelming sometimes.'

Daisy nodded. Thea always spoke good sense. Glad she hadn't blundered, Daisy let her thoughts return to Rory. She hoped she'd see him soon.

Twenty-Eight

Thea opened the door to find Max on the doorstep.

'I'll take no offence if you tell me this isn't a convenient moment for me to call,' he said.

His grey eyes regarded her steadily, free from awkwardness. Clearly he was considerate enough to understand that a visit might be mistimed and confident enough to accept a rebuff without feeling slighted.

'If you'd called ten minutes ago, you'd have found me up to my wrists in pastry,' Thea admitted. 'Now I'm about to put the kettle on so you've timed your arrival perfectly. But nothing's wrong, I hope?'

'Not at all.' He stepped through the door and followed her down the basement stairs. 'I had business in Brighton and thought I'd take the chance to let you know that Night Warrior's still doing well. It'll be a cool day in Hell before he turns docile, but he hasn't eaten me yet. I've got great hopes for him.'

They reached the kitchen where Anna was sitting sewing. 'Good morning, Anna,' Max said, and Thea liked the way his voice softened to a quietly respectful tone.

Anna needed as much kindness as possible now. She was as uncomplaining and hardworking as ever, but grief over Piers and the strain of becoming an unmarried mother were showing in her wan face. Thea was worried about her.

'What are you sewing?' Max sat down beside Anna and smiled when she held up a tiny white nightgown. 'Have you decided on a name for the little one?'

It was an innocent enough question but Anna looked stricken. She bent over her sewing as though trying to hide her face. 'I haven't,' she said.

Max gave Thea a questioning look, as puzzled by Anna's response as Thea was.

'I thought you'd decided on James for a boy,' Thea said. 'Piers's middle name.'

'I had thought of that,' Anna admitted.

'But now you want to wait until the baby arrives before you name him? Or her?' Max suggested. 'That makes perfect sense to me. One of my cousins was set on the name Samson for his son because he thought his son would be a strapping young article. But Samson was a tiny scrap when he was born and he's a tiny lad now. They've had to start calling him Sean – his middle name – to stop the teasing.'

Anna nodded but didn't look up.

'Is that what you're doing?' Thea questioned. 'Waiting to see the baby face to face?'

Anna didn't answer immediately. Then she got to her feet. 'I'm just not sure I'm the right person to name the baby. If you don't mind, I'll just…'

'Who should name the baby if not you?' Thea's unease was growing.

Max stood too and blocked Anna's way. 'Yes, who?' he asked.

Anna dashed away tears. 'I just want what's best for the baby,' she said.

'Of course,' Thea acknowledged. 'But I don't see what— 'A thought struck her and a glance at Max told her it had struck him too. 'Anna, are you thinking of giving the baby up?'

Anna sat back down and, elbows to the table, put her head in her hands. 'I want to do what's right.'

Thea sat beside her, passed her a handkerchief then stretched an arm around her shoulders. 'It's just that you've never mentioned adoption before. I understood you were planning to keep the baby.'

'I was. But then…' Anna sobbed for a moment then gulped. 'I started to wonder if that would be selfish. Other parents might be able to offer the baby a wonderful life. I've got nothing to offer.'

'You've got love aplenty and you shouldn't underestimate the importance of that,' Thea assured her.

'But does love cancel out the other advantages adoptive parents might have at their disposal? I don't even have a permanent home.'

'You've got a home here for the moment. And if that changes… Well, I'll help you to find somewhere else. You mustn't think you're alone.'

Even as she spoke Thea was aware of her commitment to Anna tightening around her like a binding. She wasn't yet sure how she'd look after herself let alone a young mother and her baby.

It was another aspect of her life that Thea was keeping from Ralph, though if she were being honest she'd done more than merely conceal it from him. She'd actively misled him when Ralph had tried – ever so delicately – to bring up the subject of Anna and her pregnancy.

'It's perfectly fine for Anna to be working in her condition,' she'd laughed. 'You've been in the army too long, Ralph. The world has changed. Some women even have the vote, you know.'

He'd smiled sheepishly. 'I know some women have to earn their livings as well as men. The pension war widows receive isn't much, and as for women who've lost their husbands since the war…'

'Anna's a hard worker and a wonderful cook,' Thea had insisted. 'She isn't the sort of person to impose.'

Anna was determined *not* to impose though all the determination in the world couldn't save her from being vulnerable just now and Thea felt responsible for her.

It was good of Ralph to be concerned that advantage was being taken of her but his words had confirmed Thea's impression of him as a man with a strong sense of gallantry who wouldn't hesitate to try to intervene in her affairs if he felt she needed protection. As far as she was concerned it was far too soon to gauge whether their friendship might grow serious. They needed time to get to know each other properly and it was important that affection developed naturally without Ralph being influenced by a chivalrous wish to rescue her from her difficulties.

After the awfulness of Herbert Ambrose, it was very pleasant indeed to spend time with a real gentleman but Thea wouldn't take Ralph into her confidence just yet.

'I can see that adoption may be the best way forward for some people,' Max told Anna. 'It may be the best way forward for you, but don't go choosing it for the wrong reason. Thea's right. A mother's love is a lot to offer a child and in my opinion it far outweighs material advantages.'

Thea smiled at him approvingly. Not because she had anything against adoption in principle. Like Max, she could see that it could be the best option for some people. It was the suddenness of Anna's shift towards the idea that troubled Thea. That suddenness suggested the idea hadn't emerged from Anna's feelings but from someone else's.

Whose, though? Daisy's? Unlikely. Daisy had often commented on what an excellent mother Anna was going to make. So—

Ah. 'Was it Doctor Maddox who suggested giving the baby up?' Thea asked.

'He mentioned it as a possibility, that's all.'

But he'd made Anna feel guilty.

'There's something else to consider,' Max said. 'Some*one*, rather. What would Piers want? I never met him, but in his place I'd trust no one more than the woman I'd planned to marry to bring up my child. Who else would tell my son or daughter that I was a decent man who'd have loved my child to bits had I lived long enough? That's an important thing for a child to know.'

'Anna?' Thea prompted.

'Piers would have made a wonderful father.'

'Don't you want your baby to know that?' Thea asked, then realised she was putting Anna under pressure of a different sort. 'Sorry. I can't pretend it'll be easy for you or the baby if you stay together because I don't know what's going to happen. If you genuinely feel that adoption is the best thing for both of you, then I shan't try to change your mind. I just want to be sure that you choose it of your own free will. Doubtless Doctor Maddox means well. But he hasn't any children of his own and I suspect he's underestimating the importance of love. Promise me you won't make your decision based on his opinion or anyone else's.'

'I promise,' Anna said. She wiped her eyes and sighed. 'I'm sorry I'm being such a bother.'

'You're not a bother. You're a friend,' Thea insisted, then got to her feet. 'Tea?' she offered Max.

He gave Anna a rueful look. 'Now *I'm* being a bother. But a cup of tea would be grand.'

Thea set the kettle to boil and Anna picked up her sewing, touching the nightgown tenderly before asking, 'How's the horse?'

'Healed and healthy,' Max reported. 'In his body, that is. He still has the devil in him when it comes to temperament, but he's only bucked me off his back three times so far.'

Anna winced but Max only shrugged. 'Falls come with the job when you work with horses. You learn how to fall to avoid injury. And he's a beautiful horse for all his temper. Strong too, and I'm hoping speed will add a third string to his bow. I'll get a professional jockey to try him out over five furlongs soon if Thea agrees.'

'A professional?' Thea questioned.

'To give an opinion on how he settles and how he might perform in a race though it's never possible to know for sure how a horse will behave in noisy race conditions until he's actually there. Don't worry about cost. The jockey's a friend of mine and he won't expect payment.'

'It sounds exciting,' Anna said, and Thea agreed.

'Will you come and see him?' Max asked Thea.

'Today?' Thea was surprised.

'I have the horsebox so I can drive you to Clareswood. The lad who works for me has the evening off so I'll have to stay and settle the horses tonight but I could drop you at Worthing station for the journey home.'

'You should go, Thea,' Anna urged. 'Daisy will be back from the butcher soon to help with the guests.'

As if on cue, the street door opened and closed above them, and moments later Daisy appeared. 'Of course Thea should go and see Warry,' she declared, after she'd heard Max's proposal.

Thea needed little further persuasion. She was curious about Night Warrior and it wouldn't hurt to take her mind off her troubles for a while. Besides, with Anna getting ever-closer to the birth, Thea might not have another chance for a day out for quite some time.

'Give me five minutes to get ready,' she said, but paused at the door to beckon Daisy to follow.

As Daisy joined her, Thea raised a finger to warn her not to speak until they were upstairs. 'What is it?' Daisy asked then.

Thea told her that Anna had started thinking about adoption. 'The decision has to be hers, of course, but I hope you'll help her to understand that she won't be a bad mother just because she's poor and unmarried.'

'I can't think of anyone who'd make a better mother,' Daisy agreed.

Pleased to have an ally, Thea continued up to her room to get ready.

The Brighton traffic was busy but Max negotiated it calmly. Thea felt pretty sure that Max had a temper beneath that self-possessed exterior but it took more than traffic to arouse it.

They headed along the coast road towards Worthing then up over the rolling hills of the Downs to Clareswood. Thea liked the look of Clareswood immediately, from the picturesque homeliness of the rambling house to the sight of horses and ponies grazing contentedly in paddocks. It was a relaxed, happy sort of place.

Max drove around to the back where there were more paddocks. Thea could see a black horse on the far side of one of them. Night Warrior? The horse looked up as they drove towards an arch that Thea assumed led to the stables. He stared at them for no more than a second or two before shaking his head as though expressing disdain. Thea smiled. Yes, that was Night Warrior.

The arch led to a courtyard which had stables around the sides and other doors that she supposed led to tack rooms and feed stores. It was far from being oppressively smart but Max obviously looked after this part of Clareswood very well indeed.

A man and a woman were standing at one of the stable doors which had the top half open to allow a chestnut horse to look out. They turned at the sound of the approaching horsebox and waved a greeting. There was a dog at their side, a lion-like creature that Thea recognised as a Chow Chow.

Max drew the horsebox to a halt and the couple walked over. The dog followed eagerly, pushing his nose into Max's hand the moment he stepped out and keeping it there as he walked round to Thea's side to open her door. She'd have got out herself but the handle had proven tricky to open from the inside.

Max introduced her to Mr and Mrs Leigh, describing her as the joint owner of Night Warrior. 'You've got a fine-looking horse there, Miss Fairfax,' Mr Leigh told her.

'He certainly lives up to his name, being as black as night and as fearsome as a warrior,' Mrs Leigh said. 'My heart has been in my mouth when I've watched Max riding him.'

'Fortunately, I'm the partner who merely has to encourage instead of risking life and limb,' Thea smiled.

'You don't ride?' Mrs Leigh asked.

'I have ridden, but not for a long time.'

Thea's father had taken her riding while her nervous mother stayed at home. She'd enjoyed both the riding and the time spent with her father, and remembering that happiness engulfed her in a sudden sense of loss. But Thea forced a smile, reminding herself that lovely memories should warm the heart rather than grieve it.

'You're very welcome to ride one of our horses while you're here,' Mrs Leigh offered. 'You'll be in good hands with Max. Night Warrior is an exception. Most animals become instant slaves to him. Like Bernard here.' The Chow Chow was basking in Max's caress.

'You're very kind,' Thea told Mrs Leigh, deciding neither to accept nor reject the offer until she could gauge whether Max wanted to be bothered with saddling a horse for her.

'It's been a pleasure to meet you, Miss Fairfax, but I'm afraid we must ask you to excuse us now,' Mrs Leigh said.

'Goodness, yes.' Her husband appeared struck by a sudden recollection. 'We're lunching with the Forresters. Good luck with Night Warrior, Miss Fairfax. Max has high hopes of him.'

Thea thanked them for their hospitality. The Leighs began to walk away but Mrs Leigh had to look round to call Bernard to follow as he showed no sign of wanting to leave Max.

'Off you go,' Max told him.

He gave Max a mournful look but did as he was bid.

'Shall we take a look at Night Warrior?' Thea asked.

Max nodded so they left the courtyard and headed for the paddock in which Night Warrior was grazing. Thea rested her arms on top of the fence. 'He looks transformed.'

'He is.' Max called to Night Warrior in a coaxing tone of voice but received only a defiant glare that made him smile. 'Transformed, but ungrateful.'

'May I see the other horses?'

'Of course.' Max introduced her to all of them, including his own mare, a nice-looking chestnut called Aurora who was obviously in foal. 'You'll sell the foal, I suppose?'

'That's the idea. The sire is a decent-looking gentleman's horse so the foal should be strong as well as handsome.'

'But not a racehorse?'

'Unlikely. I can't afford the stud fee to breed Aurora to a stallion who's proved himself in racing.'

'But if you have your own stallion like Night Warrior…'

'If he's successful in races it'll make all the difference. Breeders will pay to bring their mares to him. With luck I'll be able to buy more mares of my own and breed them to Night Warrior too. A horse can sire as many as forty foals a year.'

'Goodness.' Thea worked hard to stop a blush from rising but Max grinned anyway.

'When a horse mates, it isn't true love, Thea.'

'I suppose it isn't.'

'I'd like to have my own stables one day,' he said. 'But we'll see.'

'What'll happen to Aurora then?'

'She'll become a pensioner, stuffing her face with grass all day and taking life easy. I love horses, Thea. I'd never turn my back on an old horse whose working days are over.'

Thea was pleased to hear it.

'So?' he asked then.

'I'm sorry?'

'Are you going to ride? I can put you on old Clara. She's far too well-mannered to buck you off or run away with you.'

'I'm not dressed for riding.'

'What are you saying? That you'll only ride in a long Victorian riding habit? On a side-saddle?' He was teasing her. Challenging her too. 'Daisy rides in anything.'

'All right, then. Thank you. I'd like to ride.'

Max saddled up two horses: Clara for Thea and a larger bay horse called Constable for himself. He led them into the courtyard and Thea looked round for a mounting block. 'Here,' Max said, joining his hands together to give her a leg-up.

He boosted her into the saddle with athletic efficiency then sprang onto Constable's back. Thea leaned forward to pat Clara's neck and introduce herself then followed Max into an empty paddock. 'Don't rush,' he cautioned. 'Just give yourself time to reacquaint yourself with being back in the saddle.'

It felt strange to be riding astride like a man and Thea was glad her skirt wasn't especially tight, otherwise it would have risen up her legs rather shockingly. But as they ambled around the paddock side by side, she found her sense of balance returning and enjoyment setting in.

'I hope Anna feels better after this morning's conversation,' Max ventured after a while.

'I hope so too,' Thea told him.

'I'm not a rich man as you know. Far from it in fact. But if there's anything she needs for the baby, I'll help if I can. I could knock up a cradle, perhaps.'

'Anna has the use of my old cradle but it's kind of you to be concerned.'

'Who wouldn't be concerned? If I were in Piers's situation, I'd hope people would help my nearest and dearest.'

'I'll let you know if there's anything you can do for her.'

'What happened to Piers was tragic but Anna's lucky with her friends. She has you and my cousin too. Daisy may be a fiery little cat but she's—'

'Wonderful,' Thea finished.

Max laughed. 'She is. But don't tell her I said so or I'll never hear the end of it. Time to try a trot?'

Thea urged Clara into a trot and after a while to a leisurely canter. Then Max took them out on the Downs. She was relaxed enough by then to notice that Max rode lightly, his body so attuned to Constable's that he never had to do more than squeeze the horse's sides to make him follow instructions, and he never tugged harshly on the reins.

'Enough?' he finally said.

Thea would have liked to ride further but her muscles were already protesting from the unfamiliar exercise and she didn't want to take up too much of Max's time. He was a working man, not a gentleman of leisure.

They headed back to the courtyard where Thea insisted on helping to unsaddle Clara and rub her down before releasing her into her paddock. The morning had given way to afternoon. 'Come in and have some lunch,' Max invited.

Thea hesitated.

'A quick bite then I'll take you to the station.'

Thea followed him into a small cottage that was accessed through another arch on the far side of the courtyard. It was a pretty little place with an old oak door that opened straight into a parlour. 'Watch your head,' Max warned, and she stooped before she stepped inside.

There was nothing luxurious about the parlour or the small kitchen behind it but they were neat, clean and homely. Looking round curiously, Thea saw that Max had numerous books on horses and some novels too. Adventure stories mostly, by Sir Walter Scott, John Buchan and Joseph Conrad. It wasn't hard to picture him reading by lamplight after a hard day's work. He wasn't the sort of man who craved attention.

'Soup?' he offered.

'Yes, please. Can I help?'

'You could set the table.' He nodded to a cupboard in which she found cutlery and plates.

She took them to the little table, moved a folder of papers onto a shelf and arranged their place settings. 'Anything else?' Thea asked.

'Cut some bread?'

Thea cut slices from a loaf and fetched butter from the larder. Max had lit the gas stove under a pan and soon the smell of seasoned vegetables rose up to make Thea realise she was hungry. He poured the soup into bowls and brought them to the table, his movements relaxed and fluid.

'Tasty,' Thea complimented, but declined a second helping in case he wanted it for his supper.

'Now then,' he said, when they'd cleared away together.

He made the word sound ominous and Thea tensed.

'Shall I take you to Worthing in the horsebox or are you adventurous enough to ride on the back of my motorbike?'

It was another challenge and Thea couldn't resist accepting it. 'I've no objection to the motorbike.'

'Good,' he approved.

It was hardly a dignified form of transport. Some people – Ralph's parents being amongst them – might even call it indecent for a young woman like her. Sitting behind Max, Thea had to put her arms around his middle in order to hold on. She did so tentatively though the sudden speed when he set off made her clutch at him instinctively.

Embarrassed, she moved back from his muscled body, soon growing accustomed to the speed and beginning to trust that they wouldn't tip over when Max leaned to the left or the right as they rounded corners. By the time they reached Worthing station, she was enjoying the ride immensely even if it did make wisps of her hair fly in all directions. Fortunately, she'd pinned her hat on securely.

'Thank you for a lovely day,' she said, getting off the bike.

Max was still straddling it. 'Come again,' he told her. 'And you'll remember what I said about helping Anna?'

'Of course.'

It was comforting to know Anna had another friend in Max but the lion's share of responsibility still fell on Thea as the person who was putting a roof over Anna's head. For the moment.

It had indeed been a lovely day but now Thea could feel the weight of her problems returning. She hastened down to the kitchen when she reached Clarendon Place and found Anna and Daisy there. 'Any post?' she asked, and Anna passed her an envelope addressed in what Thea recognised as Jessie Jarrold's handwriting.

Thea tore it open, scanned the note it contained and sighed in relief. 'Jessie wants to meet me tomorrow morning.'

Was this the breakthrough Thea so desperately needed? She could only hope so

Twenty-Nine

Anna wiped the kitchen table then paused to rub her aching back. She hadn't slept well – again – and when she'd dressed this morning she'd looked in the mirror and seen lilac shadows around her eyes.

She'd been touched beyond measure by the kindness Thea, Daisy and even Maxwell Moore had shown when they'd assured her she'd be a good mother to her child. There was no doubt in Anna's mind that she'd be a *loving* mother. Neither was there any doubt in her mind that the child's life would be enriched by knowing what sort of man Piers had been. But was that enough to counteract the disadvantages the child would suffer in her care?

The stigma of illegitimacy, for one. People could be horribly cruel about such things. Poverty and lack of opportunity for another. And what use was a loving mother if she was so busy working that she had hardly any time left in which to show her love?

If only Anna could decide what was the right thing to do.

There was a loud knock on the upstairs door. A Mr and Mrs Makepeace had just left after staying for two nights and perhaps they'd realised they'd left something behind. Or maybe someone else was calling about a room. Anna hoped so. After a sudden flurry of guests, they currently had none.

Anna climbed the stairs, wincing again at the ache in her back. But it wasn't a guest who'd knocked. It was a young boy in Post Office uniform. 'Telegram for Miss Watson.' He proffered a brown envelope.

'I'm Miss Watson.' Anna was puzzled at first but then – Oh heavens, had something happened at home? Was her mother unwell? Had one of the children been hurt?

She tore into the envelope and pulled a thin sheet of paper from inside it to scan the words.

Have news Stop Please telephone Stop George Acaster.

Had Mr Acaster heard more about how the *Adiona* had gone down? Or had Piers's body been found? Anna felt a painful squeeze of distress at the thought of that beloved face battered by the waves. Or – perhaps she was mad to torture herself but the tiny flame of hope burst back into life – might Piers still be alive?

Anna had to know. She had to know *now*. Daisy was out but Thea was upstairs getting ready for her London trip. Surely Anna had time to make a telephone call?

She rushed down to the kitchen for her coat and purse, and called up the stairs as she opened the door to the street. 'I'm just popping out for a moment!'

Closing the door, she hastened down the steps and along Clarendon Place, grimacing at the ache in her back. She was about to turn onto Marine Parade when more pain gripped her, this time across her abdomen. Gasping, she came to a halt and doubled over, her fingers crushing the telegram.

Was this labour? It had to be, but it was early. A whole month early. None of Ma's babies had been quite as early as this. Anna squeezed her eyes shut and endured a wave of panic as well as pain. The pain gradually eased and she forced the panic to recede a little too. She'd known of babies in Bermondsey who'd survived being born as much as two months early. She'd known of others who hadn't survived but she wouldn't think of that now. Her child needed her to stay strong instead of giving into fear.

She opened her eyes and straightened slowly. Labour took hours. She still had plenty of time in which to telephone Mr Acaster, return to the house for her things and move into the nursing home that she'd finally booked for her confinement.

The thought that she'd soon be face to face with her baby – Piers's baby – had her hand moving to her belly. Love roared inside her with all the fierceness of a lion and she knew then that she couldn't give this baby up to others. Somehow or other she had to find a way for them to stay together.

She took a deep breath and walked on only to be gripped by another contraction. Anna hadn't expected labour to be this painful so early in the process. The strength of it left her feeling nauseous. This time she waited a little longer before moving on and this time she got a little further but then the pain struck again, making her clutch at a nearby railing for support. The railing ran across the front of a house then turned to accompany the steps that led to the door. Anna sank onto the lowest step, realising to her dismay that, in clutching the railing, she'd let go of the telegram. She leaned forward to pick it up but the breeze caught it and shifted it out of her reach.

She dragged herself back to her feet but just as she bent to the telegram a passing lorry stirred flurries of air that lifted it up and sent it swooping into the road. Another vehicle approached. Anna waited for it to pass then took a step forward and—

The pain of this contraction took her breath away. None of her mother's labours had been as swift and intense as this. Anna concentrated on staying on her feet then staggered back to the step. She breathed in and out slowly, gathering strength for another attempt at walking but when she looked round for the telegram she couldn't see it anywhere.

Thirty

'I have to go,' Daisy told Rory regretfully.

'You're a girl who knows how to disappoint a man, Daisy Flowers.'

'I'm working.'

'And here am I trying to tempt you to come out and play at the races.'

'I'd love to see you race another day.'

'Let's hope I don't break my neck in a fall in the meantime.'

'Don't say that!' Daisy cried.

'I'm teasing,' he told her, grinning. 'I can't promise *not* to break my neck – horseracing is a risky business – but I'm unlikely to do so.'

'Good.'

Daisy was horribly aware of time passing. Thea needed to leave for London soon and neither she nor Daisy wanted Anna to be left alone at the moment. But the note Daisy had received from Rory that morning had brought a thrill to her heart. Somehow or other he'd persuaded a man with a lorry load of vegetables to deliver it.

I was supposed to be trying a horse for a trainer near Seaford, but the horse got a touch of the colic and his trainer cancelled. Do gladden a poor Irishman's heart by spending the morning with me and coming to see me race this afternoon.

He'd left the telephone number of the Mermaid where he was staying again. Daisy had called to explain that she couldn't have the whole day off and been delighted when he'd suggested they still meet for an early stroll along Brighton seafront.

'Would it be all right if I walked down to the beach for a breath of fresh air before you leave?' she'd asked Thea that morning.

'Of course,' Thea had said, smiling. 'It must be hard for you to be cooped up inside all day when you're used to being out in the country air.'

Daisy's conscience had wriggled with guilt at keeping quiet about Rory but the thought of admitting she was walking out with someone was just too embarrassing. Besides, she still wasn't sure if she actually was walking out with him. Rory's teasing was nothing like Max's. It felt close to flirting instead. But why would a man like Rory – well born, successful and charming – be interested in a slip of a girl like her?

'Goodbye, then,' Daisy told Rory now. 'Good luck in the race.'

She stepped back but he took hold of her arm. 'There's a better way of saying goodbye than that,' he said. Bending, he placed a lingering kiss on her cheek very close to her mouth.

Warmth flooded her face and Rory released her with a laugh. 'I hope to see you again soon, Daisy Flowers.' Winking, he loped away.

Goodness. How lovely the kiss had been. But she hadn't time to stand and daydream over this gorgeous glow of happiness. She had to get home.

Daisy broke into a run because it would be terrible if her lateness made Thea miss her train. The thought took a little of the shine off Daisy's happiness. With Thea on the trail of Jessie Jarrold and Anna's baby due in another month's time, Daisy would be tied to Clarendon Place more and more. Would Rory lose interest if she was rarely free to see him? Hopefully, he—

Daisy frowned. Was that Anna sitting on a doorstep? It was. Knowing that only illness or serious upset would make a quietly dignified person like Anna trespass onto a stranger's property, Daisy ran even faster. She reached the step and crouched down beside her friend. 'Is it the baby?'

'I—'

Anna broke off to curl forward in pain. It was the baby, all right, but coming weeks too soon.

'Can you walk back to the house if I help you?' Daisy asked.

'Yes, but I need a telephone first. A telegram—'

Another spasm of pain brought beads of perspiration to Anna's forehead.

'We need to get you some help,' Daisy said.

'What I need is... Oh!'

'I'll fetch Thea.'

Daisy burst into the house calling Thea's name. 'You've got to come! Anna's having the baby!'

Thea raced up from the kitchen, her eyes wide with concern. 'Already? I heard her call out when she left but I couldn't catch what she said. I was just looking to see if she'd left a note.'

'She mentioned something about a telegram but she probably meant a telephone. She must have gone out to call the nursing home. She's in a lot of pain.'

They were running as they talked. Reaching Anna, Thea crouched down the way Daisy had done. 'Let's get you home.'

'I need to call—'

'Daisy can call the nursing home once you're home,' Thea insisted.

Between them Thea and Daisy got Anna back to Clarendon Place and helped her into the drawing-room as that was the first room they reached. 'I think the baby's coming quickly,' Daisy told Thea. 'I'm not sure there'll be time to move Anna to the nursing home.'

'Then run to the doctor's. He'll know the best thing to be done. And could you take the *Vacancies* sign out of the window? We can't manage paying guests just now.'

Daisy grabbed the sign and stuffed it behind some books on the hall table. She was enormously relieved to find the doctor at home though he didn't appear to share her sense of urgency. 'Babies take time,' he commented mildly.

'Not this one.'

'A midwife, are you?'

'No, but I've lived around animals all my life.'

'Animals!' Clearly, Daisy's limited experience counted for nothing with the doctor. But Anna's contractions were coming fast and hard, and she was the last person to exaggerate pain.

'Clarendon Place, isn't it?' the doctor checked.

'Number eighteen.'

He nodded and Daisy considered herself dismissed. Hoping he'd follow quickly, she hurried back to the house. 'The doctor's on his way,' she announced. 'Did you hear that, Anna? The doctor's coming.'

Anna managed a grateful smile.

Thea raised an eyebrow as though to ask how long he'd take and Daisy shrugged to show she didn't know. But just then a car pulled up outside and, looking through the window, Daisy saw the doctor get out. She let him in and brought him to the drawing-room.

'Thank you for coming,' Anna said, then paled as another contraction struck.

'I'll take a look at you then arrange for you to be moved to the nursing home,' Doctor Maddox told her.

Daisy and Thea withdrew to the hall. When Doctor Maddox appeared a few minutes later, his attitude had changed. 'There's no time for the nursing home now,' he said briskly, and Daisy resisted the urge to retort that she'd told him so.

They got Anna up to the nearest guest bedroom. 'What about your trip to London?' Daisy whispered to Thea. 'You need to meet Jessie.'

'I'll have to hope she doesn't flit away just yet.' Thea was smiling but Daisy knew she must be devastated at losing this chance to save her home.

Anna groaned and Thea went to her, taking Anna's hand between both of her own. 'Don't worry, darling. You're going to be seeing your baby very soon.'

What a good person Thea was.

Thirty-One

Thea's emotions were in a whirl as she rushed around gathering sheets, towels and soap for the doctor to use. It was exciting to know that Anna's baby would soon be born but it was worrying too and not just because the baby was coming early. Childbirth could be a dangerous process for the mother as well as the child. Even if all went well, Anna would be distraught if she gave birth only to part with the child to parents who could give it a better life than she could. Or *thought* she could.

As to her own situation, Thea could only hope she was managing to hide her dismay at missing her appointment with Jessie, thereby losing her trust and probably the only chance of overturning the Will.

'You'll stay?' the doctor said, when Thea carried the things in to him. 'There isn't time to send for a midwife or nurse.'

'If that's what Anna wants,' Thea said.

'It is,' Anna confirmed, adding, 'Please?'

Daisy stayed too and Anna's baby entered the world only fifteen minutes later. It was a magical moment that had Thea and Daisy blinking back tears.

'You have a son,' Thea told Anna. 'A beautiful son.'

'He's so lovely!' Daisy added.

'Small, but seems healthy enough,' Doctor Maddox pronounced, as the baby let out a cry.

Wrapped in a blanket, the baby was passed to Anna. 'Hello, darling,' Anna said, and the baby quietened instantly, looking up at her with all the appearance of curiosity.

Anna gazed back at him in wonder then burst into tears. 'Piers must have looked just like this when he was born,' she said. She sniffed then said fiercely, 'I'm calling him James and I'm not giving him up to anyone else.'

The doctor's lips pursed slightly but it felt like the right decision to Thea though heaven knew how they'd cope if she lost the house. *When* she lost the house, rather. Thea's imagination pictured Jessie waiting at the tea shop she'd appointed as their meeting place, growing increasingly angry, then flouncing out and dismissing Thea as an unreliable waste of time.

'Shall I arrange for you to be moved to the nursing home?' Doctor Maddox asked Anna as he prepared to leave.

'That would be kind,' Anna answered, but Thea had seen the momentary pang on Anna's face at the thought of it.

Doctor Maddox disapproved of Anna for being an unmarried mother and doubtless some of the nursing home staff would feel the same. Perhaps they'd even put pressure on Anna to reconsider adoption.

'Is it necessary for Anna to be moved?' Thea asked.

'She's weak. She needs to be looked after.'

'Can't she be looked after here?'

'No, Thea.' Anna spoke up. 'I've caused you so much trouble already.'

'What matters is what's best for you and the baby,' Thea insisted. 'Doctor?'

'I suppose I can look in each day and send a nurse to look in too. And I'm not far away should there be any difficulties. It'll be tiring work for you, though.'

'We're up to it,' Daisy insisted.

The doctor shook his head as though he thought all three of them were fools but didn't argue further. 'You need to rest now,' he told Anna.

'He's right,' Thea said, as Daisy showed the doctor out.

'I can't rest until I know the news,' Anna said.

'News?'

'That's why I went out. I had a telegram from Mr Acaster. He asked me to telephone because he had something to tell me.'

'Daisy mentioned a telegram but thought you were confused. Where is this telegram?'

'I dropped it and it blew away.'

'No matter. I can still call Mr Acaster for you.'

'Now?'

'The moment Daisy comes back. But promise me you'll rest even if he isn't available to speak to me.'

'I promise to try.'

Thea told Daisy where she was going, located the business card Mr Acaster had given Anna and walked briskly to the telephone kiosk, her thoughts in a jumble as joy over the baby jostled with the mental image of Jessie packing her things and quitting Roper Street leaving no trail for Thea to follow.

The Exchange put Thea through to Mr Acaster's secretary. 'I'm afraid Mr Acaster is in a meeting,' Thea was told. 'If you'd like to leave your name and telephone number I can—'

'I'm calling on behalf of Anna Watson. Mr Acaster sent her a telegram asking her to call urgently but she gave birth this morning and—'

Thea frowned. She could hear another voice but distantly as though someone was coming into the room. It was a gruff voice. Mr Acaster's?

There was a clunking sound as the phone was handed over. 'George Acaster here.'

'Theodora Fairfax. We—'

'I remember you, Miss Fairfax.'

'I'm calling on Miss Watson's behalf. She can't call herself because she had her baby this morning.'

'She's well, I hope?'

'Doing splendidly. The baby too. It's a boy and she's calling him James because that was his father's middle name. You have some news?'

'I do.'

Thea listened. A moment later she was racing back to Clarendon Place.

Thirty-Two

Anna knew from the way Thea was rushing upstairs that Mr Acaster's news must be momentous. Hope spread tingles of excitement through her body.

'He's alive,' Thea said, bursting into the bedroom. 'Piers is alive.'

Thank God! Anna closed her eyes and hugged the moment close, one part of her wanting to cry with relief and the other part wanting to whoop with joy.

'There's something you need to understand, though.' Thea came to sit on the edge of Anna's bed. 'He's badly injured.'

'Injured?' Anna opened her eyes again and searched Thea's face for information.

'Mr Acaster hasn't any details at present.'

'I see.' Anna took a deep breath then breathed out slowly. 'Piers survived the shipwreck and survived the last few weeks too. He's strong. I've every reason to hope he'll pull through, however badly he's hurt.'

'He's a tough one, your Piers,' Daisy said.

'Tough, and lots of other lovely things.' Anna stroked her baby's cheek. 'Hear that, darling? Your wonderful father is alive and hopefully you'll see him soon.'

She looked back at Thea. 'Is he in a hospital?'

'Mr Acaster believes Piers *has* been treated in a hospital but arrangements are being made for him to be brought back to England. His information is sketchy at the moment.'

'I need to write some letters,' Anna announced. 'Would you mind fetching paper, pen and envelopes?'

'All right,' Thea agreed, 'but then you must rest.'

Thea left the door open when she left the room and a moment later Anna heard her talking to someone in the hall. The nurse? No, the voice was male and Anna caught the name of Ralph. He must have stepped inside because his voice grew louder. 'I've called in the hope of taking you to luncheon.'

'Bless you,' Thea told him. 'But I'm going nowhere today. Anna had her baby this morning.'

'All well, I trust?'

'Very well, thank you.'

'But it's disrupted your household. Perhaps dinner would—'

'I can't go out because Anna and the baby are here.'

'Good Lord. Wouldn't a nursing home or relative's house be more appropriate?'

'I'm happy to have them here.'

'Won't it inconvenience you?'

'I'm sure Daisy and I will manage. Besides, we'll have a nurse looking in.'

'Even so... Forgive me, Thea, but it doesn't feel quite proper.'

Thea's silvery laughter rose into the air. 'Because I'm an innocent spinster?'

'You're mocking me.'

'I'm not a child, Ralph.'

'Certainly not. But you're still a young lady and… Well.'

'It's sweet of you to be concerned, Ralph, but I'm more robust than you think.'

'Evidently. Is tomorrow too soon to take you out?'

'I'll have to take each day as it comes for a while but why don't you come and take tea here one day? I'll telephone when I know I'll be free.'

'I'll look forward to it. And if I happen to be passing in the meantime, might I call in to check that you're coping? I needn't stay long.'

'Of course. You'll give my regards to your parents?'

Ralph must have moved back outside because Anna couldn't catch his reply. A moment later the door closed and Thea returned.

'I'm sorry,' Anna said.

'Sorry about what?' Thea looked puzzled.

'I'm stopping you from seeing the major,' Anna said. 'I made you miss your appointment with Jessie too.'

'I can see Ralph another day. As for Jessie—'

'You should go to London tomorrow,' Anna urged.

'I can't leave you tomorrow!'

'Daisy will be here. And the nurse will look in.'

'It's much too soon. New mothers are supposed to have bed rest for… well, several weeks, aren't they?'

Anna laughed. 'Rich women, perhaps. Ordinary women have to get back on their feet quickly. They have to cook and clean, and look after their families.'

'It would be foolish to risk your recovery by getting up too soon,' Thea insisted.

'If I promise not to get up, will you go to London tomorrow? For my peace of mind as well as yours? You could call in on my mother to tell her about the baby and ask her to let me know urgently if a letter comes from Piers. I could give you money to leave with her. To pay for a telegram.'

'Not tomorrow.'

'The day after, then. I'm going to write to Piers's parents now. Shutting me out when they believed Piers was no longer alive was one thing. Refusing to see me when he's on his way back to me is quite another.'

'Tell them about James,' Daisy suggested.

'They had their chance to help James before he was born and they never took it. Piers should be the first to hear about James now,' Anna said firmly 'I'm going to tell them I'd like to know when Piers arrives and give them a note to pass to him.'

Anna saw Thea and Daisy exchange looks. 'You're thinking Piers might not be well enough to read a note. I haven't forgotten what Mr Acaster said about serious injuries and I'm prepared for whatever that means. But I believe in staying hopeful instead of assuming the worst.'

'That's a good attitude,' Thea approved. 'I'm going to heat some soup while you write your letters.'

'And I'll take them to the post box for you,' Daisy promised.

'Thank you. I need to write to my family too if you're not going to London tomorrow. Ma will be delighted to know she's a grandmother and the little ones will love being aunts and uncles.'

She began with her note to Piers.

My darling Piers,

No heart could have been thrilled with more joy than mine when I heard of your survival. Thank God! Thank God!

I know you're injured, though I don't know the details yet. Whatever the extent of your injuries we'll find a way to cope because we love each other. We might not have stood up in church to vow to love each other in sickness and in health but the commitment we made over the buttercup holds as good for me today as it did then.

She decided not to tell him about James until she could see him face to face and share the magical moment when he realised he was a father. She also wanted to be sure that he loved her and wanted to marry her free from the sense of obligation that might come from knowing they had a child. Not that Anna doubted him, but others clearly did.

Please get a message to me just as soon as you can and then we'll be together again.
Your devoted,
Anna x

She folded the letter and put it into an envelope which she sealed and addressed to Piers. Then she began her second letter.

Dear Mr and Mrs Rutherford,

Please accept my good wishes on the wonderful news of Piers's survival. We met briefly some weeks ago when I called at Ashfyld House and tried to introduce myself as Piers's fiancée. At that time, you were too consumed with grief to acknowledge me. However, now that Piers will be able to confirm the nature of our relationship, I trust that another attempt at an introduction will be more successful.

I enclose a note for Piers and should be grateful if you would pass it to him or have it read to him if you see him before I do. Would you let me know when he arrives?

Kind regards,

Anna Watson

Everything she'd written was true and, far from showing resentment at the way they'd treated her, she'd offered them an olive branch of peace. Whether they'd accept the olive branch remained to be seen.

Whether they'd pass her note on to Piers remained to be seen too. But surely they wouldn't be so dishonourable as to keep it from him?

Having done all that she could for the moment regarding the Rutherfords, Anna settled down to write to her mother and the children, assuring them she was well and describing James, from his shell-like fingernails to his soft gold hair. She sighed with regret when she thought of the impossibility of her family rushing down to Brighton to visit but, with luck, it wouldn't be too long before she could introduce them to James.

Afterwards Anna ate her bread and soup then settled down to sleep. Despite all she'd endured during the birth her mind was too full for sleep to come easily but she drew long slow breaths until she finally floated away.

The next morning Thea insisted it was still too soon to leave Anna but finally agreed to go to London on the following day if all remained well. Doctor Maddox and a nurse called in but otherwise the day passed quietly.

When morning came Thea was still hesitant about leaving but Anna insisted. 'I'll fret with anxiety if you don't go.'

'All right, but I shan't be away for long.'

Thea kissed baby James's head as he lay in Anna's doting arms then rushed off to catch a train.

Returning some hours later, Thea came straight upstairs and Anna saw from her carefully neutral expression that she hadn't had a successful trip. 'You didn't see Jessie?' Anna asked.

'I'm afraid she and her father had moved on. The landlady said they'd been arguing a lot so Jessie might still realise I'm offering the best chance for her to get away. I left a note for her but the landlady wasn't hopeful of seeing her to pass it on.'

'I'm sorry.'

'You've nothing to be sorry for. I don't regret staying here for James's birth. How could I? He's a darling.' Thea leaned over the cradle and smiled at the sleeping child but Anna knew she must be worried sick inside.

'Have you any news?' Thea asked.

'I've had a letter from Ma and the children but nothing from Piers's parents.'

'They might be away from home.'

'They might,' Anna agreed, or they might be taking time to decide how to respond. 'If you're wondering where Daisy is, she's downstairs making supper.'

'Oh dear. I'd better go down and try to save it from incineration.'

Burnt or not, Anna would eat it. She needed to be strong again. Not only so she could cope with a new baby and Piers's injuries, but also so she could help Thea to get back on the trail of Jessie Jarrold.

Thirty-Three

Daisy felt guilty about taking time away from Clarendon Place but four days had passed since James's birth and Thea had insisted that Daisy should have some time to herself on the following day. 'Surely it's more important that you try to find Jessie?' Daisy had argued, because Jessie hadn't replied to the note Thea had left with her landlady.

Perhaps Jessie hadn't received the note because she'd left the area. Or perhaps she'd curled her lip over it and thrown it into the fire.

'You can't give up on saving your house,' Daisy had added.

'I'm not giving up. If you can describe Rose to me I'm going to wait outside Wainwrights tomorrow and ask if she knows Jessie's new address. But Rose will be at work until later so there's no need for you to spend all day cooped up inside.'

'Would you like me to see Rose for you?' Daisy had offered.

'Thank you, but Anna suggested that it's time I met her myself.'

'Good idea.' It couldn't hurt for Rose to see the person who needed help face to face. It might stir her conscience.

Hoping Rory would be free to see her, Daisy had gone out to telephone him only to pace up and down in front of the telephone kiosk, gripped by uncertainty. Yes, he'd told her she could find him at the Mermaid but perhaps that was the sort of thing he said to lots of girls. Perhaps he kissed their cheeks too. Moving around the country from racecourse to racecourse must be a lonely sort of life, after all.

What if he already had plans to take out another girl? Daisy would be mortified.

She walked away, deciding to spare herself from humiliation. But then she walked back, deciding it was cowardly to be so afraid of embarrassment that she'd miss out on—

Daisy wasn't sure what she might miss out on, but at the very least it was the chance of a wonderful day out.

She made the call, but still felt nervous as she waited for the Exchange to put her through to the Mermaid. Rory might not be staying there any more, of course, but just in case he did come to the phone Daisy was determined to sound casual instead of desperate, as though it might be pleasant to spend time with him but hardly heart-breaking if—

'The top of the morning to you, Daisy Flowers.' It was Rory's voice. 'I'm glad you called.'

'Are you?' Oh, dear. How unsophisticated she sounded.

'To be sure I am. I hope you're calling to tell me you can keep me company on a little adventure?'

'I have some time free tomorrow.'

'Grand. Where shall we meet?'

'Beside the pier?' Daisy suggested.

'The perfect place. Ten o'clock?'

'The perfect time.' Daisy was glad to feel she'd been clever with her answer for once. 'Where are we going? It's just that I have to be back by five.'

'Didn't I say we should go on the high seas in a boat?'

The paddle steamer from Eastbourne. 'I'd like that,' Daisy confirmed.

She wondered what she should say next, having no experience of ending a telephone call to a man who was taking her out. Having little experience of telephone calls in general. 'I'll see you tomorrow,' she said, and put the phone down only to wish she'd had the presence of mind to say goodbye.

Hopefully, Rory wouldn't take offence. He wasn't the stuffy sort.

'What are you planning to do with your time off?' Anna asked her later.

Daisy bent over to admire baby James and hide her blush. 'I'm hoping to go to Eastbourne. They have paddle steamers there.'

'That sounds lovely.'

'Eastbourne isn't so far on the bus,' Thea said.

Daisy simply reached out to stroke James's podgy little hand.

Wearing her Sunday best dress of dusky pink, Daisy arrived at the pier five minutes early but ten o'clock came and went, and there was no sign of Rory. Five past, ten past, a quarter past… perhaps he wasn't coming. Daisy's disappointment was crushing.

But here he came in the red Aston Martin. Relief made Daisy feel she might float off into space.

Rory drew the car into the kerb and leaned out through the window. 'Jump in.'

She ran round to the passenger's side and got in beside him.

'We've got a fine day for a boat trip,' Rory said, and Daisy agreed.

It was only as they were walking along the pier to board the boat that she was stricken with sudden doubt. She'd never been on a boat before. What if she were to be sea sick? It would be a terrible thing to disgrace herself in front of Rory.

She studied the water warily. It wasn't rough but neither was it still.

'Come on!' Rory had got ahead of her.

Deciding she'd just have to hope for the best, Daisy rushed to catch him up only to feel puzzled when she realised a section of the pier was sloping downwards. 'A storm washed part of the pier away and this is how they've mended it,' Rory explained.

A storm strong enough to wash a pier away? If a storm blew up today…

Rory laughed. 'You'll be fine, Daisy Flowers.'

She *was* fine. In fact, she loved every aspect of the boat trip along the coast to Brighton – the salty air, the breeze ruffling her hair, the raucous screeching of gulls overhead and, of course, the views of the coastline they passed. There were towns, villages, beaches and, in time, Brighton itself. It was fun to pick out the white-painted buildings in Thea's part of town, the domes of the Pavilion, the clock beside the aquarium and, further along, the smart Grand and Metropole Hotels.

Most of all, she enjoyed Rory's company and didn't mind at all when he laughed at her enthusiasm for everything she saw because his laughter was accompanied by warm looks from those dancing blue eyes. 'You're entertaining company for a jaded old jockey like me,' he said, and Daisy felt delight sparkle inside her.

Not that he was either jaded or old. He wasn't the tallest or biggest man on the boat but he had to be the most noticeable with his natty checked suit and easy, loose-limbed confidence. Even men stepped out of his way as though it were the natural thing to do. As for women, Daisy didn't miss the admiring looks they sent his way and she wondered again why he'd chosen to spend time with an ordinary girl like her. Perhaps he'd had his fill of sophisticated girls.

Some passengers alighted in Brighton. Others got on and the boat set off to return to Eastbourne.

'That was wonderful,' Daisy told him, when they finally stepped back onto Eastbourne pier.

'We should take another trip one day. We could go to the Isle of Wight or even across to France. Have you ever been to France?'

'I've never even been to London.'

'So young! So innocent! So delightfully fresh! You've got a lot to look forward to, Daisy.'

She wondered if he'd suggest a date for another trip but life as a jockey meant he didn't always know in advance when he'd be free.

'We should have something to eat,' he said.

When he took her arm and guided her away from the harbour she guessed he had the Sombre Sailor in mind. Not fancying eating in a bar filled with smoke, Daisy nodded towards the Harbour Café. 'That looks a nice place.'

Rory hesitated, and for a moment she thought he'd disagree but he glanced down at her face and her hopeful expression appeared to amuse him.

'There's a menu card in the window,' Daisy pointed out. 'We don't have to go inside if you don't like the look of it.'

They walked over. 'Beef, tongue, eggs, ham, soup… It sounds lovely,' Daisy said.

'If you think it sounds lovely, then lovely it must be,' Rory declared.

A pretty waitress came over as they settled at a table. 'What do you recommend for a jockey who needs to watch his weight,' Rory asked, smiling up at her.

'You ride horses?' she asked, impressed.

'He might be Champion Jockey soon,' Daisy said, not wanting to feel left out, though the waitress's gaze remained on Rory.

He winked at her. 'Serve us a good lunch and I'll give you some tips for the races.'

The waitress laughed. 'My dad would kill me if I put a bet on with a bookie.'

'Your dad wouldn't need to know.'

'Get away with you,' she said, then got down to business. 'The ham's looking tasty.'

'Then I'll have the ham,' Rory said. 'With eggs, please.'

Daisy ordered the same.

'Would you like tea with it?' the waitress asked.

Daisy nodded but Rory grimaced. 'I suppose whisky would be too much to hope for?'

'I'm afraid it would.'

'Then I'd like water, please.'

Daisy ate her meal hungrily but Rory merely pushed most of his food around the plate.

'I'll never be Champion Jockey if I'm weighing the poor horses down,' he explained.

'You're very dedicated.'

'I have to be. I want to win. And I want to restore the fortunes of Castle Kerwig.'

'What's Castle Kerwig like?'

'The most beautiful house on God's good earth.' He described ivy-clad walls, vast rooms with high ceilings, immense fireplaces, windows twice as tall as a man and a tower from which a person could see for miles. 'Thirty-two rooms in all,' he said.

'Thirty-two?' Daisy's cottage in Pixfield only had four.

'Acres of parkland with the greenest grass you've ever seen. As for the views across the Atlantic Ocean… you don't know what a beautiful sunset is until you've been to Castle Kerwig.'

It was with regret that Daisy finally reminded him she needed to return to Brighton. Rory didn't argue but called for the bill. She reached for her bag, wondering if she should contribute but Rory looked amused when she suggested it. 'Certainly not,' he said.

'But you paid for the paddle steamer and you need all your money for restoring Castle Kerwig.'

'The house needs a lot more money than the price of a plate of ham.'

Rory took her arm as they walked back to the car and it felt delicious. He opened the passenger door for her but before Daisy could get in said, 'Wait.'

She turned towards him, wondering what was wrong. Nothing, it seemed. Rory put his hands on her shoulders and drew her closer. He smiled down at her and Daisy's heart beat faster. Lowering his head, he touched his lips to hers and began to kiss her. It wasn't at all the sort of kiss a man gave to a mere friend.

He grinned at Daisy's flushed face when the kiss was over. 'You can get in the car now,' he laughed.

Daisy got into the passenger seat, wanting to touch a fingertip to her mouth to see if the kiss had left its mark, but knowing she'd only look hopelessly naive. She moved her lips together instead. They felt soft and swollen.

He said little on the journey though he cast amused looks in her direction from time to time. 'It's been a grand day but now it's time for you to wish me well on my travels,' he said, as he pulled up beside the pier.

'Travels?' Daisy felt a pang of dismay.

'I'm driving north later. I have races to ride.'

'Of course. You'll never be Champion Jockey and restore Castle Kerwig if you don't ride in races.'

'Indeed. Do you need me to—'

'I can open the door.' Daisy got out of the car. Would he tell her how long he'd be away and when she might expect to see him again?

He only raised his hand in a mock salute and drove off. Daisy walked back along Marine Parade hoping he'd return soon and not be distracted by pretty girls in the meantime.

The major was walking up the steps to Thea's door when she turned into Clarendon Place. He'd rapped out a knock before she could reach him to tell him she had a key.

Thea opened the door and Ralph stood aside to let Daisy enter first. 'I'll put the kettle on for you,' Daisy whispered, expecting Ralph would be staying to tea again.

Squeezing past, she accidentally nudged the hall table and the books that had been standing on it fell sideways, exposing the *Vacancies* sign that she'd stuffed behind them. Pausing to rearrange them, Daisy saw that the sign had caught the major's eye. A puzzled frown cut a line between his brows but then the meaning of the sign sank in and his eyes widened in shock.

'Thea?' His voice was incredulous. 'Are you running some sort of… *boarding house* here?'

Oh, heck. What had she done now? Daisy looked at Thea, wondering if she should make herself scarce, and received a small nod. With that Daisy glided hastily away.

Thirty-Four

'Come and sit down, Ralph,' Thea invited, walking into the drawing room and gesturing to a chair.

'Thea, I'm concerned.'

'So I see. But it needn't stop you from sitting down.' She was trying to tease him out of his shock.

It wasn't working but at least he came in and sat. Sitting opposite him, Thea braced herself to tell him the truth. 'I'm running a guest house because I need the income.'

'I hadn't realised. I suppose I'd just assumed…'

'That my parents had left me well off?'

'Comfortably circumstanced, at least.'

'It wasn't their fault.'

'I suppose that man your mother married was responsible. But you didn't have to hide your circumstances from me, Thea.'

'I didn't hide them precisely. I'm sure you've been here when the sign was in the window.'

'I never noticed it.'

Why should he have noticed it when it had never crossed his mind that she should need to let rooms? Thea was being unfair. Even if she hadn't precisely hidden her situation, she hadn't been open about it either.

Ralph shook his head wonderingly. 'To think you should be reduced to—'

'Earning a living?' Thea smiled. 'Millions of people earn their livings, Ralph. You're one of them.'

'That's different.'

'Because you're a man and I'm a woman?'

The question flustered him. 'Many women earn their livings, I know. But not… not…'

'Women of my social class?'

'You're making me feel like a crashing snob but yes. You weren't brought up to it.'

'Needs must.'

'You're very brave.'

'Not really. In fact I'm lucky in having help.'

'Your staff?'

'Anna and Daisy aren't staff. They're partners. Friends.'

'Yes, but…' He shook his head as though it didn't matter what she called them. 'Thea, I know it isn't my place to interfere.'

'It isn't,' she told him gently.

'Not yet, perhaps. We've only just renewed our acquaintance so it's far too soon, but one day I hope…' He took a deep breath, clearly trying to order his thoughts. 'It might not be proper for you to accept help from me, but from my parents… old friends of your mother's… just to tide you over.'

Until he married her? Thea enormously flattered by his interest and honoured too because Ralph was thoroughly decent. Some men might have looked down on her and her reduced circumstances. Ralph wanted only to help her.

Thea was fond of him in return. Perhaps she might even come to love him but he was right when he said it was too soon and, just now, she had too much on her mind to think clearly about a possible future with him.

In the meantime it felt more important than ever to remain independent of him. Already Ralph was trying to rush to her rescue. It was noble of him, but chivalry on his part and obligation on hers were hardly firm foundations for marriage. They also stung Thea's pride.

'I'm grateful, Ralph, but I can't accept money even from your mother.'

'But—'

'I'll consider it a kindness if you drop the subject.'

He looked keen to argue further but Ralph was a gentleman. 'If you change your mind—'

'I'll let you know.'

'Or let my mother know if that would feel more comfortable.'

'Thank you. I'm afraid I can't offer you tea today because I have to go out.'

'I didn't come for tea but to extend an invitation from Bunny and Charlotte Catchpole. Remember them from the dinner party? They're holding a tennis party on Sunday. It's early in the year for tennis but they're keen to shake off the winter. You're free, I hope?'

'I can't commit yet.' And perhaps she shouldn't commit anyway. Slowing things down with Ralph felt like a good idea though his crestfallen look tugged at her conscience. 'Might I let you know?'

'Of course. Don't worry about tennis clothes. Charlotte told me she has plenty.' He got to his feet and Thea showed him to the door.

He paused, looking at her warmly, then leaned over to kiss her cheek. 'Remember I'm your friend, Thea. If I can help in any way…'

She waited for him to walk down the steps then closed the door and leaned against it. She'd still told him nothing about her mother's so-called Will. Doubtless he'd argue forcefully that a solicitor should carry out enquiries into the witnesses and offer her money for the fee but Thea wouldn't have gone to a solicitor now even if she could have afforded the fee herself.

The situation needed more delicate handling. As things stood, the only way of proving that the witnesses had signed the Will fraudulently was through Jessie and, having met the girl, Thea was convinced that only personal appeal and tact would persuade her to help. If Thea ever got the chance to use them, that was.

On that thought Thea ran upstairs to get ready to see Jessie's friend, Rose. Daisy called her into Anna's room. 'We've been talking and we agree I should come with you to see Rose,' Daisy said. 'At the very least I can point her out to you.'

Thea opened her mouth to protest but Anna cut her off. 'You can see how well I am. You can see I'm coping with James. We can be left alone for an hour or two.'

Anna's dark eyes were determined. What a strong person she was. 'All right,' Thea conceded. 'We shan't be out for long.'

They hastened to Wainwrights and stood waiting for the staff to emerge. 'That's her,' Daisy pointed.

Rose sighed when she saw them. 'I've nothing to say,' she told them. 'Jessie offered help but you didn't bother to see her. You can't expect her to jump to attention to suit your convenience.'

'I don't expect that,' Thea said. 'I was all set to go to London when a friend went into labour prematurely. The baby was born very swiftly at my house. I couldn't leave.'

'It's true,' Daisy said. 'Thea *had* to stay and help.'

'Humph.' Rose's hostility abated but only a little.

'Jessie has changed address again but you know where she is,' Thea guessed.

'What makes you think that?'

'How else would you know I didn't keep my appointment with her?'

Rose looked annoyed with herself for slipping up but Thea also sensed the beginnings of grudging respect.

'There'll be countless moves for Jessie unless she breaks free of her father,' Thea said. 'I may be able to help to get her father out of the picture. Would you deny Jessie that opportunity because I was prevented from keeping an appointment by an emergency?'

Rose glowered, as though she wished she could think of a clever answer but couldn't manage it. 'Jessie is upset. You got her hopes up then let her down.'

'My hopes were high too.'

Rose thought for a moment. 'All right. I'll tell Jessie what you've told me, but I'm not telling you where she is.'

Thea swallowed down frustration and nodded. 'Please tell her I hope to hear from her soon for both of our sakes. Thank you for listening.'

Rose walked away.

'If Jessie doesn't write soon, I'll just have to go back up to London and try to find her,' Thea said to Daisy.

'I'll look after the house. I won't need any more time off for a while.'

'You should visit your father soon. He must be missing you.'

'I miss him too but he won't mind waiting for a visit. Tough as old boots, is my dad.'

The next day Anna got dressed and declared herself ready to take up the reins of everyday life. Thea had to admit that Anna looked well and was coping with James as though she'd looked after babies all her life. Which she had, when you took her brothers and sisters into account.

'I'm moving back into the attic room and we should put the *Vacancies* sign in the window.' Anna said. 'You've already lost money by closing to paying guests. It would be silly to lose more money for no good reason, especially as more people are coming to Brighton now the weather's improving.'

'Let's see how you get on today before we put the sign in the window,' Thea cautioned, thinking that it would indeed be useful to have some money coming in but not at the expense of Anna's health.

'I'll be sensible,' Anna assured her. 'I shan't run up and down stairs, or attempt any cleaning, but I can still make myself useful in the kitchen. I can peel vegetables and do the ironing sitting down, and I'll take things carefully when I stand.'

The post brought Anna a letter from Mr Acaster. Piers would be in England in less than a week and Mr Acaster believed he'd be going straight to his parents' home.

'It doesn't look as though they're going to write back to me so I'm going to write to Piers directly,' Anna announced.

'Would you address the envelope, Thea? Just in case his parents recognise my handwriting and destroy it.'

'I'll be glad to,' Thea said.

The afternoon brought another visit from Ralph. He came in carrying a basket of carrots, potatoes and spring greens. 'A gift from my mother. Our gardener has grown more than we can possibly consume, and when I mentioned I'd be calling…'

Ralph was trying to help her and Thea hadn't the heart to decline the gift. 'How kind. You'll thank your mother for me? Your gardener too? But please don't worry that I'm not coping. I am.'

'I'm sure. Do you want to call your girl to take these? Dolly, isn't it?'

'Daisy, but I'll take them down to the kitchen myself. Anna's cooking tonight. She's recovering well.'

'I'm pleased to hear it.'

Thea hesitated then said, 'She's had some wonderful news. Her fiancé was missing, presumed dead, but he's been found alive and he's on his way back to England.'

'Fiancé? I thought… I understood she was a widow. She wears a ring. A wedding band.'

'That's my grandmother's ring.'

'Good Lord. And now she has a child.'

An illegitimate child, born under Thea's roof. 'Please don't judge her, Ralph. And please don't judge me for taking her in.'

'I'm not judging *you*, Thea! Taking her in was a testament to your good nature.'

'I certainly hope so but don't make the mistake of thinking it was a naïve decision. I knew some people would be shocked. We both did. That's why Anna took the name of Mrs Rutherford. I suppose that might be considered a deception but, frankly, Anna's marital status is no one's business except hers. And Piers's, of course.'

'Piers? He's the man who— Good God, you don't mean Piers Rutherford?'

'The explorer,' Thea confirmed.

'But he's… he's…'

'A different social class? I think that's something else that's their business and no one else's.'

'I can't see the Rutherfords sharing that point of view.'

'Perhaps not. But Piers is a grown man and capable of making his own decisions.'

The look on Ralph's face gave Thea a moment of unease. Anna couldn't have been mistaken in Piers, could she? Surely she was too intelligent and sensible to have been taken in by a man whose flowery compliments were simply cynical ploys to persuade her to succumb to his charms? Thea had every respect for Anna's judgement but there was no denying that Anna *had* succumbed to his charms and borne a child as a result. Oh, heavens.

'What sort of man is Piers Rutherford?' Thea asked.

'I can't say I know him well. We attended different schools then I went to Sandhurst for officer training while he… I'm not sure what he did, actually. We've crossed paths the way one does at parties and balls, but I don't recall exchanging more than a few words with him.'

Which meant that Ralph couldn't judge Piers as a man. Thea hoped so anyway, though she couldn't shift the unease completely.

'I must get to an appointment,' Ralph said.

Thea showed him to the door. 'I'll write to your mother to thank her for the vegetables.'

'She'd like that. But I'd be grateful if… My mother is of a different generation. Her views on life are… traditional.'

'You'd rather I didn't mention Anna's marital status or Piers Rutherford,' Thea guessed.

'I'd consider it a favour. Does Anna's recovery mean you're able to come to the Catchpoles' tennis party on Sunday?'

'I'm still not sure. I really don't want Anna to overtax her strength. I could telephone you to let you know, but I'll quite understand if you'd prefer to invite a different guest.'

'I wouldn't. Prefer to take another guest, that is. I'll look forward to your call.' He kissed her cheek. 'I know you think you don't need help, but if you change your mind I hope you'll seek help from me.'

Encouraged by Anna and Daisy, Thea called Ralph to confirm she could go to the tennis party. 'But you need to understand that I won't lie to hide my circumstances,' she told him.

'Are you referring to your paying guests? Or to your girl, Amy? Your woman, I should say.'

'Her name is Anna,' Thea corrected. 'I'm referring to both. I'm not ashamed of my decisions or my situation, and I won't lie if they come up in conversation. I don't suppose they *will* come up, but it's only fair to warn you.'

'I appreciate your candour, and if they do happen to come up… Well, I hope people will agree that you're being terribly brave.'

Thea wasn't brave. She was just making the best of an unfortunate situation.

The Catchpoles lived a short drive away through rolling green countryside. Their house was old and pretty with large gardens. As they got out of the car, Thea could hear distant voices and the thwack of a tennis ball.

A maid opened the door but Charlotte came into the hall, looking thrilled to see them. 'You go through, Ralph, seeing as you're already changed.'

Ralph was wearing white flannel trousers, white shirt and a cream jumper.

'Miss Fairfax – Thea – you come upstairs with me.'

Charlotte took Thea's arm and led her up a grand staircase then along a landing to a large bedroom. 'My cousin, Madge, is tall like you and won't mind at all if you borrow her dress.'

Charlotte crossed to a four poster bed and held up a white tennis dress on a satin-padded hanger. It was a pretty V-necked dress with small triangles of green fabric set between the panels of the skirt.

'Thank you, it's beautiful,' Thea told her.

'I've put out a cardigan too because it's chilly. And here's a scarf to tie around your forehead to stop your hair from falling into your eyes. There are several pairs of tennis shoes. Hopefully, you'll find your size amongst them. Come out when you're ready. We're at the back.'

The bedroom overlooked the rear gardens. Beyond them were trees between which Thea caught flashes of white tennis clothes.

'Thank you,' Thea said again.

Alone, she changed into the dress which fitted perfectly except in the length. It barely covered her knees but it would have to do. She put the white cardigan on over it, tied the scarf around her head, and found some shoes that fitted. Hoping Charlotte would also provide a racquet, Thea went downstairs where a maid waited to show her to the court.

There were twelve people present, all young and all welcoming. Thea's skirt was shorter than those worn by the other young women but Ralph's eyes glowed with pride at the sight of her so it couldn't have been scandalously short.

Fortunately, there were several spare racquets. 'I must apologise in advance if I play badly,' Thea said, testing the weight of several racquets before selecting one. 'It's been many years since I've been on a tennis court.'

It took her a while to find the rhythm of the game but once she'd found it she proved to be as good as any of the women. 'It's just that I'm tall and can reach the ball more easily,' she explained, when one of the men complimented her on a winning shot.

'It also has something to do with talent.' He smiled rather too warmly for his fiancée's liking and she gave his arm a possessive squeeze.

It appeared that Ralph had already explained that Thea had been living quietly due to her late mother's ill health because several people expressed condolences and the hope that they'd see more of her now. 'You'll find us a fun set of people,' one said, and Thea couldn't help wondering if this fun set of people would have been quite so welcoming if they'd known that she cooked and cleaned for paying guests.

There was no doubt in Thea's mind that there was a general expectation that her engagement to Ralph wasn't far away. Only one person appeared to be disappointed about the prospect. She was a young woman called Edith

Hale who was pretty in a quiet sort of way. 'You've known Ralph since you were children, I believe,' she asked Thea.

'Indeed, though we hadn't seen each other for years until recently. Have you known him long?'

'Not terribly long.'

But long enough to develop a soft spot for him. No wonder. Ralph was a fine-looking man. Kind and entertaining too. Poor Edith. Unrequited love must be terrible.

'I'll be away in London on business for the next few days,' Ralph told Thea as he drove her home. 'I'll be staying at the Camborne in Piccadilly. I wish I didn't have to go, but—'

'Needs must,' she finished, conscious of feeling relieved that she'd be free to concentrate on her own affairs without worrying that she was offending him.

Unless she heard from Jessie or Rose in the next day or two, she'd return to London and try to pick up Jessie's trail for herself. There was no danger of running into Ralph in the London slums. Perhaps she'd also make another attempt to find someone who knew of the other witness, Albert Strupp.

Thirty-Five

'Was it fun?' Anna asked when Thea returned from the tennis party looking flushed and lovely. Those green eyes were incredibly striking.

'More fun than expected actually. I fitted in surprisingly well.'

'You're a lady,' Anna told her. 'You're not haughty or anything like that. But you look elegant in whatever you wear. You're gracious and beautifully spoken too.'

'It's true,' Daisy agreed, but Thea only laughed and walked over to the basket in which James was sleeping. 'How has this lovely boy been behaving?'

Daisy joined her. 'He's hardly cried at all,' she reported proudly.

Watching them smiling down at James, Anna was tempted to ask them there and then to be his godparents. But Piers had missed out on so many aspects of fatherhood already that she wanted him to be involved in the arrangements for James's christening.

'We have two new paying guests,' Anna announced instead. 'The Misses Penfold. Elderly sisters. They want to stay for three nights.'

'Are they upstairs?' Thea asked.

'Out taking the air on the pier. But they'll be back for dinner.'

'Wonderful. I'll change my clothes then help to get the dinner ready.'

Thea sounded enthusiastic but Anna guessed her feelings must be as mixed as her own. The income from the Misses Penfold was a godsend as they couldn't live on air but their presence might limit Thea's chance to pursue her witnesses as well as Anna's chance to see Piers when he arrived home. Hopefully they'd manage with Daisy's help.

It was Anna's intention to keep James away from the paying guests but she chanced upon the Penfolds when they were out for another stroll the next day. James was in the perambulator she'd bought using some of Mr Acaster's money as she hadn't had to pay for the nursing home. She'd hoped to buy one second-hand but had seen none listed in the *Items for Sale* section of the local newspaper so had spent almost eight pounds on a new Harford model. At least she'd be able to sell it on after James outgrew it. Unless she had another baby by then, but she wasn't getting her hopes up about that. Only once she knew the facts about Piers's injuries would she picture the sort of future they might have.

'Look, sister, isn't he a beautiful baby?' the elder Miss Penfold said.

'Such an angel with all that golden hair,' the younger one agreed.

'He gets that from his father,' Anna told them.

'We haven't met your husband.'

'He's been away,' Anna explained. 'But he's on his way home.'

'You must be so happy, my dear.'

The Misses Penfolds exchanged wistful looks and Anna guessed that no men had ever come home to them. Knowing she was loved by Piers gave her a warm glow of gratitude. Anna had sensed that Thea and Daisy both had doubts about the strength of Piers's feelings after all this time but Anna was sure he *did* still love her. She knew him best, after all, and she was keeping faith with him.

'If there's no news of Piers by Tuesday, would you mind if I went up to London?' Thea asked, on Anna's return. 'I want to try to pick up a trail to Jessie. Daisy's willing to help out here.'

'Of course I don't mind,' Anna assured her, but the morning brought two visitors.

The first was Mr Acaster. 'I won't come in,' he said. 'I'm just calling to let you know that Piers has arrived home.'

Anna's heart gave a leap of excitement coupled with anxiety. 'Have you seen him? Is he well?'

'I went to Ashfyld House hoping to see him but his parents told me it's too soon for him to receive visitors when he's so exhausted from the journey. I did learn that he fractured both his skull and his pelvis.'

That sounded serious. Anna realised she must have paled because Mr Acaster reached out and patted her shoulder. 'Take heart, young lady,' he advised. 'He's survived thus far and been allowed to travel. Clearly, young Piers is made of strong stuff.'

'Thank you for calling in.'

'I'll let you know when I hear more.'

'That would be kind,' Anna told him.

She waved Mr Acaster off and returned downstairs to share the news with Thea and Daisy.

'That's wonderful!' they agreed, then Daisy glanced up through the window as the sound of a motorbike reached them.

'It's Max,' she reported.

Anna went to let him in and was taken aback by his sombre expression. 'Is Daisy downstairs?' he asked.

'Yes.'

Realising the situation was urgent, she didn't linger to ask him what was wrong but led the way to the kitchen. He walked over to Daisy and put a hand on each of her arms as though steadying her. 'Your dad's had an accident. You need to come.'

Daisy's face whitened. 'What sort of accident?'

'He was kicked by a horse.'

'And?' Daisy's voice rose higher. 'How badly is he hurt?'

'I don't know yet. Daniel called me and I agreed to come and get you before heading over there.'

'Go, Daisy,' Anna urged.

'Yes, go,' Thea echoed. 'Take some clothes, though. You may need to stay for a while.'

Daisy ran from the kitchen to pack.

Anna looked at Max in concern. 'You really don't know how badly Daisy's father is hurt? You weren't just being kind to Daisy?'

'I really don't know. Hopefully, I'll learn more soon.'

He noticed the cradle and walked over to smile down at baby James. 'It's going to be difficult for you two with Daisy away,' he predicted.

Anna and Thea exchanged glances. 'We'll manage,' Thea said, though Anna guessed that both of them were wondering how they'd cope with guests as well as spend time away from Clarendon Place – Thea to go to London and Anna to go to Ashfyld House now she knew Piers was there.

'I'll come back and tell you more just as soon as I can,' Max promised.

'We'd appreciate that.'

Daisy ran back in with clothes hanging out of a hastily stuffed bag. She hugged her friends, apologised for leaving them in the lurch then rushed outside. 'Come *on*, Max.'

Max nodded to Thea and Anna. 'Don't come up. I'll make sure the door's closed.'

Moments later they heard the motorbike drive off. 'You can still go to London, Thea,' Anna said.

James began to cry so she picked him up and rocked him in her arms.

'The Misses Penfold have requested lunch as well as dinner,' Thea pointed out. 'One of us will have to go to the shops to buy supplies. Then the meals will have to be cooked, the beds made, the rooms dusted and swept...'

And a two-week-old baby needed to be looked after too.

'Let's do as much as we can today and see what tomorrow brings,' Anna suggested.

Clarendon Place was sparkling by the time Max returned that evening. Furniture had been polished, floors swept, the bathroom cleaned and beds made-up while down in the kitchen there was enough food to last for two days apart from fresh milk which would be delivered by the milkman on his cart.

'Frank took a kick to the shoulder,' Max explained. 'It broke his collar bone and caused a lot of deep bruising. It'll take a while to heal but he's going to be fine.'

'Thank goodness,' Anna said.

Thea nodded. 'It must still have given Daisy a fright.'

Max grinned. 'She hasn't stopped fussing over Frank. I have to hand it to you two ladies. Daisy's domestic skills have improved while she's been with you though they've still a long way to go before they reach average. Still, there'll be no better incentive for Frank to get well than having to endure Daisy's cooking.'

He met their smiles with gleaming eyes but then his face sobered. 'Joking aside, Frank's going to need Daisy to stay and help him for a while. She told me the news about Piers. Are you hoping to go and see him, Anna?'

'If I can.'

'I could come over tomorrow and take you to the Rutherfords' house in the horsebox as long as I'm not out too long.'

'That's kind of you,' Anna said. 'Incredibly kind. But Thea needs to go to London.'

'I'm afraid I can't promise to be free any other time this week.'

'This is too good an opportunity to miss,' Thea said. 'I can go to London another day.'

'But the trails to your witnesses are growing colder,' Anna argued.

'At the moment I have no trails,' Thea pointed out. 'If Max takes you tomorrow, James can stay with me because you'll be back in no time.'

Thea was being sensible as always. If Anna had to make her own way to Ashfyld House it would take her hours and James would have to go with her because he'd need to be fed. She wanted to be alone the first time she saw Piers so she could gauge exactly how things stood, but—

'I insist,' Thea said, then turned to Max. 'What time can you be here?'

'Eleven o'clock,' he told her. 'After morning stables.'

Anna's head felt icy-cool and determined when Max helped her up into the horsebox the following day but her stomach squeezed with nerves.

'Why hasn't Piers written back?' a voice whispered in her ear.

Because he might not be well enough to write, of course. Or he might have written only to have his letters intercepted by his parents.

'Ah,' the voice argued, 'but Piers knows his parents and their snobbery. Why hasn't he asked someone he could trust to write on his behalf or post his own letter?'

Ask whom exactly? The servants were in his parents' pay. Presumably, so too were any doctors and nurses who were attending him.

'Humph,' the voice dismissed. 'You've been apart for almost nine months. Feelings change.'

Anna blew out hard as though to rid herself of the voice as well as air.

Max glanced across at her. 'You should keep faith with Piers until you hear from his own lips about any change of heart,' he advised.

'I will,' Anna assured him.

She asked him to park the horsebox in the lane then walked to the house alone. She'd been in a state of wretchedness the last time she'd passed down this drive but she was stronger now

A maid answered the door. The same maid as before.

'I'm here to see Mr Piers,' Anna told her, tilting her chin proudly and investing her voice with confidence.

Recognition dawned in the maid's eyes. 'I'm afraid Mr Piers isn't receiving visitors.'

Had she been warned that Anna in particular should be denied entry? 'He'll want to see me,' Anna insisted. 'Please tell him I'm here. My name is Anna Watson.'

'I can't do that.'

'Then I'm afraid you have a problem because I'm not going anywhere until I've seen him.'

The maid must have realised Anna was serious because she sighed and said, 'Wait here, Miss.'

The door closed in Anna's face. A minute passed. Two minutes. Three…

The door opened again and Mrs Rutherford stood there, nostrils flaring and eyes flashing as though launching daggers. 'This is an outrage.'

'I apologise for imposing but I need to see Piers,' Anna said, calmly. 'If I could see him anywhere else I'd do so, but he hasn't replied to my letters and—'

'Of course he hasn't replied to your letters. He doesn't *want* to reply to them. This persistence proves only that you don't know my son at all. He's fastidious. And when he finally marries… Well!'

It wouldn't be to a woman like Anna.

'Please leave before I have the gardener remove you by force,' Mrs Rutherford continued. 'If you come here again, I'll call the police.'

The nostrils flared anew as a vehicle came down the drive. Turning to look, Anna saw that it was a large, chauffeur-driven car. It came to a halt on the sweep of gravel in front of the house and the chauffeur leapt out to help his passenger to alight. She was young and pretty, dressed exquisitely in a lacy cream dress with pearls at her throat.

Mrs Rutherford glared at Anna and made shooing gestures with her hands before walking forward to greet the new arrival. 'Lavinia, dearest. How good of you to come and keep our poor invalid company.'

The girl noticed Anna and whispered something Anna couldn't hear. 'She's no one,' Mrs Rutherford told her guest, ushering her into the house and closing the door abruptly to leave Anna outside, abandoned and alone.

Thirty-Six

Daisy still felt guilty despite Max pouring scorn on the reason for her troubled conscience. 'I shouldn't have said it,' she'd muttered, when he'd driven her home from Brighton.

'Said what?'

'That Dad could wait for a visit because he was as tough as old boots.'

'You're not suggesting that there's some sort of mystical connection between Frank's accident and what you said?'

'I was tempting fate.'

'Nonsense.'

'You're Irish. You're supposed to believe in mystical things.'

'I don't even believe in leprechauns,' Max told her. 'You shouldn't either. Stop being fanciful.'

Daisy had been tempted to scowl but very real anxiety over her father had prevented her from doing anything so frivolous.

Their neighbour, Mrs Beddows, had been in the cottage when they'd arrived. 'Where's Dad?' Daisy demanded.

'Upstairs.'

Daisy raced up to her father's bedroom and found him in bed, propped up against pillows. His face wasn't white exactly – he was too much of an outdoors man to lose colour quickly – but he looked drained and pinched with pain. Daisy let out a small gasp and ran to hug him only to come to a sudden halt as she realised that hugging an injured man might not be a good idea. 'Dad, I'm so sorry you're hurt.'

'It's hardly your fault, girl.'

'I'm here to look after you anyway.'

'Oh dear. I'll brace myself, shall I?'

Daisy was tempted to give him a playful punch but that too was probably a bad idea. Still, it was good to know Frank hadn't lost his sense of humour. He reached for her hand. 'It's nice to see you, girl, but I'm sorry to tear you away from your Brighton friends.'

'Can't be helped,' Daisy said brightly. 'They understand you have to come first just now.'

'Hopefully, it won't be for long.'

'What has the doctor said?'

Frank told her about the broken bone and bruising. 'I'll mend,' he said, but clearly his recovery would take time. 'I'm lucky it wasn't worse and I'm lucky in having good neighbours. Daniel's been a rock.'

Daisy forced a smile.

'He was the one who found me and got the doctor out. He arranged for Mrs Beddows to keep an eye on me until you got here, and he's gone to see a young farrier he knows who might be able to help out in the forge to keep the urgent work ticking over.'

'How kind.'

Frank looked behind Daisy to Max who'd followed her upstairs. 'Thanks for fetching the prodigal daughter home.'

'It was the least I could do. How are you feeling?'

'You know what it's like to be on the receiving end of a kick.'

'I do.' Max had had his share of kicks, falls and bites over the years.

'Which horse kicked you?' Daisy asked.

'Jim Barker's Geoffrey.'

'He's always difficult. If I'd been here to hold his head, he might not have—'

'Don't start,' Max and Frank chorused.

'If you're going to bully me, I'm going to talk to Mrs Beddows.'

Daisy kissed her father's cheek and went down to the kitchen. 'You needn't worry about supper because I've got a stew ready for you,' Mrs Beddows said. 'Best beef from the butcher and vegetables from Daniel who's promised to bring more when you need them. No one grows better vegetables than Daniel. I'll get off home now you're here, Daisy. You know where to find me if you need help.'

Daisy walked her to the door, thanking her for the help she'd already given. Max left soon afterwards, promising to call in on Thea and Anna to give them the news.

Frank dozed much of the evening away, his sleeping features craggy but tugging love out of Daisy's heart every time she looked at him.

The next morning was spent quietly too but during the afternoon Frank said, 'Enough hovering over me. Go out and get some fresh air, girl. I shan't get into trouble lying here.'

Daisy hesitated then rushed to get ready though it wasn't eagerness to enjoy the air that made her hasten into the village but eagerness to reach the post box. It was unbearable to think that Rory might return to Brighton and be unable to find her. She'd told him Thea's address but had he remembered it? Fearing he might give up on her and turn his attention to some other girl, Daisy decided to write to explain what had happened.

Not knowing where he was staying, she wrote four letters and addressed them to Rory at Brighton's Grand Hotel and Mermaid Inn, at Brighton racecourse and at the house of the friends he'd mentioned – the Morrells. She spent an agonising few minutes trying to remember their address – something to do with monks? – but finally recalled the house name of Friarsgate, in or around Plumpton though she didn't know the name of the road. A grand house might be known to the postman anyway. There was no guarantee that any of the letters would find Rory as he might be away riding anywhere in the country but Daisy would hope for the best.

She reached the post box, took the letters from her pocket and paused to kiss the topmost one before sliding them into the slot. Turning, she saw Daniel Oaks approaching with his children.

Hot colour scalded her face though she'd done nothing wrong. He'd done nothing wrong either. There were envelopes in his hand so he was here for the perfectly valid purpose of posting them.

There was no doubt in her mind that he'd seen her kiss that topmost letter. If he mentioned it to her father or Max, Daisy would never hear the end of the teasing.

Appallingly embarrassed but trying to hide it, she smiled at the children – Lily, a pretty girl of about six, and Jack, a good-looking boy who was two or three years older. Finally, she looked into Daniel's eyes. 'Thank you for helping my father.'

He shrugged as though he'd done nothing much. 'I'll be over tomorrow with Joseph, the lad who might be able to help in the forge while your father's laid up.'

'Thank you,' Daisy said again. 'Well, I'll…'

Daniel nodded to show he knew she was trying to say goodbye.

She walked back down the lane, still cringing in embarrassment but telling herself that it was actually a good thing for Daniel to know she had a romantic interest in someone else as it would draw a line under his own advances. To be fair, he'd shown no resentment at being rejected. Perhaps he too had realised they wouldn't have suited.

He arrived at the forge the following day bringing the children and also Joseph, a tall, lanky young man who worked with his farrier uncle. Frank insisted on coming downstairs and sat in an armchair propped up by cushions. Daisy pulled chairs around for the other two men. Feeling she had to say something, she repeated her thanks for everything Daniel had done.

'It's what friends and neighbours are for,' he answered pleasantly.

'I'm grateful anyway.'

She turned away to make tea as the men talked about Joseph's experience and agreed he'd work three days each week for Frank, sleeping at Daniel's.

'We've brought a basket for you,' Lily told Daisy, all waves of thistledown fair hair and vivid blue eyes.

'Vegetables?' Daisy asked.

'And herbs to help your dad. Like comfrey for healing.' Lily placed the basket on the table. 'My dad helps people to get better. Animals too.'

'So I've heard,' Daisy said with a smile. Daniel Oaks had developed quite a reputation for healing through natural lotions and potions though he was neither a doctor nor a vet. 'Would you like some milk?'

She poured milk for both children.

'May I see the chickens?' Jack asked.

'Of course.'

'Jack loves animals,' Lily confided when he'd gone.

'Don't you?'

'Of course. I love flowers too. You suit the name of Daisy.'

'Really?'

'It's because you're as pretty and fresh as the daisies in our paddock.'

'What a lovely thing to say. You're a pretty girl with a pretty name too.'

'You should wear daisies in your hair when you marry that man,' Lily said.

Suddenly self-conscious, Daisy was tempted to look around to be sure no one was listening but feared she might only draw attention to herself.

'I mean the man whose letter you kissed,' Lily explained.

'That didn't mean... Goodness, Lily, I've no plans to marry soon.'

'But when you do get married you should wear daisies.'

'Perhaps I will.' Daisy was keen to change the subject. 'How's your pony?'

The visitors didn't stay long after they'd drunk the tea she'd made. Daisy settled down for another quiet evening and was glad when Frank fell into a doze because it allowed her to lapse into thought. She wondered how Thea and Anna were getting on without her. She'd done the right thing in coming home but still felt guilty over letting her friends down. Hopefully, they'd write to her soon.

Would Rory write too? Daisy suspected he'd consider letter-writing to be dull but surely he'd write her a line or two just to let her know he understood why she was here? If he received any of her letters, that was.

A sound out in the lane roused her. It was Max on his motorbike. 'This is just a quick visit,' he said.

He exchanged a few words with Frank then drew Daisy outside.

Her heartbeat skittered wildly. Had he news of Rory? A message from him, perhaps?

'Anna went to Piers's house but his parents wouldn't let her in,' Max reported. 'They told her Piers didn't want to see her.'

'Poor Anna!' Daisy was outraged on her friend's behalf. 'Does she—'

'Believe it? She says she'll believe Piers has lost interest in her only when she hears it from Piers himself.'

'Good for her. But how is she going to get to see him?'

'That's one of the reasons I'm here,' Max said. 'I have a plan for helping her.'

Thirty-Seven

Thea was finding it hard to resist the feeling that she was wasting her time. She'd delayed coming to London for an extra day because James had been fractious and she'd wanted to be sure he wasn't sickening for anything. He'd been fine today and Thea had travelled here fired with purpose. But she'd knocked on door after door in Roper Street and the surrounding streets and been given no information at all to point her in the direction of Jessie.

She reached the end of Embry Street and paused to summon the energy to continue. A group of four boys ran past her and into Roper Street. They'd made a cart out of a wooden packing case lashed to a set of old perambulator wheels and were taking turns to ride it, pushed from behind by the others. An idea took root in Thea's head and she walked towards them.

'Excuse me,' she called, and four urchin faces turned towards her. 'I'm looking for Jessie Jarrold. She lived at number twenty for a short time. Do any of you know her?'

'Not me, Miss,' one said, eager to take his turn on the cart.

He pushed the shoulder of the boy who was already riding it. 'Shove off, Tommy. You've had your go.'

'I've only been down the street twice!'

All four boys had turned away to argue so Thea stepped into their line of vision and took out her purse. Suddenly she had the boys' complete attention. 'You might not know Jessie by name but perhaps you've seen her.'

Thea described Jessie in as much detail as she could remember. Three faces remained blank but Thea saw recognition dawn in the face of the boy the others had called Pip. 'Walks around like a cat who wants to spit at you for treading on its tail?' he asked, and proceeded to demonstrate what he meant by walking up and down with a pursed-up mouth and eyes that glared with accusation.

'Perhaps,' Thea told him, thinking that it wouldn't be surprising if Jessie's precarious way of living had made her bitter.

'I've seen her,' Pip said, his gaze dropping to Thea's purse.

'Recently?'

He thought about it and appeared to be fighting a battle between honesty and the answer that might earn him a coin or two. 'I can't remember,' he finally admitted.

'If you find her for me, I'll give you a reward.'

'What sort of reward?'

'Half a crown.'

His eyes widened and Thea guessed he'd never owned as much as half a crown in his life. But his brain kept ticking over. 'Is that half a crown each, Miss? There's four of us, see?'

Oh, heavens.

'Four pairs of eyes looking for the hissing cat woman means we're four times more likely to find her,' he pointed out.

The hero-worship he'd win by enriching his friends wouldn't hurt his standing either. 'All right. Half a crown each if you find her. But she mustn't know you're looking for her so you need to be careful.'

'We can be careful,' Pip confirmed.

Thea had addressed several envelopes to herself and stamped them too. She passed one to Pip. 'There's a sheet of notepaper inside,' she explained. 'If you find her, I want you to write her new address on the notepaper and post it to me straight away. Can you write?'

Pip was insulted. 'We're not stupid, Miss. We learn reading, writing and reckoning at school.'

'Excellent. Keep the envelope safe, won't you?'

Pip gave her another look that told her he wasn't an idiot. 'Hang on, though, Miss. No disrespect, but how do we know you'll give us the money if you live…' He glanced at the address on the envelope. 'In Brighton. That's the seaside, ain't it?'

'If it makes you feel happier, let me give you a payment on account.'

She dug in her purse for four sixpences and handed them over. 'You'll have another two shillings each if you find Jessie. That's a promise.'

'This is how we seal promises on Roper Street,' Pip told her. He spat into his palm and held his hand out.

Hiding a grimace, Thea did likewise and shook his hand. 'I'm assuming you're clever boys so I hope to hear from you soon,' she said.

She walked away, smiling as she heard them talking in awed terms of their unexpected riches.

Catching the bus to Bermondsey, Thea spent a few minutes with Anna's mother sitting in the little parlour of her neighbour's house. 'You'll be glad to hear that Anna and baby James are well,' Thea said.

'Has she seen Piers?'

'Not yet.' Thea didn't explain that Anna had been turned away from the Rutherfords' door. No useful purpose would be served by making Mrs Watson anxious until Anna knew for certain how things stood.

Declining an offer of tea, Thea stood to leave. 'I'm sorry this is such a short visit.'

'It's good of you to visit at all,' Mrs Watson said.

With messages for Anna ringing in her ears, Thea caught another bus to Tea Street where the other witness, Albert Strupp, had lived. Having appointed Pip and his friends to look for Jessie, she wondered if she might find more young people willing to look for Mr Strupp.

She found two brothers called Fred and Mattie, and agreed the same terms with them as she'd agreed with Pip and friends. Not that she thought Fred and Mattie had much chance of locating Strupp. Neither boy remembered him so they'd have to base their enquiries on his name alone. It was a name he might well have shed in favour of an invented identity in the hope of outrunning his creditors but Thea was determined to leave no stone unturned.

Having done all she could for the moment, she headed for London Bridge station to catch the train back to Brighton. She was walking towards her platform when she saw a handkerchief fall from the sleeve of an elderly woman who was passing in the opposite direction.

Thea scooped it up and was about to call, 'Excuse me!' when her eye was caught by a man in the distance. He was standing with his back to her but something about his bear-like size and camel hair coat flashed an image of her stepbrother into her mind. Surely it wasn't…

She realised the elderly woman was getting away. Thea chased after her, restored the handkerchief then turned back to look for the man.

He was no longer there. Thea turned in a circle, scanning as much of the station as she could see but he was nowhere. Still, it was highly unlikely that the man had been Stanley Ambrose because he wasn't expected in England for another five weeks.

She moved towards her platform and tried to put him from her mind.

Thirty-Eight

Anna kissed the top of James's head and rocked him gently, hoping to soothe away any tension his instincts might be picking up from her.

'You don't need to be involved in this part of the plan,' Max had explained, but Anna felt there was every need.

Not because she had a part to play but because she was desperate to know if the plan would work and – if it *did* work – how things stood with Piers. Not that she doubted him even now.

Seeing nothing but indignity in trying to persuade Mrs Rutherford to admit her that day, Anna had walked away, blinking back tears but holding herself proudly. Max had taken one look at her face and guessed what had happened. 'You weren't allowed in?'

Anna had shaken her head and been grateful when Max hadn't pressed her for details. It was as they were re-entering Brighton that Anna recovered enough to say, 'I need to get inside the house.'

At exactly the same moment Max said, 'You need to get inside the house.'

They smiled at each other wryly. 'Actually, it doesn't have to be you who gets inside the house,' Max said then. 'In fact, you're the last person who should attempt it as the servants have probably been given instructions to watch out for you. Someone else will have a better chance.'

He paused then added, 'Thea might be the best person to—'

'Not Thea,' Anna told him firmly.

Thea was indeed the person most likely to be allowed through the front door of the Rutherfords' house. With her ladylike voice and bearing, the Rutherfords would doubtless think she moved in similar circles. But there was a complication. 'Her major knows the Rutherfords. It could make things awkward for her,' Anna explained.

Max's nod suggested he'd worked that out for himself. 'We need a different sort of plan.'

We? How kind he was to help her.

'Give me time and I'll think of something,' he promised.

It had been typical of Thea to be outraged on Anna's behalf when she heard of Mrs Rutherford's appalling behaviour. 'That woman is behaving like a jailer!' Thea said, green eyes flashing emerald-coloured sparks. 'Perhaps I could get in to see Piers. I'll speak to Ralph and —'

'Please don't,' Anna urged. 'I'm grateful, Thea. Truly grateful, but I'd be a poor friend in return if I made things difficult for you with the major.'

'Once I explain—'

'The Rutherfords won't take it kindly if he interferes. And if he goes behind their backs and they find out...'

'There'll be some awkwardness,' Thea admitted. 'But your future with Piers is more important.'

'Which is why we're coming up with an alternative plan,' Max said.

'Which is?'

'Well…' He ran a hand through his dark, springy hair. 'This is only the beginnings of a plan, but I think it might work.'

He explained what he had in mind. Anna was impressed and so, clearly, was Thea though the plan wasn't straightforward. 'Will Daisy be able to leave her father?' Anna asked.

'For a while, yes.'

'And your friend, Daniel?'

'He'll help if he can.'

Anna looked at Thea, thinking Daisy might be embarrassed to be pushed together with the man she'd rejected, but Thea took a practical view.

'Daisy will want to help.'

Anna refused to entertain the idea that all their help would come to nothing because Piers had changed his mind about her, not even after she overheard the major talking to Thea when he called in after seeing a client.

'Mother met a mutual friend of the Rutherfords in Worthing yesterday,' he said, as he stepped into the hall. 'Apparently, Piers is recovering well. One of his regular visitors is Lavinia Belwood, the daughter of old friends. The Belwoods and the Rutherfords have known each other for years and both families have… Not expectations, exactly. But I was led to understand that nothing would please them more than for Piers and Lavinia to…'

The drawing room door closed and shut off his words though it wasn't hard to guess what he was saying. But

Anna wouldn't believe that Piers could have loved her so intensely only to pass her over for someone else. If he wanted to be with Lavinia he could have been with her long before he'd even met Anna.

Thea didn't mention the conversation and nothing happened to alter the plan.

'Are you sure you don't want me to look after James?' Thea asked now.

'Thank you, but you need to be free to look after the guests.' The Misses Penfold had extended their booking and persuaded two friends to join them. 'Besides, we hope we shan't be out for long but can't be sure. James may need feeding.'

She laid him in a large basket that had spent years in Thea's attic. It had two strong handles so was perfect for carrying a baby. Max arrived on time and swung out of the horsebox with long agile strides. 'It's very kind of the Leighs to let you use it,' Anna told him.

'They're decent people. When I explained my reason for wanting it, they wished me – and you – the best of luck.'

He paused to speak to Thea. 'We'll return as soon as possible.'

'Take as long as you need,' Thea said, and stood at the door to wave them off.

It didn't take long to reach the agreed meeting point. Max pulled the horsebox onto a patch of waste ground beside a field and three minutes later a van appeared, bringing Daisy and Daniel. They all got out of the vehicles to talk.

Anna was surprised by Daniel. He was tall, upright, much younger than expected and considerably more handsome. But Daisy was still only eighteen and perhaps that made all the difference to how she saw him. Poor Daisy. She looked uncomfortable at being with him though he looked perfectly at ease with her.

Daisy hugged Anna then climbed into the horsebox to kiss James where he lay in his basket. As Max introduced Daniel, Anna's first impression of a sensible man was confirmed. She liked the good-humoured twinkle in his eyes as well.

'Thank you all for helping,' Anna said, once Daisy had climbed back down again. 'What you're doing for me… It's incredibly kind of you.'

'We're doing what's right,' Max said.

Daniel nodded. 'The Rutherfords are behaving appallingly if they're keeping Piers from his fiancé and son. I'd find it unbearable to be kept away from my children.'

Anna saw that he'd go to the ends of the earth for his little ones. She turned to Max. 'Actually, I'll be grateful if you don't mention James to Piers for the moment.'

'You want to be the one to tell him he's a father,' Max guessed.

Anna also wanted to choose the right moment. Which would be after she'd been assured that he loved her as much as ever.

Max had devised the plan after surveying the Rutherfords' property through binoculars.

'It's time to get started,' he said now.

He got into the van with Daniel and Daisy, and Anna stood watching as they drove away. Her stomach was awash with nerves.

She breathed out slowly and watched the hands of her watch pass through five achingly slow minutes. The van should be in place by now, parked in a lane behind Ashfyld House and separated from it by the property's gardens and a paddock. Daniel and Max should be changing one of the van's good tyres for a punctured one that until this morning had been hanging from a tree on Daniel's property as a makeshift swing for his children.

Another five minutes passed. Daisy should be heading over the paddock and across the gardens to the back of the Rutherfords' house, making no secret of her approach. Max should be heading towards the house too, but stealthily, hidden by the hedgerows that flanked the adjoining lane that ran next to the side of the house.

Anna pictured a maid opening the Rutherfords' kitchen door to Daisy's knock. 'Sorry for the intrusion,' Daisy would say, 'but we've had a puncture and wonder if your gardener might help to change the tyre? We're in the lane over there.' She'd point a vague finger in Daniel's direction.

'I'll have to ask,' the maid would reply – or so they hoped.

She'd go back inside, consult the housekeeper then, with luck, give Daisy permission to approach the gardener who was working in the garden and needed to be got out of the way. Once the gardener had set off to help Daniel, Daisy would return to the house to ask if she might trouble the housekeeper for a glass of water.

'This is the Carmichaels' house, isn't it?' she'd ask, assuming she was invited inside.

'The Carmichaels are further down the lane,' she'd be told. 'This house belongs to Mr and Mrs Rutherford.'

Daisy would nod then give the impression of being struck by a sudden recollection.

'Wasn't it their son who was shipwrecked?'

She'd comment on the terror of the experience and draw out the information that he was recuperating at home. 'It must be nicer here than in a hospital,' she'd say. 'He can lie in bed looking out over that lovely garden I just walked through. If his room's at the back of the house, that is?'

Having learned the approximate location of his room, she'd take her glass of water outside, saying she didn't want to keep the staff from their work. Max would be hiding around the side. Daisy would wander in that direction and whisper the location to him. After a minute or two she'd go back inside as though bored with her own company and keep the staff talking. Meanwhile Max would climb a drainpipe to get to the balcony that ran across the back of the house then pass through a balcony door or window to locate Piers.

It was a simple plan in theory but fraught with risk in practice. The Rutherfords' staff might not cooperate. Max might be seen climbing up or find all the doors and windows locked. Even if he did get into the house he might be discovered by a doctor, a nurse, a visitor or Piers's parents…

Anna's breath caught in her throat. She breathed out slowly to calm the panic. It was stupid to torture herself with everything that *might* go wrong when she'd know for certain soon enough.

Fifteen minutes became twenty, twenty-five, thirty – and Anna heard the sound of a vehicle in the distance. She ducked behind the horsebox as it passed but looked out in time to realise that it was the car that had brought Lavinia to visit Piers the last time Anna had been here.

If Lavinia was visiting again, her arrival would surely scatter the staff about their duties. Max might be caught and—

But no. Here came the van with Max, Daniel and Daisy visible through the windscreen.

Anna waited to hear what had happened.

Thirty-Nine

Daisy felt awkward sitting in silence as Daniel drove them back to Pixfield. Not that he was doing anything to make her uncomfortable. Perhaps he really had recovered from the momentary madness that had persuaded him she might make a suitable wife. Or perhaps he was simply above holding a grudge. If only she too could stop feeling embarrassed.

Deciding she needed to say something she settled on, 'Thanks for helping Anna.'

He glanced across at her. His eyes were green but while Thea's eyes flashed like dark emeralds, Daniel's were the softer green of open spaces and the sea. They suited a man who spent most of his time outdoors. 'She needed help and she deserved help,' he said, simply. Then he shook his head. 'Those people…'

There was disgust in the way his mouth tightened at the thought of the Rutherfords but there was something else about him that was puzzling Daisy. It was a kind of energy. A breeziness. 'You enjoyed getting the better of them,' she realised.

Daniel glanced at her again, this time with a smile that showed strong white teeth. 'Didn't you?'

Daisy had been terrified in case the plan failed but she'd felt a fizz of excitement too. She just hadn't expected Daniel to feel it. He had to be almost thirty, after all.

His attention returned to the road and Daisy sat back to think over the scene in the Rutherfords' house. 'Keep the staff talking for as long as you can,' Max had said.

Daisy had managed to give him eight minutes according to the clock in the Rutherfords' kitchen. After that, she felt she'd overstayed her welcome. 'Well,' she said. 'Thank you for the water.'

She went back outside only to panic when she saw the gardener was already returning through the paddock. Oh, heck. If Max climbed out of a window now, the gardener would surely see him.

But a small stone landed at Daisy's feet and, turning, she saw Max waiting behind a bush. He jerked his head to tell her it was time to leave and Daisy set off on a path that would lead her to the gardener, hoping to keep his attention away from Max who was slinking his way through the greenery towards the lane.

'Did you manage to change the tyre?' Daisy asked the gardener as she passed.

'We did.'

'Thank you.' He was a miserable sort of man but Daisy beamed at him and won a reluctant nod of acknowledgement.

Seeing that Max had passed in safety she gave the man a wave and walked on briskly, catching Max up at the van where Daniel was waiting.

'Well?' Daisy demanded. 'Did you see Piers?'

'Let's get back to Anna,' Max said.

Of course. Anna ought to hear Max's news first though the suspense was unbearable. Daisy scrambled into the van then turned to look at him as he got in beside her. His grey eyes glittered with feeling. Anger was part of it, Daisy guessed, but was triumph another part?

It took only a couple of minutes to reach Anna. They saw the horsebox in the distance and Anna must have seen the van because she stood waiting for them to draw up. She was pale but dignified though Daisy noticed her hand clutched the horsebox door as though she might need it for support.

'I saw Piers,' Max reported as soon as he was out of the van. 'He told me he'd asked his parents if they'd heard from you. They said they hadn't.'

'They lied?'

'They lied about your visits and presumably destroyed your letters too as Piers never received them. They must have destroyed the letters he wrote to you as well.'

'He wrote to me?'

'Several times once he returned to England. He wasn't in a position to get to a post box himself so he gave them to his parents to post.'

Max paused then spoke the words Anna was so desperate to hear. 'He loves you, Anna. Just as much as ever.'

Anna closed her eyes for a moment. When she opened them again Daisy saw the shimmer of tears. 'I'm sorry.' Anna laughed, blinking them away again. 'It's just that… well, I'm a little overwhelmed.'

'Who wouldn't be?' Daisy stepped forward to hug her. 'So much for those Rutherfords thinking they're better than you. They're just common liars.'

'How *is* Piers?' Anna wanted to know.

'On the mend but with some way to go before he's back to normal.'

'He will get back to normal?'

'He thinks so. His broken pelvis means he can't walk yet though he's beginning to hobble a few yards on crutches. He said he's got the best possible incentive to get well now he knows you're waiting for him,' Max said, smiling.

'What will you do?' Daisy asked Anna. 'Storm the house and insist on being allowed inside now you know Piers wants to see you?'

'It's his parents' house,' Anna pointed out. 'I won't give them the satisfaction of refusing me again. No, I need to get Piers out instead.'

'How will you do that?'

'I don't know,' Anna admitted. 'But I'll work it out.'

'Let me know if you need any help,' Max said. 'Now I know Piers has a balcony outside his window and I can climb up to it from the side, it'll be no trouble for me to deliver messages.'

'I'll give whatever help you need too,' Daniel offered.

'Thank you,' Anna told them. 'You're all so kind.'

'I started out wanting to help *you*,' Max said. 'Now I've met Piers I want to help him too.'

Anna's dark eyes glowed with pleasure. 'You like him?'

'I do. He wasn't at all disconcerted to see a stranger climbing through his window. He thought it livened up the day even before I told him I brought news of you.'

'Piers sees adventure in everything,' Anna told him with a smile.

They separated then, Max and Anna heading back to Brighton while Daniel and Daisy turned for Pixfield.

Daniel's daughter, Lily, was in the lane when they entered the village. She must have been looking out for them because she waved frantically.

Daniel eased the van to a halt beside her. 'What is it, poppet?'

'An injured fawn. You've got to come quickly.'

'I'll just take Daisy home then—'

'Daisy should come too. She'll want to see the fawn because he's lovely.'

Daniel looked at Daisy.

'Perhaps for a minute or two,' she said.

Lily ran ahead and Daniel drove onto his smallholding, heading round the back of the cottage and halting outside the open doors to a barn. He swung out of the van and walked round to help Daisy but she jumped down unaided. 'This way,' he said, striding into the barn.

Daisy paused on the threshold to give her eyes time to adjust to the shadows. Half of the barn contained the usual farming implements with a hay loft above. But the other half amazed her. 'It's a hospital for animals!' she declared.

Lily and her brother, Jack, looked up from the fawn they were comforting. 'Of course,' Lily said, clearly amazed that Daisy hadn't known about it before.

'I knew your father helped sick animals but I didn't know he had a hospital like this,' Daisy explained.

Lily gave her a forgiving look. 'Come and see the fawn.'

Daisy crept forward, anxious not to startle the creature. 'Oh!' she gasped, for the poor little fawn had blood all over his chest and front legs.

'I saw him hobbling on the Downs,' Lily told her father. 'There was no sign of his mother.'

Daniel crouched down for a closer look. 'Now, young fellow, what sort of trouble have you been getting into?'

He spoke calmly, soothingly, reminding Daisy of Max's mesmeric way with horses. Very slowly, he reached out a hand and touched the fawn's head. It struggled for a moment but Daniel's voice and touch gradually made the trembling ease. 'Let's see what we can do to help,' Daniel said then.

He lifted the fawn and laid it on the workbench that stood in the middle of the barn. The movement alarmed the fawn but once again Daniel spoke in low tones to quieten it. He didn't stop talking as he examined the little deer with hands that were extraordinarily gentle considering their size. 'It's all right to be afraid. It hurts, I know…'

He looked round at Daisy and the children. 'Looks worse than it is. He's just cut himself on something.'

'What will you do?' Daisy asked.

'Clean him up, apply antiseptic, let him rest and try to find out why he was wandering alone. Hopefully, I can return him to his herd once I'm sure there's no infection.'

On cue Lily went to fetch clean water while Jack crossed to a tall glass-fronted cupboard that stood against the wall. It was filled with bottles, jars and boxes. Daisy followed curiously. 'Herbal remedies,' Jack explained, selecting a jar. 'There's comfrey for healing, carrot seeds for calming, liquorice for coughs, sunflower seeds for vitamins, hops for tonics, Golden Seal for appetite… Not all animals need the same thing, of course.'

Daisy was impressed. 'Where did your father learn about all this?'

'He's read books and he's been practising healing for years. He grows a lot of the plants himself. People come to Dad to keep their animals healthy as well as to heal them when they're sick. Vets cost money. My dad treats animals that would otherwise be left to die, especially wild animals.'

Daisy could see why Max got on well with Daniel. They were both wonderful with animals.

Working patiently, Daniel cleaned and treated the little fawn then placed him on a bed of straw in one of the pens he'd made to keep the animals safe until they were ready to be released. There were large cages too, housing wild birds.

Lily took hold of Daisy's hand. 'Come and see.'

There were currently four birds in the cages – two wood pigeons, a robin and a swift – while the pens were occupied by a cat, a rabbit and a badger.

'Will your father be able to save all of them?' Daisy asked.

'He's not sure about the badger. It must have been hit by a car. But he'll do his best.' Lily was philosophical.

Movement outside the barn caught Daisy's eye. It was a distant speck of red. A moving speck. Excitement rose up in her. It couldn't be... yet who else would travel so fast?

'I have to go,' she said, 'but thank you for showing me around. Bye, Jack. Bye, Lily.'

She turned to Daniel, sensing that he'd noticed the sudden change in her and hoping he wouldn't mention it.

It didn't feel right to call him Mr Oaks any more – too stuffy – but she wasn't ready to call him Daniel so she settled for calling him nothing. 'Thanks again for helping Anna,' she said.

'It was a pleasure.'

'You'll come back and see how the fawn is getting on?' Lily asked.

'I'd like that,' Daisy said, but she was already moving away.

She got outside, walked briskly to the lane then broke into a run, skidding to a stop as the red car screeched to a halt outside the forge.

Rory Connor swung out of the driver's seat. 'The very person I want to see.' He grinned, walking towards her with his arms wide in invitation.

Daisy was thrilled, but also shy again. Was he planning to embrace her? Kiss her, even? Goodness!

He caught her up and swung her round in a circle instead. 'Put me down!' Daisy yelled, taken by surprise.

Laughing, he returned her to her feet, looked down at her then kissed her fully on the mouth. Daisy was both shocked and delighted. It was wonderful to be liked by a man as vivid and alive as Rory but her father might be looking out of a window or someone else might chance along the lane and she still wasn't sure enough of Rory to make introductions.

She extracted herself from his embrace and smiled at him, aware that she was blushing and her hair was even more untidy than usual. 'You got my letter?' she asked.

'I did indeed.'

'It's wonderful to see you.'

'How could I come to the area and not look up my little Daisy Flowers?' he asked. 'Hop in and let's go for a spin.'

'I need to check on my father,' Daisy said. 'Cook him some dinner.'

Would Rory wait for her? Or – oh, heck – would he expect to be invited in to share her awful cooking?

'I'll let you off this once seeing as I've somewhere else to go,' he said, to Daisy's heartfelt relief. 'But let me down again and I'll think you don't care for me.'

'If you could tell me when you're coming, I could—'

'How will I know?' He shrugged. 'Jockeys live like nomads. Here one day, somewhere else the next.'

'If you could *try* to let me know…' Daisy pleaded.

'I'll do my best but a poor wanderer, that's me.'

He pulled her to him and kissed her soundly then got back into the car. Grinning, he tooted the horn and drove off in a flurry of dust.

Daisy stood for a moment, savouring the memory of the kiss. But then she remembered her father and looked anxiously at the cottage, thankful to see that he wasn't at any of the windows.

She looked towards Downs Edge too, hoping Daniel hadn't seen Rory either and particularly hoping he hadn't seen the kiss. She saw no sign of him but as she walked towards the cottage she realised that, even if Daniel had witnessed Rory's presence, he wouldn't mention it. Not to anyone. He was trustworthy.

Forty

'Of course you can bring Piers here,' Thea told Anna. 'One of the main bedrooms will be best for him.'

'But that'll reduce the number of guests we can accommodate.'

'Can't be helped,' Thea said. 'If Piers is struggling to walk, he'll never get up to the attic. Besides, we haven't time to look after many guests; I may need to return to London and you need to look after Piers.'

Thea was relieved to see that Anna knew the truth when she heard it. 'Piers and I... we'll pay you back for your kindness one day. Somehow.'

'I don't doubt it,' Thea acknowledged with a smile, though in the meantime Piers would be another person whose welfare weighed heavily on her shoulders.

Time was running out. In just a few short weeks Thea would lose the house and they'd all be out on the street – an injured man, a new mother, a baby and Thea herself.

She'd heard nothing from the boys she'd recruited to find her witnesses and neither had she heard from Jessie or Jessie's friend, Rose. But Thea couldn't just give up. Even treading old ground was better than doing nothing because who knew what might spark a breakthrough?

Getting away from Brighton was going to be tricky, though. With homelessness looming they couldn't afford to turn away all paying guests so they had a Mr Finley and his son staying, together with a Mrs Frobisher and her friend Mrs Anstey. With Anna's plans for Piers taking shape, Thea was reluctant to insist on another visit to London just now.

Max was riding over each day on his motorbike to pass messages between Anna and Piers. Daniel had driven over with his enchanting children too. 'I was expecting someone older and duller,' Thea confided to Anna.

'Not to mention less handsome,' Anna agreed. 'But Daisy's only eighteen and at that age…'

It was to Daniel's credit that he appeared to bear Daisy no ill will. His attraction to her was understandable because Daisy was both deliciously pretty and funny but perhaps, on reflection, he'd decided she was right in thinking they weren't well matched.

It was also to his credit that he wanted to help Anna too though there was something dignified about Anna that commanded respect.

'And, how are *you*?' Max asked Thea one day.

'Me?' She was making tea, thinking she was doing a good job of hiding her anxiety, but shrewd Max missed nothing. 'I have my share of worries but I'm still able to count my blessings.'

He nodded. 'Don't hesitate to ask if I can help.'

'Thank you.'

Thea honoured his kind intentions but what could he do? What could anyone do?

Worry about the house was costing Thea sleep and she was on constant alert for the postman in case he brought something of interest. Which he didn't, except for a note from Ralph saying he'd returned from London but had contracted a head cold so wouldn't visit for a few days.

Thea wrote back to wish him a speedy recovery. She didn't like to think of him feeling unwell but there was no denying that it was convenient to have him confined elsewhere for the moment.

She was alone in the house almost a week after her visit to London when she heard footsteps in the street outside and looked up, hoping to see the postman's feet through the kitchen window. But these steps weren't energetic like the postman's. They were heavy instead, like— No, they couldn't be.

Brown shoes came into view. Brown trousers too and, above them, a camel hair coat. The shoes mounted the steps and their owner banged on the door. Once, twice, a third time. Deep thuds that demanded an answer.

Clearly, Thea hadn't been mistaken when she thought she'd caught a glimpse of her stepbrother at London Bridge station. Stanley Ambrose was here and her instincts screamed that it couldn't be for any good reason.

She threw off her apron and went upstairs, reaching the hall as another thud sounded. She took a deep breath then opened the door but stepped forward, blocking the way into the house even as she forced her expression into one of polite enquiry.

Being tall, Thea wasn't often overwhelmed by the physical impact of another person but Stanley's bulk was like a brooding, threatening mountain. She squared her shoulders, raised her chin and met his gaze unflinchingly.

His eyes were hooded with hammocks of pulpy fat underneath, his mouth mean beneath a coarse-looking moustache and his neck spilt over his collar. He'd been eating breath mints but they couldn't disguise the unpleasant smell of stale whisky and hair oil that emanated from him.

'This is an unexpected visit,' she said, relieved to hear that her voice sounded almost steady.

'I'm here for the house.'

'You said I could live here until the end of May. That's a whole month away.'

'Change of plan.'

Something hadn't gone well for him, Thea guessed. He looked as hard as ever but shabbier with a wilder edge to his aggression.

'I need the house now,' he said. 'You've had more than two months to make alternative arrangements. You can have one more week.'

'That isn't long enough. There are others living here, including a mother and her baby.'

'It's your problem if you've invited them into a house that doesn't belong to you.'

'Doesn't it?'

That gave him pause. His eyes narrowed and ugliness oozed from his pores. 'You know it doesn't belong to you. It's in the Will.'

'So you say.'

'So you *saw*. My solicitor showed it to you.'

'He showed me a document, certainly.'

Stanley took an intimidating step forward but Thea resisted the urge to shrink away. 'Now look here,' he said. 'I don't know what you're suggesting but I don't like the sound of it. And I won't have it. Is that understood?'

'My mother would never have signed a Will like that. Not knowingly, anyway.'

'Then why haven't you challenged it?'

Because she hadn't any evidence, of course.

He gave a knowing nod. 'You can't challenge it because you've nothing to challenge it *with*. That means the house is mine. One week or I'll throw you out. Don't make the mistake of thinking I'm not serious.'

'I'm not afraid of a bully like you,' Thea lied. 'But I expect you're afraid of the police.'

He moved swiftly for a big man, bounding towards her with his arm raised ready to hit her. Thea was quicker still. She ducked out of his path, colliding with the hall table and hearing something fall from it to smash on the floor. Summoning all of her strength, she gave Stanley an almighty shove that sent him staggering back through the door. She slammed it shut before he could come back at her.

He thumped it with what she supposed must be his fist. 'One week or you'll see I mean business.'

Thea was trembling so much that she couldn't trust her legs to hold her. She sank to the floor and forced herself to take deep, steadying breaths. She'd never had violence threatened against her before. It was brutal and shocking. But she couldn't let it defeat her.

She saw that it was a china vase that had broken. Not a thing of much monetary value but appreciated nevertheless because it had belonged to her grandmother. Thea reached out and began to collect the broken shards.

A sudden knock on the door jolted her into dropping them again. Stanley must have got halfway down the street before he'd turned round and come back to ensure he'd got his message across.

Thea stood but didn't open the door. 'You may as well go away as I'm not letting you in,' she called.

'Is there a problem?' That was Max's voice.

Belatedly, Thea realised he'd used the doorknocker in a civilised way instead of thumping on the wood. She opened the door, hoping her cheeks weren't flushed. 'Sorry.'

'You thought I was someone else. Someone who's been throwing his weight around by the look of things.' Max was staring at the broken china. His mouth tightened and he looked back at Thea intently. 'Your charming stepbrother, I suppose. Did he hurt you?'

'No.'

'Honestly?'

'He really didn't. But he wants me out of the house even sooner than I thought. Not that I'm leaving.' She didn't want Max to think she was feeble.

She bent to the broken china and with Max's help placed the shards on a newspaper that a guest had abandoned on the table. 'Have you brought Anna a message from Piers?'

'I have.' He handed an envelope over. 'I'm also here to tell you I've arranged for a jockey to give Night Warrior a timed run on the Downs on Saturday morning. Will you come and watch?'

'I…' Watching Night Warrior would distract her from her woes but could she spare the time?

'It won't take long but don't decide now. Just let me know when you're certain of your plans.'

'Thank you. Would you like some tea?'

'Thanks, but I need to press on.' He hesitated. 'I've offered before and I'll offer again. If there's anything I can do to help, just ask. Even if you do have others to support you.'

By others, Thea knew he meant Ralph.

The thought of Ralph had Thea's conscience stirring. Was she wrong to keep her troubles from an old friend who clearly wanted to be more than a friend? Realising Max was watching her, Thea roused herself. 'I'm grateful.'

'Pride can be a good thing but don't let it get in the way of common sense,' Max said, and with a nod of farewell he left.

Thea carried the shards down to the kitchen where she disposed of them in the bin.

The only good thing about the encounter with Stanley was that Anna had been out with the baby when it happened so Thea had a little time in which to think about what was best to be done. It was neither fair nor practical to hide Stanley's visit from Anna but what, exactly, should Thea tell her?

Forty-One

'Unpleasant, you say?' Anna asked, guessing that Stanley's behaviour had been a lot worse than that.

'Yes, but I'm not going to let him intimidate me.'

Thea had courage aplenty, but Anna could also see worry in that lovely face.

'I'll move out straight away if staying here puts you in danger,' Anna said. 'I still have some of Mr Acaster's money saved.'

'I don't think I'm in danger.'

But clearly Thea couldn't be entirely sure. 'Luckily Daisy can stay at her father's,' Anna continued. 'She'll be disappointed that you're closing as a guest house, but she always knew it was only temporary.'

Anna was tempted to ask if Thea might be able to stay with Ralph's mother. It was surely only a matter of time before Ralph proposed. But Anna was reluctant to intrude on Thea's private business.

'I'm not abandoning the house to Stanley,' Thea said firmly. 'I'm staying and I want you and Piers to stay too though I don't think we should take any more paying guests for the moment. You need to concentrate on Piers and I need to concentrate on finding a witness.'

'You don't think your stepbrother might... try something?'

'He wants the house so he isn't going to damage it. He might attempt to throw us out on the street but we've got a week before that happens. And if – when – he comes, we'll just have to ensure we don't let him in until he's got some sort of Court Order requiring us to leave.'

'I won't open the door to anyone until I know who's calling,' Anna promised. 'I'll be sure to keep the kitchen door locked too.'

It was still worrying. Even if they succeeded in keeping Stanley out temporarily, the situation was fast approaching a climax and, without evidence to prove that the Will was fraudulent, the law would be on his side. Anna felt anxiety slide inside her at the thought of having to find somewhere else to stay when she had an injured Piers and a helpless James to look after, especially if Piers had no money of his own put by.

But the most important thing was to have him with her. On that thought she opened the note Max had delivered, read it through and smiled.

'Good news?' Thea asked.

'Piers will be coming on Sunday.' Joy surged in Anna's heart then reality reminded her not to count her chickens before they were hatched. 'If all goes to plan, that is.'

Forty-Two

'Are you listening?'

Daisy realised Max was speaking to her. 'Of course I'm listening.'

He was explaining the plan that he, Anna and Daniel had concocted to steal Piers away from his parents' house. It was exciting and daring, and Daisy was thrilled to know Anna would soon have the man she loved by her side. But paying attention to Max didn't stop her from listening out for a car as well.

Not that Daisy was expecting Rory to visit. In fact, much as she longed to see him, she hoped he wouldn't visit while Max and Daniel were sitting at her table and her father was sitting in his armchair. It would be better if Rory came later, after Max and Daniel had gone and – with luck – her father had slipped into a doze. Daisy might then be able to spare an hour or two to go out with him away from the curious eyes of the village. A simple drive through the countryside would be nice. Or he might prefer to take her to tea.

The thought of going out to tea brought a small quiver of anxiety as Daisy remembered how lovely Thea looked when she went out with Ralph. With her slender figure and glorious hair Thea would look lovely in anything, of course, but the clothes Anna had helped to create were much nicer than anything Daisy possessed. Clothes had never interested Daisy before – she'd have worn boys' trousers given half a chance – but she wanted to look at least a little bit smart for Rory's sake. He always looked extremely dapper.

If she knew when he was coming she could wear her Sunday best dress of dusky pink again but he might turn up at any time and give her no chance to change. She'd considered wearing the pink dress just in case he came but her father might wonder why and in any case she might dirty it as she went about her chores. She'd settled for trying to look presentable in her other clothes. She'd even gone to the trouble of ironing the three skirts she possessed.

'Are you feeling quite well?' her father had asked.

'These skirts are creased.'

'Times must be changing because I'd have sworn you were incapable of even noticing a crease. In fact you usually iron creases *into* my shirts.'

'Anna's been teaching me,' she'd offered by way of explanation but she hadn't looked up to gauge if he believed her.

Today she'd put on her newest blouse. It wasn't particularly new or smart but it did have a narrow strip of lace around the collar. She'd also used more pins in her hair in the hope of persuading it to lie flat though wisps were still escaping. Daisy knew it was wrong to be discontented with your lot in life but she couldn't help wishing she had Thea's tall, fiery beauty or Anna's Madonna-like perfection. It was hard to imagine what

Rory could see in a tiny girl with unruly hair and not an ounce of grace or dignity. If he actually *did* see anything in her beyond a passing fancy.

She was relieved when Max finally asked, 'So we all know what's expected of us on Sunday?'

Daniel nodded as though relishing the prospect of it. Daisy nodded too.

'Good,' Max said.

He got to his feet and walked over to say a few parting words to her father.

Daniel got up too. 'Lily asks if you'll come over this afternoon when she's finished school,' he told Daisy. 'She's got something to show you.'

Urged by Lily and Jack, Daisy had been to the animal hospital most days since the fawn had been found and Daniel had treated her with the sort of relaxed civility he probably showed to anyone who was visiting his children. Daisy was grateful for it. Grateful too for his tact and discretion over Rory though she still cringed at the thought of him knowing she was interested in a man.

She was also reluctant to commit to visiting at a particular time in case Rory came.

'It's kind of Lily to invite me but I'm not sure I can come over today,' she answered.

She kept her voice low but her father heard it anyway. 'Don't be soft in the head,' he called. 'I don't need you hovering around me all the time.'

He was well on the road to recovery in terms of his general health. He could walk with ease and was spending time in the forge doing what he called supervising but which Joseph, his temporary helper, probably called interfering. A vigorous man all his life, Frank was finding convalescence frustrating.

'I shan't fall into a swoon if you're away for half an hour and you don't need to get Mrs Beddows in to look after me either,' he finished.

Daisy had asked their neighbour to sit with him the day she'd gone to the Rutherfords' house.

'I'll tell Lily to expect you, shall I?' Daniel asked.

'Please tell her I'm looking forward to it,' Daisy said.

In many ways that was true and not just because of the animals. Lily and Jack were proving to be surprisingly interesting. Daisy even enjoyed watching Daniel's skilful handling of the injured creatures when she could be sure he wasn't watching her in return.

He nodded by way of farewell, had a brief word with her father and then left with Max. Daisy was relieved to see them go and thanked her lucky stars that Rory hadn't appeared while they were here. It would be rotten luck if he arrived in the half hour she spent with Lily and Jack later.

But he might not come at all.

Rory did come, just as she was walking up the lane to Downs Edge. Hearing the distant roar of an approaching vehicle, Daisy came to a halt, torn between joy at the prospect of seeing Rory and frustration that he'd timed his arrival badly.

He grinned, waved, then brought the car to a screeching halt. 'Are you here to meet me?' he asked, sliding out.

'I didn't know you were coming.'

'Then I hope I'm a nice surprise.'

'A lovely surprise.' Daisy's heart had quickened with pleasure at the sight of his smile and dancing eyes. If only he'd arrived earlier. Or half an hour later.

'Let's go and see what Worthing has to offer in the way of entertainment,' he said.

'I'm supposed to be visiting someone,' Daisy told him, hoping he wouldn't be too disappointed.

'Who is this someone? You're not playing fast and loose with a poor Irishman's heart, I hope?'

'Of course not. It's a neighbour's little girl. Lily.'

'A child? To be sure she won't hold it against you if you see her later. She probably won't even notice the time.'

'I'm afraid she would notice.' So would Daniel. Daisy dreaded the thought of him dismissing her as rude and flighty. But perhaps she could see both Lily *and* Rory. 'If you could wait for me, I'll—'

'Wait?'

'Only for a short time,' Daisy pleaded. 'Twenty minutes. Fifteen. Ten, even.'

'Daisy, I thought you understood. I have to grasp my leisure time when I can. I haven't the time to spare for waiting.'

'Not even ten minutes?'

'I see I was mistaken,' Rory said. 'I thought you had feelings for me but—'

'Rory, I have!'

'Then come along with me now and see your little friend later. I'll even buy some sweets for you to give her.'

'I wish I *could* come with you.'

'But you won't?'

'Can't. I really can't.'

'I see how it is. I'm not important to you and I shouldn't be surprised. After all, who am I but a roving sort of man trying to make his fortune the best way he can? I hope you enjoy your afternoon.'

He was moving back towards the car as he spoke. Daisy hastened after him. 'Another time,' she began, but Rory gave her a look that suggested he had no confidence in another time.

He started the engine.

'I'll see you again?' Daisy asked desperately.

'It's *you* who doesn't want to see *me*,' Rory pointed out.

'That isn't—'

Too late. He'd already driven away.

Forty-Three

Thea got up early to catch Jessie's friend, Rose, on her way into work but it did no good. Rose saw Thea from a distance and marched up with her eyes blazing. 'I hope you're proud of yourself. I was the only friend Jessie had but thanks to you she daren't even write to me in case I lead you to her.'

So Rose hadn't heard from Jessie either. 'I'm sorry, but you're blaming the wrong person,' Thea pointed out. 'It's Jessie's father who's hurting her.'

'Humph.' Rose's lip curled and, turning abruptly, she marched away.

Thea sighed in disappointment and tried to quell the anxiety that gnawed at her peace of mind. She bought bread and milk then walked along Clarendon Place deep in thought. A man was walking towards her but Thea took no notice of him until she found herself barged roughly aside though there was plenty of space on the pavement for him to pass.

'Begging your pardon, Miss,' he stopped to say, but his expression told her he wasn't sorry at all. 'Fine morning, ain't it? It would be a pity not to see more mornings like this.'

His words sounded horribly like a threat. The man walked on, leaving Thea staring after him. Was his aggression a spontaneous act of malice because she appeared to be his social superior? Or was this the first step in a campaign of intimidation organised by her stepbrother?

Thea walked on, committing the man's appearance to memory so she'd know if she saw him again. Tall. Bulky around the shoulders. Greying, greasy hair hanging in straggling rats' tails. Bulbous, misshapen nose. Thea gave him the name of Bulky Man.

'Thea!'

She realised Ralph had driven up. 'I'm here with an invitation from my mother. It would give her great pleasure if you'd join us for lunch on Saturday. It's her birthday.'

It had slipped Thea's mind that Maria Kirby-Laws shared the same birthday as Cecily Fairfax. 'It's my mother's birthday too and I'd like to put flowers on her grave,' Thea told him.

'Of course. I'll be happy to take you to the cemetery first. What time would suit you?'

'I'm not actually sure. I'll be going to Max's stables early on Saturday as he's arranged for a professional jockey to ride Night Warrior and give an opinion on whether he might have a future in racing. I don't know what time I'll be back.'

'Why don't I take you to see the horse?' Ralph offered. 'We can go to the cemetery afterwards and then on to Mother's for lunch.'

Thea hesitated. She'd prefer to miss the lunch as it would be a strain to maintain an appearance of cheerfulness for several hours that could be better spent enquiring after the witnesses. But Ralph looked so eager to please that it would have seemed churlish to refuse him. 'If you really don't mind the early start, that would be wonderful.'

Ralph beamed in delight. 'Until Saturday,' he said.

It was an uneasy week that brought Thea no closer to knowing the whereabouts of the witnesses but ever closer to Stanley's deadline which would expire on Monday. On Friday afternoon she went out to buy flowers for her mother's grave. Thea visited the cemetery often but most times she hadn't the money for shop-bought flowers. She usually took posies of ivy or jasmine cut from the small garden at home or sprigs of holly or berries plucked from trees she passed. The important thing was that they were given with love. Birthdays were special, though, so today she bought a small bouquet of spring flowers for her mother and another for Maria Kirby-Laws.

Walking home again, her attention was caught by something on the steps leading to the front door. She moved closer and realised that the steps had been scattered with vegetable peelings. Glancing around, she saw Bulky Man at the end of the road. He doffed his hat to her then swaggered off.

Tiptoeing through the mess, Thea opened the door and rushed straight to the kitchen.

'I'm glad you're back,' Anna began, only to frown. 'What's wrong?'

Thea told her about the mess Bulky Man had left. Anna had already been warned that he might – just might – be connected to Stanley and this latest incident confirmed it for her as well as for Thea. 'Your stepbrother really is a nasty piece of work.'

'One of us could have slipped on those peelings,' Thea said. 'I'm not sure I should leave you and James in the house by yourselves more than is absolutely necessary from now on. Perhaps I shouldn't go to Max's tomorrow. Or to the birthday lunch.'

'Of course you should. The house is Stanley's golden goose so he won't want to damage it. That means I'm safe here though I'll keep the doors and windows locked as we agreed, and I'll look out for hazards outside.'

Thea hesitated.

'Don't give up the fight now,' Anna urged. 'Look what the postman brought.'

She handed Thea an envelope addressed in Thea's own handwriting. It was one of the envelopes she'd left in London. Tearing it open, Thea drew out a note and felt a thrill of excitement when she saw it had been signed by Pip. The boy wouldn't have won prizes for neat handwriting but Thea still managed to read the scrawl.

Dear Miss Fairfox,

I seen her. The woman wot you was looking for. I seen her go into the ~~por poor~~ pawnbroker's on Esmerelda Street. I culdn't follow her home cos me dad wud've given me a belting if I'd been late but she'll have to go back to the shop for the locket. I knowed it were a locket she ~~por~~ pawned cos I looked through the window and saw her hand it over in return for a tiket.

Anyways, I think this is worth harf a crown.

Pip

'It isn't Jessie's address, but it's a start,' Thea told Anna, passing her the letter excitedly.

Anna read it and looked thrilled on Thea's behalf but then a shadow crossed her face. 'When will you go to London?'

'It's too late to go today, unfortunately. I'd go tomorrow but it would be awkward to miss the lunch. As for Sunday…'

Sunday was the day they were fetching Piers. Anna's face was carefully neutral but Thea could see the dread in her eyes at the thought of the plan being postponed.

'Not Sunday,' Thea said, and to Anna's obvious relief she pointed out that the pawnbroker's shop wouldn't be open. 'I'll have to go on Monday. Stanley's deadline expires then so you'll need to be extra vigilant here.'

'I'll be careful,' Anna promised. 'But I want you to tell Max about this Bulky Man. If we all go to fetch Piers as planned on Sunday, we'll have to leave the house empty and I don't think that will be wise. Max may have some advice.'

'I'll try to mention it,' Thea said, thinking it might be difficult to have a private word with Max in Ralph's presence.

'Try hard,' Anna begged.

It was chilly when Ralph collected her the following morning and drove her to Clareswood where he parked beside a shining red car that looked built for speed. Max was in the courtyard with a whippet-thin man whom he introduced as Rory Connor, the jockey. 'It's a pleasure to ride your horse, so it is,' Rory told her.

He had twinkling eyes and a ready grin, and Thea imagined he turned them on every woman he met. Ralph looked disapproving even so, and he was brisk with Max too. 'Shall we get on?' he said.

Max led Thea and Ralph onto the Downs and pointed out the posts he'd put in to mark the beginning and the end of the five-furlong run. 'If you could wait here while we fetch the horse…' he said.

He walked away and Thea saw Ralph bridle at what he doubtless thought was a lack of deference on Max's part though to her it was just the easy behaviour of friends. She commented on the beauty of the Downs to give Ralph no chance to put his disapproval into words and kept him talking about the scenery until Max returned with Rory riding Night Warrior. Predictably, the horse was trying to toss his head and skitter.

'Black horses are usually bad-tempered, you know,' Ralph observed.

As if on cue, Night Warrior bared his teeth at Ralph and might have taken a chunk out of him if Rory hadn't pulled him back.

Thea caught a wry gleam in Max's eye before he got it under control. 'We suspect Night Warrior was badly treated so it's understandable if he's a little wild,' she explained to Ralph.

'I just hope he doesn't disgrace you.'

'Max is giving him a chance to show what he can do. If he doesn't enjoy running, it isn't the end of the world.'

'But it will affect the horse's stud value,' Ralph pointed out.

'Let's just see what happens.'

Rory rode Night Warrior to the starting post. Max took a stopwatch from his pocket so he could time the run then raised his arm and swung it down as a signal to Rory to begin.

'That horse is actually rather good,' Ralph remarked, as Night Warrior thundered over the grass.

It was a beautiful sight to Thea. 'He's magnificent.'

Rory and Night Warrior reached the end of the five furlongs and Rory rode the horse in a circle to calm him down. Max ran over to them. Thea followed with Ralph. 'That was fast,'

Max told Rory.

'The boy enjoyed it, so he did. I think you've got your racehorse, Max. If he can behave himself on a real course.'

'You should think of sending the horse to a proper trainer,' Ralph told Thea.

'Max is training him.'

'An established trainer might be able to make more of the horse and increase his value.'

'Night Warrior belongs to Max as well as me.'

'I could talk to him,' Ralph offered. 'He needs to consider your interests as well as his own. Or I could buy his share in the horse.'

'Thank you, but I've no wish to change the current arrangement.'

Night Warrior represented more than just money to Max. He also represented challenge and the chance to achieve something wonderful. Thea couldn't take that opportunity away. Besides, Night Warrior might not thrive away from Max who'd worked wonders with him in a very short space of time.

'If it's a case of the training fees,' Ralph began.

'It isn't.' Not that Thea could have paid the fees.

She congratulated Rory on his ride. 'What comes next?' she asked Max.

'More practice in getting him to settle. Teaching him to gallop upsides another horse or two. And training him to jump off at the start.' Max spoke confidently but then he frowned as Ralph stretched a hand to him.

'A gesture of appreciation,' Ralph explained, and, to her horror, Thea realised he was offering a tip as though Max were a servant instead of a partner.

'Ralph, no,' Thea began, but Max answered for himself.

'There's no need for that,' he said coolly. He nodded to Rory to head back to the stables before Ralph could offer the tip to him.

Rory moved off with Max following.

'Well, really,' Ralph said to Thea in a low voice that she was sure still carried to Max. 'Your man is a little abrupt. Some might say rude.'

'He isn't my man,' Thea pointed out. 'He's my partner.'

'I'm not sure I'd use that term to describe—'

'I'm chilly, Ralph. Would you be good enough to fetch my gloves from the car?'

Ralph was taken by surprise but gallantry required him to do as she asked. 'Of course.'

Thea waited for him to set off for the car then hastened after Max. 'Ralph didn't mean to cause offence,' she told him.

'I'm sure he didn't.'

'I'm sorry anyway.'

Max shrugged. 'I'm a grown man, Thea. I won't be brought low by the likes of –' He broke off, paused, then said, 'You've done nothing wrong here, but unless I'm much mistaken something else has happened to trouble you.'

Thea told him about Bulky Man.

'Anna's right to be concerned about leaving the house empty,' he said. 'I'll think about what's best to be done, but let's assume we're still going to the Rutherfords' house tomorrow as planned.'

They reached the courtyard where Rory dismounted and Night Warrior nudged Max's arm. 'All right, all right, you haven't been forgotten,' Max assured him. 'Will you let Thea stroke you, I wonder?'

Thea advanced cautiously, ready to dart back at any moment. She touched Night Warrior's neck, hot and moist with sweat but vibrant and alive. 'You're beautiful,' she told him.

Night Warrior whinnied then stamped and tried to turn. 'Your man's coming back,' Max observed dryly.

Thea didn't need the gloves Ralph had brought her but drew them on anyway. 'Thank you for giving me the chance to watch the run,' she told Max. 'And thank you for riding him, Rory.'

'I hope to ride this devil again,' Rory said.

They parted with goodbyes and neither Thea nor Max gave any hint that they'd be seeing each other when they rescued Piers the following day.

'Wasn't that a lovely way to spend an hour or so?' Thea asked Ralph. 'Thank you for taking me.'

She wanted to cheer him up after his well-intentioned blunder with the tip and also to assuage her guilt over keeping him in the dark about so much that was happening in her life. She was rewarded with a warm smile of pleasure.

They returned to Clarendon Place. 'To collect the flowers,' Thea said, though she also wanted to check on Anna.

All was well so Ralph drove her to the cemetery. The grave which held her parents was marked by only a temporary cross, because it was too soon after her mother's burial to set the permanent headstone in place but it comforted Thea to know that a decent headstone was waiting at the mason's shop.

It had been bought for Thea's father long before Herbert had taken advantage of her mother's loneliness to drain the Fairfax family finances. It was therefore a fitting memorial – not large or showy but dignified, being a simple stone slab with a leaf design at the top and engraving across the front:

In Loving Memory of Robert Fairfax
March 5th 1875 – June 12th 1916
Beloved husband of Cecily and adored father of
Theodora

That lettering was a little weathered now but underneath there was another, newer inscription:

Also in Loving Memory of Cecily Anne Fairfax
Beloved wife of the above and adored mother of
Theodora
April 11th 1877 to September 18th 1922

Even paying for that small inscription had involved Thea in strict economy, but she'd been determined that her mother's tribute should be as loving as her father's.

Herbert had played no part at all in choosing the wording. He'd played no part in the funeral either except for turning up drunk. Afterwards he hadn't visited the grave even once as far as Thea knew.

'Happy birthday, Mother,' she whispered, crouching down beside the grave.

Ralph kept a respectful distance, standing to attention as though back in the army. Realising they were the only people in this part of the cemetery, Thea was glad to have him nearby though his presence made it difficult for her to say what she'd have liked to say to her mother. She contented herself with apologising silently for breaking the vase and failing to get the better of Stanley. Not that she was giving up.

She'd been keeping an eye out for Stanley and Bulky Man today as on every day but they reached the road to Worthing without having seen either of them. The thought of Anna alone in the house with James still troubled her but Thea tried to rise above her anxiety when they reached Beeches Lodge.

Ralph's parents welcomed her with smiles and embraces, and a big fuss was made of the flowers Thea had brought though they were modest enough.

'I'm so glad you agreed to join us today,' Maria beamed. 'I know it must be difficult, being your dear mother's birthday too, but I'm sure she'd have wanted you to celebrate her anniversary instead of being cast down by it.'

'She would indeed,' Thea agreed, and as they settled down to lunch she knew she couldn't have been more cherished by the entire Kirby-Laws family.

After they'd eaten Mrs Kirby-Laws suggested Ralph should take Thea into the garden. 'I expect you'd like to stretch your legs,' she said. 'You could see the white lilacs too. They're just coming into bloom and looking lovely.'

Thea was relieved to get outside. Ralph's family was wonderful but she had a lot on her mind and it was easier to hide it in the open space of the garden.

The lilac trees really were beautiful with their blooms of pristine white. There were clouds of pale blue forget-me-nots too, purple iris and graceful arched stems of lily of the valley. 'So pretty!' Thea said, and with that Ralph produced a penknife from his pocket and cut several stems of lilies.

'It's a pity the roses aren't yet in bloom as a red rose would be a better symbol of my feelings but I hope these lilies will be an adequate substitute,' he said, presenting them to her. 'I love you, Thea. There's nothing I want more than to marry you.'

Thea gasped. She was touched by his sincerity. She was sure she must be pleased. But above all she was thrown into panic because Ralph's timing was terrible. He was making assumptions about her circumstances that weren't true. She was holding things back from him. Keeping secrets. She needed more time to get things straight before she even considered—

'You don't have feelings for me?' Ralph looked dejected.

'Of course I do!' He was a good man. A decent man. 'I just—'

Her words were lost as Ralph swept her into his arms. 'You've made me the happiest man alive,' he declared, kissing her cheek and then her mouth.

Thea's head reeled. She wanted to explain that she hadn't actually accepted his proposal but as Ralph released her she saw he was waving to his parents, who were standing outside the house as though waiting for confirmation that all was well. The wave was the signal they needed to hasten down the garden with glasses and champagne in a silver bucket of ice.

'Ralph,' Thea began, but Mrs Kirby-Laws folded her into an embrace.

'My dearest girl! We couldn't be more delighted!'

'This is the happiest of days,' Mr Kirby-Laws agreed. He eased the cork out of the bottle and, with Ralph holding the glasses ready, poured the champagne.

Thea felt as though she was being swept away by an avalanche.

'Just think how delighted your parents would be if they could see you now,' Maria Kirby-Laws said, as Ralph handed the glasses around.

Thea did think about it and once again, her mind's eye supplied a picture of her parents beaming with pleasure at the sight of Thea surrounded by people who loved her. Ralph was certain of his feelings and if Thea was less sure of hers, wasn't that only because she had so much trouble in her life that it was crowding out everything else?

'To the happy couple,' Mr Kirby-Laws proposed.

Ralph put his arm around Thea and held up his glass. After a moment's hesitation she raised her glass too. But it still felt wrong – terribly wrong – to be engaged to a man from whom she was keeping secrets.

It was more important than ever that she should outwit Stanley soon.

Forty-Four

'It's beautiful,' Anna said, admiring the ring Thea had been given. 'With your colouring an emerald is perfect.'

The large oval emerald was surrounded by diamonds that sparkled brightly even in the subdued lighting of the basement kitchen.

'I couldn't be happier for you,' Anna added, though it seemed to her that Thea's smile was brittle and her mood troubled.

'To be honest I'm a little dazed,' Thea admitted. 'I hadn't expected a proposal quite so soon. I'd hoped... Well, I'd hoped to have resolved matters with the house before thinking about getting engaged to be married.'

'The major adores you.'

'Yes, I think he does. And I know that makes me a very lucky girl.' Thea shrugged. 'I suppose the situation with the house will be resolved soon enough. One way or another.'

Anna understood why Thea might not have wished to tell Ralph about the problems with the house when they first renewed their acquaintance. In the same way that Anna wanted to know Piers loved her free from obligation,

Thea might have wanted to know the major loved her free from chivalry. But now they were engaged, wouldn't it be a relief to her to confide in him?

Perhaps it was the plan to rescue Piers that was holding her back. Thea might feel that, if she started being open with Ralph, she'd have to tell him everything, including the rescue plan. That might lead to conflict between them. Ralph might also warn the Rutherfords what was afoot and Thea might have decided that was a risk she couldn't take.

'I don't want to make things difficult for you,' Anna said. 'I understand that being engaged means some loyalties have to come before others. If you'd rather Piers didn't—'

'Nothing's changed with regard to Piers,' Thea assured her. 'We rescue him tomorrow and bring him here.'

'But—'

'I insist.'

Should Anna insist on the opposite course? She was torn but it wasn't just selfishness that kept her silent. Thea was kind, generous and brave but anxiety was picking away at the edges of her customary calm and the last thing she needed now was an argument. Besides, she was right when she said the situation would soon be reaching a climax anyway.

Anna was glad that Thea had Ralph's family to take her in if she lost the house and glad that Daisy could live with her father. As for her own situation… Worry sat like wet sand in Anna's stomach, lurching from side to side now and then, and sending a nauseous sensation to her throat. But she refused to let it daunt her. Somehow she, Piers and baby James would find a way to manage.

The thought of Piers burst through the worry on a surge of joy. Tomorrow she'd see him again. Hold him again. If the plan succeeded.

To Anna's relief Thea had told Max of their reluctance to leave the house empty. The more Anna thought about it, the more she feared that Stanley would seize the chance to break in and change the locks. It was hard to see what Max could do about it, though, so perhaps Anna should suggest that Thea should stay behind even if it did weaken the plan a little.

Far too agitated to sleep well, Anna was up early on Sunday though Max wasn't due to arrive until the afternoon. It meant she had many hours in which to torture herself with all the things that might go wrong: a crisis with one of the horses in Max's care, Daisy's father taking a turn for the worse, Daniel's children needing him at home… All she could do was to keep busy.

Max arrived precisely on time and didn't arrive alone. He led in two gangly young men with matching grins and straw-like hair. Twins. 'Albie and Alfie,' he said, introducing them. 'Sons from the farm next to Clareswood. They'll hold the fort here while we're gone. If that's all right?' He looked at Thea.

Anna looked at Thea too, wondering what she was making of the fact that Albie was carrying a shotgun.

'Don't worry,' Max said. 'The only creatures Albie has ever shot are rats in his father's barn. The gun is a precaution. It'll send a message in the unlikely event of your stepbrother putting in an appearance. It won't hurt for him to know that you have friends.'

Thea looked a little stunned but didn't argue.

'Everything ready here?' Max asked.

Anna was galvanised into action. Excitement coursed through her when she thought that Piers might be with her in little more than an hour!

'Help yourselves to tea and biscuits,' Thea invited the twins.

She picked up the bag they'd packed with the things they needed for the rescue and Anna picked up James in his carrying basket. Outside, they climbed into the horsebox and Max drove them to the meeting point where Daniel and Daisy were waiting in the van.

Daisy hugged Anna and then Thea. Was Thea going to tell her about the engagement?

Anna caught Thea's eye and raised an eyebrow.

Thea coughed a little awkwardly. 'I got engaged yesterday.'

'Engaged to be married?' Daisy asked.

In answer Thea held up her left hand. The emerald and diamonds sparkled even more brightly in the daylight. 'Thea, that's wonderful news!' Daisy wrapped her in another hug. 'I'm so pleased you won't have money worries any more.'

Daniel stepped forward to kiss Thea's cheek. 'Congratulations. I hope you'll be very happy.'

'Indeed,' Max said, more briskly. 'Congratulations. But we need to get started.'

Anna, Daisy and Thea were already wearing their drabbest clothes. Now Anna wrapped a thick blanket around her shoulders to add bulk to her body then covered it with a cape. She also put on a hat and a pair of spectacles that had been left behind years ago by the Fairfax family cook. With Thea's permission, Anna had pushed the lenses out to leave only the frames. Hunched over, she looked much older. Quite unlike herself. Which was, of course, the idea.

Thea pulled a shawl over her head to cover her glorious hair while Daisy wrapped herself in several blankets.

Setting off again, they drove both vehicles to the lane behind the Rutherford's property, where Daniel had parked the day he'd pretended to have a puncture. It was important to move quickly now for fear of being seen.

Daniel brought his late mother's old wheelchair from the back of the van and Daisy slid into it, swathing the blankets around her so that only her eyes and nose remained uncovered. Anna got behind the wheelchair and tried an experimental push. 'I'll manage,' she confirmed.

Max brought rope and strips of old tarpaulin from the van and paused by the horsebox where Thea remained seated by the open window. She was to be their lookout and didn't need reminding of what she had to do. 'One toot of the horn if a vehicle is coming. Two toots if there's a person on foot,' she recited.

They were ready to begin. 'Good luck to all of you. And thank you,' Anna said.

The two men ran to the lane that led along the side of the Rutherfords' property and climbed through the hedgerow into the field opposite, intending to make their way parallel to the lane until they were level with the house. Daniel carried the tarpaulin strips over his shoulder and Max carried the rope.

Anna let them get ahead then pushed Daisy along the lane in the same direction, her steps laboured so anyone who happened to see her would dismiss her as an old woman who was taking an invalid out for some air. As she neared the house she saw Max and Daniel dart across the lane ahead of her and push their way through the hedgerow onto the Rutherfords' property. An electric thrill of anticipation passed through her as she watched them climb the drainpipe to the balcony then ease through a door into the house.

'They're in,' she reported to Daisy whose view from the wheelchair wasn't as clear. Then she glanced around to be sure no one else was watching.

Several minutes passed that felt like eternity. Then Max reappeared on the balcony. He threw a pair of crutches to the ground then climbed back down the drainpipe with swift and nimble movements. Daniel came through the balcony door backwards, holding someone in front of him. It had to be Piers though Anna couldn't see more than a vague shape at present.

Max had explained that the tarpaulin strips fastened together to make a harness to which ropes could be attached for lowering Piers to the ground, Daniel taking his weight from above and Max guiding him carefully from below.

Anna's heart kicked in her chest when Daniel turned Piers around though she couldn't see much of his face because his overgrown fair hair hung low. Daniel helped him over the balcony railing and lowered him slowly.

It was only a makeshift harness and Piers stiffened occasionally as though holding back cries of pain. But Max was there to take his weight as he reached the ground. Piers leaned against the wall as Max stripped the harness from him and bundled harness and ropes together. Daniel climbed down from the balcony and picked up the crutches.

Then the two men stood each side of Piers, slinging his arms around their shoulders so that he hung between them, and set off for the hedgerow.

Getting an injured man through it was difficult but Anna helped to hold branches apart and Daisy leapt out of the wheelchair to help as well. The moment the men were through, Piers was lowered into the wheelchair and swathed in Daisy's blankets.

'Back to the vehicles,' Max instructed, but Piers said, 'Wait!'

He grinned at Anna with eyes that were as merry as ever despite the purple shadows that ringed them and the thinness of his face. Reaching an arm out, he drew her to him so he could kiss her full on the lips. 'At last,' he said, and Anna wasn't sure whether she most wanted to laugh or burst into tears of relief.

'Enough of the canoodling,' Max said. 'There'll be time for that later.'

He beckoned Daniel and Daisy to climb into the field with him and Anna pushed Piers down the lane as though she were merely retracing her steps with Daisy in the chair. None of them spoke, having agreed that it was foolish to risk being overheard by a farmworker or someone who happened to be out exercising a dog or taking the air.

Thea was on the watch for them and jumped from the horsebox, though she kept looking up and down the lane in case anyone approached. She beckoned to confirm that the coast was clear and Max, Daniel and Daisy climbed from the field onto the lane.

'You must be Thea,' Piers said, keeping his voice low. 'Thank you so much for looking after my darling.'

He took hold of Anna's hand again as though he wanted never to let it go but it was essential to get away before his absence was discovered. Max and Daniel lifted him into the horsebox while Daisy, Thea and Anna loaded the wheelchair, crutches and harness into the van.

Goodbyes comprised hasty hugs and whispers then Max gestured impatiently for Anna and Thea to climb into the horsebox beside Piers. Max climbed in too though they were rather squashed with four of them sitting side by side. With a final wave to Daniel and Daisy, Max drove off.

'I can't tell you how delighted I am to be home,' Piers said. 'By home I mean with Anna, of course.'

He turned at the sound of a snuffle and saw the baby in his basket. 'Who's this?' he asked. He saw the expression on Anna's face and went even paler. 'You don't mean…?'

Anna reached around for the basket. 'This is James,' she said. 'Your son.'

Piers stared down at the sleeping baby in stunned wonder then picked him up and kissed him. 'Hello, James. I'm your father. I'm sorry I haven't met you until now. I'm sorry your mother has been through such a difficult time. But I'm here now and I'm going to make things up to you. Starting with a wedding. I want to give my name to both of you just as soon as possible. I couldn't love two people more.'

He glanced across at Anna. Tears shimmered in her eyes but she laughed them away.

'I love you more than life,' Piers told her, and no one could doubt it.

Forty-Five

'She looks contented,' Daisy told Lily, looking up from where the mother cat was lying on her side, suckling four tiny kittens.

If only Daisy could feel contented but her misery was hardly the fault of sweet little Lily or these adorable felines, even though it was this tortoiseshell mother cat that Lily had wanted Daisy to see the day she'd disappointed Rory. What a wretched day that had been.

She'd felt terrible watching Rory drive into the distance, not knowing if she'd ever see him again. Unable to hold back tears, Daisy had paced up and down the lane, but she'd known that Lily might come looking for her or someone else might happen along and start gossip circulating about why Daisy Flowers was crying. Dashing the tears away, she'd hastened to Downs Edge and found Lily waiting in front of the farmhouse.

'What do you want me to see?' Daisy asked, hoping a big smile would mask her distress.

'She's in the kitchen.'

'She?'

Taking hold of Daisy's hand, Lily led her into the cottage kitchen where a basket had been placed near the hearth. The cat lay inside it, nervous, suspicious but too exhausted to move from the welcoming warmth of her cushion. Daisy crouched down with Lily but made no attempt to touch the frightened creature. Instead she listened as Lily told her how she'd found the cat cowering behind her school in a pitiful state.

'You can see how thin she is. She's clean now but her poor fur was matted when I found her and her ear was torn and bleeding. She must have been struggling out in the wild for weeks or even months. She's expecting kittens and Daddy thinks they'll come very soon.'

Daisy made sympathetic noises and managed to get through both the visit and an evening with her father. But the moment she got into bed she burst into more tears and got up in the morning feeling gritty-eyed and listless.

'I'll manage fine if you want to go back to Brighton,' her father told her, clearly thinking she wanted to be with her friends.

'I'm in no rush to go back.'

She missed Thea and Anna badly but she wasn't convinced that her father was ready to cope alone. Besides, even with her friends, Daisy would have to pretend to be fine.

She set about her chores with as much energy as she could muster and made no objection when Lily ran down the lane after school to tell her the kittens had been born in the night and Daisy had to come and see them, 'Right now!'

Smiling wanly, she went to take a look. There were four kittens in all, three boys and a girl. 'The littlest kitten wasn't breathing when it was born,' Lily told her, 'but Daddy blew air into its mouth until it breathed for itself then he sat up late cuddling it to keep it warm. Didn't you, Daddy?'

Daniel had just stepped in from outside. 'Didn't I what, poppet?'

Lily told him and Daniel simply shrugged as though it had been the sort of thing anyone would do.

'Come again tomorrow,' Lily invited, when Daisy said she should be heading home. 'We'll be able to tell you what names we've chosen for the kittens.'

So Daisy went back again.

'The kittens are Louis, Louisa, Peter and Patch,' Jack told her. 'Lily chose Louis and Louisa, and I chose Peter and Patch.'

'They're wonderful names,' Daisy approved.

She'd been too distraught to take much notice of Daniel's home on her previous visits but wretchedness over Rory had settled to a steady misery and that third time she went into the house her curiosity finally stirred.

Mrs Beddows, the neighbour who'd helped Daisy and her father in years gone by, came in to help Daniel sometimes but mostly he managed alone and clearly he managed well. The kitchen was clean, comfortable and homely, a large table with eight chairs around it occupying the middle of the room and armchairs standing each side of the hearth. One wall had an old dresser holding willow patterned plates placed against it while shelves holding books and periodicals had been built against another. Drawings the children had made appeared here and there, and so did the small natural treasures they'd gathered – pretty stones, shells and fir cones.

There was a photograph too and Daisy leaned forward for a closer look. It was a family portrait of Daniel, a shyly pretty woman who was obviously his wife, and the children who were much younger then. Daniel's arm was around his wife's shoulder in a loving protective gesture while the children sat on their laps – Jack on his father's and Lily on her mother's. The eyes of both parents shone with pride.

Daisy hadn't given much thought to Mrs Oaks who'd died some years before Daniel moved to Downs Edge and never been known in the village. Now she realised how hard her death must have been for him. It was to his credit that he'd coped so well and brought up two delightful children. He was certainly no whiner.

Walking home again, Daisy's thoughts returned to Rory but this time a growing sense of unfairness sent small sparks into her unhappiness. Daisy understood he was committed to racing and restoring Castle Kerwig. She knew his work was irregular and he had to seize his chances where he found them.

But had it really been impossible for him to wait just ten or fifteen minutes? And could he not even have tried to understand her dilemma? She'd hoped it might have occurred to him that he'd been unreasonable but he'd neither visited nor written.

The following day they rescued Piers. Daniel said nothing to suggest he was aware of her unhappiness but Daisy still suspected he'd guessed that her romance had gone sour.

'Nervous?' he asked, as they set out. 'I know I am.'

Was that true or was he giving Daisy an excuse for staying quietly cocooned in misery? Either way it was a relief.

She was genuinely delighted to hear that Thea was engaged. Delighted to see the glowing love that Anna and Piers obviously shared too. But she couldn't help being aware of the contrast between the way their lives had taken upward swings while hers had swung downwards. Remembering the way Rory had expected her to drop everything to suit his convenience, the sparks of injustice grew stronger.

Now she was back at Downs Edge again at Lily's request. After showing her the animals that remained in the hospital – a pigeon had been released and the badger returned to the wild – Lily had brought her inside to see the cats.

'I'm going to make some tea,' Lily announced.

'Would you like me to help?'

'I can do it.' Lily appeared keen to show off her domestic abilities. 'Why don't you sit down?'

Daisy felt too restless to sit. She walked to the window that overlooked the rear of the property instead. Neat beds of vegetables, herbs and salads stretched from side to side and as far back as some distant greenhouses. Daniel was working there and Jack was helping. They worked in harmony, moving rhythmically and deftly, and exchanging occasional smiles. As Daisy watched, Daniel called his son over to show him something on a rhubarb leaf. An interesting insect? Whatever it was, it appeared to present no threat and soon they were working again.

Another question came into Daisy's mind. Rory was like a firework on a dark night. Bright. Vivid. Exciting. But where was the substance? Compared to Daniel's steady kindness, Rory appeared frivolous.

The thought surprised her momentarily but then it made her ponder yet another question. Had she kept Rory secret from everyone because she knew, deep down, that he wasn't a solid sort of person but… Daisy sought for a description and came up with a single word. Selfish. Rory was selfish

Something Max had said about him nudged at Daisy's memory. *He's full of blarney.* Certainly Rory spoke in extravagant terms of his ambition and love for his home but would a man who was serious about restoring Castle Kerwig spend money on flamboyantly smart clothes and a flashy car? Would he bet on races too?

Astoundingly, Daisy realised that if Rory drove up there and then to make things up with her, she'd accept his apology but after that… no, she wouldn't want to walk out with him again. She was over him.

'Tea's ready,' Lily told her.

Daisy turned from the window and sat at the table as Lily – tongue between her pretty white teeth in concentration – poured the tea into cups. Four cups, Daisy noticed. 'Are Jack and your father coming in?'

'I'll take the tea out to them.' Lily picked one cup up carefully.

Daisy picked up the other cup and they carried them outside.

'Lovely,' Daniel said, taking Lily's cup with a smile.

Jack grinned as Daisy passed him the other cup. 'Thanks, Daisy.'

Daniel bent to pick up a spray of blossom he'd placed by his tools. 'Thought you might like to put this into water, poppet,' he said, passing it to Lily who looked delighted.

He had a smile for Daisy too. She answered with a small smile of her own, beginning to relax with him at last.

Lily and Daisy returned to the kitchen to drink their own tea. Lily twirled the blossom in her fingers then raised it to Daisy's hair. 'You look like a bride,' she said.

Not that again.

'Are you definitely not getting married?' Lily asked.

'Not at the moment.'

'So I can't be your bridesmaid?'

'Sorry.'

The sound of voices had them turning to the window. One voice was Daniel's. The other was female. It was low-pitched and pleasing though Daisy couldn't hear the words being spoken.

'Perhaps I can be Daddy's bridesmaid,' Lily said, getting up.

Daniel's bridesmaid? Frowning, Daisy watched as Lily opened the back door and waved to the visitor.

It was Ellen Harker, a widow who lived just outside the village. Daisy had never got to know her well as Ellen was eight or nine years older but looking at her now Daisy was struck by how tall, slender and neat Ellen was. How attractive too with her glossy brown hair and pretty dress. Even her laughter sounded pleasant.

Daniel laughed too and Daisy felt as though claws were tearing at her heart. What on earth was the matter with her? The answer was startling. She was jealous, but how could this be when only a few days ago she'd fancied herself halfway to being in love with Rory? Daisy couldn't understand *how* it had happened. She just knew beyond doubt that it *had* happened. In getting to know Daniel better, love for him had crept up on her unawares along with love for his adorable children.

But Daisy had rejected him and Ellen Harker had taken her place in Daniel's affections. No wonder he felt no awkwardness around Daisy. He was long over his passing fancy for her.

Daisy's tea suddenly tasted bitter.

Forty-Six

Thea decided against wearing her engagement ring on her trip to London, afraid it might attract unwelcome attention from thieves bearing in mind that she'd be visiting the shabbier districts. She decided to wear old clothes too. 'How do I look?' she asked Anna.

'Like a genteel young woman who's down on her luck,' Anna told her.

'Which is what I am,' Thea said, pleased.

'Only until you marry the major.'

Thea couldn't think of Ralph without her conscience stirring and it didn't help that Anna appeared to be puzzled by the way he was still being kept in the dark. She and Piers behaved as though they loved, liked and trusted each other implicitly. They were two halves of a whole. But with nothing to hide on either side they'd been free to grow close in the time they'd spent together before Piers's expedition and in the letters they'd exchanged before the shipwreck.

Thea and Ralph had renewed their acquaintance only recently and with secrets standing between them so it was bound to be different. Doubtless they'd grow to be open too, but just now Thea still felt strongly that they needed to get to know each thoroughly over time instead of being catapulted into an early wedding by an urge on Ralph's part to rescue her. She'd have no choice but to tell him the full story if she found herself out on the streets but Thea was determined to fight Stanley to the last moment.

With his deadline expiring today he'd been to the house last night and thumped on the door but Thea had refused to let him in. He'd smashed a bottle on the steps, sending beer spilling down them, but had left no permanent damage. Not yet anyway. 'You'll be careful?' she urged Anna and Piers.

'We'll take no chances at all,' Piers assured her.

'Wish me luck then.'

Anna folded her into a hug and Piers kissed her hand from where he was stationed in a chair.

A final scan of the street from the drawing-room window showed no sign of Stanley or Bulky Man. Thea stepped outside cautiously then hastened to the end of the road. Turning the corner, she waited for a moment then peered back along Clarendon Place. No one appeared to be following her although a pursuer might be exercising caution too.

She stayed vigilant all the way to Brighton station but saw no one suspicious. Seeking safety in numbers, she settled into a carriage that was already occupied by two middle-aged ladies. A whistle blew, steam hissed and she was on her way.

Relaxing a little, she thought over the previous day with mixed feelings. Thea was delighted that Piers had been reunited with Anna and more than a little relieved to hear that Piers had some money put by. 'I'm not a rich man and

I'm going to have to earn a living but I've got some ideas about that,' he'd said. 'In the meantime, I have enough to pay my own way here. I won't sponge on you, Thea.'

Despite the fact that he was obviously still in pain, Piers's blue eyes had shone with eagerness and Thea had needed only a few minutes in his company to realise how much zest for life he had. It was contagious and exciting. Thea was sure he'd make his way in the world and provide for his little family somehow.

It had been lovely to see Daisy too though her natural merriness had appeared dimmed. The awkwardness with Daniel had eased a little as far as Thea could see but perhaps Daisy was disappointed because the days of the guest house were coming to an end. It was understandable if Pixfield felt quiet to her after the liveliness of Brighton. Thea would gladly give her a reference if she wanted to apply for other work. Not every job involved cooking, after all.

Despite Daisy's low spirits she'd congratulated Thea on her engagement warmly. So had Daniel. Max had been considerably cooler but he hadn't taken to Ralph and Thea couldn't blame him for that given Ralph's tactlessness at Clareswood. Poor Ralph. He hadn't meant to cause offence.

Something Max had said when they'd brought Piers to Clarendon Place had stuck in Thea's mind. He'd spoken in response to an announcement Piers had made about wanting to marry Anna quickly. 'We don't care about a big song-and-dance type of wedding,' Piers had explained. 'We'll be happy just to have Anna's family and all of you with us. You're the ones who helped my darling girl, after all.'

'Good idea,' Max had said. 'We should celebrate with Thea while we can.'

Did he think Thea would turn her back on them all once she was married to Ralph? If so, he was wrong. These people were her friends, and Ralph – and his parents – needed to understand that.

She supposed her wedding would be a much showier affair than Piers and Anna had in mind. 'You mustn't worry about the cost,' the Kirby-Laws had assured her. 'Ralph is our only child so it will give us pleasure to see him married in style. The wedding will be our gift to you both.'

How generous they were. Thea knew she was lucky to be marrying into such a welcoming family. Once her secrets were behind her she'd be able to give her good fortune the appreciation it deserved.

On that thought she turned her mind to the mission that lay ahead. She'd seen no one suspicious walking along the train corridor in search of her but still took every precaution when she arrived at London Bridge. She waited to leave the train until most passengers had got off then hastily attached herself to a group of tall men amongst whom her own height would be less conspicuous. Once outside the station, she hid in a shop doorway for several minutes. Only when she was satisfied that no one was in pursuit did she head for Pip's neighbourhood.

Pip had written his address at the top of his note but Thea didn't feel comfortable knocking on his door. His parents might think she should have asked their permission before involving him, or Pip might be hoping to keep his half-crown to himself.

She arrived at Roper Street at what she anticipated was the right time to catch him on his return from school. A few minutes later a trickle of children began to appear but

Pip wasn't amongst them. After another ten minutes she began to wonder if he'd entered his home through a back alley.

She waited a little longer and her ears picked up the sound of youthful yells some distance away. Following the sound, she rounded a corner to see Pip kicking a football around with his gang of friends.

He saw her too and his eyes glowed in anticipation of pay day. 'You got my letter?' he asked, running up.

'I did, and thank you for your help.'

His gaze dropped to her bag.

'I've brought your money,' she assured him, 'but I wonder if you might help me some more? There'll be an extra shilling if you do.'

An extra shilling met with Pip's approval.

'For one thing, I'd like you to show me the pawnbroker's shop you mentioned.'

'And for another?'

'Did the pawnbroker write the lady's details down?'

'In a book. A big book.'

'Can you remember where he kept it?'

Pip thought back. 'Behind the counter, Miss.'

'Do you think you can divert the pawnbroker's attention long enough to give me a chance to look at it?'

''Course I can.'

'I don't want you to do anything dangerous or damage any property.'

'Leave it to me, Miss. Oi!' He turned and ran back towards his friends, 'Who wants to earn an extra shilling?'

They all did, of course. Thea sighed. This mission was proving expensive but with luck it would be worth it.

Pip led her to the road in which the pawnbroker had his shop.

'Can you describe the locket to me?' Thea asked.

'It was just a locket.' Clearly, Pip thought it was unreasonable to expect a boy to notice jewellery when there were footballs and catapults in the world. But he applied his mind to the question. 'Silver. Not round exactly but….'

'Oval?' Thea suggested.

'That's right. With a swirly pattern on the front.'

Engraving, Thea assumed. 'Give me three or four minutes before you start whatever you're going to do. And remember –'

'We won't do no damage, Miss.'

Hmm.

Thea crossed the road and walked into the shop. She'd brought a narrow gold bracelet with her, one of the few items of jewellery she'd managed to hide from Herbert. The pawnbroker was a small wizened man with rounded shoulders that suggested he spent too long hunched up at a desk peering through the magnifying glass that hung around his neck.

'Forgive me,' Thea began. 'I've never done this before and I'm not sure how to proceed. I need to raise a little money and wonder if you might give me a loan if I offer this bracelet as security?'

He held out his hand to invite her to pass it to him. Probably her story was no different from those of most people who came into his shop. He raised his glass to the bracelet and at that moment the sound of shouting came from the street. Pip had got to work and Thea awarded him full marks for ingenuity.

He'd persuaded his smallest friend to play the victim in a fight. The boy was sprawled on the ground and Pip sat astride him aiming pretend but very convincing slaps at his head.

'Oh, dear,' Thea cried. 'That young boy is going to be seriously hurt.'

The pawnbroker muttered under his breath then raised a section of the counter so he could pass through and get outside where he set about ending the fight with shouting and a few attempted slaps of his own. Thea looked over the counter and saw the book. Tall enough to reach it, she leafed rapidly through the pages until she found the right date. And there it was. Just one entry for a silver locket on a twelve inch chain, oval in shape, engraved with a pattern of leaves and belonging to Jessie Jarrold of 16 Slixon Street.

Thea committed the address to memory, returned the pages to their original order then stepped away to await the pawnbroker's return.

'Bloody boys,' he grumbled.

'Actually, I've changed my mind,' Thea said. 'I think I might be able to raise the money another way. So sorry to have troubled you.'

'Humph,' he said, as though women, like boys, were nothing more than nuisances.

Thea found a grinning Pip and his friends waiting at the end of the road.

'You should be on the stage,' she told them. 'That fight looked real.'

'So it's an extra shilling each,' Pip concluded.

Thea handed the money over, asked for directions to Slixon Street and learned that it was only three roads away.

Number sixteen was as shabby as most of the other houses in the street but an effort had been made to keep it clean. Thea guessed the landlady was trying to attract lodgers, and hoped Jeremiah Jarrold wouldn't leave her out of pocket.

What next? The old problem of ensuring Jeremiah wasn't alerted to her quest remained. It seemed unlikely that he'd be out working though he might well be out drinking or gambling. If anyone in the family had a job it was more likely to Jessie. Keeping a job might in fact explain why the Jarrolds hadn't moved far from their previous lodgings.

Thea was wondering if she should ask Pip to knock on the door and draw Jessie out on some pretext or other when movement in an upstairs window caught her attention. Looking up, she saw a dejected Jessie. At that moment Jessie saw Thea and stiffened in shock.

She wouldn't want Thea coming into the house and giving the game away about their previous conversations. Or so Thea hoped. She was right. In no time, Jessie hurried out of the door, wrapped up in a shawl that she'd pulled over her head. 'How did you find me?' she hissed.

'That doesn't matter,' Thea said. 'What matters is the black eye you're trying to hide.'

Jessie glared then blinked as tears pooled in her eyes.

'You can't go on like this,' Thea said.

'Easy for you to say.'

'And not so easy for you to betray your father,' Thea acknowledged. 'Is there a café nearby? You need to eat.'

The poor girl looked half-starved.

'I can't—'

'I'll pay. Don't think of it as charity. Think of it as payment for your time.'

'For my services, you mean. So you can use me to have my father arrested.'

'I certainly hope that will happen. For your sake as well as mine. If your father is found guilty of fraud he'll be locked up long enough for you to get away, build a new life and let the trail to that new life grow cold.'

Thea bought Jessie some soup and watched her eat it hungrily, sweeping bread around the bowl to ensure she wasted not a drop. 'You're not working?' Thea guessed.

'I had a job. A decent job. But I lost it.'

Jessie didn't explain why she'd lost her job but Thea wouldn't have been surprised to learn that Jeremiah had put in a drunken appearance or that Jessie had made mistakes due to her nerves being in shreds.

The soup brought a slight tinge of colour to Jessie's cheeks. 'I suppose you're thinking I owe you some help now,' she accused.

'Actually, I was wondering when you might next get something to eat.'

Jessie's eyes registered surprise and finally defeat. Not that Thea saw it as defeat but as the first step on the road to justice for both of them. 'My father never told me he committed fraud,' Jessie said.

'But?' Thea prompted.

'I remember him arriving home one day in a new suit of clothes. He had a pocket watch too and was incredibly pleased with himself. Chuckling even. He pulled a roll of notes from his pocket – five pound notes – and said he'd got them just for signing his name. Easiest money he'd ever earned in his life, he said.'

'When was this?'

'Two years ago. I remember because it was my birthday and I thought he might give me a few shillings as a present.'

The twist of Jessie's mouth told Thea that she hadn't received as much as a farthing.

'That certainly fits with the time my mother's Will – the fraudulent Will – was apparently signed,' Thea said. 'It fits with the time my stepbrother was in the country too. Can you remember anything else?'

'Not really. My father said he hoped his friend would put him in the way of earning easy money again but it never happened. And it wasn't long before the money was gone and the watch with it.'

As evidence of fraud it was all circumstantial. What Thea needed was an actual admission of guilt on Jeremiah's part. Might there be a way of coaxing that from him?

'What does your father do with his time these days?' Thea asked.

'Very little. He soon drinks and gambles money away, whether it's money he's won or scrounged, or money I've earned.'

'So he might like the idea of going to a racecourse to bet? Brighton racecourse perhaps? There's a meeting there on Saturday.' Thea had seen posters advertising the event.

'He'd love it. But I don't see how it could happen. He hasn't a penny to his name at the moment and I'm struggling to get work.'

Thea opened her purse again and counted out some money. 'I have an idea. Hold onto this then let your father find it when I tell you to do so. Can I write to you at Slixon Street?'

Jessie hesitated.

'Where then?' Thea asked, hoping Jessie's courage wouldn't fail her now.

'There's a girl at number eight who's friendly. I'll ask her to take a letter for me.'

'Thank you.' Thea got to her feet and patted Jessie's hand. 'You're doing the right thing by helping.'

'Am I?'

'You can't go on as you are. Next time your father lashes out he could have a bottle in his hand. A black eye would be the least of your problems then. You might be scarred or blinded. You might even be killed. Look out for my letter.'

'What's it going to say?'

'I don't know yet. But I'll work something out.'

It was her last chance to save her house.

Forty-Seven

Anna paused at the door to the drawing-room, feeling a warm glow of happiness as she saw Piers rocking baby James and cooing to him lovingly. Sensing her presence, he looked around and grinned. 'Do you think James is getting to know me?' he asked.

'I'm sure he is.' Anna walked into the room and looked down at their son who was staring up at his father in apparent fascination.

She knew that at only four weeks old, James was too young to focus properly let alone understand what was said to him but there was no doubt that he felt comfortable in Piers's arms. How similar they were with their golden hair and vivid blue eyes. 'I think his eyes are going to stay that colour,' Anna said.

Piers looked confused so she added, 'The colour of a baby's eyes can change. They're often blue at birth only to darken later.'

'What a lot I've got to learn about fatherhood.'

'You're a natural,' Anna assured him.

Piers kissed James's forehead then passed him to Anna who kissed him too. As Anna laid James in his basket, Piers hauled himself to his feet and used his crutches to hobble to the window. He was taking the threat of Stanley Ambrose seriously and no wonder.

Not long after Thea had left for London on Monday, Max had surprised them with a visit. 'I can't stay more than a few minutes,' he'd said, then smiled grimly as he noticed Anna taking in his unshaven face, battered hat and ill-fitting workman's clothes. Max wasn't a dandy by any stretch of the imagination but he'd always been neat.

'Disguise, just in case Ambrose or his Bulky Man have seen me before,' he explained. 'I wanted to be sure neither of them followed Thea because it would be disastrous if she accidentally led them to Jarrold.'

Max had helped Anna and Piers because the Rutherfords' behaviour had touched his sense of outrage. He was helping Thea because Stanley's behaviour was touching his sense of outrage too. Unless…

An idea floated into Anna's mind and gave new significance to the coolness he'd shown over Thea's engagement. Had he been cool because he was in love with Thea himself? Goodness. Poor Max.

'Did anyone follow her?' Piers asked.

'Bulky Man, or at least a man who matched his description.'

Anna was aghast. 'Did you manage to warn Thea?'

'I put a crease in Bulky Man's plans instead. I'd taken a bottle of milk with me so I started to drink it as I walked.'

'And walked straight into Bulky Man,' Piers guessed. 'I hope you made a mess of his suit?'

'Jacket, waistcoat and trousers,' Max confirmed. 'I said, "Sorry, Guv'nor," in my role of scruffy working man then dabbed at his clothes with a filthy handkerchief that only added oil to the mess. Luckily he wasn't the sort of man to accept an apology graciously. He called me all the names under the sun, but that suited me fine because it meant I could call on passers-by to reason with him. Thea's train had left long before the crowd dispersed.'

'You did well,' Piers complimented.

'I thwarted Bulky Man and his paymaster today but I'm sure it's only a matter of time before they're back in action.'

'We'll stay vigilant,' Anna promised.

That had been two days ago. Thea had kept mostly to the house since returning from London though she was out on an important errand today. 'I'll be especially careful now I know Bulky Man is still around,' she'd said. 'Though I won't assume he's the only soldier in Stanley's army. I'll try to make it impossible for anyone to follow me.'

She'd pinned her distinctive hair as close to her head as possible, covered it with a hat and packed a different hat and shawl into her bag so she could change her appearance in an instant. She'd also left early so as to lead anyone who attempted to follow her in a game of hide and seek all over Brighton before she even attempted her errand.

She still hadn't returned. 'I hope she's safe,' Anna said. 'And I hope she saves her house even if we will have to move out of it. I've enjoyed living here, Piers. Not just because it's a lovely house. And not just because I've been sharing it with Thea and Daisy, wonderful though they are. I've actually enjoyed helping to run a guest house. Maybe we could run our own guest house at some time in the future.'

'You're welcoming and efficient, my darling. I can see why the idea appeals to you.'

'It doesn't appeal to you?'

'It does, now I come to think of it,' Piers said. 'Though I've some ideas of my own about how I might earn a living.'

'So you've said, but you're being terribly secretive.'

'Not secretive. Just cautious until I know how the land lies.'

Anna noticed movement along the street. It was a telegraph boy on his red bicycle. The war had been over for almost five years and these days telegrams like the one Mr Acaster had sent could relate to the happiest of tidings but she still couldn't see a telegraph boy without her mind returning to those dark days when the sight of one had made everyone in the street fall silent as they watched and waited to see which house the boy approached, praying it wouldn't be their house because telegrams often brought news of death or terrible injury.

Her stomach lurched as the boy skidded to a halt just outside. Was there bad news from Ma and the children? Or could Piers's parents be getting in touch at last?

Anna glanced at Piers and was surprised to see that he was smiling in satisfaction. 'Here's hoping this is good news,' he said, hobbling into the hall to open the door.

Following, Anna watched him give the boy a tip then open the telegram. 'I hope you don't mind, but we're having visitors today,' he announced, beaming.

Max, Daniel and Daisy were coming in the evening but clearly Piers had different people in mind. 'Visitors?' she questioned.

'Let me be mysterious for a little while longer, angel,' he said, kissing her.

Anna was relieved when Thea returned safely.

'I did see Bulky Man,' she reported, making Anna's heart jump momentarily. 'But I lured him into Hannington's as it's the biggest store in Brighton and looked at women's dresses for a while. He had to keep his distance in there because he didn't exactly fit in. Then I rushed to a different part of the store. Bulky Man came after me but I dropped a handkerchief to give myself an excuse for ducking behind a counter so he didn't spot me. The moment he turned away I tiptoed back the way I'd come and went outside.'

'I imagine that made Bulky Man happy,' Piers said, laughing.

'I slipped into an alley, changed my hat and went into another shop to see if he appeared. He raced straight past, looking furious.'

'You didn't see your stepbrother?' Anna asked.

'I dodged around Brighton for a while but saw no of sign of Stanley or anyone else who appeared to be taking an interest in me.'

'So you managed to see Jessie's friend?'

'I did. Rose jumped at the chance to move away with Jessie once Jeremiah has been arrested.'

This was excellent news.

Later, Anna smiled when she opened the door to Piers's visitors. 'Mr Acaster, how nice to see you,' she said, standing back to let the *Herald*'s editor into the hall.

It really was nice to see him because he'd been kind and generous with both his money and his time. But it wasn't the thought of a social visit that had put that satisfied look onto Piers's face. Was Piers hoping to persuade Mr Acaster to relaunch the Amazon expedition with another ship? Or did Piers have a different expedition in mind? Anna felt a pang of dismay at the thought of being separated from him for months on end again but Piers was an adventurer by nature and it wouldn't be fair to restrict him.

Mr Acaster had brought a thin, grey-haired gentleman along. 'Arthur Sinclair,' he said, introducing him.

'I'm happy to meet you,' Anna told him.

She led the men into the drawing-room and left them with a beaming Piers as she went downstairs to make tea. 'Well?' Thea asked, and Anna told her the identity of the visitors.

'Though I still don't know why they're here,' she added.

Luckily, she didn't have to wait much longer to find out. She carried the tea tray upstairs and put it on a table because Piers was holding an arm out to invite her to go to him. He looked delighted. 'I'm going to write a book and Mr Sinclair is going to publish it,' he announced.

'A book?'

'About being shipwrecked.'

'I'm going to publish extracts in the *Herald* too,' Mr Acaster told her.

'That's wonderful,' Anna said.

Piers had told her all he remembered about the sinking of the *Adiona*. Four men had survived it, floating in the ocean for two days after lashing themselves to some wreckage. Piers had been uninjured then except for some bruises but a second storm had sent them crashing into rocks off the coast of Brazil, fracturing Piers's skull and pelvis, and knocking him unconscious.

Some days later he'd learned that one of the survivors had been lost in the second storm. Piers and the others had been found by local men and taken to a village. It had been a remote village and weeks had passed before a message got through to the authorities and a rescue boat arrived. Luckily, Piers's bones had healed well despite the lack of formal medical care.

Anna shuddered whenever she thought of the suffering the shipwreck had caused but she could see that an account of it would make for gripping and moving reading.

'We're going to start a fund to raise money for the families of those who were lost,' Mr Acaster said, and Anna didn't need to look at Piers to know that this had been his idea.

'There's more,' Piers told her. 'I'm going to write adventure stories too.'

This was even more surprising. 'I wrote the opening chapter of one story while I was waiting for you to come and rescue me,' he said. 'I sent it off to Mr Acaster and he sent it to Mr Sinclair here to see what he thought.'

'Mr Rutherford's a talented writer,' Mr Sinclair told her.

Anna felt lightheaded with relief. With an income from Piers's writing they'd be able to afford a home, food, coals for a fire… Even more importantly, Piers would feel useful and fulfilled.

There was only tea to drink but Anna still called Thea up to toast Piers's new career.

Afterwards, when Anna had Piers to herself again, she asked the question that was burning inside her. 'What put the idea of writing books into your head?'

'I started thinking about it after Max shinned up the drainpipe that first time. I'd been feeling pretty miserable before then to be honest.'

'You'd been through a terrible time with your injuries.'

'I'd been through an even worse time when I thought your feelings for me had changed. After Max told me you loved me as much as ever I felt I was bursting free of quicksand. I started to plan our future together and knew I'd have to earn a living. I've been writing articles about my travels for years so writing about my shipwreck felt like a natural next step as long as I could find someone to publish the book. My imagination was fired up by then and I started to wonder if I might write adventure novels too.'

'It's marvellous, Piers. Really. But I don't want you to feel you have to stay at home all the time if you'd rather be travelling. I don't want to tie you down.'

'I hated being apart from you. I'd hate being apart from my son. Travelling still interests me and maybe one day I'll travel again. In fact maybe we can travel together. But just at this moment what I want most of all is to settle down with you and watch our son grow.'

'Travelling in your imagination for your stories?'

'Exactly.'

'I can't pretend I'm not thrilled by the idea of having you at home but you will let me know if you want to go on a trip or two? It's important to me that you're happy and free to be the sort of person you wish to be.'

'I know.'

He drew her to him again and kissed her. He nudged her lips softly and the kiss grew more urgent. Anna snaked her arms around Piers's neck and kissed him back, revelling in the passion of it. But then she drew back a little and laughed, knowing her cheeks must be glowing.

'Wrong time and place,' Piers guessed.

'Mmm.'

They both tensed suddenly as the door knocker sounded again. It was too early for Daisy, Daniel and Max to be calling.

'Careful,' Piers called, as Anna crossed to the window.

She moved the curtain aside just enough for her to see who was standing on the doorstep. When she turned back to Piers, her expression was sober.

'Trouble?' he asked.

Forty-Eight

Daisy hadn't felt as low as this since the death of her much-loved mother seven years ago. Back then she'd been able to howl her grief with all the abandon of a child. Now her feelings had to be locked up inside and examined only when she was alone.

Not that Daisy wanted to dwell on them. She was reminding herself constantly that no one had died on this occasion and a bruised heart couldn't possibly compare with the loss of a beloved mother.

But it hurt all the same. It hurt so much that it took her breath away at times. Looking back, Daisy's awkwardness with Daniel and her disappointment over Rory felt like the emotions of an inexperienced girl. The anguish she felt now was the emotion of a person who'd passed into womanhood in a few short days and she had no one to blame for that anguish except herself.

Had she not been so blind to the attractions of one man and dazzled by the frivolity of the other, she could have been with Daniel now – as his sweetheart or perhaps even his fiancée, looking forward to becoming his wife and sharing his life.

How wonderful it would have been to have had Daniel turning those outdoors-green eyes on her and smiling. To have had him folding his strong arms around her and lowering his lips to hers. To have known she was loved by a man she not only loved in return but admired and respected too.

Instead she'd dreamed of working with Max and run away to Brighton when what she really wanted – needed – was right here under her nose. The taste of self-blame was bitter indeed.

But Daisy had no choice but to endure it with as much courage as she could muster. She'd be a poor daughter and friend if she let her unhappiness trouble others.

Hearing Daniel's van coming down the lane, Daisy ignored the way her heart gave a painful squeeze and put on a show of friendliness as though she were putting on a hat. 'How are the kittens?' she asked.

'All doing well, thank you.'

'And the fawn?'

'He'll be ready to go back into the wild in a day or two.'

'Alone?'

'No, I'll place him with a herd and see what happens. If the herd rejects him, I'll have to take him home again and Lily will adopt him as her pet.'

'Another pet.' Daisy smiled, for Lily had several.

Daniel smiled back. 'We're lucky we have the space for them.'

It cost Daisy another pang to think how Downs Edge might have been her home too. She imagined feeling the warmth of Lily's smiles and Jack's grins every single day as they tugged her out to see their latest discoveries from caterpillars to sparrows then snuggled up to her in an armchair and let the fire toast their toes.

She took a deep breath and began to talk about how much his friend, Joseph, was helping her father. It was exhausting but necessary if she were to avoid the jealousy that would stab her like a knife if Ellen Harker had space to come into the conversation.

It didn't help that Ellen had so many excellent qualities that Daisy lacked. She was calm, dignified, gracious and industrious. Doubtless she'd be the perfect wife to Daniel and an ideal mother to his children. In her care Jack and Lily would be fed on delicious home-cooked food, kept clean and brought up to be as industrious and polite as Ellen. And Daniel would feel happy and contented. He'd hold Ellen in his strong arms and smile down at her with gratitude and love.

Argh! The stab had come anyway and Daisy was hugely relieved when they finally reached Clarendon Place. She leapt out of the van before Daniel could walk round to help her and hastened up the steps to the door, trying hard to put her own problems aside.

'Everything all right?' she asked, as Anna let her in.

'We've had visitors,' Anna said.

'Oh?' Daisy was alarmed.

'Not Stanley or Bulky Man. Piers's parents.'

They'd reached the drawing-room by then, a room they were using because it gave a better view of the street outside. Daisy glanced at Piers to see if the visit had upset him but he looked calm. Pleased in fact.

He was sitting in an armchair with his crutches beside him and Anna went to stand at his shoulder. They didn't cling to each other but it was clear that each was happier being close to the other and it cost Daisy another pang to know she might have shared that sort of intimacy with Daniel.

'I suppose I'd call my parents... chastened,' Piers told her. 'They insisted that they'd thought they were doing the right thing by keeping me apart from Anna.'

'They also said they hadn't fully appreciated the strength of our feelings for each other,' Anna added.

Daisy wanted to scoff and say snobbery probably had a lot more to do with their attitude than misunderstanding but she saw that Anna and Piers already knew it.

'The important thing is that we're on speaking terms,' Anna continued. 'I might not be the woman they'd have chosen as their son's wife but they'll tolerate me if that's the only way they'll get to see Piers and their grandson.'

'At this stage we're calling a truce,' Piers said. 'But they were thrilled to meet James and I think he's going to build bridges.'

'They've agreed to come to the wedding,' Anna said.

'That's wonderful news,' Daniel said.

Daisy had been aware of him coming in behind her. How could she not be aware when his presence sent a tingling sensation across her skin? Now he went up to Anna and kissed her cheek then shook Piers's hand.

'It *is* wonderful.' That was Max's voice. He must have come in with Daniel.

He too kissed Anna and shook Piers's hand but it seemed to Daisy that her cousin was feeling grim. She supposed he was thinking of the seriousness of what lay ahead. 'Shall we get started?' he asked.

Everyone sat, and with her usual quiet efficiency Anna handed round cups of tea.

'Thea?' Max asked, inviting her to begin.

'I've written to Jessie and told her to let her father see the money at noon tomorrow. I've suggested she should drop it as she moves it from her pocket to her handbag. I just hope her father is too excited by the money to punish Jessie for hiding it.'

'Let's hope he never gets the chance to hurt her again,' Max agreed. 'She's certain he'll go to the Red Lion for a drink?'

'Not certain, but it's his nearest pub and he's been spending time in there.'

Max looked at Daniel. 'We shouldn't rely on it. Let's keep an eye on his house then follow him wherever he goes.'

Daniel nodded. 'If we follow him into a pub, it'll be easier to get chatting as we wait at the bar to be served.'

'I'm so grateful to you all for giving up your time,' Thea said.

'Ambrose has to be stopped,' Max said simply.

'It's still good of you to help.'

For a moment there was silence. Max looked at Thea as though he had a reply in mind but, on reflection, thought it best left unspoken.

Daisy supposed he'd intended to say something about Thea needing her friends to rally round her but that would have drawn attention to the fact that Ralph wasn't helping. By the look on her face, Thea was supposing the same. Thea must have her reasons for keeping Ralph in the dark but now they'd got engaged it puzzled Daisy. Thea had her pride but surely it shouldn't stand in the way of letting Ralph help her, especially when other friends were helping?

Daisy looked to Anna to see what she thought. As usual Anna's face had the calm stillness of a Madonna but those dark eyes missed nothing and, just now, they were looking thoughtfully from Thea to Max and back again. Which meant what exactly? That she was of the same opinion as Daisy? Or something else?

Anna roused herself. 'So you're going to persuade Jarrold to come to the races on Saturday,' she said to Max and Daniel.

'That's the idea,' Max confirmed. 'We'll tell him we have a tip for a dead cert in the three-thirty and have every intention of winning big though we won't tell him what the tip is. We'll just say he's welcome to come along with us.'

'We'll walk him home after the pub so he won't think it strange that we know where he lives when we call to take him to Brighton,' Daniel added.

'Then we'll loosen his tongue with drink and manoeuvre him into admitting that his signature on your mother's Will was part of a fraud,' Max continued.

'I'll have a policeman ready to hear the confession,' Piers promised.

'And Daisy, Thea and I will keep our eyes open for Bulky Man and Stanley Ambrose,' Anna finished, because it was absolutely essential that they should be kept away from Jarrold.

Would the plan work, though? Quiet descended once again as they considered all the ways it might go wrong. Max and Daniel might be unable to meet with Jarrold in London or to persuade him to come to Brighton. Jarrold might agree to come to Brighton only to do another moonlight flit before Saturday. Even if they got him to the races he might refuse to talk about the Will, or the policeman might not be prepared to linger long enough to hear a confession.

'It's the best plan we've got,' Max reminded them. 'The twins will look after the house again while we're out and—'

He broke off as three loud thumps landed on the front door. 'I'll find out who it is but I'll keep the door shut,' Thea said.

She went into the hall while the rest of them stayed in the drawing-room but they all got to their feet in case they needed to act quickly.

'Mr Ambrose,' they heard Thea say. 'I'm afraid I haven't changed my mind about—'

'Get out of my house!' The words came as a roar accompanied by the sounds of the door bursting open and Stanley barging inside.

Piers was the first into the hall as he'd been sitting closest to it. 'I shouldn't use violence, if I were you,' he said coldly.

'I'm not afraid of a cripple,' Stanley jeered.

'I'm younger and stronger,' Piers pointed out with icy calm. 'I think I'd beat you in a fight.'

'Not that that he needs to tackle you alone,' Max said, joining Piers in the hall and being followed by Daniel, Daisy and Anna.

This was Daisy's first look at Stanley and the sight of him disgusted her. He was big, fat and oily with pouches beneath his eyes and coarse red lips. Even from a distance she could smell him.

'Who the hell are—'

'We're Miss Fairfax's friends and we'd like you to leave,' Max said.

'It's my damned house!'

'Tell that to a court of law,' Max taunted. 'If you dare.'

Daniel stepped forward, rolling his sleeves up purposefully. 'Shall I—'

'I think Mr Ambrose is leaving,' Max told him. 'Isn't that right, Mr Ambrose?'

Stanley glared at him and for a moment Daisy thought he might launch himself at Max. Instead he kicked an angry foot at the hall table and left. 'You'll not get the better of *me*!' he shouted.

Max closed the door behind him. 'This lock has a couple of screws loose. I'll fix them before I go.'

In the meantime he drew the bolt across. 'I don't know anything about that man's circumstances,' Max said. 'But it looks to me as though things have gone badly for him and he's lost most, if not all, of his money.'

'I agree,' Thea told him. 'He looked prosperous two years ago. Even in February he looked smarter.'

'This house may be his last chance of avoiding bankruptcy and that makes him a dangerous man,' Max suggested.

There was a sombre feel to the rest of the evening and when they parted they took care to ensure there was no sign of Stanley, Bulky Man or anyone else who might be associated with them.

Daisy got into the van quickly to escape any offer of help from Daniel and was vexed when he noticed she'd trapped her dress in the van door. Releasing it, he tucked it around her, sending her one of those impersonal smiles he might have given anyone. Torture.

Neither of them spoke much on the drive home but as they drew close to Pixfield, Daisy felt she had to say something about his trip to London with Max. 'You *will* be careful when you meet Jarrold tomorrow?' she asked. Pleaded, rather.

'Of course,' he said, but his tone was paternal and he might have been reassuring Lily that there were no bogeymen hiding under her bed.

Not that Daisy blamed him for treating her like a child. It was only recently that she'd stopped behaving like one.

'Well?' her father asked, when she walked into the cottage.

She told him what they were planning. 'I'm worried something might go wrong but I'll just have to keep my fingers crossed,' she added.

'Hmm,' he said.

Hmm? She frowned at him, unsure of his meaning.

'Strikes me that there's more bothering you than your Brighton friend's house.'

Daisy stiffened.

'Don't worry, girl. I won't pry. But I'm your dad and I love you. And if you ever want a chat...' He patted her arm then picked up his newspaper and began to read it. Or pretended to read it.

Tears welled up in Daisy's eyes. She was trying to be brave but it was hard. So hard. All she could do was to try harder.

Daniel had promised to call in after he'd been to London with Max to let her know what had happened. All day long Daisy steeled herself to behave as though she had no special feelings for him. It would be terrible if she embarrassed him by letting him see into her heart.

'I can't stay long,' he said, when he came in during the evening, and for that Daisy was grateful. He didn't even sit down. 'All went well with Jarrold. He's the sort of man who'd sell his own mother for a shilling. Max and I took him home before he could spend all of Thea's money and agreed to call for him tomorrow to catch the train to the races.'

'He really thinks he's going to make his fortune?' Frank asked.

'He thinks Max's cousin works for the stables where this dead cert is in training. Not that he knows Max's real name or mine. We're going by the names of Mick and Davie.'

Frank snorted laughter.

'I'll come for you at ten tomorrow,' Daniel told Daisy. 'I'll drop you at Thea's house then catch the train to London with Max. Mick, I should say.'

'So you're all set for your adventure,' Frank said, when Daniel had left. 'I hope it all works out.'

He didn't say he also hoped a smile would return to Daisy's face but she knew it was in his thoughts.

She wore her dusky pink dress for the races. It was the dress she'd worn when meeting Rory but she felt like a different person now.

Daniel wore his best clothes too – a suit of dark grey cloth and a tie. How handsome he looked with his upright figure, shining bronze hair and warm green eyes. Keeping her observations to herself, Daisy aimed for a smile that suggested amusement at them both being dressed like actors in a play.

'You'll look after my girl?' Frank asked him.

'I'll look after myself,' Daisy said swiftly.

Frank drew her to him and kissed the top of her head. 'You may be growing up but you'll always be my little girl.'

Daisy couldn't see Daniel but imagined he was exchanging indulgent smiles with Frank. It was another painful reminder of how immaturely she'd behaved and how she only had herself to blame for this misery. 'I'll see you later,' she told Frank, and walked out to Daniel's van.

'Here's hoping for a successful day,' she said, as Daniel drove onto the lane.

Daisy had brightened her voice in the hope of recovering some dignity, but her spirits were suddenly cast into a deep crevasse.

Ellen Harker was in the lane. She saw them coming and waved. Daniel pulled up beside her and spoke to her through the open window. 'Good morning, Ellen.'

Ellen? But of course they were on Christian name terms. How fresh and neat Ellen looked in her lace-trimmed blouse and simple skirt. There was nothing of the flirt about her but regard for Daniel shone in her hazel eyes. Doubtless Daniel's eyes were shining with equal regard. Daisy squirmed, feeling very much in the way.

'I was bringing you some scones,' Ellen said, holding up a basket in which a crisp white napkin had been folded into a parcel.

'How kind,' Daniel told her. 'Shall I take them now? I'll be out for much of the day but they shouldn't spoil in the van.'

Ellen passed the basket through the window. 'I'll call in for it later.'

When she'd be able to have Daniel to herself.

Ellen realised Daniel wasn't alone. 'Good morning, Daisy.'

'Good morning.' Daisy felt like a gauche pupil greeting a teacher and Ellen's attention returned to Daniel.

'I thought I might teach Lily to make scones one day soon,' she said.

'Lily would like that.'

'But I can see you're on an errand now so I'll let you go.' Smiling, Ellen stood aside and Daniel drove them away.

Silence descended but it was an awkward silence to Daisy. She thought of filling it with questions about the animals in the hospital but the awkwardness wasn't about the absence of words in general. It was about the absence of words that related to Ellen. After the warmth Daisy had shown on Thea's engagement and Anna's reunion with Piers it felt ungracious not to acknowledge that Daniel was set fair for happiness too. Ungracious and… childish.

The silence grew more oppressive. 'What a nice lady Mrs Harker is,' Daisy finally said, though it made her feel as though her heart were being squeezed through a mangle.

'Indeed,' Daniel agreed.

Something more seemed to be required. 'Jack and Lily like her too so that's nice.'

Daniel smiled but what sort of smile was it? A smile that acknowledged she'd said all that the circumstances required? Or a smile that encouraged her to continue? Oh, heck. Daisy decided it was better to be too gracious than not gracious enough. 'Mrs Harker will be a wonderful mother to them.'

Daniel concentrated on overtaking a cart that was laden with baskets of vegetables. 'I'm sure she *would* be a wonderful mother,' he said then. 'Unfortunately, she won't have the chance to prove it.'

'Won't have...?' Daisy was puzzled. She was sure she hadn't been mistaken in reading Ellen's feelings. Could natural modesty be preventing Daniel from reading them the same way? Oh, heavens. Daisy wasn't going to have to help him along by playing matchmaker, was she? The thought of it almost choked her.

'I'm a lucky man to have won Ellen's regard,' Daniel acknowledged. 'I value her highly.'

So what was the problem?

'But it wouldn't be fair of me to marry her. I'm not in love with her, you see.'

'You're not?' Daisy was missing something. But what was it?

'It's hopeless, I'm afraid. I can't love Ellen because my heart belongs to another.'

Another? There was someone else in Daniel's life? Why not? He was a special man.

Daisy rode out a wave of agony but then a thought swooped into her head that made sense of it all. Daniel meant that his heart still belonged to his late wife. Daisy had been right all along about him only taking an interest in her because he wanted her to look after his house and children but she felt no satisfaction in having been right. She only felt hurt.

'My heart belongs to you, Daisy,' Daniel continued.

Awash with misery, it took a moment for Daisy to register his meaning. Then she turned to him in utter amazement. '*Me?*'

His smile combined affection with amusement. 'Yes, you.'

'But I thought… I thought…'

'That I was only ever interested in you as a housekeeper? I've been in love with you ever since I met you, Daisy. But I realised I'd spoken too soon and that you needed time to get to know your own mind.'

In other words, she'd needed time to grow up. 'You've been waiting for me?' Daisy's voice was soft with wonder now.

'I'm a patient man,' he told her, only to laugh and add, 'What am I saying? I'm not patient at all.'

He drew the van into the roadside then turned to her. Reaching out, he touched a hand to her cheek then cupped her chin and ran his thumb across her mouth in a way that had delight leaping up inside her. 'It's been torture to have to keep a distance, Daisy. It's been especially hard not to do this.'

He drew her to him, kissed her, then rested his forehead on the top of her head. 'At last!' he groaned, and then he kissed her again.

This was a different sort of kiss. A needy kiss that lit an equal urgency in Daisy so that she kissed him back as though she never wanted to let him go.

Even after the kiss was over she stayed in his arms and Daniel looked happy to keep her there. He smiled down at her. 'Happy?'

'Blissful. But I can't believe you still want me when I've behaved like a silly child.'

'You're not a child now. That's what matters. Will you marry me?'

'I can't think of anything I'd like more. But what about the children? They like Mrs Harker.'

'No disrespect to Ellen, but they like you more. They adore you.'

'I adore *them*.'

'Which makes everything perfect.'

'Not for Mrs Harker.' Daisy felt sorry for the woman.

'I've never given Ellen any encouragement to think we might be more than friends and I'm sure she knows deep down that I'm not the man for her. I hope she won't be unhappy, but if she is disappointed I have a shrewd idea it won't be for long. She's an attractive woman and I know of at least three men who'd like to pay their addresses to her. Good men too.'

'I'm glad,' Daisy said, then suddenly remembered that time was passing. 'Goodness, we need to be on our way.'

'We do,' Daniel agreed. 'Today has been wonderful so far. Let's hope it stays wonderful.'

Forty-Nine

Thea felt dismay wash over her when Piers turned from the drawing-room window and reported that Ralph was approaching.

'Ralph?' she questioned stupidly. But what she really wanted to know was why Ralph had turned up today of all days.

Was he worried because she'd been distracted when they'd last gone out to dinner? Thea had found it impossible to relax because her thoughts were in a tangle and kept veering off in different directions – to her parents, her friends, her stepbrother, Bulky Man…

'Thea, are you quite well?' Ralph had finally asked.

Luckily, her subconscious had registered the fact that he'd been talking about how much he was looking forward to their wedding but she'd felt a pang of guilt on seeing that her quietness had carved frown lines into his forehead. 'Forgive me,' she'd said. 'I'm a little tired tonight.'

'I'm not surprised. I can't wait until we're married and I'm able to take on some of your burdens.' He'd reached for her hand and cradled it between his much larger ones, his dark eyes earnest and loving.

Once the issue of the house was resolved, she'd be able to love him back the way he deserved instead of with only half of her attention. But right now she needed to get rid of him.

Opening the door, she schooled her expression into the appearance of a welcome she didn't feel. 'Ralph! This is a nice surprise.'

Even as she spoke, she scanned the street for Stanley and Bulky Man.

'Bunny and Charlotte are getting up a small party to go to the races,' he said. 'A last-minute arrangement. They've invited us to share the fun.'

Thea was horrified. 'Brighton races?'

'There's a meeting this afternoon. Do say you'll come.'

Thea could see no escape. If she declined to go to the races with Ralph, she wouldn't be able to go at all because he'd see her there. That meant there'd be fewer people looking out for Stanley and Bulky Man. Even if she stayed at home Ralph would wonder what was going on if he spotted her friends pretending not to know each other.

'Thea?' Ralph prompted, and at that point the situation became even more hopeless.

Max arrived with the twins, Albie carrying his shotgun again.

Ralph heard them approach and turning to see them, took instant umbrage. He stormed down the steps to the street. 'Now look here,' he said to Max. 'I know Miss Fairfax has a loose sort of business arrangement with you, but that doesn't mean you can bring all and sundry to her house.'

'Ralph, don't,' Thea called.

'Darling, I'll be obliged if you let me handle this for you.'

'No, Ralph.'

Chasing after him, Thea put a restraining hand on his arm then looked at Max. 'Please go inside. You too, Albie and Alfie.'

Max gave her a long look in which she read challenge though she wasn't sure what sort of challenge he intended. But then he beckoned to the twins. 'I think Miss Fairfax is capable of handling this… situation,' he said.

The twins grinned and climbed the steps behind him.

'My dear girl,' Ralph began, 'I really think—'

'Come inside, Ralph. We need to talk.'

She took his arm and led him into the house. He looked around when they reached the drawing-room and said, 'Humph,' as though relieved to find that Max and the twins had at least known their place well enough to go down to the servants' quarters.

Thea closed the door for privacy.

'Darling, it's wonderful that you're so kind,' Ralph said, 'but that man—'

'Max is helping me, Ralph.'

He opened his mouth to argue but Thea put up a hand to silence him. 'Please sit down and listen. You may be surprised – even shocked – by what I tell you, but I'll be grateful if you don't interrupt.'

'Really, Thea, I—' Something in her expression quietened him. 'Very well. The sooner I know what's going on, the better.'

'Then please sit down.'

Ralph hesitated. It wasn't gentlemanly to sit while a lady remained standing but Thea didn't care about that. She wanted him confined to a chair while she was free to pace the room and keep her head clear.

Finally, he sat and Thea told him everything. Ralph was neither still nor silent as she spoke. He fidgeted, he ran his hand through his hair, his Adam's Apple bobbed up and down, and several times he muttered, 'Good God!'

He tried to interrupt too but Thea wouldn't allow it until she'd finished. 'I'm appalled,' he finally said.

'Perhaps I was wrong to keep things from you,' Thea conceded.

'I'm not appalled with *you*. My darling girl, how could you think so?' He got to his feet and took her in his arms, cradling her head against his shoulder in a protective gesture. 'It's that stepbrother of yours who appals me. And to think you've had to suffer his evil all alone.'

'Not alone,' Thea corrected. 'I've been lucky with my friends.'

'Hmm. Well, you've finally confided in me so you can leave the matter in my hands.'

'No, Ralph. I know you want the best for me, but we already have a plan.'

'We?'

'Max, Daniel, Piers, Anna, Daisy—'

Ralph's pained look told her he thought that, as allies, they couldn't have been more inappropriate. 'We need the police and our family solicitor. He's a good chap who—'

'Please do nothing.' Thea stepped away from him. 'Stanley has a Will that looks to be in perfect order. The only way I can fight it is with evidence of fraud and that means extracting a confession from Jarrold. There's no way he'll confess if you frighten him off or lead Stanley to him.'

'But—'

'We're not excluding the police. Piers has an acquaintance in the force. He's arranged for an officer to overhear the confession and there'll be other policemen at the racecourse anyway.'

'But how are you going to extract this confession?'

Thea explained the plan but Ralph was still unimpressed. 'With all due respect, my love, it sounds hopelessly unlikely to me.'

'I know it might not work. But we've thought about it carefully and—'

'*We*,' Ralph scoffed.

'I'm sorry I didn't involve you. I didn't want my circumstances to influence how you felt about me.'

'You couldn't have thought I'd love you less if you hadn't a penny to your name?'

'Quite the opposite. I was afraid you might feel obliged to rescue me. Chivalry is an excellent quality, Ralph, but it isn't a solid foundation for marriage. The only firm foundation for marriage in my opinion is for two people to love each other freely as equals.'

'I can't pretend to understand, Thea. A girl is entitled to look to a chap for support. But everything's out in the open now. Obviously, I want to do my bit to help.'

'Thank you. The best thing you can do is to let the plan proceed and explain to Bunny and Charlotte that I'd already agreed to attend the races with another friend. I'll come over and say hello, but please support me when I say I need to get back to Anna.'

'There must be something more I can do.'

'Doing as I ask will be enormously useful, Ralph.'

'It won't feel entirely honest.'

'The most important thing is to bring a criminal to justice. Not just for my sake but also for the sake of Jessie and all the other people Stanley, Jarrold and Bulky Man might harm in the future. You can tell the truth to Bunny, Charlotte and everyone else afterwards if it'll make you feel better.'

'Of course. I'm sorry, darling. I'm not used to... subterfuge.'

'Did the army never use it?'

Thea had him there.

'Think of it as a battle,' Thea advised.

She made him promise to do nothing to acknowledge the presence of her friends at the races, and not to stare at Jarrold. 'He can't be given any reason to suspect he isn't just having a day out.'

'You won't put yourself in any sort of danger?' Ralph asked. 'I couldn't bear it if—'

'There'll be thousands of people at the races.'

'I suppose that's true.'

Thea kissed his cheek and sent him on his way but could she really trust him not to interfere? Thea wasn't sure. Ralph would do whatever he considered to be right.

Daisy arrived with Daniel soon afterwards. 'Max here yet?' Daniel asked.

'Downstairs,' Thea confirmed.

They hastened down to the kitchen and no one could doubt what had happened because Daniel stood with his arm around Daisy's shoulder. 'It's about time my little cousin saw sense,' Max said, getting up and shaking Daniel's hand.

'Less of the "little cousin", please,' Daisy scolded, but Max only aimed a playful punch at her shoulder before kissing her cheek.

Congratulations rang out from the rest of them. There were handshakes, hugs and kisses but eventually Daniel looked at his watch. 'Daisy will have to explain how it all came about. Max and I need to catch that train to London.'

Daniel and Max went off, and Daisy told the story of Daniel's proposal over a cup of tea. 'I'm delighted for you,' Thea said again, her words swiftly echoed by Anna and Piers. Even the twins looked on with amusement.

'So we're all settled now,' Daisy said. 'Me with Daniel. Anna with Piers, and you with Ralph, Thea.'

'Indeed.' Thea realised she hadn't sounded quite as delighted as the circumstances justified. 'Sorry. I just need today to be over before I can relax.'

Anna made soup for lunch but Thea could manage only a few spoons of it. 'Tension,' she said, patting her middle.

She hoped it wasn't the uneasiness of foreboding.

Daisy went ahead to the races on foot, the idea being that she'd stay apart from Thea and Anna so as to provide a pair of eyes operating from a different direction. Thea would have stayed apart from Anna too but Ralph's visit had put paid to that idea as the Catchpoles might think it odd if they saw her wandering around alone or hiding in shadows when she was supposed to be with a friend.

Piers also went ahead in a taxi so as to meet the police officer and settle in the stand ready for Max and Daniel's arrival. Not that they'd acknowledge each other.

Thea and Anna walked to the races too, pushing James in his perambulator. Albie planned to leave the house by the back door to follow them at a distance until they were safely inside the racecourse. Crossing Eastern Road, Thea glanced around as though checking the traffic and was glad to see him sauntering behind them.

The nearer they drew to the racecourse the more people they saw heading in that direction on foot, in cars or on coaches. Many of them were elegantly dressed and clearly comfortably-off. Others were ordinary working people but they all shared a festive air and winter wear had been cast off in favour of lighter dresses, hats and suits.

'I've lived near this racecourse all my life but I've never been inside it,' Thea said.

'I've never been to the races either,' Anna admitted. 'My father used to put a bet on in the bookmaker's shop near home occasionally but it was a squalid little place.'

She nodded towards the big stone building that stood ahead of them. 'Not so long ago I thought I might end up in there.'

'The workhouse?' Thea was shocked.

'I'll always be grateful to you for helping me. Now it's my turn to help you.'

As soon as they were inside Thea realised she'd underestimated the crowd. There were many thousands of people here. It was hard to avoid being jostled and James's perambulator made forward progress slow though Thea could see one advantage to having a baby with them.

'If we need to hide our faces quickly, we can lean over the perambulator as though we're paying attention to James,' she said.

The problem would be spotting someone from whom they needed to hide in this ocean of humanity. Even with the advantage of height, Thea could barely see past the immediate press of people. It would be harder still for Anna and as for little Daisy...

Racing hadn't yet begun so the crowd had spread out onto the course itself and the grassy area beyond the opposite rails. Making their way onto the course Thea and Anna walked past the tall viewing stand. The seats rose steeply but there was a flatter area in front that was heaving with people.

Cleverly, Daisy was standing on steps but keeping to the side of them so as to avoid being in the way. She appeared to be studying a racing programme but she must have noticed Thea because, as agreed, she gave a slight nod in the direction of the seats to confirm that Piers was inside with his tame police officer.

Where was he, though? There were just too many hats and heads to—

There he was, on one of the lower tiers. He'd been clever too because he'd taken his hat off to show hair that glowed brightly despite Anna having cut it into a neater style. The man who sat next to him was presumably the police officer wearing civilian clothes. No one sat on Piers's other side. Hopefully, this was because he'd managed to place his crutches over the seats, reserving them for Max, Daniel and Jarrold so they'd be close enough for the police officer to overhear what they said.

The next person they saw was Ralph who was obviously looking out for her. It made him conspicuous and several people turned to look at him as he approached Thea with an anxious purposefulness that stood out in this merry crowd of pleasure-seekers. 'There you are, darling.' He kissed her cheek then greeted Anna with a stiff, 'Good afternoon.'

Anna took it philosophically. 'Good afternoon, Major.'

He turned back to Thea. 'Could you come and speak to our friends? They're keen to see you.'

'Of course.' Thea parted from Anna with a look that said she'd return as soon as possible.

Ralph's group comprised seven people and included Bunny, Charlotte and Edith Hale, the young woman from the tennis party who was sweet on Ralph. Bunny and Charlotte sprang forward to congratulate Thea on her engagement and the others joined in.

'Yes, congratulations,' Edith echoed, with a fair stab at sincerity.

Thea pitied her.

'Are you sure you can't join us?' Bunny asked.

'I'm afraid I'm committed to a friend.'

'That's the trouble with getting up a party spontaneously,' Charlotte said. 'People tend to be unavailable. But then it wouldn't be spontaneous if invitations were sent out weeks in advance.'

Thea smiled as everyone laughed. 'I'll see you again later if I can manage to find you in the crush,' she said. 'If I can... well, I hope you all have a lovely afternoon.'

Ralph moved to accompany her back to Anna but Thea stilled him with a hand. 'Stay with your friends, Ralph.'

Fire was blazing in Anna's dark eyes when Thea reached her. 'Don't look round but Max and Daniel have just arrived.'

Thea's heart kicked against her ribs. 'Is—'

'There's a man with them. I'm pretty sure it's –' Anna broke off at the sound of a voice, a coarse whine that Thea recognised as belonging to Jarrold.

'What time is it? I need to put some money on Franklyn's Fancy.'

'Save your money for the big one,' Max advised him.

The three men walked past and Thea got her first look at Jarrold. He was much shorter than Max and Daniel, thin in the legs but with wide, hunched shoulders and overlong, greasy hair. Glancing back, Max winked.

She watched them move inside the stand where Daniel made a show of looking around. Thea was too far away to hear what was said but judging by appearances the scene stuck closely to the agreed script. 'Let's sit here,' Daniel said.

Piers looked up innocently at his approach.

'Sorry to be a trouble,' Daniel continued, 'but would you mind—'

'Oh! Of course!' Piers gave a good impression of having forgotten he'd left his crutches in the way.

He moved them aside then resumed his conversation with the police officer as though Daniel was a stranger. Meanwhile Daniel and Max sat down with Jarrold between them.

Thea studied Jarrold's face – ferret-like, with untrust-worthy eyes that flicked around as though searching for opportunities to cheat. His gaze came to rest on someone or something and, looking around, Thea saw a uniformed policeman. Jarrold watched him until satisfied that he was simply wandering through the crowd then sat back and said something to Max.

Thea had noticed several policemen on duty. Some were on foot. Others were mounted on horses. Remembering that the racecourse had a reputation for attracting pickpockets, she drew her bag closer.

'They're about to begin racing,' Anna said. 'We need to move.'

Thea needed to move anyway. Even in a crowd of thousands she risked drawing Jarrold's notice if she simply stood staring up at the stand.

It was impractical to take a perambulator into the stand so they joined numerous others who were watching the race from the rails beside it. A great cheer went up when the race began and through the people in front of her Thea caught a glimpse of the jockeys' colourful silk jerseys flashing by like fast-moving rainbows above a forest of horses' legs.

The roars of the crowd were deafening, cries of, 'Come on!' mixing with cries of, 'Run faster, you little bleeder!' and groans of disappointment as money was lost on horses that couldn't – or wouldn't – run any faster.

Thea's shoe suddenly felt loose. The button that secured the strap across her instep had come off. 'Bother,' she said, but then an idea occurred to her. 'I don't suppose you've brought your little sewing kit?'

'I have.' Practical as always, Anna produced it from her bag. 'Sewing the button back on is your excuse to go into the stand,' she guessed.

'Exactly.'

'I'll stay on look-out,' Anna said.

Daisy was still on the steps looking one way so Anna positioned herself to look the other.

Thea found a seat just along from Jarrold. She got to work with needle and thread, using a silver thimble to push through the leather. A cobbler would do a better job but Thea's repair might get her through the day.

She worked slowly, ears pricked to catch the nearby conversation, and, so she could cast secret looks at Jarrold, holding her shoe up for inspection now and then. Daniel had produced a couple of hip flasks to loosen Jarrold's tongue with alcohol though they'd already got him half-drunk before they'd arrived. Max said something about how much cheaper it was to bring whisky in from home rather than buy it in a bar. 'Though there's nothing to beat having enough money to walk into a bar and buy whatever you like. Remember that time I made close on a hundred in one week, Davie?'

'A hundred pounds?' Jeremiah asked.

'Yes, and all thanks to that cousin of his,' Daniel said.

'Ssh!' Max gave a performance of glancing over his shoulder to be sure no one was listening. When he spoke again he began in a whisper. 'Cousin Tommy expects his share, o' course. He tips me the wink about the horses, I put the bets on and we share the spoils.'

'Fair enough,' Jeremiah agreed.

Max shrugged as though life was just perfect. 'Who needs a steady job when there's easy money coming in? Not me.' His voice had got louder again. 'O' course I have to move around a bit, putting a bet on here and a bet on there so I never look suspicious. But I don't mind that, especially when Davie comes along to keep me company.'

'You can get by on these tips too, can you?' Jeremiah asked Daniel.

'Let's call my winnings an occasional bonus. I've got a little scheme of my own going, haven't I, Mick?' Daniel grinned at Max, tapping the side of his nose conspiratorially.

'Oh?' Jeremiah prompted.

'Vehicle repairs, that's me. Only the dozy fool who inherited the business from his pa leaves most of the work to me. Which means not all of the money goes through the books. Some goes straight into my pocket.'

'And you?' Max asked Jeremiah.

'Me?'

Max nudged him with his elbow. 'Smart chap like you must have some scheme or other going?'

'Well, I...' Jeremiah's words trailed off.

Max looked at Daniel who pulled his mouth down to suggest that Jeremiah had disappointed him.

'About this tip your cousin gave you,' Jarrold began, seeing it getting away from him.

'I only share tips with friends,' Max said.

'Useful friends,' Daniel agreed. 'Friends who give something back.'

'What sort o' something?' Jarrold asked.

'Tips for the horses or the dogs,' Daniel explained. 'Only good tips, mind. What you'd call *informed* tips, like Mick's. Or ideas for other ways of earning a few bob. Clever ideas we haven't thought of.'

'I'm a good man with the cards,' Jarrold said, growing desperate. 'I've got this special way of marking the backs.'

Max only grimaced. 'Doesn't look like it's done you much good.'

He turned to Daniel. 'We should be getting on. We've bets to place.'

Daniel nodded. 'Be seeing you, Jerry.'

He got to his feet and so did Max.

'Wait!' Jeremiah cried. 'Clever ideas, you say? Ideas you 'aven't thought of?'

'That's right,' Max said.

'There was something I did that earned me a nice little bundle.'

'Oh?' Max and Daniel sat down again.

'There was this Will,' Jeremiah began.

'Will?' Max queried. 'Like a Last Will and Testament?'

'The very same. I didn't have to go to any trouble. All I had to do was sign it. Five minutes work for fifty pounds.'

Max looked confused. 'You made a Will and what? Promised to leave someone money if they gave you money now?'

'I didn't promise anything. It wasn't my Will. It was someone else's.'

'You were a witness?'

'Precisely.'

'Don't you need two of them? I remember when my Uncle Mordecai was—'

'There *were* two of us. Me and my old friend, Albert.'

'You got paid for being a witness?'

'That's the point,' Jeremiah said proudly. 'Witnesses aren't usually paid but this Will needed... discretion.'

'Meaning what?' Daniel asked. 'The person making the Will didn't want his family to know he was cutting them out?'

'Bit more complicated,' Jeremiah said. 'Actually, there were two Wills.'

'Two?'

'One was fine and dandy. Above board, so to speak. That was the Will of my friend, Herbert. His Will left everything to his son, Stanley.'

'What was wrong with that?'

'Nothing. But the other Will... Herbert's wife's Will... that left everything to Herbert.'

'I still don't see the problem,' Max said.

'The other witness and me... We were supposed to watch this lady sign her name but we never even met her. Stanley – that's Herbert's son and not a man you'd want to get on the wrong side of – got us in the back room of the Golden Anchor to sign our names. We were told this lady was the frail sort and couldn't be troubled with visitors so she'd signed it already.'

'Had she signed it?' Max asked.

'Somebody had. But no one pays fifty pounds each to witnesses unless there's something a bit... *devious* going on, do they?'

'So this Will left property to Herbert and then Stanley when it should have gone to... who?'

'Don't know,' Jarrold said. 'Don't care. I was paid to sign my name and ask no questions, and that's what I did. A man has to look out for hisself in this world.'

'Clever,' Max approved. 'I suppose you'd call what you did fraud.'

'I suppose you would.' Jeremiah was proud of it. 'If you're lookin' for easy money, Mick... you too, Davie... you could do worse than ask around and find some lawyer who might have need of special Will-signing services like that.'

Jarrold broke off as Piers's police officer got to his feet and loomed over him. 'Oi, what's this? You shouldn't be listening in on other chaps' conversations.'

'I'm a police officer and I'm arresting you on—'

Jeremiah gave the officer a hard push that sent him crashing into Piers. Then he bolted, scrambling down the steps and forcing his way between people and railings onto the course itself.

Max and Daniel raced after him but so did Thea and it was she who reached him first, bringing him down by swinging her handbag at the back of his head and sending him staggering to the ground.

'Excellent shot,' Max complimented, catching her up.

Daniel grinned then went to Jeremiah, rolling him onto his back and saying, 'I shouldn't fancy your chances in a fight with me, Mr Jarrold. I'm twice your size.'

'You tricked me!' Jeremiah spat. 'You, you—'

'Careful now. Ladies present. You don't want me to have to shut you up, do you?'

Piers and his police officer appeared. 'Are you all right?' Thea asked them anxiously.

'In fine fettle,' Piers assured her, his blue eyes dancing with pleasure at a job well done. 'We heard everything.'

'We certainly did,' the police officer confirmed, bending to Jeremiah to make the formal arrest and secure him in handcuffs.

Anna and Daisy had got through the crowd too. 'You're making a habit of getting the best of villains, Thea. That was another magnificent hit,' Anna said with a laugh.

'You were like a warrior queen,' Daisy agreed.

Thea breathed in deeply, feeling that even the air tasted of triumph. But then she saw Ralph approaching, eyebrows drawn together in concern.

'My darling girl, what on earth happened?'

'She brought this sleazy criminal down with her handbag. That's what happened.' Daisy giggled, and Ralph sent her a disapproving look.

Jarrold had been hauled to his feet. 'We're going to see he's safely locked up in the police van,' Max said.

He, Daniel and Piers walked off with the police officer, heading for the side of the stand behind which Thea assumed there to be offices and vehicles.

'We need to talk.' Ralph took Thea's arm and steered her further along the course and away from the crowd so they could speak more privately. 'I should never have sat back and let this plan go ahead,' he told her.

'The plan worked,' Thea pointed out. 'It worked perfectly. We brought a criminal to justice. We saved my house. My inheritance.'

'But this unseemliness...'

Thea realised she was still holding her shoe. Bending, she put it on and fastened the button. 'I didn't break my shoe chasing after Jeremiah, but it would have been a small price to pay for capturing him.'

Straightening, she saw he was frowning still. 'Ralph, aren't you pleased that the plan succeeded?'

'Of course I'm pleased you have the house that means so much to you. But this exhibition... this scene... It lacks dignity, Thea.'

'Lacks dignity?'

'I'm blaming myself. It's my job to protect you and I was wrong to let myself be persuaded against intervening. But I've learned my lesson so you can rest assured that I'll waste no time in getting you away from these people and into my care.'

'These people are my friends.'

'I know how difficult things have been for you. It was natural to make friends of convenience when—'

'Friends of convenience?'

'People you were drawn to by desperation rather than natural affinity. But that's all going to change, darling. Don't worry.'

Thea understood then what she hadn't fully understood before, though perhaps she'd suspected it all along. Ralph saw only part of her. He saw her elegance and gracious good manners and thought they fitted into his world.

But he didn't see the woman beneath the surface. The woman who admired and valued people of all classes. Who thought life should be an adventure instead of traditional and predictable. Who wanted to welcome that life with a man as her companion instead of her shield.

In short, she wasn't the woman Ralph needed as his wife and he wasn't the man she needed as her husband. 'Ralph, I'm sorry. I'm truly touched by your feelings for me but you've built me up in your mind to be the sort of person who's a mirror image of yourself and I'm not that sort of person. Sooner or later you'll realise it and you'll be disillusioned. Miserable. We both will.'

'I don't follow, Thea. What are you saying?'

'I'm saying you're a dear man who has the best of intentions but your world isn't my world. Not any more. So I'm releasing you for both our sakes.' She pulled the emerald ring from her finger and tucked it into the top pocket of his jacket. Then she stepped forward and kissed his cheek. 'I wish you well, Ralph.'

'But—'

'You're disappointed now. Hurt too, and I'm sorry for that. But one day you'll realise that what I'm saying makes sense and you'll be happy again.' She paused then said with a smile, 'You could make Edith Hale happy too.'

'Edith?' Ralph looked puzzled, but Thea's meaning soon sank in and she saw that the idea of Edith as a prospective wife wasn't something he instantly dismissed.

It was enough to reassure Thea that, even if he wasn't quite ready to admit that she herself was wrong for him, it wouldn't be long before he did so. Ralph wasn't a calculating man but he'd met Thea at a time when he was thinking of settling down and had been all too ready to be dazzled instead of taking the time to get to know her. Edith would make a much more suitable wife for him.

'I'll write to your parents to explain and wish them well,' Thea said.

Bunny bounded up with his party of friends close on his heels. 'We heard there's been a commotion.'

Thea looked at Ralph, pleading with him to understand.

'Yes, but it's over now,' Ralph said, and as he stepped amongst his friends Thea was pleased to notice Edith moving to his side.

She watched them walk back towards the crowds and sighed. What a day this had been, triumphant but tinged with sadness as far as Ralph was concerned, and with a future that… well, who knew what her future might hold now he was no longer a part of it?

She set off walking too but froze when she heard a scream. What on earth…? It had come from the stands and, looking up in that direction, she saw people racing for the steps as though desperate to get out. Then someone pointed a finger and Thea realised they were pointing behind her.

She turned and saw Stanley further along the course. He must have made his way round the stand and the crowds on each side of it so she wouldn't see him approach and there would be fewer people around to get in his way. To her horror she realised he was holding a pistol.

He aimed it at her and fired. The bullet missed its mark but the crowd erupted into full panic. 'Thea, run!' she heard above the screams. Daisy's voice.

Turning, Thea did run but another shot rang out and she knew then that, wherever she ran, she'd be taking danger with her and putting other lives at risk. She stopped running and looked back at Stanley who was still some distance away. He'd lost his hat and his camel haired coat flapped open like the wings of a demented bird. He lurched from side to side as he walked towards her and that gave her hope because drunkenness would surely mean his aim was awry. And how many bullets could a pistol hold? Not many. If she stood here and let him continue to fire at her – and only her – the pistol would soon be empty or the police would intervene to save her.

A glance around showed her two policemen at the side of the stand between her and Stanley, agitatedly trying to decide what to do. A mounted officer joined them but none were armed and none appeared to fancy their chances against a man with a gun.

Stanley paused to fire again. And again. Thea winced each time but stood her ground, supposing they were now the only two people left on the course itself.

Stanley came on and passed the policemen. Surely they'd intervene now they could come at him from behind? But another glance showed that they were still doing nothing, even though Max had joined them and was arguing furiously.

Stanley was close enough now for Thea to see his crazed expression. Which meant that she was a much closer target for him. He levelled the gun and took aim.

But the gun was empty. Thea slumped in relief as he tossed the gun aside with a roar of rage. But then he tugged another gun from his pocket and Thea's bones felt as though they'd turned to liquid. Raising it, he screwed his eyes up then blinked rapidly as he tried to line it up on her.

'Ambrose!' a voice yelled.

Stanley turned his head to look and saw Max coming for him on the police horse. Staggering a little, he swung the gun around to take a shot at him but wasn't fast enough. Lying low over the horse's withers Max stretched out an arm and knocked the gun to the ground. The force sent Stanley into a spin and he fell. But he got up on his knees, frantically searching for the gun then crawling towards it.

Again, Max was faster. Leaping off the horse's back, he snatched the gun off the grass just before Stanley reached it.

The policemen finally ran up. Two of them got hold of Stanley and Max passed the gun to the third. As Stanley was dragged away – presumably to join Jarrold in the police van – Max walked to Thea and touched her arm, his expression probing. 'All right?' he asked.

She was trembling so hard that all she could do was nod though she was desperate to thank him for having had the courage to help her. Max's grey eyes lightened to a twinkle. 'We got him,' he said with satisfaction, and Thea gave a choked sort of laugh that broke through the worst of her tension.

All of her friends had reached her now. 'Thank God that man didn't hurt you but why didn't you run?' Anna asked, amazed.

'Because she didn't want to put anyone else in danger,' Max replied and he looked at Thea with obvious approval.

'How incredibly brave,' Anna said.

Thea finally found her voice. 'Max was the brave one.'

'You were both brave,' Rory Connor said, having walked up leading the horse which he'd caught.

'Rory!' Thea was surprised to see him though she knew she shouldn't have been. He was a jockey after all and the colourful silks and cap he wore indicated he was here to race. She was even more surprised to realise that he and Daisy knew each other judging from the way Daisy's face had suddenly flushed with embarrassment.

'Hello, Daisy Flowers,' Rory said, turning to her with a grin.

Daniel put a protective arm around Daisy's shoulder.

'Like that, is it?' Rory said then. 'I was going to ask you for a second chance, Daisy, but I see I'm too late.'

'You are,' Daniel told him firmly.

'What's this?' Max frowned at Rory accusingly. 'You don't mean you and my little cousin were...?' He rolled his eyes to show it didn't matter now. 'She's made a better choice than a wastrel like you,' he chided.

'Alas, I fear 'tis true,' Rory agreed. 'Well, it's time I restored this horse to our fine constabulary so I'll bid you all good day.' He smiled round at them, winked at Daisy and loped away.

Daniel gave Daisy's shoulder a reassuring squeeze.

'I know I'll have to talk to the police about everything that's happened but what I want most of all just now is to go home,' Thea said.

'To celebrate being in the house that's well and truly yours again?' Max guessed.

'Exactly.'

They headed towards the exit and Thea caught a glimpse of Ralph's face in the crowd. He smiled and nodded, and Thea was delighted to realise it was his way of telling her that he understood her decision and wished her well.

'So,' Max whispered. 'The emerald ring is gone and I'm glad of it. The major had a lot to offer in terms of worldly goods and social prestige but he wasn't the man for you.'

'No.'

'I've got little to offer in terms of worldly goods and nothing at all to offer in terms of social prestige. All I've got is ambition, a hard working attitude and the possibility of making something of myself one day. But I think I might still be the right man for you. What do you think?'

It all made sense to her now. She'd seized on reasons for keeping the truth of her situation from Ralph because she'd needed barriers between them. All along, instinct had warned her that they wouldn't suit each other. But she'd trusted Max from the moment they met. Now she realised that she loved him too and he loved her. Just the way she was.

'I think you might be,' she said.

He turned to her, stopping her in her tracks, and smiled down at her with wry humour as well as love in those shrewd grey eyes. 'You know I am,' he said, and he kissed her in a way that ignited flames inside her and left her in no doubt that he was most definitely the man for her.

'Marry me?' he whispered against her cheek.

'I'd love to.'

Thea laughed when he finally released her, flushed, embarrassed but fizzing with a happiness that was shared by their friends judging from the delighted looks on all their faces.

They walked back towards Clarendon Place, taking their time and savouring their triumph. It felt wonderful to have her arm linked with Max's and sparks of excitement passed through her every time they glanced at each other and exchanged smiles.

'It's ironic that you've saved your house on the very day it becomes clear you won't be living there any more,' Daniel said, as they approached it. 'At least, I assume you'll move to Max's cottage?'

'He needs to be near the horses,' Thea confirmed. 'But I shan't sell the house just yet. I've actually enjoyed running it as a guest house. In fact I wonder if we might continue to run it for a while as most of us could benefit from the income. You and Piers need somewhere to live, Anna, so might you take charge while I come over only some of the time?'

'I'd love to!' Anna cried.

'Daisy could help out sometimes too, if she's minded?'

Daisy looked at Daniel excitedly. 'Best of both worlds,' he said.

'We can always get extra help in if needed,' Thea said. 'So that's settled.'

She let them all inside and went into the drawing-room to put the *Vacancies* sign in the window. The Brighton guest house was back in business and very satisfactory it felt.

Acknowledgements

Books are collaborations and warmest thanks are due to my editor, Rosie de Courcy, for helping to shape this story (particularly the horsey bits), Claire Windrush for copy-editing and to all at Team Aria/Head of Zeus for their support – Lauren, Hannah and Vicky especially. One of the themes of this book is friendship and I'd also like to thank my friends for all the fun.

About Lesley Eames

Born in Manchester but currently living in Hertfordshire, LESLEY EAMES' career has included law and charity fundraising. She is now devoting her time to her own writing and to teaching creative writing to others. In addition to selling almost 90 short stories to the women's magazine market, Lesley has won the Festival of Romance's New Talent Award and the Romantic Novelists' Associations Elizabeth Goudge Cup.

Hello from Aria

We hope you enjoyed this book! Let us know, we'd love to hear from you.

We are Aria, a dynamic digital-first fiction imprint from award-winning independent publishers Head of Zeus. At heart, we're avid readers committed to publishing exactly the kind of books we love to read – from romance and sagas to crime, thrillers and historical adventures. Visit us online and discover a community of like-minded fiction fans!

We're also on the look out for tomorrow's superstar authors. So, if you're a budding writer looking for a publisher, we'd love to hear from you. You can submit your book online at ariafiction.com/we-want-read-your-book

You can find us at:
Email: aria@headofzeus.com
Website: www.ariafiction.com
Submissions: www.ariafiction.com/
we-want-read-your-book
Facebook: @ariafiction
Twitter: @Aria_Fiction
Instagram: @ariafiction

25460298R00237

Printed in Great Britain
by Amazon